Lisa Walker is an award-winning short story writer. Her play *Baddest Backpackers* aired on ABC Radio National in 2008. She has worked as a wilderness guide and environmental communicator. She writes, surfs and works in community relations on the far north coast of New South Wales. *Liar Bird* is her first novel.

www.lisawalker.com.au

Liar Bird

Lisa Walker

HarperCollins*Publishers*

HarperCollins*Publishers*

First published in Australia in 2012
by HarperCollins*Publishers* Australia Pty Limited
ABN 36 009 913 517
harpercollins.com.au

HarperCollins*Publishers*
Level 13, 201 Elizabeth Street, Sydney NSW 2000, Australia
31 View Road, Glenfield, Auckland 0627, New Zealand
A 53, Sector 57, Noida, UP, India
77–85 Fulham Palace Road, London, W6 8JB, United Kingdom
2 Bloor Street East, 20th floor, Toronto, Ontario M4W 1A8, Canada
10 East 53rd Street, New York NY 10022, USA

National Library of Australia Cataloguing-in-Publication data:

Walker, Lisa.
    Liar bird / Lisa Walker.
    ISBN: 978 0 7322 9412 0 (pbk.)
A823.4

Cover design by Darren Holt, HarperCollins Design Studio
Cover images by shutterstock.com
Author photo by Tim Eddy

For John.
Thanks for all the happy days.

Part One

after such a fall as this,
I shall think nothing of tumbling down stairs

Alice, from *Alice's Adventures in Wonderland*,
Lewis Carroll

Chapter One

Down the plughole

If it wasn't for the long-footed potoroo, I might never have heard of Beechville. But I suppose I can't entirely lay the blame at the potoroo's door — Warren Corbett must also take his share.

There have been many influential figures in my life, people who have opened doors at the right time, given words of advice, turned me onto a path I might not have taken. Of all of these, Warren Corbett looms largest.

Wazza, as he's widely known in PR circles, was my first boss. More than that, he was my mentor. *Do what it takes, girl, but don't let them catch you,* was his favourite saying. Second was, *When in doubt, deny, deny, deny.*

He's old school, Wazza. PR Ethics hadn't been invented when he made his first million. It was my luck — some would say karma — that I ended up at Winning Edge Public Relations still wet from my Communications degree. That was when the learning really started.

Wazza taught me everything I knew — how to set up 'grassroots' front groups that look and act just like the real thing; how to infiltrate real groups if need be and, most importantly, how not to let your conscience stand in the way of your career. He said it was important to *look* ethical; actually *being* ethical was optional and probably unwise.

He was the learned master and I the eager student. I sucked up his wisdom as thirstily as any magician's apprentice. Good old Wazza, he's still there, doing his thing. God knows there's no shortage of clients ready to fork out for his golden touch.

Out of all the graduates who'd applied to his company — fifty or so — he picked *me*. Why?

'I trust my instincts, Cassandra.' He'd leant over his massive glass table, a whiff of cinnamon aftershave drifting towards me from his shiny cheeks. 'In this game, you have to. And you … I can sense something. You're smart, but they're *all* smart. You look good, but they *all* look good. You've got something different, though.' He'd placed his hand-rolled cigar in an ashtray and pointed his immaculately groomed, gold-ringed finger at my chest. '*You* are hungry.'

He was right.

He told me later — only half joking — that he'd been worried I'd leap over the desk and sink my teeth into his jugular if he'd knocked me back. I'd laughed politely, showing just a hint of fang to keep him on his toes.

We had five great years together, Wazza and I. Years that bought me my Manly harbour-front apartment, my Ferrari and my five-star investment portfolio. We were the PR 'A' team and all Sydney knew it. There wasn't a company director or charity queen who didn't have our card pinned to their board. I never stopped to question where we were going. Why would you when the phone never stopped ringing, the invitations to parties kept coming, and the bank account was bursting at the seams? I was on a fast ride to glory, leaping up the ranks of society like a cheetah on speed.

My life was mapped out in front of me — partnership in a year or two, my own business one day, a PR realm stretching its tentacles through Sydney, Australia, the world. Why not? After where I'd come from, I deserved it.

But it was thanks to Wazza that on Monday the 23rd of September at six am the phone woke me. Sliding my hand out from under the doona, I grasped the receiver and pressed it to my ear.

'Simon McKechnie here.'

Simon was a rabid anti-progress leftist greenie and columnist for the *Herald*. McKechnie at six am was never good news.

'From the *Herald*,' he added, when I didn't reply.

Like I didn't know.

'The People's Council for Better Community Services. What can you tell me about it?'

Luckily my wits didn't desert me. I made a *chchch* static noise, placed the phone down gently, unplugged it, checked my mobile was turned off, drew the curtains and, striding into the lounge room, poured myself a neat whiskey. It hit my belly like a bolt from God.

Anthony, of course, was useless.

'What's up, Cassandra?' he called from the bedroom. 'Are you making coffee? Make mine a skinny.' He was using his pathetic little sleepy-boy voice.

I could expect no help there.

I knew I had about ten minutes, maybe twenty — plenty of time. My feet sank into the hand-woven Turkish carpet as I padded to the meditation room. Pulling out my tattered copy of *The Annotated Alice*, I opened it randomly, closed my eyes and pressed my finger to the page. *'You don't know much,' said the Duchess, 'and that's a fact.'*

I nodded — so true. Spot on, in fact.

Why *Alice in Wonderland*? I know it's not what most thirty-year-old PR executives read. Well, we all have our means of coping. Some people are into Oprah; others, Buddha; and some — well, me — rely on Alice.

I first discovered the wisdom of Alice at the age of eight ...

☙

It was the day of the school fete — a much anticipated event that hadn't gone to plan. My 'best friend' Jessica and I had had a falling out, but that's another story. Suffice to say, I was deflated, dejected, down and out.

Alone at the book stall I shuffled through the Enid Blytons and out-of-date *Women's Weekly*s laid out on the trestle tables but my eyes were drawn to a battered copy of *The Annotated Alice*. Stuffing the last morsel of Chiko Roll in my mouth, I picked up the book in my chubby freckled hands.

I liked books. Ours was a TV, not a book, house. At night we all lined up on the sofa in front of the box. If I tried to leaf through a book at the same time, Mum would frown at me.

'Put that away, Cassie. You're distracting me.'

As a result, books had an almost illicit appeal.

The flushed and sweaty woman behind the stall eyed my greasy hands as I opened the book at random. I saw a picture of a fierce, regal-looking woman frowning at a girl with long, blonde hair and the following words: *Never imagine yourself not to be otherwise than what it might appear to others that what you were or might have been ...*

My thumb smeared a trail of oil across the page. I read the words over and over. They made no sense at all, whichever way I looked at them. I liked that. I liked the way it made me feel. As if I was poised on the edge of a well of wisdom. Oh yes, there was meaning there, I just needed to find it, dive in, explore ... Handing over my last twenty cents, I took my treasure home.

It has stayed with me, that book, a 1972 edition containing both *Alice in Wonderland* and *Through the Looking-Glass*. Its pages were yellowed and stained when I first bought it, but they're more so now. The soft texture of the paper speaks of many hands fondling it before me. A faded inscription in the front reads, *To darling Tessie, from Mum.* I think of Tessie as my blood-sister. I'd like to meet her one day. Discuss *Alice*; share what it means to me. You don't get that kind of connection with an e-book.

So … forget the I-Ching and the Tarot — I find *Alice in Wonderland* much more likely to provide wise advice at the right moment. It may need interpretation, but doesn't all the best advice?

'You don't know much,' said the Duchess. See what I mean? Perfect. What did Simon McKechnie know after all? Not much, *and that's a fact.*

I glanced at the clock as I closed *Alice*. I still had a few minutes.

Folding my legs into lotus pose, I rested my hands, palm up, on my knees and meditated, using the mantra Wazza had taught me: *deny, deny, deny.* It was a well-practised routine. By the time the knock on the door came, I was ready.

'Just a minute,' I called. Rinsing my mouth to remove the smell of whiskey, I wrapped myself in a blue velvet robe. Lips pursed, I applied my pale pink Innocence lipstick and inspected myself in the mirror.

The baby-faced looks I'd relied on to get me this far hadn't let me down.

Running my fingers through my spiked and highlighted hair for a just-out-of-bed tousled look, I centred myself as I walked to the door.

Deny, deny, deny.

As I expected, McKechnie was there, sandy hair poking out at all angles, a holier-than-thou expression on his pale face. *Puhleese.* We all had to make a living. That he got to make his playing an environmental saint was his good luck, I suppose.

'Why, Simon, what brings you to Manly at this time of day?' I widened my eyes in mock surprise.

His pale green eyes narrowed, ready for his specialty: the inquisition. He would have been in great demand in sixteenth-century Spain, would Simon. *Bring on the thumbscrews ...*

We're old sparring partners, McKechnie and I. We were in the same year at university until our paths diverged. His to the gods, mine to the devil, some would say. But where would journos be without PRs? We do their job for them most of the time.

Oh, I'd thought about journalism, but PR attracted me more. What's wrong with PR anyway? It's illusion, smoke and mirrors, storytelling ... Everyone loves a story, don't they? I suppose journalism is about stories too, but it's like the difference between non-fiction and fiction. And we all know fiction's *much* more fun.

'Phone lines down?' Simon's voice was flat.

'Possum must have chewed them again.' I eyeballed him, daring him to call me a liar. It was funny to think he'd asked me out in first year uni. I'd kind of liked him then. He was sharp, and witty, in a slightly try-hard way. I didn't mind that. Most men tried hard around me.

But girls like me didn't go out with guys like Simon. I was totally out of his league. Let's face it, he might have been posh Woollahra to my rough-as-guts Blacktown, but my personal real estate was way more exclusive.

Anthony was out of bed by now; he hovered behind me, a towel around his waist. 'What's up, babes?'

I wished he wouldn't call me that. Not in front of the media anyway. Anthony is very sweet, but brains are not his strong point. He has other Unique Selling Features, as we say in the PR world.

'Why don't you make coffee, Ant, and let me talk to our visitor?' I said.

It was a difficult interview, but I think I handled it well.

Lashings of wide-eyed ingénue, a touch of sharp-edged denial and a dash of honesty — yes, I was handling the Rainforest Runaway project. There was no point in denying it. If there was one thing Simon was noted for, it was his attention to detail.

I thought I'd got away with it.

'What was that about, babes?' Anthony handed me my skinny latte. Sometimes I found Ant a little too ... frothy, but we were a good team. I knew it wasn't fair to expect mental stimulation from a hairdresser to the stars. In other areas, he was very stimulating indeed.

'Nothing you need to worry about, snookiepants.' Energised after my bout with Simon, I wiggled my shoulders playfully.

Ant correctly interpreted my mood. Taking my coffee cup from me, he ran his hands inside my dressing gown and lifted me onto the breakfast bench.

Outside the window, the Manly ferry thrust itself across the sun-studded water of the harbour. The commuters on the front braced themselves for a fast, wet ride.

It was a Harlequin Mills & Boon Sexy Sensation moment. With my bare bum cold on the black granite and my legs wrapped around Ant's waist, I permitted myself a moment of smugness. For a girl from Blacktown, I'd done pretty well.

I arrived at work right on time and nicely relaxed.

Suzie, the junior on the front desk, looked up as I pushed open the glass doors. 'You look good, Cassandra. New makeup?'

I flashed a smile. 'Morning Glory — you should try it.' She scribbled a note as I went into my office. I shouldn't tease, but there was something about her that invited it — a sweet naivety that reminded me of myself at that age.

Wazza wandered in soon after, puffing on his cigar, a phone held to his ear. He finished his call. 'How's tricks, Cassandra?'

'All good, Wazza.' There was no need to trouble him with news of Simon McKechnie. The situation was under control. Wazza's shiny silver phone directed a ray of light across my desk. It flashed in my eyes, blinding me for a moment. 'Hey, when do I get *my* iPhone?'

'It's coming, darling. You know I can't refuse you anything.' Wazza blew me a kiss as he left.

I spent the next half-hour or so ringing the people on the ground, telling them to sit tight — put a rain check on the day's recruitment. The People's Council for Better Community Services wasn't disbanded, just lying low.

Once that was done, I put it out of my mind. Rainforest Runaway was only one client. Twenty others were panting for the Winning Edge touch.

There was nothing on the TV news that night, which was a promising sign, but the proof of my escape would be next morning's *Herald*.

At six am I prodded Ant. 'Go get the paper.' I sat up while he was gone and gazed out at the harbour. Was there any better view in the world? With the sun rising it was like an abstract painting — triangles of gold light, triangles of red boats.

I pulled on the sunglasses I kept on my bedside table for this purpose. I'd worked so hard for a bed with a view like this. It was unfair someone like Simon McKechnie could threaten it. He'd coasted into *his* job on the tails of his famous journalist parents.

The only place I'd be coasting on *my* parents' tails would be the Blacktown TAB. I think my mother still holds the record for the largest loss in one race. She has other vices too — nothing illegal, though. We don't talk about my father.

Ant handed me the paper and I gnawed my lip as I picked off the plastic. Bloody plastic wrap. The more of a hurry you're in, the harder it is to get off. I ended up ripping at it with my teeth while Ant watched anxiously.

Unfurling the paper, I checked page one — nothing. Page two — nothing. Page three — nothing. I flicked to the back, to be sure. 'Yay.' I punched my hand in the air. I was in the clear.

Ant rolled over on top of me. 'Feeling sexy now, poochy?'

'I think I might be, snookie.'

We were just getting all hot and steamy when the doorbell rang.

Chapter Two

You look a little shy

I knew it was him — McKechnie again. I have a sixth sense about these things — call it my PR antenna.

I pushed Ant off me. 'Shit, shit, shitty shit.'

'Don't answer the door, babes. Come on.' Ant nibbled at my earlobe, which I normally love, but it did nothing for me at that moment.

'Damn that Simon McKechnie and his frigging Walkley Award.' It was no secret in journalism circles — Simon was after a big story to set him up for the award.

'What's a warklyward? Do you want me to get rid of him for you?'

It was tempting. I eyed the gym-toned muscles in Ant's arms. Simon would be no match. It wouldn't solve anything, though. 'No, shit, I'd better get it over with.' I felt a surge of fondness for Ant. He did his best. 'Thanks anyway, snookie.'

There was no time for meditation, but I did consult *Alice*. Flipping the book open I pressed my finger to the page.

Beware the Jabberwock, my son! The jaws that bite, the claws that catch!

I slammed it shut. *Right*. Thanks for those stirring words, Alice. I didn't say it was an infallible system, did I?

Bing bong, went the doorbell again. I pulled on my J-Lo velour tracksuit for a casual 'at home' look, ran fingers through my hair, et cetera, and opened the door.

I almost slammed it shut again when I saw how many of them were out there. McKechnie I'd been expecting, but not The Terror and the TV stations. I'd have to be careful — one of the TV journos was a woman and they're not as easy to fool as men.

Simon's eyes were glinting. It suddenly dawned on me: this was personal. He still hadn't forgiven me for knocking him back; it was payback time.

I'd have sorted something out if it had just been him. Men are usually pretty straightforward that way. I might even have enjoyed it. I had to admit he had something — a certain ruthless charisma. But that wasn't going to happen with this melee outside my door. Was that why he'd brought them — for maximum embarrassment?

Straightening his face, he opened his wallet and handed me a cheque. I glanced at it, a surge of nausea running through me. It was made out to the People's Council for Better Community Services. No prize for guessing whose signature was on the bottom.

The TV woman thrust a microphone at me, practically breaking a tooth. I hate the way they do that.

'No comment.' I slammed the door and leaned up against it. *No comment.* I may as well have put my head in the stocks and passed them the rotten tomatoes. Public shaming in the media is the modern version of that medieval punishment.

On Wednesday, Ant brought in the *Herald*, laid it carefully on the bed and backed away — I'd been known to throw things when I was angry. It was on page three, not that this was any surprise. The story had made the TV news last night. My *no comment* and door slamming made great visuals. The same close-up of the J-Lo tracksuit disappearing behind my Grecian Blue door on ABC, Nine, Ten and Seven. SBS, bless its multicultural heart, had other fish to fry.

What I couldn't get over was how guilty I looked. Even if you turned the sound down, I still had a 'caught in the spotlight' face — like someone who'd been selling fake shares to kindly grannies. Even *I* wouldn't have believed I was innocent after seeing that face. 'Coffee, Ant,' I muttered, snapping the newspaper pages straight.

He was glad of an excuse to get out of there.

Simon had pulled out all the stops. It ran to almost a page. I figured he had that award in the bag.

It was all there. How I'd used telemarketers to find people to write letters in support of Rainforest Runaway. The 'spontaneous' outbursts of support I'd funded. The 'activists' I'd paid to lobby for the developers. Note the 'I' — no-one else was mentioned. It was like I'd dreamed up the whole idea myself. Where were all the executives who'd been singing my praises just yesterday?

I didn't know how Simon managed to sound so surprised — it was standard practice. I knew he knew that. He knew I knew he knew. Oh, shock, horror — the evil spin-doctor. Give me a break. It's an elaborate charade — journalists and PRs — played out in front of an unsuspecting public.

'Standard for us, not standard for most people,' said Wazza, when I rang him for support. 'Remember the first rule of public relations.'

'Do what it takes?'

'And the second part?'

'But don't let them catch you.'

'I'm going to have to let you go, Cassandra.' He lowered his voice, adopted a mournful tone. 'You know that, don't you?'

My stomach contracted. I hadn't known at all. It hadn't even occurred to me. Yes, Wazza was my boss, but I'd thought he was more than that. I'd thought we were friends. I opened my mouth, but no words came out.

'This is *nothing* to do with Winning Edge Public Relations. I'm *shocked* and *saddened* by these techniques.' Wazza's voice dripped with sincerity; he was in his element. 'This sort of thing brings the whole public relations industry into disrepute.'

I realised he was practising his sound bite. 'Save it for the media, Wazza.'

He snapped back into his normal jovial tone. 'Give it six months, maybe a year, it'll all blow over, darling. Then it'll be business as usual.'

And that's how Wazza hung me out to dry.

I cried for most of Wednesday — most of Thursday too. When I wasn't crying I was eating. When I wasn't crying or eating I was drinking. Sometimes, in a feat of multitasking that no-one but me will ever appreciate, I did all three things at once. Even *Alice in Wonderland* provided no solace. Knowing that everything has a moral if only you can find it might have been apt, but it did nothing to pull me from my gloom.

Ant tiptoed around me like I was an unexploded mine. 'I know you didn't do anything wrong, Cassandra,' he ventured once.

'Shut up. What would you know?' I sobbed and threw a chocolate muffin at him. 'Dickhead.' Yes, I was mean. Not everyone can be Zen-like in the face of adversity.

It was the unfairness that pissed me off most. It's not like my clients were selling tobacco — they just wanted to build some nice houses with rainforest frontages ... and backages.

A community group called Save the Long-footed Potoroo was making it difficult for them. I mean, what is a long-footed potoroo anyway? A rat with big feet? I'd looked it up on the internet. Turned out they'd left their run a bit late when it came to saving the long-footed potoroo. Only by about fifty frigging years. That's how long it was since one had been sighted in that area. The last of these big-foots were holed up in a national park on the Victorian border — nowhere near Rainforest Runaway.

The group was made up of a bunch of nutters who for no good reason had decided their backyard supported a bunch of long-footed potoroos. Their case was based on two sightings, both — coincidentally — on a lonely road shortly after pub closing time. They had the moral high ground, though. The wish fulfilment brigade was out in force. The long-footed potoroo had returned. Hallelujah! It was the second coming of Christ as far as they were concerned. The media loved them.

You can't fight a community group with news releases, it doesn't work. So I'd just done what any good PR would have — created my own community group.

The newly formed People's Council for Better Community Services was doing a great job of lobbying for increased services on the South Coast. A minor part of their role was to lobby for the Rainforest Runaway development, which would bring with it sporting fields, a community centre and a skate park. The fact that this group didn't really exist was obviously just an oversight on behalf of the community. Who wouldn't want a skate park? I knew they'd love it once they had one.

On Friday afternoon I pulled myself together. The show must go on. I was due to attend a gala launch of a new perfume by one of my clients, Cosmonauts, at the Art Gallery that night. Chin up, I told myself as I sorted through my dresses, carefully selecting one that wouldn't show the spot where all those muffins and whiskies had lodged. *Razzle dazzle 'em. It takes more than this to get a girl like Cassandra Daley down.* Wazza might have let me go but I still had connections. Wasn't I the hottest PR in town?

I was jumpy, though; I couldn't shake it. Would people be mean to me? I hadn't felt nervous about a social function for a long time, but now, the old insecurities came knocking at the door. *Remember to make eye contact, smile, think of conversation starters …*

I even pulled out the little notebook I'd started when I was twelve. It was stuffed full of useful questions to get a conversation going. I flicked through, in search of inspiration, but it seemed to have dated badly. *Do you like guacamole? Have you ever been in a food fight? If you could have a superpower, what would it be? What did you have for lunch yesterday?* I tossed it back in the cupboard; I really needed to update that book …

I've come a long way since I was twelve. No-one ever picks me for a shy person these days. At least I don't think they do. I hide it well. *Years of training, years of training …*

'Cassandra, phone for you,' said Ant at five o'clock.

'Coming.' I fixed my diamond teardrops to my ears as I traipsed down the corridor.

It was Jessica O'Callaghan, the client and, yes, my former 'best friend' from Blacktown. Like me, Jessica had escaped Western Sydney at the first opportunity. She was now the marketing executive for Cosmonauts, a cosmetics giant. Our shared desire to bury our less-than-glamorous origins created an uneasy bond between us.

Growing up in Blacktown didn't add to one's allure in the rarefied world of the Sydney A-list crowd. East, yes, north, yes, inner-west, maybe, but far west … never. It was our dirty little secret. I'm not sure if you could call my relationship with Jessica a friendship; it was more of a strategic alliance or trading partnership.

'I just wanted to let you know, Cassandra,' Jessica's voice trilled down the phone, 'we're not expecting you to come tonight. I'm sure you'd rather not, after the week you've had. You must be wrung out.' Her voice dripped concern, but I understood.

'Oh, I'd forgotten it was on, Jessica.' I laughed gaily. 'Ant and I are off to the opera. Life is such a whirl, isn't it, ha ha ha?' I slammed the phone down. 'Bitch.

Bitchy bitch. *I'm sure you'd rather not*,' I mimicked. 'Damn right I'd rather not go to your stupid launch, Jessica. And did I ever tell you your platform wedges are just *so* yesterday?' I think when the term frenemy was coined, they were probably thinking of Jessica.

Ant, his white silk shirt half-buttoned, gave me the kind of look you'd give a sick kitten.

'And stop looking at me like that. I'm not dead yet.' A hiccoughing sob burst from my lips. 'Oh, Ant, why are people so ho-ho-horrible?'

Ant and I got takeaway from the local Thai and watched repeats of *Six Feet Under.* He licked my calves and attempted to massage my feet while we lay in front of the box but I kicked him away. 'I'm not in the mood, Ant.'

On Saturday morning I woke up even crankier. I'd hardly slept a wink and felt like crap. Getting dumped by Jessica — who'd been lucky to have me do her PR in the first place — was the final straw. I'd be networking with the underworld snitches on the bottom of the harbour if I sank any lower.

I still found it hard to believe things could change so quickly. One minute I was the Golden Girl, the next incredibly tarnished. I felt for Britney Spears now, I really did. What did they want me to do? Shave my head, get drunk and attempt suicide? Would they forgive me then? I doubted it. Knowing Sydney's A-list as I did, they would pretend not to notice, while enjoying a secret thrill.

Schadenfreude — isn't that a great word? We don't have one like it in English even though it's one of our favourite pastimes. Maybe the Germans take delight in others' troubles even more. It's possible.

I ground my teeth, thinking of the source of my misfortunes. The way Simon had looked as he handed me the cheque. It reminded me of something. Yes, that's right, Sydney University, 1997 …

The quadrangle was seething with chanting students. *IMF?* Shut it down. *World Bank?* Shut it down. *G8?* Shut it down …

Flicking back my long, pink-streaked hair, I punched my fist in the air. I'd been doing a lot of protesting in my first year. The cause wasn't as important as the sense of power it gave me. At the centre of a yelling mob of students I felt alive, energised, part of something bigger than myself.

'Cassie?'

I turned. It was that sandy-haired guy from my Communications tute — I couldn't remember his name.

'Do you want to go get a beer after this?'

I checked him out, out of the corner of my eye. I was about to say no when something made me hesitate — maybe it was his green eyes. He was clever too, I remembered that, always had lots to say. My eyes flicked up and down, maybe, but nah, not in my league.

'Get nicked,' I muttered, then turned back to the front. 'The banks have blood on their hands …'

In my defence, it was the way we all spoke. Revolutionaries have no time for niceties. I did feel a quiver of guilt as his eyes bored into me, before he pushed his way through the crowd ...

'I thought you might like to read the colour mag, Cassie?' Ant laid the paper on the bed like a dog that's not sure if it's done the right thing.

'Cassandra,' I snapped, snatching it off him. Would he never learn? No-one calls me Cassie. Not since uni, anyway.

Outside, the Manly ferry chugged towards the city — my city that had turned against me. *Oh, Sydney, you gorgeous, callous bitch*. I flicked through the paper. I was old news. One of the columnists pontificated on the evils of spin-doctors, but there were no letters, no follow-up. *Spin-doctors*. That was me, I suppose. At the moment, though, I was more spun-out than spinning.

The city had moved on, but it wouldn't forget — not yet. Like Wazza said, six months, maybe a year. Until then I was dog food — no-one in Sydney would touch me. What was I going to do with myself? I couldn't mope around — what if people saw me? I'd look pathetic. The last thing I needed was for someone to see me hanging about on a weekday. It would kill my reputation.

I imagined the commuters eyeing me out of the corner of their Ray-Bans. *Did you hear? She used to be ...* they'd shudder as I gorged myself on muffins at the café, my stomach straining at my size 26 tracksuit. No — I couldn't let that happen to me.

I needed to get away for a while, act like it was my choice, return refreshed, revitalised and triumphant. What I needed was another job — some place they'd never heard of Cassandra Daley and her astroturf. Somewhere Sydney people would never find me.

Ant was still sitting on the end of the bed, doggy eyes following my every move.

'For chrissakes, Ant, stop watching me. Get me a coffee … and a fresh muffin from the bakery, will you, snooks?' That would keep him out of my hair for a bit.

As he left the room I grabbed *Alice* from my bedside table. *'You look a little shy; let me introduce you to that leg of mutton,' said the Red Queen.*

Ha. I would be lucky to be introduced even to a leg of mutton if I stuck around here. A pathetic, friendless loser, that's what I'd be.

I opened the jobs section. There were lots of PR jobs, but all in Sydney. I kept flicking. There at the end was a small box: *Public relations specialist for wildlife agency, North Coast — Beechville.*

Beechville? I shuddered. There were good parts to the North Coast. Come to think of it, one good part — Byron Bay. Byron was tres chic — most of Balmain was there in summer. You had no trouble getting any sort of latte in Byron. Somehow I suspected Beechville wasn't like that. It sounded like the kind of place where Instant Roast and teabags were the order of the day.

Getting out of bed, I turned on my computer and typed the name into Google. There it was: Beechville — a small dot near the Queensland border. Why on earth would they need a public relations specialist there? What could happen in a country town like that? Something about that appealed, though. I'd had enough action for the time being.

I pictured myself in a rocking chair on a wide verandah — maybe strolling in to work to have my photo taken with a koala or on a rainforest walkway …

At least it wasn't too far from civilisation — if you could call Surfers Paradise and Brisbane civilised. Anything north of Hornsby was the wilderness as far as I was concerned, but, given the circumstances, you take what you can get. It would be quiet, boring maybe, but quiet. I'd have time to plan my comeback; recuperate my energies for a big re-entry.

Wazza would take me back; he'd never find anyone else as good as me. No, stuff Wazza, I'd set up in opposition to him. I might find my reputation to be an asset; in fact, I'm sure I would — once people had the chance to reflect on it. It showed I'd go the extra mile. Clients liked that.

The good part was, Beechville was North Coast and Rainforest Runaway was South Coast. Separation of these two places could only be beneficial.

The door clicked as Anthony let himself back in. Ripping out the ad, I placed it in my top drawer.

Beechville. I felt half-asleep at the thought of it.

Chapter Three

Three o'clock is always too late

As I'd expected, I had no trouble getting the job. They must have been in a hurry to fill the position — they flew me up for an interview the day after I emailed them my résumé. It was a one-hour flight to Coolangatta, then I hired a car and drove back across the border and inland.

It was amazing how fast the vestiges of civilisation died away as you headed west. One minute it was high rises and shopping malls, the next, tiny villages interspersed with lots of nothing. Never mind skinny latte, I didn't think they even ran to cappuccino out here.

Talk about winding roads — and dusty. Every five minutes or so some cow cocky in a battered ute would raise one finger from the wheel in a subtle salute as I went past. There was etiquette to this — it was always the pointer finger, and only lifted a smidgen off the wheel. I was pretty much in the swing of it by the time I got to Beechville.

The town itself was tucked in at the base of a range of mountains — probably the Queensland border. It was pretty — if you liked that kind of thing. A zigzagging road headed towards the gap between two mountains. The trees were thick up there, like a shag pile carpet — rainforest, I guessed.

Why *do* people get so excited about rainforest? Think about it — 'rain' forest. Those places are muddy. And what about leeches? I was yet to experience them and didn't plan to.

Beechville was basically one street — a pub, motel, petrol station, school, general store, council chambers, farming supplies shop, skatepark and … wildlife office — sleepy as. *Perfect*. It was the type of town you could hide out in forever. I straightened my skirt as I got out of the car. Without the air-conditioning it was warm and humid. A light breeze lifted my hair.

Over at the petrol station a round-bellied farmer type leaned on the back of his ute, watching me as he filled his car. I waved — I figured I'd better start making friends if I was planning on moving in. His nod was so subtle I'd have missed it if I blinked. As I turned away, a woman joined him.

I felt a tingling sensation between my shoulder blades. I always know when people are staring at my back. Maybe they didn't get a lot of passing traffic. Why would you come to a crappy place like this unless you had to?

The wildlife office was a Queenslander-style weatherboard building. Only one thing spoiled its folksy charm — the graffiti on the picket fence outside. You don't expect that in the country. I paused, deciphering the scrawl. *LOVA*, read the black curling letters — it was a gang, I supposed. Or maybe one bored, sunburnt farm kid in baggy jeans and a backwards-facing cap who liked to imagine himself on the bad streets of New York. My brother had been like that as a teenager. He'd retired his spray can since, but otherwise not much had changed.

Opening the gate, I climbed the creaking stairs to the office. A freckle-faced man — Rodney, his name badge said — showed me through. He seemed startled to see me for some reason.

'Oh, you're here for the interview?' He sounded like it was the last thing he would have expected. His eyes flicked over me in a frightened way.

I nodded slowly, not wanting to make any sudden movements. I suspected Beechville was the kind of place where people were easily startled.

I totally blitzed the interview, of course. Talk about a laugh — they got me to do a mock news release for a fox-baiting program. I mean who'd run a story like that?

I tried to sex it up, toying with headlines like *The Crimes Foxes Commit* and *Innocent Victims of a Fox's Greed*. Eventually I settled for *Secrets of Better Fox Killing*. Anything secret has to be good, right?

My interviewer — think Steve Irwin in drag — was a dauntingly capable woman, fortyish, brusque. She would have done well in the army. *Sam Patton, District Manager*, read the words on her shiny badge. A pager on her khaki hip went off several times during the interview. Each time she glanced at it quickly before continuing. She radiated a kind of suppressed energy, like a racehorse at the starting gate. I had no doubt she could have jumped up and run a marathon. Sitting down was clearly *not* her preferred posture.

I did ask why she needed a public relations consultant.

She seemed surprised that I would doubt it. 'It's not only this office you'll be responsible for, it's the whole region. We've got offices all over the place. It's *extremely* busy.' The muscles in her legs tensed, like she was dying to start hosing down all that busyness right now.

I nodded. Privately, I thought she and I had a different understanding of the word 'busy'. No-one who'd organised an A-list pirate-themed launch on a pontoon in Sydney Harbour could ever find a place like Beechville busy.

It was obvious she'd never heard of the astroturf scandal. It's funny, you feel like you're the centre of the universe in Sydney, but up here in the sticks that kind of news didn't rate. I'd flicked through the local paper while I was waiting for my interview. The price of stock — the four-legged kind — and roadworks had featured prominently. I didn't suppose the *Herald* even made it to Beechville.

The front-page story was about a feral pig the size of a pony holding a woman hostage in her house. Apparently every time she tried to go out, it charged the door. Eventually the Rural Fire Brigade had rescued her. Scary stuff. Who knew life in the country was so dangerous?

I'd put Wazza down as my referee. He'd been delighted. The last thing he wanted was me hanging around casting my shadow on him.

Sam pumped my hand as I stood up after the interview and almost crushed it. 'We'll be in touch.'

By the time she released me I was ready to cry for mercy. I winced as I straightened my fingers. I knew I'd got the job.

On the way out I saw the admin guy, Rodney, absorbed in some computer work. A mischievous impulse seized me. 'Byee,' I called loudly as I passed his desk.

He looked up, gasped, turned pale and stuttered, 'B-b ...'

I couldn't wait for him to finish, so I waggled my fingers and walked out.

The footpath back to my car crossed over a bridge. Stopping, I leaned over. The creek below was clear and golden brown; something splashed in the shallows. For a moment I had a strange urge to take my shoes off and paddle. I glanced at my phone — three o'clock.

Who was it who said three o'clock was always the wrong time for anything? That's right: Jean-Paul Sartre. Ah, the French philosophers, I hadn't thought about them for a while ... Jean-Paul Sartre, Blaise Pascal and, my favourite, René Descartes ... Those guys had loomed pretty large in my life at one stage.

I looked down at the creek again; I could almost feel the water between my toes. But no, in this case three o'clock was too late. The car lights flashed as I pressed the button on my key. If I was quick I'd have time for a whiskey at the airport before my flight.

By the time I landed in Sydney there was a message on my phone. They wanted me to start as soon as possible. That suited me just fine.

Back home, Ant took it harder than I expected. He wanted to come with me, which was cute, but I told him to sit tight. 'There'll be nothing for you there, Ant. These people don't go to hairdressers. You'll be better off here. You can visit, and I'll be back in six months. You can still stay in the apartment while I'm gone.' It was only fair, seeing as he'd given up his studio in Darlinghurst to move in with me only nine months ago.

I don't think he believed I was really going to Beechville. He probably thought it was all a front for a secret affair. Even when I was throwing my bags in the back of the Ferrari on Sunday he was still trying to talk me out of it. 'Where are you going to live? Have you thought of that? There mightn't be any suitable accommodation.'

'I'm living in one of the ranger houses.' I glanced at a printout of the email they'd sent me. 'Frog Hollow.'

Ant screwed up his nose. 'You don't even like frogs, Cassie.'

'Cassandra. And I *may* like frogs. I don't know yet.'

Ant ran his hands through his blond-streaked hair. 'You won't be able to.stand it up there, Cassandra. They won't have heard of skinny latte, and I bet their Thai restaurant won't be authentic.'

'There is no Thai restaurant, Ant.'

That shut him up. I think he was embarrassed for me.

There was one thing that couldn't be avoided before I left town.

Mum had been leaving increasingly frantic messages on my phone since the scandal had erupted.

'Cassie, what have you done? All my friends are talking about it. Is it a mistake? It must be a mistake. Call me back.'

'Cassie? I haven't heard from you — how do you attract these events into your life? You didn't used to be like this. Call me back.'

'Cassie? When are you going to call? You need to work out what you want from life. You know you only need to ask and the universe will provide. Call me back.'

This last message hinted at a new obsession. Like me, my mother believes there are guiding forces at play in our lives. Unlike me, she isn't satisfied with allowing a children's book to channel these forces for her.

Twirling the car keys in my hand, I dialled her number. My brother Brian answered the phone and for a glorious moment I thought Mum might be out.

'Cass? You are *so* in the shit. You've upset Mum. Mum, it's Cassie,' Brian called, dashing my hopes.

'Like *you* never upset her.' I can't speak to my family without sounding like a fifteen-year-old. The funny part is, I never used to sound like that when I actually *was* fifteen.

At that age I was Blacktown's sole gothic-punk French philosopher — *I think, therefore I am* — and so on. Yes, René Descartes and I were very close in those days.

I dressed in black, head to toe; black lipstick, beret and nail polish too. A copy of Descartes's *Passions of the Soul* was usually tucked under my arm and, like all teenagers, I was serene in the knowledge of my superiority to all those around me.

Why Descartes? It was mutiny, I suppose — a desire to cut myself free from the suburb I inhabited. Dinner might have been sausages in front of *Neighbours*, but the Paris Left Bank beckoned. *I am not one of them*, I thought, as I jostled with pimply boys and peroxide-haired girls on the train. I pictured myself strolling along the Seine discussing philosophy and love. Oh to be in love in Paris. Oh to be in love with René Descartes. What a shame he had the face of a walrus.

A demand to *clean your room, Cassie* would

be likely to bring a retort of *what is this bourgeois tidiness thing, Mother?* I'd regressed in some ways over the years since, I suppose, but I wasn't sorry to have ditched the Cartesian philosophy. I mean, who cares if *everything is self-evident*? It's all such a downer.

'That is totally beside the point, young lady.' Mum had snatched the phone off my brother.

By now I wasn't sure which point it was beside, but it didn't really matter. The horse races were on the radio in the background, so I knew I only had fifty percent of her attention. That was plenty for the half-baked script we were following.

I sighed and delivered my next line. 'I'm not fifteen anymore, you know.' I'm not sure that even *Home and Away* would get away with dialogue like this. Somehow, my family does, though.

'Exactly my point. Come on, Daylight Dancer.'

It's hard competing with a four-legged animal for your mother's attention. No wonder I avoided ringing home.

'I'm very upset, Cassie. Did you hear who won that one?' she said to Brian.

I ground my teeth.

'Cassie?' Mum sniffed.

'Yes, Mum.'

'Is it true what they say in the papers?'

I paused. I couldn't argue that the facts were true — it was the interpretation that was wrong. Just because I'd done those things, it didn't make me public enemy number one.

'Cassie. Answer my question.'

'Yes, Mum, but ...'

'I don't want to hear any excuses, Cassie. If it's true, then you need to ask for forgiveness.'

I tapped the toe of my boot on the ground; mothers can be so infuriating. 'Who's going to forgive me, Mum? Buddha? Shiva? Allah? Or have you moved on — Apollo, maybe, or Ra?' My mother is devout, but not in a monogamous way. I guess it shows an independent spirit.

'That is totally uncalled for, Cassie. There is no harm in leaving yourself open to the truth in whatever form it manifests itself.'

'No, Mum.' As in most dealings with my family, after frustration comes guilt. 'So, what is the truth?' I bit my tongue to stop myself adding 'today'.

'Well, I'm very into the Egyptians, as it happens, but I've also been reading this fantastic book.'

'A book?' This was something new. Most of Mum's information came from television.

'Yes, I saw a program on the telly, then I bought the book. You probably won't have heard of it.'

'Try me.'

'It's called *The Secret*. Because it's all about this secret that's been suppressed for centuries. People in power have tried to keep it hidden. Some of the greatest minds in history were teachers of —'

'I've heard of *The Secret*, Mum.'

'Have you really?' Her voice was breathless. 'That's not coincidence you know, Cassie.'

'Yes, Mum. Anyway, I'm going away for a while so I won't be able to come to the barbecue on Sunday.'

'Oh, Cassie … I've already bought your favourite sausages.'

'Don't tell me she's not coming to the barbecue.' Brian's voice carried from the background. 'Typical. Got a better offer, has she? Oh, come on, Golden Dream. Tell her the one about the interrupting cow, Mum.'

'Tell her yourself,' said Mum.

'I'm sorry, Mum.' Funnily enough, I *was* sorry. I hated the weekend barbecue at Blacktown, but now that I was leaving I viewed it through a soft-focus lens of nostalgia. Brian and his crappy jokes, Mum and her pineapple salad, *Gladiators* on the box afterwards … Who knew when I'd get back there? 'I won't be gone for long.'

But Mum had already moved on. 'Rhonda, who's the author of *The Secret*, says you need to focus on your goal and you will get what you want. It's the Law of Attraction. I found a fantastic statuette at Kmart yesterday. I went in there thinking, I'm going to find a nice inspirational statue for the garden, and there it was.'

'What sort of statue?'

'It's a frog. I've got it on the bench here, right now. It's Heqet, the Egyptian frog goddess of resurrection, which is not the type of thing you usually find in Kmart at all. Well, they didn't say it was Heqet in the shop, but it's quite obvious. She's the daughter of Ra. You should try this Secret thing, Cassie.'

'Maybe I will, Mum. Soon as I figure out what I want.' My mind wandered. This Rhonda Byrne was making squillions from *The Secret*. My *Alice in Wonderland* Theory of the Universe couldn't be any more stupid. Was I missing out on a big marketing opportunity here? *The secret they tried to hide ... the secret of ... Alice.* It had possibilities.

'I'll stick the sausages in the freezer and we'll have them when you get back.'

'That'll be great. Thanks, Mum. Bye.'

I placed the phone down carefully and picked up my handbag — time to go.

So that is how I was ejected from the Garden of Eden. Is it any wonder there was no love lost between wildlife and me?

Chapter Four

Who are you?

I can't say leaving Sydney didn't hit me hard. It was my town and I loved it. Sadly, it no longer loved me back.

It's not like I'd never been anywhere else. I zipped up to Noosa or Byron once a year, and down to Melbourne every now and then for the clothes and music. I'd done the tax-deductible PR conferences in Europe, America and Japan. But every time I flew back into Sydney it was a homecoming.

I hadn't always felt that way — not when I was growing up in Blacktown. What shy, gothic, René Descartes-reading teenager does? I'm not sure there even *were* any other teenagers who shared my interests. If there were, I never met them. It was lonely out there in the west. When people talk about their school days I generally go quiet. There's not a lot I want to remember, really.

But the new and improved Cassandra fit Sin City like a cork in a champagne bottle. Only someone had shaken the bottle and out I'd popped — *bang* — onto the dreaded Pacific Highway heading north.

I was uncomfortable, like I'd been in the bath and someone had pulled the plug. It wasn't life threatening, but ... I was definitely losing buoyancy. *The Country. The Country and me.* The idea was outlandish. I felt like I might be about to fall right through the centre of the earth, like Alice, and come out where people walked upside down.

Ant — that sneaky bastard — had given me a special compilation CD. He'd slipped it in my hand as he kissed me goodbye and I'd tossed it onto the passenger seat.

I pushed it into the CD player at Hornsby and almost did a U-ie as 'Darlinghurst Nights' started. After that came 'From St Kilda to Kings Cross', 'Miracle (in Marrickville)', 'King Street', 'Khe Sanh', 'Sydney from a 727'...

He surprised me sometimes, Ant. Just when I thought I'd got him figured out, he pulled a stunt like this. He wasn't relying on his own attractions to bring me back; he'd got the whole city on his team.

I dialled our number on my car phone as I drove over the Hawkesbury River. I was officially out of Sydney now. It was lucky he wasn't home or I might have said something I'd regret later. As it was I contented myself with, 'Hey, big boy — nice move on the CD. Be good.'

Six months, I told myself again. *Six months max.*

I was still singing along to 'King Street' as I drove into Beechville. After ten hours on the road I was ready to put my feet up. Whatever form of comfort was on offer in this godforsaken town, I wanted it, and I wanted it now.

Beechville looked like it had been struck by the Black Death — not a soul in sight. I'd thought it was quiet when I came up for the interview, but it had been like Pitt Street rush hour compared to the way it was now. Only a couple of cars outside the pub suggested any sort of life — *but not as we know it, Jim.* I drove through without stopping. A grassy paddock with roaming cows fringed the town and then — all signs of human presence ceased.

Amazing.

I was used to a city that never ended. You could spend all day driving in Sydney and never leave it. Here it was in and out, just like that. *In. Out.* It suddenly hit me: there was more bush than town, more *out* than *in*. It sounds obvious, but it was a revelation — a disturbing one.

They'd told me 'Frog Hollow' was on the left, ten minutes out of town, on the way to the border. I pulled over to the side of the road after ten minutes and got out of the car, sliding into my sandals. It was almost dark. The sun had already sunk behind the mountains. A black shape loomed out of the sky and flapped past me, almost brushing my face. *Ew, a bat.* I jumped, squeaked and climbed back in the car.

Look for a dirt track, the email had said. This direction had seemed okay at the time, but out here in the middle of nowhere it now revealed itself as ludicrously vague. Turning on the headlights, I drove slowly, looking for turnoffs. There were no friendly cottages or beaming farmers to give directions — nothing except bush right up to the edge of the road.

The corridor of trees reminded me of a program I'd watched on lost tribes of the Amazon. This was the kind of forest you could hide a group of cannibal pygmies in without anyone ever knowing. I heard drumbeats, then realised my CD was still playing softly. I turned it off, my ears scanning for threatening sounds.

A dirt track headed off to the left. Stopping my car at the junction, I cursed the composer of the stupid directions. I'd have something to say to — picking up the printout, I flicked my eyes down to the signature block of the email — *Mac*, when I saw him.

It was a dirt track, but was it *the* dirt track? Why hadn't they tied a balloon to a post or something? That would have been the friendly thing to do. Weren't people supposed to be friendly in the country?

Gritting my teeth, I turned up the track and was immediately swallowed by darkness. Dense forest enclosed the road, blocking out the last of the daylight. My car bumped and bottomed out a couple of times as I edged forward. It was like that scene in *Rocky Horror* where Brad and Janet get lost. *Any minute now I should come across the Frankenfurter castle ...* Eventually a cottage appeared in my headlights.

Hallelujah.

There were no lights on. Maybe this was Frog Hollow. How would I know?

Chickens clucked as I climbed out of the car. A wire chicken pen stood beside the house and a hammock hung on the verandah — signs of habitation. So maybe this wasn't Frog Hollow, but I could ask for directions anyway.

I walked towards the house — sneaked was a better description. It was so quiet, and I was miles from anywhere. I wasn't used to being surrounded by so many trees. More and more it felt like the opening scene in a horror movie.

And then I noticed the arm hanging down from the hammock.

It looked lifeless.

I stopped, gnawing my fingernails, something I hadn't done for years. Surely, if that person was alive, they would have heard me drive up? The arm was suntanned, muscular, with a tattoo of a wolf on the shoulder. No, not a wolf, a tiger. It had stripes — a funny-looking tiger. The tattooist must have been drunk.

I tiptoed towards the hammock. Pausing a short distance away, I peered over the edge. A man lay inside it. He wore only a loose pair of khaki shorts. A camera was tucked in beside his waist. He was also, as I had suspected, dead. No-one sleeps that soundly. Not at six thirty in the evening. I held my breath, chewed my lip, inspected the body, wondered what the usual protocol was in this situation.

Behind me the chickens clucked in an agitated way. Why were they doing that? I was suddenly deeply freaked out. Was there someone out there? Behind me? My heart beat double-time as I swung around. I needed to get out of here — report the body.

Then I heard a sound from the hammock — a moan.

I turned.

The man's eyes opened.

I screamed.

'What the fuck?' He sat up.

I screamed again.

He rubbed his eyes. 'Who are you? Can you stop screaming?'

I stopped screaming. *How embarrassing.* 'Sorry. I'm lost. Do you know where Frog Hollow is?'

The man was slow to answer, like he was having trouble waking up. There was something odd about him, even if he *was* alive. Maybe he was a drug addict. Probably. *Definitely.* There was a lot of that around on the North Coast, I'd heard. The heavy stuff too, *heroin, ice* ... Not just coke, like the Sydney PR crowd. I took a step backwards.

He gazed at my face intently, but still didn't say anything. I noticed he was sort of cute-looking — for a heroin addict.

'Over there,' he said eventually, pointing.

I followed his finger. Another bush track headed off the one I'd driven in on. I'd missed it in the dark. 'Okay, thanks. Sorry to bother you.' I backtracked to the car, noting the lack of any polite response on his part. *No trouble, pleased to help, welcome to the country ...*

I glanced in the rear-vision mirror as I drove off. The arm was hanging over the edge of the hammock again. *Great, I've got a drug addict for a neighbour.*

I found Frog Hollow at the end of the rutted laneway. It was a tiny weatherboard cottage badly in need of a paint job and about as welcoming as a Sydney airport cabbie. After a few deep breaths I summoned the courage to go in. The key was under the front doormat, as they'd said in the email. As I opened the door a dank, unused smell almost bowled me over.

My mobile rang; it was Ant. His voice was crackly — the mountains weren't helping reception. 'Hiya ... Okay? Did you ... CD?'

Assuming a fake cheeriness, I walked down the lino-clad corridor. I didn't want to worry him or he'd be on the next plane up here. 'Yeah thanks, darl, great CD, loved it. It's a pretty little cottage they've given me.' I reeled back at the sight of the kitchen — peeling lino benches, no dishwasher, two-ring gas oven, cobwebs over the windows. 'Very ... rustic. Nice garden.' That was a total lie; there was no garden, just bush right up to the house. I was busting for a pee. 'Gotta go, snooks.'

I suddenly missed him. If Ant were here, he would whisk me away to a five-star hotel as soon as he saw this place. 'Love you.' I didn't say that very often, but right now I felt like I did love him, or if not him, our life together. I definitely loved that. *Six months at most, maybe five.*

'Love … poochy,' said Ant, as I opened the toilet door, '… you biiig time.'

I folded my phone shut, lifted the lid of the toilet and, for the third time in ten minutes, screamed. Looking up at me from the toilet bowl were two black eyes. The owner of the eyes — a green frog the size of my hand — was doing slow laps around the bowl. My house was not only froggy by name, but by nature.

'Crawk.'

Yes, it was you, my little listener, soul mate and muse — our very first meeting. Not an auspicious start to our relationship at all. And things did get worse before they got better, didn't they?

I slammed the toilet lid shut, then hesitated. What if it wanted to get out? I lifted it again, went outside and peed on the grass. A weird cough-like bark sounded nearby as I stood up. A brown shape the size of a chicken scuttled through the bushes. God only knew what animals were out there. The forest rustled around me — *all the way to Queensland and beyond.* It was primitive and untamed — the opposite of the Garden of Eden. All that forest, and only a freaky drug addict and me to call it home. It was a scary thought.

I sniffed the air. It smelt of dirt and rot and bark. I'd never smelt anything like it before. I sniffed again, searching for an odour I associated with the outdoors I knew — grass clippings, flowers, dog poo … Any of these would have done. But nothing about the smell of this air was familiar.

I ran inside, but it was no better in there. The tiny house was scant protection against such a vast outdoors. There were scuffles and creaks all around me — like the *out* was coming *in*.

A single bed with rusty springs graced the bedroom, but no sheets or blankets. I hadn't thought of that — for some reason I'd imagined motel-style living. *Stupid, really.* Making a nest out of my extra-large beach towel and pashmina shawl, I crawled inside.

My handbag was on the floor next to the bed. I lifted it up by its strap and scrabbled around inside. For a terrible moment I thought I'd forgotten it, but no, there it was, under the phone, tampons, water bottle, lipstick, business cards, hairbrush, deodorant, notebook, pen, headache tablets and peppermints: my lavender. Thank goodness. Opening the lid, I sprinkled a few drops on the towel that was my pillow. This was a habit I'd picked up from Mum in her aromatherapy phase. *Men find it irresistible, Cassandra. Just look at Cleopatra. Julius Caesar and Mark Antony wouldn't have been nearly as much in love with her without the lavender.*

It's a pity Mum didn't discover lavender before Dad left. You never know, it could have made all the difference. Anyway, I don't know if lavender makes me irresistible, but it does help me sleep.

I pulled out *Alice* for some bedtime wisdom. '*Who are* you?' *said the Caterpillar.*

That's what I love about *Alice* — the philosophy. All right, I admit it: you can take the girl out of Descartes, but you can't take Descartes out of the girl. The question was one worthy of René himself. Who *was* I? Was it really *me*, here in this hideous house? I certainly didn't feel like the Cassandra I knew anymore.

But who *was* the Cassandra I knew — the shy kid, the punk teenager, the rebellious uni student or the glam PR exec? I thought I knew, but now I wasn't so sure. Was there another version of me out there somewhere? Could I pretend to be someone else and see what happened? There was something tempting about that idea.

I curled up under my shawl, listened to the alien sounds of the bush and wondered how I'd ended up here, miles from my natural habitat. Headphones in my ears to block out the noises, I finally fell asleep to someone singing about a bus to Bondi.

Some hours later I woke up with a start — sweating. It was the dream, the one I'd had every night since it happened — a large and menacing long-footed potoroo lurked outside my window. It opened its mouth in a sinister smile, showing long, sharp teeth. *Where to now, Cassandra?* it said.

Part Two

*so many out-of-the-way things had happened
lately, that Alice had begun to think that very
few things indeed were really impossible*

Alice's Adventures in Wonderland

Chapter Five

Of pigs and men ...

The Beechville Wildlife Office was empty when I got there on Monday, ready for work. I was jaded and ratty after a night full of wildlife dreams and noises, but I put on my best PR face as I climbed the stairs.

Standing at the front counter, I tinkled the little bell. I'd dressed down for my first day on the job — a simple black suit. I couldn't resist wearing my Jimmy Choo backless sandals but I was pretty sure no-one here would notice.

Eventually a figure in ranger uniform appeared. As he got closer I realised I knew him. What a surprise — it was the man from the hammock, my strange neighbour. He still looked exhausted. His hair was sticking up from his head like he hadn't had time to comb it, and a two-day growth blackened his chin.

It must be tough holding down a job when you're a drug addict. He frowned as he saw me.

It wasn't the reception I was used to but I smiled brightly — you work with what you've got. 'Hello, you must be the lone ranger. I'm Cassandra. I'm starting work here today. We met last night. We're neighbours, I guess.'

He was taciturn to the point of grumpy. 'I'm Mac,' he grunted.

Author of the dodgy directions, no less. Given his mood, I decided to let it pass.

'They've left some reading for you,' he said.

He definitely wasn't bad-looking. In a *Raiders of the Lost Ark* kind of way — square-jawed, broad shoulders in crumpled khaki, curly dark hair, bright blue, if slightly bloodshot, eyes. The uniform did it for me, I must say — sexy as. The waves of irritation that radiated off him weren't as much of a turn-on, though. I'm sensitive to that sort of thing.

I followed him across the office. It was small, just a few workstations. The only signs of habitation were the wildlife posters that covered every wall. 'Where is everyone?'

'Been an outbreak of plant hoppers.'

I nodded sagely. Judging by his tone this was not a good thing. 'That's a bugger.'

Mac eyed me strangely. 'Yeah, it is. There's only three of us anyway.' He paused. 'Four now. That's your desk.'

'Okay, thanks. I'll get straight onto it.' My desk had not escaped the plague of wildlife posters. Shiny eyes and pointy beaks surrounded me as I sat down. *Threatened birds of the North Coast*, read the title on one poster. *Threatening*, would have been more to the point.

Another poster was adorned with frogs. I recognised my toilet bowl companion — it was a green tree frog. *Why wasn't it in a tree then?*

A note lay next to my computer. It was from Sam — the female Steve Irwin — my new boss, and it looked like it had been written while driving a car with one hand. *Hi Cassie.* I mentally snorted. Cassandra. *Sorry I couldn't be here to settle you in. The main thing to do is organise the Feral Pig Awareness Morning. I've left some detailed notes on the file. See you later, Sam.* Her name trailed off the edge of the paper as if she'd run off while finishing it.

Feral Pig Awareness Morning. It sounded kind of new-agey. I imagined incense burning, pigs in kaftans sipping green tea. *Breathe deeply and raise your awareness, piggies.* What next? *Discover your inner sow? Rebirth as a piglet?* It *was* the North Coast, after all, even if a decidedly un-funky pocket. A giggle exploded through my nose. Mac looked up.

'Feral Pig Awareness Morning,' I spluttered. 'Is this for real?'

Mac frowned. 'S'pose so. They're a bit of a problem.' He turned back to the maps he was shuffling on his desk.

I bit my lip. *Okay. Feral Pig Awareness Morning here we come.* It wasn't what I was used to, but you can cope with anything for a few months, right?

I flicked through the files on my desk. There was some background on feral pigs and suggested speakers. Sam was obviously something of a control freak. She had listed all the contact details on an Excel spreadsheet. Paper-clipped to the back was a flowchart showing the project management stages for the event. I ignored that. Event management was my forte. *Flowchart, shmowchart.* Taking a deep breath, I attempted to banish all amusement; this was my job now.

Working the phones diligently for the rest of the morning, I lined up the program. I was pleasantly surprised by how helpful people were and how easy to contact. It was like they were sitting by the phone waiting for my call. There was none of that phone tag game you play in Sydney. There, it's almost embarrassing if people can get you on the first call. It implies you're not busy, which is like admitting you're a failure. People here seemed fine with admitting they had nothing better planned than attending a feral pig morning. They also seemed fine with chatting on for at least ten minutes in order to ascertain my life history and tell me theirs.

Mac glanced over in my direction with a frown every now and then. Maybe the office was usually quieter than this. There wasn't much I could do about that. Building relationships was part of my job. A few people came into the office and he got up to deal with them.

It was a slow morning, but I *did* learn a lot about

pigs. You never know when that sort of thing will come in handy as a conversation starter. I imagined myself at a cocktail party: *Did you know that in dry conditions groups of up to a hundred pigs will gather around waterholes, dahling?* Maybe not.

Mac stood up at twelve o'clock. 'Keep an eye on the front desk while I'm at lunch, will you?'

He'd barely left when the bell tinkled on the front counter. I rose, with some trepidation. I'd heard Mac dealing with phone calls and counter inquiries and I wasn't sure if I was up to it. I hadn't realised how *annoying* wildlife was.

One didn't really have to think about wildlife in Sydney at all. I know some Americans think kangaroos bound down our main streets, but it isn't true. I do remember watching a remake of *Skippy the Bush Kangaroo* in my teens. There wasn't much on television that escaped my family. That was the extent of my wildlife experience, apart from the odd chip-stealing seagull in Manly.

Here in Beechville an army of surly wildlife was hell-bent on harassing its innocent citizens. From the bits I'd heard, queries had ranged from angry people who'd:

(a) been swooped by a magpie,
(b) had their gardens ruined by bandicoots,
(c) had their sleep disturbed by possums or,
(d) had rabbits in their backyard they wanted
   Mac to catch.

Mac had dealt with each of these inquiries with incredible politeness. More politeness than he'd shown me, I had to say. A muttered, 'Dickhead,' as he put the phone down on the rabbit call was the only sign they were getting to him.

So, I approached the counter with caution, not sure what I was going to find. *Maybe someone with*:

(a) a snake wrapped around them,
(b) a bat tangled in their hair, or
(c) a dingo gnawing at their ankles?

The woman at the counter seemed harmless enough. She was middle-aged, short-haired and wore a T-shirt and track pants. A shoebox was clutched in her hands.

She looked at me suspiciously. 'Where's the ranger?'

'He's out to lunch. Can I help?'

She pushed the shoebox towards me. 'Found this swimming in my pool.'

I took the box warily. It was light and something scuttled around inside.

'I think it's a Hastings River mouse. You put a brochure out about it.'

I nodded, not wanting to admit my ignorance. 'I'll get the ranger to have a look when he gets in.'

The woman scribbled her name and phone number on the box. 'Let me know what it is.'

I placed the box under my desk and promptly

forgot about it in the excitement of getting ready for the feral pig morning. It was scheduled, I now realised, for Thursday. Better get cracking. I looked at my list of things to do. I'd already done almost all of them. On second thoughts I'd better slow down if I didn't want to run out of work. Perhaps life in the country required a more measured approach to task management.

Several hours later, in the midst of the mid-afternoon torpor, something ran over my Jimmy Choo sandal. I jumped up, shrieking. A small, furry creature scuttled across the floor and under a filing cabinet.

Mac leapt to his feet. 'What was that? It looked like a Hastings River mouse. Where'd it come from?'

He was quick off the mark — mouse identification in a flash. *Pretty impressive.* I pulled the box out from under my table. A small hole had been gnawed in the side. 'Oops.' I explained about the woman who'd come in while he was at lunch.

Mac stalked over and snatched the box off me. Her contact details were written on the outside. 'Shit, Christine Bowles. We're in for it now.'

'Why?'

'She's the most bloody-minded woman in Beechville. She's a local councillor with a hotline to the *Beechville Star.* She hates us because she reckons we don't do enough weed control and ... now you've lost her Hastings River mouse.' He was about as happy as a bride with no seating plan.

'What's the big deal with the Hastings River mouse?'

Mac pointed to a poster on the wall. It showed a mousey creature sitting on its haunches under a shrub.

Have you seen the Hastings River mouse?
The Hastings River mouse hasn't been sighted
in this area for ten years. If you think you
have seen one, please report it to your local
wildlife office.

'It's critically endangered. If she's got a Hastings River mouse on her property it's big news. It means more funding — more funding for weed work and that's what she wants.'

I pursed my lips and nodded. It was hard to believe a mouse was so important, but Mac obviously thought so. 'I'll catch it.'

'You'd better, or we're up shit creek.' Mac stalked back to his workstation.

That was the longest conversation we had all day.

I placed the box on my desk, ready to jump if the mouse ran past, but it was still at large when I went home.

The sun had dropped behind the mountains, leaving Frog Hollow in shadow as I jolted up the driveway. I shivered as I got out of the car. Wasn't it supposed to be warm on the North Coast? As if it wasn't enough to be plagued by animals at work, I now remembered my little problem here. Walking cautiously to the toilet, I peered inside.

The frog was there — its black eyes regarding me with Buddha-like calm. I met its gaze. It was a beautiful shade of green — like last season's colours. I had a handbag in exactly that shade. Lime green was so hot last year.

You're a little out of fashion now, but I know you don't care about that sort of thing.

It had me — I must admit — at a loss. *I need toilet. Frog is in toilet. I can't use toilet while frog is in it.* My mind was stuck in *Fun with Dick and Jane* early-reader mode. There was also the alarming possibility that if the frog could get in my toilet, other things could too. Maybe things that weren't as charming in last season's colours. *Things like snakes and rats …*

Meanwhile, it gazed up at me innocently. There was no way I was going to the toilet on top of it. It wouldn't be nice. And it might jump. Maybe it had sharp teeth. It *looked* harmless, but so did cows and apparently they killed more people each year than sharks.

I plodded out to the kitchen. Noodles and bananas were on the menu for dinner — not very satisfying, but probably slimming. After dinner I was at a bit of a loose end. I looked in all the cupboards in case they'd hidden a television somewhere, but of course there was none.

Sitting on the couch, I tried to read the *PR Weekly* I'd brought with me. I needed to keep up-to-date if I was going to make a successful comeback. What was I thinking? *If.* Of course I was going to make a successful comeback. What else *could* I do? I turned the pages, but not much went in. Maybe I should try something lighter? I put it down and picked up *The Sydney Magazine* instead.

I flipped through the pages. A face jumped out at me — Simon bloody McKechnie. The article was titled *Hard Drinking Journalists — Why Abstinence is the New Black.* That bastion of hard drinking, the news room, was now, if you could believe the article, full of herbal tea-sipping reformed alcos. Simon had been a heavy drinker even at university. Dancing bare-chested on the table at the pub was his usual Saturday-night routine. So he was on the wagon now, huh? *Wish he'd bloody drunk himself to death.*

An insect scuttled across my foot. I jumped up. It was a cockroach. In the corner of my eye I saw something else move — another one. As I looked around, I realised my lounge room was like a version of *Where's Wally?*. For *Wally*, substitute *Cocky*. Once I got my eye in, there were millions of them. I rolled my magazine up and clenched it in my fist.

Cockroach killing turned out to be quite satisfying. Who would have thought? Visualising Simon Teetotal McKechnie's face on each insect made it even more fun. Once I'd killed twenty I sat down again. *Now what?* An owl hooted outside, an unknown animal walked heavily across my roof, a lime green frog swam silently around my toilet. What was I doing here? *'Who are you?' said the Caterpillar.*

I walked into the bathroom and looked inside the toilet. 'If you take away my six-figure salary, my Manly beach lifestyle and my social whirl, am I still Cassandra Daley?'

'Crawk.'

I could tell you thought it was a good question.

'You're a bit of a philosopher, aren't you?'

My voice echoed around the bathroom. I didn't like it. I know we enter and leave this world alone, but I do like a bit of company in between. I started to leave.

'Crawk.'

I came back again and looked at the frog. I'd heard a voice in my head. A voice with a French accent. 'What's that? *Cogito ergo sum?* I think, therefore I am?'

*You didn't answer, of course. I didn't expect
you to. But I recognised the quote — my old
mate Descartes was making a comeback.*

'René, is that you?'

It was my mother who first introduced me to René Descartes. She had been at a dream workshop where his name was invoked. Descartes was a great one for dreams. It was, in fact, a dream that got him started on the philosophy lark in the first place. Three dreams, to be precise, all taking place on the one night.

In the first, he was buffeted by a whirlwind. In the second, he was woken by thunder to see sparks coming from his stove. In the third, he found a dictionary of Latin poets on the bedside table and read a verse beginning with the words, *What path shall I take in life?* He took these dreams as an instruction to follow a path of wisdom.

The teenage Cassandra liked his style. A man not afraid to take direction from a dream — it showed intuition and daring. And his philosophy got right to the heart of things — existence, meaning, mind ... *Am I a person dreaming of a butterfly, or a butterfly dreaming of a person?* What more do you need? Descartes was a worthy companion to Alice. I would have liked to introduce him to her. In their quirky way, both were seekers after truth.

Leaving René to paddle in my toilet bowl, I went outside to pee again. It was incredibly dark. The trees towered over the house, blocking out the starlight. No lights showed over at Mac's house. He was a hard man to work out. Why was he so tired if he went to bed early? It would be nice to be friends, but I couldn't see that happening. My only neighbour seemed to dislike me intensely. Why? I didn't know.

The bushes rustled next to me and again I heard that coughing bark. I scurried back inside. *Five months max, maybe four.*

'Darlinghurst Nights' serenaded me to sleep.

Chapter Six

Keep in touch

Rodney, the admin officer, returned from the plant hopper front on Tuesday.

He was startled all over again when he saw me, although he must have known I was coming. 'Hello, er, Cassandra. Have you settled in all right?' A tide of red swept over his freckles.

I swung my Calvin Klein handbag. I'd got into the spirit of things today, in a khaki mini-dress, with army overtones, and ankle boots. 'Yep, right into it, thanks.' I glanced around the office. There was no sign of my boss, Sam.

Rodney correctly interpreted my look. 'Whale stranding down the coast. Big surf bringing 'em in. Sam's the expert on that kind of thing.' He sounded like he was having trouble talking.

Rodney looked like the surf had brought him in

too. His hair was plastered flat to his head and strips of sunburnt skin peeled off his nose. Had the man never heard of sunscreen? By the time he was thirty, he'd look fifty. He propped a surfboard up next to his desk.

I gazed at the surfboard. Maybe I was disorientated, but I'd been thinking we were miles from the sea. It had felt like at least a few hours from the ocean when I drove here. 'How far is it to the beach?'

''Bout forty-five minutes.' Rodney's Adam's apple worked furiously. 'If you push it. Bit of a drive. Worth it, but.' He coughed.

I tapped the toe of my boot on the floorboards, wondering what would happen if I asked him another question. Would he hyperventilate and faint? It could be fun to see.

'How was it?' Mac wandered in, flinging his backpack on the table. Red streaks crisscrossed his eyes and dark circles stained the skin beneath them. He must have been hitting it hard. Funny, he didn't seem like a party boy.

Relieved from the battle front, Rodney's face relaxed. *Was I that scary?* 'Unreal, really pumping. Where were you?'

Mac smiled. So he did know how to do that. 'Slept in.'

Rodney sat down at his desk and Mac's smile turned to irritation as I pulled a piece of bread out of my bag, placing it near the filing cabinet where I'd last seen the mouse.

He snorted. 'Here.' Walking to his desk, he picked up a metal box. 'Use this, then at least we might catch it. There's some carrots in the fridge. That's what they like.'

He was gone before I could ask him what the box was. I fiddled with it and one of the ends pushed down. Fetching the carrot, I placed it inside and put the trap on the floor.

Next on the agenda was reading the paper. One of my duties, apparently, was to scan the pile of local papers each morning for wildlife-related stuff. I didn't have to go far this morning. *Rogue Magpie Holds Street Hostage*, screamed the headline. The accompanying photo showed a woman with an umbrella over her head racing for her car while a magpie dived towards her. I tagged the article and moved on, but there was nothing else of note.

There was, however, a message on my phone. 'This is Christine Bowles — have you got an ID on the mouse yet?' Her voice was terse. 'I'm sure it was a Hastings River mouse. I've called the paper. They want to come over and take a picture of it.'

Shit. Now what? The woman was as dogged as a Nigerian spam emailer. I glanced around the office. Why was this *my* problem? Mac was hunched over his computer, typing. Rodney — judging by the action in my email inbox — was busy with filing, car booking and stationery orders. For an office with only four staff — one missing in action — there was a lot of administration required.

My phone rang. It was Rodney, which was strange. If he'd raised his voice it would have had the same effect. '*Beechville Star*,' gulp, 'at the front counter,' gulp, 'for you.'

Damn, that was fast. *Deny, deny, deny?* That hadn't gone so well for me last time. *Tell the truth?* Impossible. 'Mac?'

He looked up.

'The *Beechville Star* wants to take a photo of the mouse. What do I tell them?'

'You're the PR guru.' He turned back to his computer.

Jesus. And I'd thought this job would be so simple.

Smoothing down my skirt, I strode to the counter. A well-scrubbed young man with a camera over his shoulder leaned against the wall in the lobby. I reckoned he was straight out of a Journalism degree. *Lucky me.*

I gave him my best smile. 'Hi, I'm Cassandra Daley. You're here about the mouse?'

His cheeks coloured as he straightened up. I hadn't lost it then.

'I am *so* sorry, we had to send it to the vet. It had a sniffle and we didn't want to risk it — you know, being such a rare mouse.'

'Oh.' He pulled at the knot of his tie. 'When will it be back?'

'Not until tomorrow, I'm afraid.' I eyed the trap out of the corner of my eye. 'Maybe the next day if it's a bad cold. Shall I give you a ring and let you know?'

He pulled his card out of the camera bag and handed it to me. 'Anything else on?'

'I'm running a Feral Pig Awareness Morning on Thursday,' I glanced at his card, 'Justin.'

He flushed again.

'Did you realise feral pigs inhabit sixty-one percent of Australia?'

Justin shook his head.

I leaned over the counter and lowered my voice, like I was imparting a secret. 'Female pigs produce up to twelve piglets every year. They inflict terrible damage on the environment.' Knowledge retention has always been one of my strong points. 'You'll be there, won't you?' I knew he would be.

As Justin departed, a woman carrying a plastic cage with a little joey in it came up the stairs. She opened her mouth to speak but I pre-empted her. 'I'll get the ranger, shall I?'

'Front counter,' I said to Mac as I sat down at my desk. 'You're the wildlife guru.' I jumped as the mouse ran over my foot towards the kitchen, totally ignoring the tasty carrot in the trap.

Given the media interest, I decided I'd better do a bit of background research on the Hastings River mouse. A library cabinet in the corner of the room held a surprisingly thick volume titled *Threatened Species of the Far North Coast*. I carried it back to my desk and flicked to 'H'. Apparently the Hastings River mouse had now vanished from most of its former range in Queensland and New South Wales and was thought to be extinct until 1981, when one was found in the Tablelands, a day's drive south of here.

The main threats it faced were loss of forest, bushfires, grazing and being eaten by foxes, feral pigs and cats. Conserving vegetation next to streams was the best way to help it recover. That was obviously where Christine Bowles and her weed work came in. And, now I thought of it, me and my feral pig day.

For the lack of any other tasks, planning for the pig morning continued. I pulled out my usual event checklist.

- *Establish goals and objectives of the event — what does the client want to achieve?* Sam hadn't left me any details about that, but it was pretty straightforward — improve awareness of feral pigs, I imagined. *Check.*
- *Establish target audiences the client wants to reach.* I glanced at the file. Sam had said mainly farmers ...

I couldn't resist a sigh at this point. *Farmers.* It was a far cry from the last event I'd organised. There, my target audience had been the newspaper social pages, the *Vogue* entertainment round-up, the eastern suburbs socialites ... Had Wazza replaced me yet? I'd thought I was irreplaceable, but I suppose no-one is really.

I sighed again, then shook my head to clear it of these thoughts, focusing on my checklist. There was no point in feeling sorry for myself. *Farmers.* I could do better than that. *Check.*

- *Set the time and date.* Already sorted. *Check.*
- *Do celebrities need to be booked?* Celebrities might be hard to come by, however ...

Mac had finished with the injured joey. It was in a box beside his desk awaiting collection. 'Do you know much about feral pigs?' I said.

Mac yawned. 'More than I want to.'

'Want to launch the Feral Pig Awareness Morning?'

'Launch?'

'You know, give a little speech, tell some funny tales about feral pigs you have known, introduce the speakers, sign programs, that kind of thing ...'

Mac looked at me like I was speaking a foreign language. 'That's not how we usually do it.' He paused, like he was on the verge of saying no, then apparently reconsidered. 'But yeah, okay.' He pulled out his diary. 'When is it?'

'Thursday, ten am.'

He scribbled a note. 'Fine.'

'Thanks.' I was speaking to the back of his head. He'd already turned to his computer. I continued with my list.

- *Establish venue — consider quirky location, space, water views ...*

I glanced at the file. Sam had suggested the Beechville CWA Hall. Looked like I'd have to go with quirky. 'How do you book the CWA Hall?' I called to Mac again.

His eyebrows drew together. 'Maureen, the CWA President.' He hesitated. 'At the supermarket.' He turned abruptly and picked up his phone.

I slid my Jackie O sunglasses on. 'Going out for a minute,' I called to Rodney.

The so-called supermarket was across the road from the office. I hadn't made it there yet — I'd been living on the instant noodles, crackers and bananas I'd bought on the drive up; penance for my binge-eating episode in Sydney.

It was warm out on the street and very quiet — a cow mooed in the distance. Rural noises were still a novelty to me. The town was pretty much dead in the middle of the day. In the mornings the school kids at the bus stop added a bit of action with their chattering and shoving but right now you could have fired a rocket down the street without hitting anyone.

As I strolled across the empty road I noticed the graffiti artist or artists had struck here too — *LOVA* was scrawled across the shop's red brick facade. I was surprised they didn't get someone to scrub it off — maybe they were beyond caring. It's not like Beechville was the kind of place that attracted tourists.

There was only one person on duty at the shop — two dusty rows of tinned goods and a few wilted vegies do not constitute a supermarket in my books. As I got closer I read the woman's name badge — it was Maureen. 'Hello.' I gave her a cheery wave. 'I'm here about the hall.'

She had the face of a pit bull terrier, only twice as scary. I don't think she liked the look of me either. Her eyes flickered up and down as she stood at the checkout, her vivid orange hair glowing under the fluorescent light. Anthony would have had a fit. He sometimes got physically sick if he saw people with a bad hair job. She bagged groceries while I hovered behind her sole customer, a farmer in a battered Akubra hat.

As the man left the shop she folded her arms, giving me the sort of look usually reserved for Mormons at your front door. 'Where'd you come from?'

'Sydney.'

'Thought as much.' She said it like I'd come direct from Osama Bin Laden's cave.

Negotiations ensued.

It was touch and go there for a while. Even the head of the United Nations would have had his work cut out for him, I reckon. Signing the Kyoto Agreement wouldn't come close. But she didn't know who she was dealing with. Namely, the 2008 Public Relations Institute of Australia 'PR to watch'. Frankly, she was no challenge for someone with my skills.

I sucked up like mad. *Yoga classes leave scuff marks on the walls?* Outrageous. *Some people don't sweep the hall properly?* Shoot them at dawn. *Kids run amok?* Exterminate them.

Finally she leaned down and pulled the keys out from under the counter. They were attached to a piece of wood the size of a coat hanger with *Return to Maureen* written on it in blood. That's what it looked like anyway.

'You sound like you've got your head screwed on ... for someone from Sydney. So, I suppose it's all right.' She pushed the keys over the counter. 'There's a parcel here for you too.'

'A parcel?'

She pointed at the Australia Post sign below the counter. 'I'm the post office as well.'

She leaned down, pulled out a small box and slid a clipboard across to me. 'Sign here.'

I looked at the back of the parcel. It was stamped *Winning Edge Public Relations*. Wazza. I turned it in my hands. I'd open it later. In private.

I figured I may as well stock up while I was there. I glanced at the refrigerator. 'Do you have Lean Cuisine?'

She put her hands on her hips and shook her head. 'Never had any call for that. Got McCain's frozen meals, if you want.'

I bought a lamb dinner and a chicken curry.

'Can get that other stuff in for you, if you want.' Maureen bagged my dinners.

'You could? That would be wonderful, Maureen. Thank you.' *While I was on a roll ...* 'Is there any chance you can get in Australian *Vogue* and *PR Weekly*?'

I thought I'd stretched the friendship for a moment, but no, Maureen nodded. 'S'pose I could do that.'

'You're a darling. When my boyfriend, Anthony, comes to visit I'll get him to do your hair, if you like. He's a hairdresser — Felicity Holden is one of his clients.'

Maureen's face was blank.

'He does Kylie too, when she's in town.'

'Oh, Kylie.' Maureen patted her lurid locks. 'Well, that would be nice.'

'I'll let you know when he's coming. Cheers then, byee.'

I walked back into the office swinging the piece of wood like a baton in one hand and my frozen meals in the other. I'd slipped Wazza's parcel in with the meals. My mind was churning with the possibilities of what might be inside, but I wanted to open it in privacy.

Rodney's mouth fell open as he saw me. 'Are those the keys to the CWA Hall?'

'Yeah, why?'

'Wow, that's amazing.' His sunburnt cheeks crinkled. 'No-one except Mac has ever been able to get them off her before. Not even Sam. She's got a soft spot for Mac.' He looked at me like I'd just conquered Everest. 'I can't believe it. Hey, Mac,' he called. 'Your girlfriend's cheating on you. Cassie got the keys off Maureen. How bizarre is that?'

I decided to let the *Cassie* pass this once. I held the keys up so Mac could see them. He nodded, his gaze lingering.

So why'd you send me over there then, Mr Unhelpful? What was this guy's problem? I plonked the keys on the desk with a meaningful thud then went into the kitchen. Pulling out my parcel, I slid the frozen meals into the fridge.

Now what had Wazza sent me — a present and a letter begging me to return, maybe? I ripped off the brown paper. Inside was a state of the art iPhone. Wazza's business card fell out onto the floor. I picked it up. *Keep in touch*, he'd scrawled on the back. It wasn't an apology, but it was something.

I blinked away tears as a maudlin attack of homesickness threatened to overwhelm me. Wazza had let me take the rap, but at least he still cared. *You know I can't refuse you anything*, he'd said, shortly before he'd sacked me. I ran my fingers over the phone as I walked back to my desk. It was a beautiful object, shiny and sleek. It reminded me of Sydney. It reminded me of home.

Placing the phone on my desk, I continued with my Feral Pig Awareness Morning checklist.

- *Develop key media messages to reach target audiences.* I'd put out a news release of course, but a personal touch is always good. Let's see if I couldn't broaden our audience a little …

Opening my hotmail account for anonymity reasons, I sent an email to the advice column of the newspaper.

Should I go the whole hog?

My boyfriend has aksed me to the feral pig awareness morning at the Beechville Hall on Thursday. It sounds like fun, but I'm not sure if our relationship is ready for this type of event. I've heard they can get pretty raunchy. We've only been going out for two weeks. Is it too early?

Satisfied, I pressed the 'send' button. The killer combination of pigs and raunch should get the crowds in. The spelling mistake, *aksed*, was a nice touch too.

It was a busy day, but nothing I couldn't have handled in my sleep. First, I called the media reps and got them hyped. I spread my net wide, all the way to the Gold Coast. They all seemed desperate for copy so I was hopeful of a good turnout. Next, I confirmed with the local sign maker that he'd have my banner ready for collection in the morning and double-checked that the caterers were on track. Lastly, I called my guest speakers, the feral pig experts. As before, they were on for a chat, so this took a while. They seemed pretty excited about the event, which you couldn't knock. An enthusiastic speaker is a good speaker.

At the end of the day I picked up my car keys and iPhone. Mac was still at his desk doing something complicated with a multi-coloured map and a pen. Strangely, I found that very sexy. It's odd, this attraction thing — it must be hard-wired into our brain. Maybe it was the idea that he knew his territory. From a cavewoman's point of view I could imagine that being a turn-on.

He rolled out another map with a flick of his wrist, inspected it closely and made some notes on the side. *Mmm, definitely sexy.* Maybe it was just that what he was doing was incomprehensible to me, but he seemed to be good at it. I watched him for a few moments. 'Um, Mac?'

He grunted.

'What do you do if you've got a frog in your toilet?'
'Get it out.' He didn't even look up.
'Thanks.' *Thanks a lot. Not.*

I inspected the toilet when I got home.

You were still there, René Treefrog, you obstinate thing, you. Something about the way you gazed at me made me feel bad about disturbing you, but I figured it was time for action; I couldn't keep peeing on the grass.

Sliding on a pair of washing-up gloves, I snapped them like an evil scientist.

'Yeah, look, I know you've been here longer than me and it's pretty nice down there in the toilet bowl, but, well, it's my toilet bowl now.'

Reaching in, I grasped the frog. It kicked its long green legs in a panic. I squealed, but hung on.

'Sorry, it's you or me, RT.'

Running outside, I placed it on the grass at the bottom of the back steps. It didn't move, but its shiny, shiny eyes burnt into my back as I went inside.

'Crawk.'

I swung around. 'Did you say something, RT? There is nothing absolutely in our power?'

The frog was inscrutable as always.

'Yeah, that's what I thought. You don't want to take on this girl with your Cartesian philosophy, frog, or *you* are going *down*.' It looked tough, but I'm pretty sure it knew where I was coming from.

Peeling off my gloves, I slapped them on the sink. Damn, I was good. Only three days out of Sydney and already I was frog wrangling with the best of them. I was taking this here wilderness and taming it. I now knew how the first settlers felt as they beat back the bush to make their homes. You had to be vigilant out here in the sticks. Give the wildlife an inch and it takes over. You only had to listen to all the complaints in the office to know that.

There was no peeing on the grass that night while some freaky animal coughed in the bushes. Everything was as it should be — bum on the plastic seat and mistress of all I surveyed.

Chapter Seven

Look on both sides

My iPhone rang just as I was about to leave for work on Wednesday morning.

'Cassandra darling, how are you travelling?' It was Wazza.

I pictured him leaning on his desk with the view of the harbour, puffing on his morning cigar. 'Yeah, um, pretty good.' I searched my mind for something to say that would make him feel like I was the kind of girl he needed back on his team. 'I had a frog in my toilet, but I got rid of it.'

'Good, Cassandra, good.' Wazza's voice was hearty.

I heard him tapping on a keyboard as he spoke. I had a feeling what I'd said hadn't registered at all. 'And I'm planning a feral pig symposium. Pigs are a terrible menace.'

'Excellent.' *Tap, tap, tap.* 'Sounds like you've settled right in.'

'Yes.' *No.* 'How are things going there?' I wanted to ask if he'd replaced me, but I was too afraid he'd say yes.

'Busy, busy, busy. Thanks, Sophie,' said Wazza, his voice slightly muffled.

Sophie? There never used to be a Sophie.

'Got to go. Hope you like the iPhone.'

'I love the i—' It was too late, the phone had gone dead.

When I got into work, Mac and Rodney were leaning over the newspaper, laughing.

'What's the joke?'

The smile dropped off Mac's face quicker than a green light in Pitt Street. He looked even more exhausted today. His eyes were red where they should have been white and he was pale beneath his suntan — a man of mystery.

Rodney pointed at the paper, still snickering. I smiled — they'd printed my letter. I think they'd been a bit stumped for an answer, but the advice columnist had had a stab at it.

> *Dear 'Should I go the whole hog?'*
> *It might be best to stay away from raunchy events like this in the early stages of dating if you think they'll make you uncomfortable. Maybe a movie or a picnic would be more suitable.*

'Where'd she get the idea the Feral Pig Awareness Morning was going to be raunchy?' Rodney snorted.

I shrugged lightly, but Mac's eyes met mine and his eyebrows twitched. Mr Enigma had a keen sixth sense.

I glanced around the office, but there was still no sign of Sam.

Rodney pre-empted my question. 'Sick turtle,' gulp, 'on the beach.'

'Does she ever come in?'

Rodney and Mac glanced at each other. 'She was in one day last week wasn't she, Mac?' said Rodney.

'Might've been the week before.'

'She's just really,' gulp, 'into marine wildlife,' said Rodney.

'And really *not* into doing anything involving paperwork,' said Mac.

'I suppose there are advantages in having a boss who's never in,' I said.

'What you don't want to do ...' Mac paused.

I waited for him to go on. Was he about to address a whole sentence to me? 'Yes?' I prompted.

He frowned, maybe regretting his rash volubility. 'Don't underestimate her, that's all.'

'He means.' Rodney took a deep breath. 'She's not here, but she's here, if you know what I mean.'

I didn't, but I let it pass.

'We're pretty much self-managing, aren't we, Mac?' said Rodney. He was much better at talking to Mac than to me. 'She sends us,' gulp, 'emails. That's a good way to get in touch,' gulp, 'with her if you need to.'

I checked the trap at my desk. The carrot was untouched. There were a couple of messages on my phone from newspapers wanting to do stories on the Hastings River mouse. I'd only just sat down when it rang.

'What's this about the mouse having a cold?'

I moaned internally — Christine Bowles. It was too late to change stories now so I summoned my best on-top-of-it-all manner. 'Yes. It's at the vet on the Gold Coast — a special mouse vet.' I figured she'd have the local vet on speed dial.

She snorted. 'What — at Fleay's?'

I did some quick thinking. I didn't know what Fleay's was, but no doubt she had them on speed dial too. 'No, not Fleay's, it's a new place.'

'Surely you've got an ID?'

The mouse ran out from under my desk and straight past the carrot. Wasn't it supposed to be keen on a carrot? Mac followed it with his eyes. I tried to signal at him in sign language, making waves with my hand to indicate *river*.

He shrugged.

'Ah, no ID yet. It's too fast.'

'Too fast?'

'Not fast, faded. Their colour fades when they're sick. It needs to be healthy before they can ID it.' I thought I saw Mac smile out of the corner of my eye, but when I swivelled my chair he was as glum as ever.

'This all seems incredibly inefficient,' Christine snapped. 'But that's what I've come to expect from you lot. I'll be writing to the minister if I don't have an answer by Friday.'

'Wildlife is very unpredictable,' I said.

She snorted and put the phone down.

Satisfied that I had put that problem on hold, I picked up the newspaper. There were no wildlife-related articles in the paper today, but at the back an advertisement for the local theatre company, the Beechville Dramatic Society, caught my eye. The troupe was putting on *The Sound of Music* and there, in a nun's habit, was my boss — she had the lead role, no less. Interesting.

When I turned on my computer there was an email from the singing nun herself.

Can you do a news release about threatened shorebirds hatching on the beach? Some of them shelter in the tyre ruts on the sand and get run over. You'll find some information in the file under ...

Reams of detail about where exactly to look followed. *Tyre ruts?* What kind of animal figures tyre ruts are good places to hang out? They almost deserved to be threatened for that kind of behaviour — survival of the fittest and so on. I looked up the birds in my book — it turned out an affinity for tyre ruts was only one of their problems.

Who knew that migratory birds came all the way from Russia and Japan each year? It was bizarre. Why did they go there in the first place? Why not just stay here? Japan, I could understand, Japan was fab, but what was the big attraction in Russia? Vodka? The book didn't explain.

Imagine how tuckered out you'd be if you were a little bird who'd flown all the way from Moscow under your own steam. And then when you finally get here, you can't even rest on the beach without being chased by dogs.

Yes, I know swimming is tiring too, René, but you didn't swim from Russia, did you?

I paused, realising I'd just been talking to the frog again. The shock of moving to the country seemed to be making me regress to my teenage self. Descartes had been my most constant fantasy friend during my chaotic teenage years. I shook my head and returned to the task at hand.

It took me about thirty seconds to think of a headline with the right amount of innuendo. I figured *Watch Out for Chicks on the Beach* would do it. They'd open the email expecting Elle McPherson and get — I scanned the photo library — cute, fluffy hatchlings. *Ooh. Perfect.* Clicking 'send' I emailed the news release to all media outlets.

Within a couple of hours I'd done two radio interviews and lined up a trip to the beach with the

Beechville Star for next week. 'Yeah, I'll take you down in the four-wheel drive to get some shots of the chicks,' I assured Justin. 'No worries.' That would be a morning out of the office at least.

Mac glanced over as I put down the phone. I think he was pretty impressed. There really wasn't much to this wildlife officer thing. I'd never driven a four-wheel drive before, but it couldn't be too hard. Look at the morons you see in mud-splattered Land Cruisers. My eyes fell on the carrot-baited trap near my feet. If only I could capture the mouse I'd have this job in hand. Perhaps I needed a second opinion on correct mouse-trapping procedure.

For the remainder of the day I double-checked my Feral Pig Awareness Morning event list and tied up loose ends.

- *Determine total number of guests expected to attend.* I'd already figured out the hall held up to one hundred and catered accordingly. *Check.*
- *Establish budgets available.* 'Just get invoices for catering, etc. and we'll sort it out later,' said Sam's note. Pretty much open slather. *Check.*
- *Familiarise yourself with the topic/theme of the event.* I eyed the book Sam had left for me: *Feral Pigs in Australia.* I'd read it later. Maybe.
- *Establish if merchandise needs to be organised.* I toyed with the idea of some pig-themed mugs, but decided it was too late. *Pity.*
- *Consider any potential PR risks with holding this event.* What PR risks could there be? *Nil.*

'See you at the hall at nine thirty tomorrow,' I called to Mac as I left, before I realised he was on the phone.

'Yeah, that's right, Hannah. Ten o'clock at the CWA Hall,' he murmured.

At least he was spreading the word.

As soon as I got home I checked my toilet — all clear. *Yee hah*. I figured I had this here wilderness pretty much tamed.

Take that, René Treefrog. I bet you don't doubt all things now, right?

Talking to a frog philosopher, even an absent one, was beginning to feel very natural.

My bedtime words from *Alice* seemed somewhat ominous, however, considering it was the eve of my big pig morning. *'You may look in front of you, and on both sides, if you like,' said the Sheep, 'but you can't look all round you.'*

I slammed the book shut. There was no point in getting too hung up about these things.

Chapter Eight

We're all mad here

I'm not sure when it first occurred to me that I might have played this thing wrong.

It wasn't when I was unfurling the banner — *Welcome to the Beechville Summit for Feral Pigs*. I was pleased with the title. 'Summit' gave it the right amount of gravitas — like the Kyoto Summit, but different.

'Quirky' was the right word for the venue. The Beechville CWA Hall Committee ruled with an iron fist — no velvet glove. I'd keep it in mind for a masochists' convention if I ever had to run one. There were signs everywhere.

**CHILDREN MUST NOT ATTEMPT TO ENGAGE
IN PLAY UPON THE STAGE
NO NAPPIES IN THE BIN BY ORDER
OF THE COMMITTEE**

THE FLOOR MUST BE LEFT SWEPT AND CHAIRS ARRANGED ALONG THE WALLS

I pitied any poor child who attempted to play in that hall. It was sad, really, to imagine a child so starved for fun they'd get over-stimulated on a visit to the Beechville Hall.

Beechville was like that, though. The best you could say about it was that it was a 'make your own fun' kind of place.

Everything was still going well when the caterers from the Gold Coast arrived — friands, mini quiches, espresso coffee and a selection of teas. It was all just as it should be — chic and delicious.

The media turned up right on schedule, which was unusual but welcome. I had the local TV station there, the radio ready for a live broadcast, and not one, but four local newspapers. I'd never realised before what a hotbed of media action these little towns were. The papers were like Russian dolls, slotting one inside the other: *The Border Monthly*, *The Hills Fortnightly*, *The North-East Weekly*, and — a tremendous coup — *The Gold Coast Daily*. Justin from the *Beechville Star* was there too, of course. He blushed when I greeted him. *So cute*.

My guest speakers had arrived — a motley crew, but you take what you can get. There was the local trapper, in his tight grey moleskins and highly polished riding boots. The pig expert from the university — I hate to say it, but it's true — had grown to resemble his subject: not so much the feral as the domestic variety. He was decidedly pink with sparse bristles on his head and cheeks.

And lastly, there was Mac, my 'celebrity' launcher. I eyed him where he stood with the other speakers. His hands were in his pockets and his shoulders pushed at the back of his tres sexy ranger uniform. I drummed my fingernails on the table. I wasn't sure why we hadn't hit it off yet, but there weren't many men I couldn't bring around eventually.

Five minutes to ten — my spine tingled as I surreptitiously scoped the empty seats. That was, I suppose, my first presentiment of disaster.

In times of social anxiety I try to keep busy — at school dances I'd usually be found serving drinks or taking tickets at the front door. So now, I rearranged the friands, made sure the coffee was hot and tidied the stack of course notes I'd arranged on the welcoming table. At five past ten, my first actual participant arrived. A stout man I assumed was a farmer peered in the door, taking off his felt hat. He eyed the banner and the table with the two white-capped girls from the catering company and backed out again.

Oh no you don't. I swooped down on him, wrote out a name badge — Trev — steered him gently towards the coffee and resumed guard at the door to prevent escape. Out of the corner of my eye I saw him frowning at the friands and tea selection before finally selecting English Breakfast. By quarter past, five bemused-looking farmers were huddled together for protection in the back row. The word had obviously been passed around: they'd all chosen English Breakfast tea, and rejected the friands and coffee.

Every now and then one of them looked at me as a sheep would at a sheep dog — ready to make a break for it if I let down my guard. Ten empty rows of seats stretched towards the stage. At the front, two greasy-haired teenage boys — presumably in search of the advertised raunch — sat chewing gum. I pondered some conversation starters, but none of my usual ones seemed right for either of my client sectors. And I'd always thought that 'you're looking fabulous, great shoes' would never let me down.

I peered out the door. No-one else was in sight. Walking up to Mac, I pulled him aside. 'How many people do you usually get to these things?'

He gazed past my shoulder. 'About three or four. This is a good turnout.'

'Why didn't you tell me?' I hissed.

'You didn't ask.' Mac's shoulders lifted slightly. 'How was I to know you were planning for an Olympic-sized crowd?'

I narrowed my eyes at him. *You'll keep*. My gaze went to the rows of untouched pastries. The catering girls — giggling at some witty remark from the teenage boys — stood ready for the onslaught. The banner looked exactly as it should. The venue was decidedly quirky. No-one could fault my event management.

Except that there was no-one here.

Panic fluttered in my stomach. I quelled it. I'd

had worse events than this, surely? I tried to think of one, but there wasn't time for that now. I needed to concentrate on the media — distract them from taking footage of the rows of empty seats. I could see the headline now — *Who Gives a Pig?*

I picked up copies of my media kit and put on a brave face. Striding over to the media contingent, I handed them their packages. 'We're here today to strike a blow against these terrible pests,' I said. 'Did you know feral pigs are responsible for the loss of squillions of native animals?'

The bitch from the TV station thrust out her microphone. Red lipstick was smeared on her teeth and her enormous breasts strained at the buttons of her blouse exposing a lacy bra beneath. It was obvious why she was stuck out here in the sticks. 'What animals are actually at risk from feral pigs?'

'Well ...' I glanced over at Mac for help, but he was deep in conversation with the pig expert. I racked my brain, but only one animal came to mind. 'The Hastings River mouse ...'

She frowned, apparently feeling a mouse was no big deal.

I knew where she was coming from — visuals are everything in television. 'They're very cute, big ears —' I held my hands up next to my ears to demonstrate, then paused as voices carried up the street towards me. *Hooray — the feral pig enthusiasts at last!* A group of about ten women marched into view. Alas, as they came closer I saw their placards.

The TV camera swung away from me.

'Stop the killing! Pigs have rights too!' The voices were clearer now. 'Stop the killing!' yelled the woman at the front, her curly grey hair jiggling with indignation. *Animal Liberation* read the large black letters on her purple T-shirt.

The five farmers got to their feet and walked in unison towards the door, like plumper versions of Texas gunslingers. The teenagers swivelled, probably hoping the raunchy part was about to begin.

The red-faced farmer who'd arrived first stepped forward. He pointed at the grey-haired woman. 'Get out of here. Next time I catch you on my property interfering with my traps you're going down for six months. You animal libbers wouldn't know if your pants were on fire. You wouldn't have lasted a minute in 'Nam.'

'Pigs are intelligent, sensitive animals. They don't deserve to be cruelly killed just because they're in the wrong place at the wrong time. It's humans who are the real pests,' the woman yelled back.

The cameras swung back to me.

'Can you tell us how the pigs are killed once they're trapped?' said the red-toothed reporter.

The farmers and animal libbers turned towards me. I looked for Mac, but he'd vanished, as had the other guest speakers. Was there a trapdoor leading to a secret tunnel? Then I noticed the Emergency Exit door swinging shut. I couldn't believe this. I was meant to be on a quiet sabbatical from the city. I was supposed to be falling asleep in my armchair from the boredom.

I eyed the microphone thrust at my lips; the cameraman moved in closer, the animal libbers stood poised to attack, the farmers puffed out their chests ready to take them on. I tried to calm myself with a quote from *Alice*, but only one came to mind — *We're all mad here.*

There was a word for these country folk and that word was — feral.

I made it to the office early the day after the fiasco. I couldn't face anyone else until I'd faced the worst myself. Turning on my computer and Googling the news channel, I prepared to be horrified.

I'd been totally over pigs by the time I'd got home the night before and not in a fit state to stream the news live. I was still totally over pigs, but it had to be done.

'Angry scenes at feral pig awareness morning,' said the newsreader.

I shuddered as the red-toothed woman did her piece to camera. There was me in the front mouthing platitudes about putting pigs to sleep in a loving environment. I even mentioned hand — that is, trotter — holding. In the background farmers faced off animal libbers. There was chest prodding on both sides.

What a debacle. My stomach squirmed. The worst part was that with syndication the story could go anywhere. I moaned, closing my eyes — what if Sydney people saw it? It didn't bear thinking about.

It could end up as a humour segment on *Media Watch* or *Rove*. I'd hate to think what *The Chaser* would do with it.

What could I say in my defence? There have been worse events? That is certainly true. What about the fashion show where Miss Universe's skirt fell off? I wouldn't want to have organised that one.

Yes, disasters in event management were not unprecedented. But, I had to admit, the combination of an empty hall and a near riot made this one a low point in my career. I knew there was no excuse — I'd skipped the risk analysis section of my checklist. That was my fatal mistake. I'd been lulled into thinking nothing could go wrong in a town like this. Things were supposed to be simple in the country.

I moaned as I watched the footage. There had to be a good chance I'd be packing my bags in the fallout from this one. It was hard to imagine the organisation's profile had been enhanced by my efforts.

Where would I go next if I got the sack? Not Sydney, that's for sure. It could only be downhill from here — Mount Isa or the Simpson Desert, maybe? Did they have any call for public relations in places like that?

I paused the video. It was a great news story. Action, colour and conflict — it had it all. The only thing missing was sex. They could have got that in there too if they'd been more vigilant.

The only saving grace for the day was that there was so much happening outside the hall the cameras never made it back inside. If they had, they would have found my raunchy pig day had become a self-fulfilling prophecy ...

I had to hand it to those Beechville kids — they were quick off the mark. When I'd stumbled in after my interview the teenage boys and the girls from the catering company were nowhere to be seen. Then I'd heard some scuffles in the kitchen. I peered around the corner. The boys had the girls backed up against the wall and the only time I'd seen more tongue action was in a Maori war dance. They didn't even notice me.

As I'd backed out I'd noticed the boys' T-shirts. Both had *LOVA* plastered across the back. This LOVA thing was pretty popular — maybe it was a local band.

Slamming the door behind me, I'd headed home to nurse my wounds. I'd thought the day couldn't get any worse. But then it did ...

I was almost on the toilet when I saw you.
You were back, René, you little Houdini, you.

I jumped, pulling up my pants. 'How did you do that?' I'd left the seat cover down as a precaution, but there was the frog — bold as a Kings Cross hooker, a smile on its glossy green face. It was spooky, like it had supernatural powers. Was it going to appear everywhere? Would I open the fridge to find it sitting in the crisper? Open my underwear drawer and find it cosied up in my knickers?

'I'm going to pee on you,' I said.

René called my bluff, giving me a look of supreme philosophical indifference. 'Crawk.'

'What's that, René? Illusory joy is worth more than genuine sorrow? Yes, I'd have to agree.'

I'd peed outside on the grass again. *Round two, frog.* I really needed to do something about this. Peeing on the grass was all very well, but there would soon come a time when the timing of my, well, *other* requirements would not be met by the office loo. And I didn't want to think about that too much.

An animal moved in the bushes and I wondered how my life had come to this. Not only could I not run a feral pig awareness morning, I couldn't keep my toilet frog free. I'd always seen myself as capable, confident, a good woman in a crisis. But now — I wasn't so sure.

Curling up in my makeshift bed, I'd listened to a heavy-footed creature dance a polka on my roof. What had happened to the woman who'd organised the Cointreau Ball, generally agreed to be the best party Sydney had ever seen? Surely that woman wouldn't let herself be done in by a green frog and a pack of placard-bearing grannies?

I remembered the Caterpillar's words on my first night in Beechville: *Who are you?* Well, I knew now. I was a city girl and that was final. The sooner I was back in my natural environment, the better.

I'd fallen asleep at last but frogs in black berets spouting philosophical insults marched through my dreams.

Now, I yawned as the screen went blank, and leaned back on my chair. Was there any chance my boss might not find out about the shambles I'd made of my first task?

'Saw the news last night.'

I jumped and came back to an upright position. Surprise, surprise, Sam was in — just when I didn't want to see her. Life's like that, isn't it?

She leaned against my cubicle wall, hands deep in the pockets of her khaki shorts. Her posture was casual but she looked like she meant business.

I smiled apologetically. 'Sorry. You get that sometimes …'

'Well done.' She cut across me, nodding at the computer screen. 'We haven't had that much media coverage in ages.'

Was she being sarcastic? 'But, the animal libbers …'

'Yeah, great stuff.' A broad smile split her suntanned face. 'Shows people what we're up against. You see, it's a matter of balance, Cassie. On the one side, we've got the farmers.' She held up one finger. 'They're always trying to get us to do more feral pig control. On the other side,' she held up a finger on her other hand, 'we've got the loony left — there's a lot of them too. If we can get both sides thoroughly pissed off we know we're doing our job. It was great to see them taking on the animal libbers, that Hannah Dobrovsky, she's a f—' Her pager beeped as if it had been programmed to censor. She pulled it off her belt. 'Got to check on a pelican.'

Her eyes flickered up and down my yellow halter-neck sundress. 'Get Rodney to order you a uniform. Keep up the good work. I hear you've got Maureen on side too. That's no mean feat; she's never warmed to me — only talks to Mac.' She rolled her eyes. 'Mind you, I suspect she might be hiding a kind heart underneath that crusty exterior. I'll email you later about another news release.' She jogged out of the office like a giant boar was snapping at her heels. The melody of 'How do you solve a problem like Maria?' drifted towards me as she vanished. She had a deep but tuneful voice. I made a mental note to buy a ticket for *The Sound of Music*.

She was an intriguing woman. There was no doubt she was on top of things — she knew about me and Maureen. Like Rodney said, *She's not here, but she's here*. How did she do that? The way she appeared and disappeared at critical moments ... it was almost like a comic book superhero. But which superhero would she be? I couldn't think of any existing ones that fit the bill — she was way too individual. I'd call her Whale Woman. I gave her disappearing back a mock salute — *thanks for your vote of confidence, Whale Woman*.

A smile stretched across my face. Well, that wasn't the outcome I'd expected, but in the PR game perception is reality. *Cassandra the PR queen strikes again*. I punched my hand in the air. *Yeah*, I wouldn't be buying that one-way ticket to the Simpson Desert just yet.

Mac had come in while Sam and I were talking; his

eyes were on me as I swivelled in my chair. He didn't look happy. I gave him my killer smile. He frowned. No, it was more than a frown — he *glared*. He was always grumpy, but today he'd gone one step beyond — he was the über-grump. What was biting him?

Sam's words suddenly repeated in my mind, *that Hannah Dobrovsky* ... Hannah, I'd heard that name before — *ten o'clock at the CWA Hall, Hannah*. Had Mac stirred up the animal libbers? If so, why? What had I ever done to him?

I met his eyes. He stared back. Yep, I was definitely reading some major antagonism there. Had he tried to set me up? If so, it had backfired. What was wrong with him? Had he had someone else lined up for this job? *Anyway, Cassandra one, Mac nil, in this round.*

Which reminded me ...

Rodney was just depositing his surfboard next to his computer. I called over to him. 'Hey, Rodney, what do *you* do if you have a frog in the toilet?'

He frowned. 'It's tricky. Can't just take them out. They get back in again.'

I twitched one eyebrow in the direction of Mac, who was pretending not to listen. 'Oh, you can't just take them out, huh?'

'No.' Rodney leaned down and pulled a sheet out of his filing cabinet. Walking over, he handed it to me. 'Here's our,' gulp, 'information sheet. Sometimes they come in through the,' gulp, 'sewer.'

I wrinkled my nose.

'Who's got the frog? You?' he said.

I nodded.

'You have to check your breather pipe. Make sure it's netted.' He pointed at the diagram. 'Then you need to frog-proof your toilet. Seal the windows and doors ... and put a board on top of the toilet. They can lift the lid.' He breathed deeply, like he'd just run a race.

They can lift the lid?

He must have noticed the look of dismay on my face. 'I can come over and give you a hand. If you want.' He blushed and coughed.

Sensing an opportunity, I glanced at Mac. I had to sort this out. I couldn't afford to have him trying to nail me at every turn. This wasn't much of a job, but right now I needed it and that, apparently, meant keeping Mac on side — at least while I learnt the ropes. The last thing I wanted was a colleague who was hell-bent on making me look bad.

He knew this town, I didn't, and knowledge is power when it comes to PR. The pig morning had turned out in my favour more through luck than good management. If I was honest with myself, I knew I'd made a mistake in my assessment of the community. The spectre of the Simpson Desert had retreated for now, but ... 'Or Mac's right next door ...' I said.

Mac looked up; his eyes went from Rodney to me. 'What?'

'You'll come over and give me a hand with my frog, won't you?'

His mouth twitched.

Rodney and I waited; Rodney looking puzzled and me … I was aiming for innocent.

Mac sighed. 'Yeah, okay.'

'Tonight?' I asked.

He inclined his head briefly.

Rodney went back to his workstation, looking a little deflated.

My eyes met Mac's. 'Well, must have been news to you that the frog's come back. Guess you're learning all the time, hey?'

He shrugged. 'Sometimes they don't come back.'

I let it pass. I had other fish to fry while I had his attention. Pulling a jar of peanut butter out of my desk drawer, I placed a spoonful in the mouse trap while he was watching.

He turned back to his keyboard quickly.

Ha! He'd known that carrot wasn't going to be any good, but did he tell me to try peanut butter? No. This I also had to get from Rodney. I'd cornered him in the lunch room yesterday and asked for a second opinion. *I don't know why Mac told you to use carrot,* he'd said. *Peanut butter's what we normally use for trapping. Mac's the expert, though, I'm just the admin officer …*

Placing the trap on the floor, I flicked through the newspaper, avoiding the feral pig morning coverage. Instead, I tagged an article, *Local Boy Rushed to Hospital After Encounter with Bullrout*. Goodness — another danger I'd never heard of. Apparently these spiky fish lurked among the weeds in creeks. One false step and you're in agony so excruciating you want to cut your foot off. I guess that's why cities were invented — to escape from the many menaces of nature.

My mind was still on Mac as I cut the article out. I wasn't used to meeting men who didn't like me. It was making me cranky. The way to most men's hearts was through their ... well, it's sort of obvious and I fully intended to try that angle. But maybe Mac wasn't most men? He was a ranger and perhaps the way to *his* heart was through his wildlife ...

On the wall opposite was a big poster — *Stop the Cane Toad*. That had possibilities. 'So, I hear cane toads are a big problem around here.'

Mac nodded, not taking his eyes off the keyboard. 'Yep.'

'Do you want to take me out some time to get a few pics? I could do a story — drum up some awareness.'

'You want to run a cane toad awareness morning?' His voice was dry, but he looked up from his computer and I almost detected a trace of amusement in his bright blue eyes.

He really was kind of cute. If only he weren't such a grouch. 'Just some pics at this stage. Maybe we could have a round-up or something later.'

'It would need to be at night.'

'The round-up?'

'Yeah obviously, but the pictures too.' His voice had a strained patience. 'They come out at night.' He articulated each word clearly, as if talking to someone with a poor grasp of English.

I pretended not to notice. 'Okay. So … can we make a date?' I gave him the old eyebrow flash of innuendo. 'To go toading?' I almost giggled. *Listen to yourself, Cassandra. A toading date — what have I been reduced to? What would Jessica say?*

But Mac's expression was discouraging. 'I'm pretty busy. I'll let you know when I'm free.' He turned back to his computer.

Ouch. I was dismissed. Dismissed, but intrigued. What was he *so* busy doing every night? He wouldn't be as grouchy if he was worn out from all-night shagathons. But he'd turned down a chance to be alone. In the dark. With me. That had never happened to me before. It pissed me right off. I glared at his back.

Just you wait. One of these days you'll come to me begging to go toading.

Chapter Nine

Disenchantment

I knew Mac was coming over to sort out my frog issue, so after dinner — chicken cacciatore Lean Cuisine (thanks to my new friend, Maureen) — I tarted myself up a bit. I had a hunch he was an au naturale kind of guy, so I spent about half an hour making myself look like I had no makeup on at all. Then, in the spirit of 'just another night at home' I changed into my nightie.

That done, I relaxed with the *PR Weekly* Maureen had ordered in for me. It probably wasn't a good idea. Flicking through pictures of PR events just made me more and more despondent. There was Wazza on a yacht on Sydney Harbour, Jessica at the perfume launch I'd organised ... I could practically taste the champagne bubbles in her slender glass, the Sydney rock oysters on the tray that hovered next to her.

But I know these things mean nothing to you, René. Stop frowning. You're such a downer sometimes. Live a little, why don't you?

I gazed at the picture of Jessica; her long blonde hair was ever so slightly dishevelled and smoky black eye shadow contoured her eyes. Yeah, she really had it going on. That 'just been fucked' look takes a long time to achieve. Even if I'd made it to the perfume launch I wouldn't have come near her style.

Jessica ...

I'd never really understood why Jessica was my friend when we were growing up in Blacktown. She was so pretty and popular and I ... well, wasn't. Jessica played netball and excelled at swimming squad and modern dancing. I dropped any ball that came my way — not that many did — and never mastered breaststroke. I loved to dance, secretly yearned to be a star, but couldn't do the fancy gymnastic moves required by our teacher, Mrs Archer. I think maybe Jessica had needed a fall guy, someone to make her look good. I was good at that.

A mosquito buzzed around my ankle. I slapped at it, leaving a smear of blood. The old house creaked in the breeze from the mountains. Would I ever get back where I belonged? Who would have thought I could go so quickly from worries about the correct number of chilled oysters per guest to an obsession with a frog in my toilet?

I wiped at the blood. *Patience, Cassandra, just a few more months …*

Mac took his time coming. I was out on my verandah with a whiskey and soda when he lurched out of the bushes. I'd been expecting a car, so it startled me. In silhouette he looked rather menacing — like a hunchback, or yowie. I think I might have screamed, before I realised it was him and the hunch was a backpack.

'Doctor Livingstone, I presume?' I said, when I recovered. He had that look about him — like a long lost explorer. I smelt beer on his breath. Maybe he was an alcoholic, not a drug addict.

He just sort of grunted in that charming caveman way he has. He was wearing a faded T-shirt with a rip under the armpit and baggy khaki shorts. For some reason he was covered in leaves, like he'd been rolling around in the forest. I didn't want to inquire further — the mind boggles. He certainly hadn't gone to a lot of trouble with presentation — unless, like me, he was after a minimalist look.

If he was, it was working. Despite, or perhaps because of, the rips, leaves and beer odour, I found him very, very intriguing. He was quite a contrast to the Sydney pretty boys (sorry, Ant).

'I was expecting you to drive,' I said. 'That's why I screamed.'

'Why would you drive when you can walk?' he grunted.

'Well, lots of reasons actually — mainly to do with footwear …' I trailed off — he didn't look sympathetic to my line of argument. 'You're a bit late,' I added. 'I was expecting you at seven o'clock.'

'I don't wear a watch,' he said.

'Neither do I, I use my mobile.'

'Don't have a mobile either.' He scratched his head and a beetle with a shiny red back fell out of his curls and crawled away.

Curiouser and curiouser. I followed it with my eyes. I didn't know what to say to that. 'You're not one of those Amish or something are you?'

His mouth twitched, like he was about to smile, but he nipped it in the bud. 'I like the feeling of being cut off — telling the time by the rhythms of the day.' That was a long sentence for him — he tightened his mouth like he'd said too much.

I scanned his face. 'Well, who doesn't? But, you know, there are practical difficulties. Places to go, people to meet ...'

He shrugged. 'I get to work on time, mostly. It's not a problem.'

I gave him a long look. I'd just figured something out. It was a hallelujah moment — why hadn't I worked it out before? I'd known subconsciously there was something strange about him, but it had just clicked. His body language was all mixed up.

I'm a bit of an amateur expert on body language; you need to be in PR. It's so much more revealing than what people say. If a client's saying yes, yes, yes, but they're sitting back in their seat with their arms folded, then you know you have to work a bit harder.

With Mac, it was the opposite. His words were all no, no, no ... But if I looked at him and didn't listen, I'd be thinking: *mmm, I'm in with a chance here.*

Even while he sounded as grumpy as hell, he had his hands thrust into the pockets of his pants with his feet pointing towards me. It was the classic male *I'm interested* pose. To test him out, I scratched my neck. Sure enough, a moment later, he followed my lead. *Interesting ...*

Taking him down the lino corridor to the toilet, I opened the door. A huge cockroach ran out in front of me and I jumped backwards, almost crashing into him. As I switched on the light he burst into a coughing fit. When I turned around, he'd gone all red. I had a fair idea what was going on. Let's just say I'd chosen my outfit carefully. *The way to a man's heart ...* Backlighting can be very flattering to a girl. 'Frog in your throat?' I said.

'I'll be right.' He studiously avoided looking at me.

We stepped towards the toilet. Inside the bowl, there was René, circling his pool, back legs kicking strongly. Mac's shoulder brushed mine as we looked down at him. He jumped away, like I'd burnt him.

'Why do they like toilets so much?' I said.

'Combination of moisture and shelter.' He wet his hands under the tap.

'Shouldn't you wash your hands afterwards, not before?'

'Need wet hands or you'll damage their skin. I'll wash after as well, so I don't transmit any diseases.'

'Diseases?'

'Nothing *you* need to worry about, only frogs. They're getting pretty knocked around at the moment.'

Then he just reached into the toilet, grabbed René with his bare hands, took him outside and let him go on the grass. 'Go on, mate, find a pond,' he said.

René didn't move, of course — just gave him the old shiny eye treatment. He looked undaunted. 'Crawk.'

It is not enough to have a good mind, huh?
The main thing is to use it well?

'We'll see about that.'

'What's that?' said Mac.

'Nothing.' Had I spoken out loud? *How embarrassing.*

'Got to check the breather pipe now.' He pulled a torch out of his backpack. 'Have you got a ladder?'

'A ladder?'

'Yeah, to get on the roof.'

I had no idea what he was talking about.

'The breather pipe?' He pointed up to the roof, where a curved, white pipe protruded from the corrugated iron.

'Oh, that. Is that the breather pipe? I thought it was on the ground. How do the frogs get all the way up there?'

'They're tree frogs. They climb up the trees.' He pointed at some overhanging branches.

There was no ladder, but he climbed up a tree next to the house and got on the roof that way.

Mmm, very sexy, very caveman … I watched him do his thing for a while.

I could see how you got in now, René, the cap that should have fitted over the end of the pipe was missing — if there'd ever been one.

It seemed to be a bit of a process to fix it. He kept on pulling things out of his bag, measuring up bits of netting, banging at the pipe with a hammer …

The whole time he was trying — rather unsuccessfully — not to ogle me in my see-through nightie, which was cute. I had a fair idea what he'd be thinking about when he went to bed, though.

When I figured he'd seen enough, I left him to it.

I was pretty pleased with myself that night after he left. I reckoned he was hooked; now I just needed to reel him in. It was a case of keep your friends close, and your enemies closer, when it came to Mac.

What about Ant, you say?

Well, Ant and I didn't have the kind of relationship that involved being faithful to each other, René.

Or at least I didn't think we did — we'd never explicitly discussed it. Anyway, a week is a long time — a girl's fancy tends to wander.

And right now, my fancy had wandered to Mac. I had to admit my interest in him was only partly motivated by a desire to keep my job. He was annoyingly hard to get — which only made him all the more desirable. And there was just something about him ... I wanted to get my hands on his tattered T-shirt and rip it right off his back. My feelings were primitive, raw and totally cavewoman. *Want man. Oog.*

It was with these thoughts on constant replay that I wandered to my newly de-frogged toilet before going to bed. Mac had left the lid down, so I flicked it up and was centimetres — centimetres! — from the seat when I saw this ... *thing.*

It registered in some primal part of my brain. I leapt up with a screech that came from deep in my stomach. A chimpanzee in the jungle would have done the same. The wail kept on coming. It was a cry of alarm and distress, like a warning to other monkeys ... I'd never heard a noise like that come out of my mouth before.

There was a fucking snake in my toilet.

As I slammed the toilet door behind me all I could think of was going home — home to Ant — home to Sydney. I suddenly hated this place — snakes, frogs, uppity grumpy rangers ... The fact that I'd fancied Mac a moment ago flew out the window as I ran down the corridor.

Country life wasn't at all what I'd imagined. There were many things I could tolerate: trains running late, traffic jams in Pitt Street, aggressive people in koala suits wanting money ... However, snakes lurking beneath my bottom ... Freud would have had a field day with that one.

Forget raw and primitive; I needed to get back where I belonged — even if it meant public humiliation in front of my peers. Damn it — being seen in a tracksuit on a weekday would be preferable to this. Maybe I could have radical plastic surgery and start over under a new identity? Yes, that was definitely a viable option.

Or maybe Wazza could slip me a bit of contract work on the sly while I waited for my name to be rehabilitated? Why not? I pulled out my iPhone and selected his number. It went straight to the message bank. 'Wazza? It's Cassandra. I'm coming back to Sydney. I was wondering if we could get together for coffee this weekend? Throw around a few options?' There, that sounded suitably non-desperate and breezy.

Sprinting around the bedroom, I shoved my clothes into bags. It didn't take long, I only had two suitcases. I needed to get out of that horrible snakey house. I was pretty sure the snake wouldn't be able to get out of the bathroom, but who knew? If the frog had superpowers maybe the snake did too. The diamond-shaped head poked out of the toilet bowl over and over in my mind. I shuddered. Frogs, maybe; snakes ... never.

Slamming the front door behind me, I placed the

key beneath the mat. I'd email from Sydney and let them know where to find it. Flattening my foot, I accelerated out of the driveway, bounced over the ruts, bottomed out on the ridges and turned south. *South. Home. Sydney. Caffè lattes. Thai restaurants. Yay.*

Autopilot took over. I was south of Coffs before I pulled over for petrol and realised I was still in my transparent nightie. What the hell — I didn't care. I was on the road and going home; there was no stopping me now. The petrol station attendant — a teenage boy — blushed as I paid. I bet he copped an eyeful as I walked out.

Dawn broke somewhere around Newcastle. Tears pricked at the back of my eyes as the sun caught the sides of the road cutting on the freeway. I ticked off the landmarks: the Hawkesbury River, the end of the freeway at Hornsby, the inevitable rude taxi driver ... Beaming at him as he gave me the finger, I turned into the home strait humming along to 'Miracle (in Marrickville)'.

Pulling into my driveway, it was hard to believe it had only been a week since I'd left. Already, it was a revelation to be on a driveway with no ruts, at a house with no wild animals, about to be greeted by a man who'd be thrilled to see me. *God bless Sydney.* I practically kissed the pebblecrete driveway I was so happy to be there.

An early morning jogger pounded past as I let myself in through the front door. The familiar smell of furniture polish and carpet shampoo greeted me.

Friday was our day for the cleaner so the surfaces still sparkled from her visit yesterday. Pulling off my nightie, I padded down the corridor. Ant was in for a treat.

The curtains were drawn in the bedroom, the sheet buckled over the shadowy hump of Ant's body. With a leap I pounced on top of him. 'Surprise, Ant. I'm home.'

It was a nasty moment — not at all what I'd imagined. There was no thrilled Ant, no cries of joy at my return, no vigorous reunion rumpy-pumpy.

Not one, but two sets of eyes peered up at me from the pillow. And, no, the other set didn't belong to a dog or a stuffed teddy bear.

Has that ever happened to you, René? No, I suppose that kind of thing doesn't go on much in the frog pond. Well, you're lucky.
Crawk.
Yes, it was rather disenchanting.

'Sorry, Cass, I didn't know you were coming,' Ant stuttered. Rather lamely I thought.

Well, obviously. 'Cassandra.' My haughty retort probably mixed badly with the fact that I was only wearing a G-string, but I was beyond caring. 'Are you going to introduce me?'

'Sorry, this is Damien. Cassandra, Damien. Damien, Cassandra.'

That's right — Ant's bed mate wasn't a woman.

Ant peered up at me from between my legs. 'You might have met?' He sounded like a good host. I almost expected him to add, *you and Damien have lots in common.*

Which would have been true — I now realised I was straddling one of my former clients. 'Hi, Damien. Fancy running into you here. How's Rainforest Runaway going? Is Wazza still doing your PR for you?'

Damien blushed as he attempted to pick up his Trent Nathan boxer shorts from the floor. I didn't make it easy for him, pinning his torso to the bed with my knees. 'Ah, y-yess,' he stuttered.

'Don't go,' I said. 'I'm pleased we bumped into each other, because I've been meaning to ask you — were you happy with the work I was doing? It's just that, you know, I didn't get much support from you guys when the shit hit the fan.'

Damien wriggled out from under me and gathered up his clothes. 'Tricky business, that,' he muttered.

'Don't rush on my account.' I swivelled on Anthony's chest to face him. 'Stick around — let's catch up on old times. We never really debriefed properly. And guess what? I'm available again if you need some work done. How lucky is that?'

He mumbled something about a breakfast meeting and ran out the door, pulling his Lacoste polo shirt on as he went.

'What's eating him?' I said to Anthony.

Beneath me, Ant's eyes were wide. 'Cass, Cassie ...'

I jumped to the floor. 'Shut up, Ant. Coffee. I've been driving all night.'

Striding into the kitchen, still wearing only my G-string, I thrust coffee beans into the grinder and helped myself to Ant's homemade organic yoghurt. 'Good morning.' I waved at the startled couple in the next door apartment, whose kitchen windows looked into ours. They twitched their blinds closed.

Ant pattered after me, draped in a sheet. He looked like a dog that'd been caught stealing the dinner. 'It was the first time, Cassandra, I promise. I don't know what came over me.'

I ignored him, shovelling the yoghurt down my throat with a wooden spoon.

'You know I'd never do anything to hurt you,' Ant said.

I turned on him. 'What, you just woke up and thought to yourself, I'm feeling a bit gay today? Seeing as Cassandra's away, maybe I'll go to bed with Damien? You do realise you've become a stereotype — the gay hairdresser?'

I finished the yoghurt, flung the tub in the sink, and opened the fridge door to see what else I could eat. I was taking this remarkably well, I thought, as I devoured a whole Camembert.

Ant hovered next to me — poised to run if I turned violent.

'The thing is ...'

He jumped as globules of Camembert flew out of my mouth towards him.

I finished my mouthful. 'The thing is, I can't decide if you cheating on me with a man makes it better or worse. I'm away one week and you realise you're homosexual?'

He backed away as I stepped towards him. 'It wasn't like that, Cassandra. Damien came in for a haircut and, well, I was lonely without you.'

Closing the gap, I jumped at him, my breasts jiggling, and pulled his hair. 'You could have got a dog or something. Did you think of that? Ferrets are very in at the moment.'

'Stop it, Cassie, ow ...' Ant covered his head protectively.

I kicked his shin.

'I'm sorry, Cassandra. I feel really bad about it.' He rubbed at his leg.

I snorted and went back to the fridge. '*You* feel bad about it? How do you think *I* feel?' I scanned the racks for sustenance. There was way too much fruit and vegetable and not enough fat, sugar and salt. 'You on the Israeli Army Diet again?'

Ant was slumped at the table. He shook his head. 'Pritikin. I didn't know if you were ever going to come back, Cassandra. I thought you'd meet a sexy ranger or something.'

I looked around sharply.

'I know how you feel about uniforms,' he added.

Ant and I had first met when he was hired as beefcake for a military-themed launch of a new fashion label. Modelling was a little sideline for him. He'd been wearing a white uniform with gold epaulettes and buttons that I'd enjoyed undoing later.

Ant's big brown eyes followed me. 'I suppose it's over between us now.'

'I suppose it is.' I tested my emotions. They were very quiet. Was I repressing a deep grief or was I okay with the concept? I wasn't sure. Folding ten slices of smoked salmon in half, I slid them into my mouth as a pre-emptive measure.

'Can we still be friends?'

'Todd Rundgren, 1989,' I muttered through the salmon. I have a photographic memory for song titles from my childhood years.

'What?'

'It doesn't matter.' Joining him at the table, I sipped my coffee. A desperate need to share the horrors of my past week overwhelmed me. 'Oh, Ant,' I sighed.

'What?' Ant eyed the coffee warily, visibly relaxing as I drained the last of it.

'You've got no idea what it's like up there. There are frogs in the toilet. And snakes ...'

'Snakes?' Ant's eyes bulged. 'How many?'

'Just one,' I admitted. 'But it was in the toilet. I almost sat on it.' I shuddered.

Ant reached out and took my hand.

I didn't shake him off.

'That's awful, Cassie. I don't know how you put up with it for so long.'

I let the 'Cassie' pass. 'It's only been a week.' I'd forgotten that one of the nicest things about Ant was the way he listened.

'It seems like longer,' he said. 'I'm so sorry, poochy.'

I waved my hand at him. After all, he'd just beaten me to the inevitable infidelity. It's not like I'd been totally guiltless. I remembered Mac's ripped T-shirt with a pang. A lost opportunity ...

'I hate to see you looking so sad,' said Ant.

'No, no, I'm fine, fine.' I forced a smile. 'So, you and Damien? Is it serious?'

Ant blushed and shrugged. 'I'm a bit confused right now. I feel like an idiot. I've missed you, but then he just came along and ...'

'Mmm.' I knew what he meant.

'So, this snake, how did it get in the toilet?'

'Umm.' My brow furrowed. 'I'm not sure. Through the roof, I suppose, there's this hole ...' *The roof ...* Suddenly, as if someone had turned on a switch, I remembered what I'd seen as I'd looked up before going inside.

Mac had glanced down to check I was going. I replayed that glance: hadn't there been a touch of guilt there? And then, out of the corner of my eye, I'd seen him pull something out of his backpack ... My memory homed in on it. It had been a sack. And, now that I thought about it, hadn't there been a faint suggestion of movement? My face flushed red with rage.

'What is it, Cassandra?'

'That bastard. I'll show him.'

Chapter Ten

A silly phase

The drive back from Sydney on Sunday night gave me plenty of time for reflection. Retracing the landmarks I'd passed with such excitement on Saturday could have made me feel bad, but it didn't. My focus was elsewhere.

It was funny, but I wasn't as hung up about Ant as I felt I should be. After all, he'd cheated on me. With a former client. In my bed. I weighed it up. It was irritating, certainly, but was I heartbroken? No. Maybe I was in denial. Would I break down in tears at Newcastle? Port Macquarie? Kempsey? As each town went past I glanced at the block of chocolate on the car seat next to me and decided I didn't need it.

Ant had seemed more cut up about being sprung than I did.

'It doesn't mean I don't love you, Cassandra. This Damien thing, it's not like I'm in love. I'm just going through a silly phase,' he'd said as I got in the car.

I don't think he even realised he was almost quoting from an old song again — 'I'm Not in Love', 10CC. He just happens to think in mushy song lyrics. 'Look, Ant, chill out. Take your time to figure out which way you're swinging, right? You can stay in my apartment if you want, or come and visit me in Beechville — not that I'd recommend it. It's not what you're used to.'

'Why are you going back there, Cassandra? It sounds horrible, not your thing at all.'

It was a good question. It wasn't like Beechville held any attraction for me. Sydney was my town and I longed to return to its embrace, but it wasn't ready to take me back yet.

Ant and I had gone out to breakfast at our usual spot on Sunday morning ...

It had been a funny feeling to be back in Café le Mer at Manly. I'd felt like I'd been away much longer than a week. I was a soldier returned from the war zone, an explorer back from the jungle ...

I'd soaked up the passing parade of well-dressed walkers and yachts on the harbour like a child with her nose pressed to a lolly shop window. I'd spied a few familiar faces but quickly looked away before they could snub me, pulling my sun hat lower. Their eyes had skated over me with the merest flicker of recognition.

My iPhone had lain switched on next to my perfectly brewed skinny latte but Wazza was notably silent. 'Give me a call,' I'd said to Ant, when I couldn't stand it any longer. 'I don't think my phone's working.'

He'd flicked open his mobile and pressed my number.

'Dirty Deeds' sang my phone. I do like that old AC/DC stuff. I'd picked it up. 'Hello?'

Ant waved at me across the table. 'Hi.'

Pressing 'end', I'd banged it back down. I'd shovelled down my eggs Benedict, but they tasted like rotting seaweed. *Why didn't Wazza call?*

So Beechville was still my bolt hole, my burrow, the cocoon I could hide in until I emerged as a reformed PR butterfly.

But something else was drawing me back too. *Why are you going back there?* Ant's words hung in the air. Sheer bloody-mindedness pretty much covered it. 'I've got scores to settle,' I drawled, as I slammed the car door.

I waved at Ant as I drove off. The sun shone on his white polo shirt and caught the highlights in his hair. It was a little sad that I'd probably never have him on the kitchen bench again. My body tingled at the thought. We'd had some fun, hadn't we?

Now, I slowed down as I cruised through Coffs Harbour. Looking back on the last nine months, I realised there'd been something missing in my relationship with Ant. It was annoying, after a while, having a partner who did what you told them to all the time. Maybe for some people that would be good, but for me it wasn't. I liked Ant; he was sexy, obedient and a good listener, but I needed more than that.

And what I needed was a bit of resistance, a touch of unpredictability, a dash of bad attitude ... That feeling with a man of never knowing what you're going to get back — like a game of ping pong. Mmm, now *that* was sexy. And when you finally hit that winning stroke that leaves them in awe ... *well,* the sense of achievement. You can't beat it. Cross-gender verbal ping pong should be an Olympic sport.

This brought me back to Mac. If putting a snake down a girl's toilet didn't qualify as resistance, then what would? As I drove past the Big Banana it occurred to me that I was looking forward to the challenge of getting him right where I wanted him.

Now that I didn't have a snake looking up between my legs it was almost funny. He clearly wanted me gone, but why? I thought about it off and on all the way back to Frog Hollow. Why did he want me gone *so much*? I had that quiver in my stomach I get when my PR antennae are vibrating. That man was hiding something, and I wanted to know what.

I tuned to the North Coast radio as I got closer to Beechville. *An angry emu threatened a bike rider at Broadlake National Park today,* said the announcer. I smiled. I wouldn't say I was exactly glad to be back in a place where emus made headlines, but, well, it beat home invasions and drive-by shootings. And Sam had been right when she'd said it was busy up here. It was amazing just how busy wildlife could keep you.

No lights showed at Mac's house when I got there on nightfall, or I would have gone over and confronted him. A package was sitting on my doorstep, though. I ripped it open — my uniform had arrived. I tried it on in front of the mirror. *Wrong, wrong, wrong.* Too much Girl Scout, not enough va va voom. Luckily I had a stapler and some sticky tape left over from the feral pig morning in my car. It took a couple of hours to get the look I wanted, but I was happy with the result.

There was another task I needed to complete before I went to bed.

Living in a house with a snake in the toilet was going to be problematic, but I'd come prepared. I pulled the heavy-duty duct tape out of my handbag, slammed the toilet seat down, not checking to see if it was still at home, and started wrapping. Fifteen minutes later I had the seat completely encased in silver tape. There was no way that snake was getting out of there — not this way anyway. It could go back out the way it came in if it wanted.

It's all right, René, don't look at me like I'm a serial killer. I'd Googled snakes at home before I came back, so I knew they could hold their breath for twenty minutes, and they could certainly climb. It wasn't going to die in there; I didn't want that on my conscience.

You probably thought I didn't have a conscience, didn't you? Well, it's not true.

Crawk.

Was I missing you? Strangely enough, I was. Your philosophy had been annoying — who needs that from a frog? Not to mention the way you'd commandeered my toilet, but, yes, the house did seem quieter without you.

Crawk.

Never accept a thing as true? There you go again ... see what I mean? Who needs it? Where's the relevance?

Anyway, the bathroom was now useable, and as for the toilet, I'd sort that tomorrow. In the meantime, there was the grass.

I gave Mum a ring before I went to bed. I knew I should have called in to see her while I was in Sydney. Manly to Blacktown is a long way, though — I could get to Coffs Harbour, almost, in the time it would take me to get there and back.

She picked up the phone, sounding breathless. 'Cassie? You should know better than to call on Sunday at this time.'

My mind ticked over. 'Sorry, Mum. I forgot about *Gladiators*.'

'I'll have to be quick, darl, they're about to have the elimination round. I'm afraid we ate your sausages. Brian's girlfriend came around for the barbie so we had to defrost them. How are you going up there?

Is Anthony going up to visit? I really need to get my tips done. I don't suppose he'll be coming over here anytime soon …'

'Tell her the one about the interrupting cow,' yelled Brian in the background.

'Tell her yourself,' said Mum.

'Mum, I —'

'I might need to find another hairdresser. Don't tell Anthony, will you? I don't want him to think I'm playing the field or anything.'

'Mum, Ant and —'

'I hope you're still using that lavender sachet I gave you next to your underwear. It will keep the insects away — very calming scent, too.'

'Yes I am, Mum, but Ant isn't —'

'Oh, got to go, Cassie. They're about to duel with the Sumo ball. Talk to you soon, darling. Bye-bye.'

'Bye, Mum.'

Mac's house was still dark when I went to bed; no doubt about it — he was a man of mystery.

I stopped short as I came into my bedroom. That was strange. My pashmina shawl was neatly folded on the end of my bed. I eyed it — I was pretty sure I hadn't done that before I left. In fact, I was positive. I hadn't even realised I'd left it behind.

A faint aroma rose from it as I picked it up. There was my lavender, and something else — an earthy, sweaty, beery smell. It sounds disgusting, but it wasn't. It wasn't at all …

Climbing into bed, I pulled the shawl up to my nose and pressed my knees together as I breathed in deep. It smelt like Mac.

I consulted *Alice* before I went to sleep. *'Oh my ears and whiskers ...' said the White Rabbit.* I remembered the ripped T-shirt. Oh my ears and whiskers indeed.

At work the next day he was trying for Mr Innocent. I'd got there before him and stuck a note on his computer — *I'm onto you.*

He glanced at the note, then crumpled it up without looking at me.

So that's the way you want to play it. I opened a new email — I DON'T KNOW WHAT YOUR PROBLEM IS, BUT IF YOU THINK YOU CAN GET RID OF ME THAT EASILY, THINK AGAIN BUDDY. I pressed 'send'.

I thought I detected a certain amount of fluster as my email arrived. But then my inbox went ting, there was one from him — Sorry, don't know what you're talking about. Has the frog come back? I snorted and deleted it. He'd soon find out who he was dealing with.

Grinding my teeth, I moved on to scanning the newspaper — *Local Man Nets Record Cane Toad Haul.* A blurry image of a man in a battered felt hat accompanied the article. He held a cane toad in one hand and a bucket, presumably containing the record haul, in the other. People in Beechville didn't have to wait long for their fifteen minutes of fame. Everyone got a turn in the limelight. There was something nice about that, I supposed.

My inbox had a couple of grenades I needed to deal with, notably an angry email from Christine Bowles. *Where is the mouse? The Minister will want to hear of this.*

With everything else that was going on, I'd completely forgotten the mouse. I'd had to pack the trap away for the weekend as apparently it was a breach of animal ethics or some such to leave it unchecked for longer than a day. I set it up again with a blob of peanut butter before I checked the rest of my emails.

Then another one arrived from Christine Bowles.

My letter to the Minister goes in the mail at eleven a.m. unless I hear from you with identification.

Just as I finished reading this there was a metallic click. The trap had snapped shut. I picked it up, pushed the door down a fraction and peered inside. There it was, trembling in the corner — that furry little problem. 'Ohh, it's so cute.'

'What've you got there?' Rodney had just come in. He did a double take as he noticed my uniform. 'You, you look good in that,' he mumbled and blushed.

I smiled at him sweetly while he got over it. 'It's a mouse. I think we'd better ask the ranger to identify it for us.' I looked over at Mac. His head was pressed against his computer screen; heavy breathing drifted towards me.

'Mac,' said Rodney loudly. 'Have a look at this.'

He started and pulled himself upright. 'Just, um …' He yawned, gave up on finding an excuse, and got up from his chair at the speed of an arthritic ninety-year-old. 'Let's have a look.' Taking the trap from me, he pushed the door down a fraction. 'Hmm, *Mus musculus*.' He handed the trap back.

'*Mus musculus*? Is that the rare one?' I said.

'House mouse,' he grunted.

'House mouse? But why did Christine think it was the Hastings River mouse? And you — you said you thought it was a Hastings River mouse too.'

Mac shrugged. 'Mistaken identity. Happens a lot.'

But I couldn't let it rest there this time. 'You knew, didn't you?' Mac frowned and wandered back to his computer. I pursued, prodding him in the back as Rodney looked on, bemused. 'You knew it was a house mouse all along. Didn't you? You did, didn't you?'

Mac slipped some headphones into his ears and pressed the power button of his iPod. His eyes met mine for a moment. I took that as a yes.

'Jesus.' I stomped back to my chair and replied to Christine's email. Sorry – mistaken identity. The mouse is Mus muscoolus. I hoped I'd spelled it right. 'What do I do with it now?' I called to Rodney, pointing at the trap.

'I'll take care of it for you. Green Dream.'

'Green Dream? That sounds nice.' I imagined a grassy playpen.

Rodney gave me a baffled look. 'It's what we use

to euthanase animals.' He drew his finger across his throat as he picked up the trap.

'Oh.'

Before I did anything else, I had to take care of the basics. Flicking through the yellow pages to T, I found a company that hired out portaloos at a very decent rate. Good — now I could withstand a siege.

My next email was from Whale Woman.

Seeing as you've settled in now, I want you to do an audit of all PR aspects of our office and make recommendations on how things can be improved. Please don't feel constrained by the way it is at the moment. You have my full support to make any changes necessary. I'm just tied up with a couple of marine mammal issues; otherwise I'd be there to talk you through it.

I smiled. Now here was something I could get my teeth into — an image audit. This was a good chance to show my true colours. Image audits were my bread and butter. A company's image is so important. It's not just a matter of sticking a logo on things — it's all the little details, like how staff answer the phone and what they say when people ask them about their job in the pub. Most people don't realise that.

I opened a new page on my computer.

Image audit

Now, where to start? My eyes roamed around the office and fell on Mac. He was nodding his head to a tune on his iPod. He looked like he hadn't shaved for a few days, his shirt was crumpled and a smear of some blackish stuff stained his khaki shorts. His hair was still doing whatever it had been doing when he got out of bed. Was that moss in it? His mud-splattered boots were only half laced and some kind of plant seemed to be using his socks as a home. His legs and forearms looked like they'd been lashed with a cat-o'-nine-tails. What *had* he been up to? My fingers moved furiously across the keyboard.

Item examined – ranger
Image conveyed – scruffy and uncorporate
Desired image – stylish and welcoming
Action required – get him to dress and groom better
Budget – nil

Now, what next? I picked up my notebook and went for a walk.

Item examined – office

What could you say about the office? The furnishings, the carpet, the signage — it all seemed to be stuck in a seventies time warp. It certainly needed an image makeover, but what to do? Although — sometimes shabby is chic. There was one client of mine who I'd advised to cultivate a down-at-heel look — it projected

132

an image of sincerity and being careful with clients' money.

What sort of image were we trying to convey here at the wildlife office? Caring, concerned, friendly, environmentally aware … Who did that kind of thing really well? Steve Irwin, of course. My mind whirred.

What we needed were big blown-up pictures of a ranger. It would have to be Mac — once he'd had his image makeover. We could have stand-up cut-outs of Mac holding a frog, a snake, a mouse … He'd have to smile; he wouldn't like that. That was a bonus. And then there was the merchandising …

I eyed the brochures and other printed materials that lay on the desk at the front of the office. Where were the ranger dolls, the kids' ranger shirts, the ranger line of surf wear? It was boring, boring, boring — and unprofitable. There was no harm in making a profit if it went back into wildlife, was there?

Picking up a brochure on cane toads, I read it. Whoever had written this material had no idea about copywriting. It might have made a good academic thesis, but no layperson was going to wade through it. *The cane toad,* Bufo marinus, *was introduced to eat cane beetles, but showed no interest in these pests … blah, blah, blah.*

We needed cane toad Playstation games, maybe a word of mouth cane toad whispering campaign, something on YouTube and Twitter … I really needed to run a cane toad focus group to see what would connect with the punters. *Tell me, what do you think of when I say cane toad? Um, warty, I'm thinking warty.*

This office was so far behind the ball game; it hadn't even entered the stadium, let alone got itself onto the field.

Racing back to my desk, I started to type.

By the time I emailed my report off to Sam, it was eleven o'clock — time for the media 'famil' I'd organised last week. Justin from the *Beechville Star* was keen for a first-hand look at the survival-challenged shorebirds. Or that's what he'd said. I think it wasn't so much shorebirds as this bird. Still, any puff is good puff.

The phone rang as I was about to leave. I picked it up. 'He-llo, Cassandra Daley.'

'It's Simon McKechnie here.'

Well, that was a surprise. *Simon*, what did *he* want?

'From the *Herald*,' he added when I didn't say anything.

I was tempted to hang up, but curiosity got the better of me. 'Oh, really? Wow. I think I knew that — what do *you* want? Run out of backs to stab? A bit light on for witches to hunt?'

'I was just wondering … how you're going up there.'

'Who told you I was up here?'

'I can't reveal my sources.'

'Pig's arse you can't.'

'Funny you should mention pigs,' he said.

I groaned internally; somehow he'd found out about my pig morning. 'You know, Simon, that was actually a very successful event.'

'Really? It didn't give that impression. I was thinking of a follow-up …'

'You're joking. You think people in Sydney are interested in feral pigs?'

'I think they might be interested in the combination of feral pigs and *you*. It's an intriguing dichotomy — quirky. Might suit the *Weekender*.'

My stomach sank; this was the last thing I needed. And he was right — *Disgraced PR queen, Cassandra Daley, comes to grips with feral pigs* was a story with legs. 'Leave me alone, Simon,' I hissed. 'Haven't you done enough, without a "where are they now" article?'

'I was joking, Cassandra.' His voice was soothing.

'What are you ringing for then?'

'No ulterior motive — just checking up on you.'

'I'm fine.' I banged the phone down. *Weird.*

Looking up, I noticed Mac's eyes on me. He had a thoughtful look on his face. I'd probably been speaking too loudly. As soon as I caught his eye he looked away.

Shaking my head, I shut down my computer. What was Simon up to? Sneaky little bastard probably just wanted to gloat. I picked up my iPhone and, for about the tenth time that day, checked for messages, but Wazza hadn't called me back. The door to Sydney was still closed; I just needed to make the best of it for now.

Picking up the keys to the four-wheel drive, I adjusted the dashing Akubra hat that came with the uniform and strode from the office. *Ranger Cassandra to the rescue.*

Chapter Eleven

High tide

The radio crackled and faded as I reached the beach. I'd been singing along to Johnny Farnham's 'You're the Voice' until it died. '1987,' I said to Justin. 'A good year for music.'

He flashed me a funny look. 'I was born in '88.' In his cap and sandshoes he looked like a school kid on an excursion. Journalists, like doctors, get younger every year.

'Well, *I* was only in primary school,' I muttered. 'Grade Four. I just have a good memory, that's all. This is Whitey's Beach,' I explained as I veered onto the sand track through the dunes and turned north up the beach. 'It's a nature reserve the shorebirds use for nesting. It's also popular with fishermen, illegal campers, dog walkers and drug dealers. Apparently it's a gay beat too. You've got to hand it to those birds: they're determined.'

Whitey's Beach was a far cry from Manly — no cafés, bike paths or lifeguards; just miles and miles of sand. The media 'famil' was going very well. The fruits of my research were paying off, judging by the copious notes Justin was taking. 'Every year we have egg and chick losses from dogs, foxes and four-wheel drives. People put their tents up next to nests and party all night, but still the birds keep coming back.' I liked the 'we'. It implied a long-standing relationship with the birds.

'I suppose they've got nowhere else to go,' said Justin.

'No, they don't.' I pulled up a short distance from a group of birds digging for shellfish on the sand. They looked like the right ones, from what Sam had said. The pied oystercatchers' long orange beaks and feet contrasted nicely with their black and white feathers. It was a good look. Maybe I could emulate them. *Orange boots would go well with my black and white checked skirt …* 'Why don't you take some pictures?'

Justin jumped out and started clicking, walking further along the beach towards another group of birds. I figured I may as well drive up a bit.

Starting the car, I put it in gear and pressed the accelerator. Nothing happened apart from the engine revving. I tried again, but it still wouldn't move. A loud whining accompanied my efforts, then a movement outside caught my eye. Sand was spraying up outside the window. Turning the car off, I jumped out. *Shit.* The tyres were half buried. How did that happen? Kneeling down, I scraped at the sand ineffectually, before giving it up as a bad job.

Getting to my feet, I glanced up the beach, tapping my fingers on the car bonnet — Justin was still happily involved with the birds. He looked like he was getting into it — setting up lots of creative angles. *Good.* My eyes came back to the tyres. There was no way I was going to get that car out of there. Not without a lot of digging anyway. And wouldn't the same thing just happen again?

This was just what I didn't need. I eyed the waves licking greedily towards me. *Please let the tide be going out.* This job was turning out to have a multitude of unforeseen pitfalls. The feral pig morning fiasco had — bizarrely — turned out all right for me, but wrecking a car … That could be cause for dismissal, particularly with on-the-spot media coverage. I knew Justin was sweet on me, but that wouldn't stop him filing the story. Journalists were like that.

I looked from the car to the tyres to the waves to Justin and back again, seeking a solution. *Car. Tyres. Waves. Justin.* It was a quadrangle of evil with no apparent means of escape. I jumped back in the car and tried again, praying for a miracle. There was no miracle. When I jumped out of the car, the tyres were buried even deeper. This definitely wasn't looking good for my job prospects.

I couldn't go back to Sydney. Wazza wasn't returning my calls and now Anthony was gay. That would be an über-loser whammy as far as the in-crowd was concerned. *Did you hear — she turned her boyfriend gay? No wonder — look at her stuffing herself ...* The plastic surgery makeover didn't seem such a good idea anymore either. I was used to my face; I didn't want to change it.

And then there was Simon's phone call. It had shaken me a bit. I'd thought I was safe — a few more months and I'd be in the clear — but he'd reminded me that with the right fuel, stories can run and run. He wasn't really thinking of doing a follow-up, was he?

Oh, René, what would you do in this situation?
Crawk.
An optimist may see a light where there is none? Are you saying there is no light?

The sand shimmered like a desert as I gazed down the beach. It reminded me of *Wolf Creek* — a movie I wished I'd never seen. I'd probably end up selling Kombis to crazed outback killers if I lost this job. A wave washed over my foot and I came to a decision. I didn't like it, but it was the lesser of two evils.

I selected the office number on my phone; Rodney put me through to Mac. 'I need some help.' I clenched my teeth. He was the last person I wanted to ask, but who else was there? Part of me was interested to see how he'd react. Would he tell me to get stuffed?

'What's up?' he said.

It was different hearing his voice on the phone — more intimate somehow than face to face, like his mouth was up against my ear. It surprised me that I could enjoy that, even in this awkward situation. Perhaps I'd fallen for him a bit more heavily than I'd meant to. I pushed the thought aside. 'I seem to be stuck,' I said.

'Uh huh?'

He didn't say much, but what he did say was strangely sexy. Once you're attracted to someone it really doesn't matter what they say, does it? It's the voice that counts. His was deep, but not too deep — masculine, but not macho. It hit the low notes like a fine cello.

'I need someone to give me a hand.' Without intending it, I found I was purring like a cat. I sounded like a phone sex operator.

'Have you got your Akubra hat on?' His voice was dry, though still sexy.

'What's that supposed to mean?' I touched the brim of my hat. Was he having a go at me?

'Nothing. Have you tried winching?'

'Winching what?'

'There's a winch on the front of the car.' He spoke slowly, as if to a two-year-old. It was pretty uncalled for.

I snapped out of my erotic haze. 'It's all right, I speak English.' I glanced at the car. There was a roll of wire below the bumper bar, but — really. I mean, I called the NRMA if I got a flat tyre. Winching was way beyond my repertoire. There were two things I did to cars: put petrol in and clean the windscreen. 'Oh come on. Just drive down and give me a tow out, will you?'

I lowered my voice. 'I've got a journalist with me. I've managed to keep him busy photographing birds so far, but it won't be long before he notices we're not going anywhere.'

'Could be tough turning that into a good news story.'

'You're enjoying this, aren't you?' He was a total bastard; how could I have forgotten? I stamped on any romantic thoughts. This was going absolutely nowhere.

'How far above the sea-line are you?' he asked, ignoring my question.

'About a metre. Why, is the tide rising?'

There was a pause. 'No, it's going down. You should be right.'

'Oh, good. So, are you coming?'

'Yeah, I suppose so. Sit tight.'

I thought I heard him whistle as he put the phone down. *Bastard.*

Forty minutes later Justin was getting restless. 'So, I've got all the shots I need, I guess we'll be off now.' He wiped the sweat off his forehead. It was pretty warm out there in the sun. He must have been as much of a four-wheel-drive novice as I was — he hadn't even noticed we were bogged.

I leaned against the car, adjusting my hat to keep the sun out of my eyes and thought quickly. I'd been checking the time on my phone every ten minutes or so. *When was Mac going to turn up?* Contrary to his advice about the tide, the waves seemed to be getting closer, not further away.

'There's another bird down there you haven't photographed yet.' I pointed at a lone long-legged bird with a pointy beak about a hundred metres away. 'It's a rare one too.'

Justin brightened up, pulling out his notebook. 'What's its name?'

I inspected the bird. 'The long-legged pointy beak.'

Justin scribbled. 'Haven't heard of that one. I'll go get a picture then.'

I rang Rodney while he was gone.

'He should be there by now,' Rodney said. 'He left ages ago. I'd come down myself, but I can't leave the office unattended.'

'The tide's going out, right?' I eyed a wave that almost touched the back wheel.

'Hmm, let me have a look at the tide chart … no — tide's coming up. It'll be high in about an hour.'

'Great.' As I hung up, a rogue wave washed over my foot. Where *was* that lying bastard?

Justin trudged back towards me, shimmering in the sun like a serial killer on an outback highway. I was about to break it to him that we weren't going anywhere, when a black shape appeared in the surf in front of us.

'What's that?' Justin lifted his camera.

A flipper came out of the water, then a whiskered snout. What *was* that? I blinked and refocused. It was a seal, rolling around in the breakers like it didn't know what to do with itself. Surely that was unusual for the North Coast? Weren't they supposed to live in cold places? I frowned, doubtfully, but then its head came out and its round black eyes looked towards the beach. Yes, it was definitely a seal.

'What do we do?' said Justin, clicking off a few shots. 'Is it sick?' The uniform had him fooled — he thought I knew what I was doing.

'Don't touch it,' I said sternly. I wasn't keen on getting wet, and I've heard seals attract sharks. 'I'll contact my manager.' I hadn't wanted to call her before — for obvious reasons — but the arrival of the seal put a whole new complexion on things. Seals were right up her alley. I smiled: events were taking a turn for the better.

Whale Woman appeared within fifteen minutes; it was uncanny. She took control of the situation immediately, snapping at the two grizzly fishermen who'd stopped to stare.

'Keep your distance — let it rest. Not you,' she said to Justin. '*You* take photos.'

He knelt down in the surf on command, the waves soaking his jeans.

Like I said, she'd have been good in the army. Her gaze swung to my car. The waves were washing at the hubcaps. 'I'll just get that out of the way while you do the media thing.' She jumped in the car, turned it on, then turned it off again and jumped out. 'Need to lock in the hubcaps. You're right, it's good to keep it in two-wheel drive on the hard sand, but now the tide's coming in …' Kneeling down, she did something to each of the hubcaps, started the car and — just like that — drove it up closer to the sand dune.

Lock in the hubcaps, hey? I'd remember that for next time.

The car would have been underwater by the time Mac finally arrived.

I was on the phone to ABC radio when he drove up. 'Yes, that's right, Colin. It's a young New Zealand fur seal here on Whitey's Beach. The vet's on the way and we're going to assess its health and see what we can do. I'll call you back in time for your four o'clock bulletin …'

I saw Mac assess the situation — my car, up above the high tide mark, Sam on the phone to the vet, the fishermen … He looked disappointed. What was he hoping for — the car bonnet vanishing underwater?

'Where have you been?' Sam snapped her phone shut. 'I've been calling you on the radio for about an hour.'

'Sorry. I must have been out of range.'

'It's lucky Cassandra was able to respond so promptly.' She nodded at Justin. 'Got onto the media too.' Sam gestured at the seal. 'Do what you can until the vet gets here.' She looked him up and down. 'We've got a couple of other things to discuss too, but that can wait for now.'

Sam took Mac aside after the vet came and the seal departed. It had rested on the beach for about an hour, then hauled itself into the sea and swum off — to the Land of the Long White Cloud, presumably. The words 'image audit' drifted towards me. I pricked up my ears.

'I want you stylish and welcoming,' Sam said.

'Pigs might fly,' Mac muttered.

'You've been letting things slide lately too — sleeping on the job.'

'Who told you that?'

'I have my sources.'

The look Mac gave me after Sam left was indescribable, but I'll have a go. It was the kind of look you might give to someone who'd just robbed a blind beggar, or maybe tossed their rubbish on the ground right next to a bin.

No-one had ever given me a look like that before.

It didn't faze me. I returned the favour — or tried to. Total contempt is a difficult look to master. Still, the main thing was, Sam had instructed Mac to assist me with my office revamp and cane toad campaign.

Oh, he hated it so much.

'Oo, oo,' I sung as I climbed the stairs to the office, doing the understated dance moves like the girls in black from the video clip 'Addicted to Love' — Robert Palmer, 1986, the year I turned seven ...

Everything was going my way — for once. The seal incident had been a triumph — a public relations triumph and possibly one for the seal too. New Zealand fur seals are pretty uncommon in these parts, so it caused a bit of media stir.

I stopped singing for a moment, remembering the seal's big, dark eyes. I'd liked that seal, and not only because it had come along in the nick of time and saved me from a public relations disaster.

Oh yes, and the image makeover? It was going fabulously too ...

The last couple of days Mac had arrived at work neatly pressed, shaved and grime free. I'd found a fashion photographer from the Gold Coast to do the shoot and the local wildlife carers had brought in some cute animals.

He'd posed with a blue-tongue lizard — their tongues really *were* blue — a flying fox and a carpet python — he seemed terribly at home with that one. Which reminded me — I narrowed my eyes at him as the python coiled around his neck — I still hadn't got to the bottom of the toilet-snake incident. But I would ...

Anyway, it was totally fab.

'This is going to do wonders for our image,' Sam said when she saw the proofs. Her brow crinkled as she looked closer. 'Was that the best smile you could manage?' she said to Mac.

He glowered.

'It's all right, you can do a lot with airbrushing,' I said. 'That'll get rid of that gritted teeth look.' I beamed at him.

I was glad Sam was there to protect me at that point or I think he might have bitten me.

So, phase one of the revamp in motion, it was time to get the cane toad campaign rolling. This morning, to kick it off, I was holding a focus group. I bustled around the meeting room getting it all ready — pens, paper, easel, tape recorder. I ran through the ABCs of focus groups in my mind: *planning, recording, moderating, analysis and reporting ...* Yep, I was ready.

My group filed in at ten o'clock. I'd managed to get a good demographic spread. I had Generation Y — one of the boys from the feral pig morning; Generation X — Rodney; and a Baby Boomer — Maureen.

I'd had to offer Maureen and Tyler — that was the boy's name — a twenty-dollar voucher, to be reclaimed out of my new merchandising range, when it arrived. Rodney, of course, was getting paid for his time.

Once they were all settled, I wrote *Cane Toads* in big letters on the butcher's paper clipped to the easel and tapped the words with my marker pen. 'How do you feel about cane toads?'

'They're gross,' volunteered Tyler.

'Nasty,' said Maureen.

'Make good golf balls,' said Rodney.

There was a knock on the door. A curly grey head poked in from the corridor. 'I heard there was a workshop on cane toads?' It was Hannah, the animal liberationist from the feral pig morning.

I sighed, tapping my foot. *And I wonder who told you?* It appeared Mac was cowed but not beaten. I thought about asking her to leave, then decided against it. She could cause trouble; besides, a spread of opinion was always good. 'Take a seat. How do *you* feel about cane toads, Hannah?'

'I like them. I've got to know the ones that visit my garden each night. They co-exist quite peacefully with the other animals. And they control garden pests.'

The other three looked stunned.

'Bonkers,' Tyler muttered to Rodney, who nodded.

I stretched my lips into a smile, scribbled *co-exist peacefully* and turned the page of the flipchart over. *War Against Toads* read the heading on the next piece of paper. 'What do you think about this as a campaign title?' I asked, deliberately not looking at Hannah.

Maureen nodded approvingly. 'I like it.'

'Yeah,' said Rodney.

'What about "crusade"?' said Tyler.

I looked at him in surprise. 'Good suggestion, thanks.' I wrote it down.

'Or counter-strike,' said Rodney.

'Attack,' said Maureen.

'Jihad,' said Tyler.

'Blitzkrieg,' said Maureen.

'Conciliation,' said Hannah.

I reluctantly turned in her direction, my hand sore from writing.

Her cheeks were pink. 'How would *you* feel if people wanted to bash you with a golf club, just because you're warty?'

'We're not talking about golf clubs,' I said soothingly.

'*I* am,' said Rodney.

Tyler leaned across to Rodney. 'She should move to Byron Bay, they're all like that there,' he whispered.

I decided this was a good time to hand out my written questionnaire. 'If you could just fill this out before you go. I need to get feedback on my draft brochure ...' I handed them each a copy of the brochure and the questionnaire.

They all scribbled furiously for a few minutes, then I managed to get rid of them without too much of an altercation. Sitting down, I opened up the first questionnaire.

This is what I got from Tyler.

What do you think of this brochure?

It's good to hit cane toads with golf clubs, but there are many other ways of killing them too.

Would you change anything about it?

A lot of people like to run them over in their cars — I like that, but I think it's better to drop them in a vat of boiling oil.

Would you recommend it to your friends?

Or shooting them with an air rifle is also good.

What did you most like?

Or I wouldn't mind trying a James Bond thing, where you suspend them over a

What didn't you like?

tank filled with really fierce sharks, or a knife pit, or a fiery furnace ...

Hannah's response was a stark contrast, although she'd ignored the questions too. *I think people's true nature comes out when it comes to cane toads. Just because they are considered a 'pest' people feel like it's all right to be cruel. I find them very gentle creatures.*

I've picked them up and stroked them and never come to any harm. The toad did not ask to be put here and the damage it supposedly causes could never be compared to that done by humans.

Rodney and Maureen actually did have a crack at answering the questions, so I supposed the session wasn't totally wasted.

I filed the questionnaires and my notes away. I'd have to try to make sense of it all later. What I really needed right now were some images for my brochure. I bailed Sam up as she was rushing out. You almost needed a net to catch that woman. 'The focus group went really well. I'm going to develop a whole new range of cane toad collateral, but I'll need some pictures first,' I said.

Sam glanced at Mac, who was doing his best to pretend he didn't know what was going on. 'Take Cassandra out to get some shots,' she commanded.

He looked up slowly and nodded.

'That boy you had here ...' said Sam to me.

'Tyler?'

'Yes. He's a genius on the football field. You should see him play some time.' She carolled the opening line of 'My Favourite Things' as she strode out the door.

Mac gave me the total contempt look again once Sam was gone.

I gave him my version back, with bells on — I'd been practising in the mirror.

He raised one eyebrow — I could tell he was impressed.

Chapter Twelve

With what porpoise ...

Yodelling the chorus of 'I Still Haven't Found What I'm Looking For' over the splashing of the shower, I rinsed off my hair. U2, 1987. Getting out, I picked up my towel off the tape-encased toilet.

It was toading night. I treated it as I would any other big date: waxed my legs and eyebrows, moisturised every inch of my body and padded down the hall to my bedroom to select my nicest undies.

A bit presumptuous? Maybe, but it never hurts to be prepared — even when your hot date holds you in total contempt. Things can change.

That was the easy part. Now, what to wear? Subtlety was the name of the game — I'd scare him off if I dressed like a vamp. I pulled on a pair of cargo shorts and a little T-shirt that flashed glimpses of my stomach, then I applied my 'no makeup' makeup. A pair of Blundstone boots completed my look. It was very Lara Croft Tomb Raider, I thought as I looked in the mirror. My boobs weren't as big as hers, but whose were — outside the computer gaming world, anyway? Even Angelina Jolie in the movie version hadn't come close.

It was a big night, so a quick consultation with *Alice* was in order before I left. I opened the book. '*… if a fish came to me, and told me he was going on a journey, I should say, "With what porpoise?"*'

I considered that. What *was* my porpoise? *Purpose.* Ostensibly, to find cane toads, but *really*? Well, obviously what I wanted was Mac. My heart fluttered at the thought of him pressed up against me. I sighed. How likely was that? He hated me. Although, on the other hand, hatred is closer to love than indifference is. You never knew …

What was going on with him? I sensed he was attracted — there was the body language … But his grumpiness went beyond the usual male lack of eloquence. Maybe a few hours in a car together would loosen him up.

As I closed *Alice*, the phone rang.

'Knock knock.' It was my brother, Brian.

'Who's there?'

'Interrupting cow.'

'Interrupting cow wh—'

'Moo moo.' Brian cackled with laughter.

I joined in. It was actually pretty funny.

'You get it?' said Brian.

'I get it. Interrupting c—'

'Moo moo.'

We chortled again.

'How's it hanging, bro?' Brian always brought out my inner rapper. It was probably something to do with his baggy jeans and backwards-facing cap. I pictured him leaning on the kitchen bench, one eye on the television.

'Yeah, yeah, cool. Had a good barbie last Sunday. Shoulda been there.'

'Mmm, would have liked to be.'

'When are you coming home, Cass?'

'Soon as poss, bro.'

'You pretty much got hung out to dry, huh? Who's that bloke you worked for?'

'Wazza.'

'Yeah. What's his story? How come he let you take the rap?'

'That's the way it works, Brian.'

'Well, that sucks, Cass. You don't drop your mates in it like that. But that's what you get for hanging out with that poncy eastern suburbs crowd.'

I smiled. Brian made life seem so simple. Things were either black or white with him. With me they were a million shades of grey. He was right, though. *Why hadn't Wazza called me back?*

'There's a job going for an admin girl in the real estate down the road. Mum reckoned it might suit you. You could move back home.'

I visualised myself filing leases in the Blacktown Real Estate; moving back into my old bedroom with the posters of Che Guevara and Mao Tse-tung. It would be like the parallel universe I had escaped by going to university. I shuddered. 'I'll think about it. How's Mum?'

'She's into some Chinese thing now. Brought in all these mirrors to direct the energy around the house and shit.'

'Feng Shui?'

'Something like that. She says it different, though. You know that frog statue?'

I thought about it. 'The one from Kmart that she put under the tomato plant out the back?'

'It's not under the tomato plant anymore, Cass. She's got it at the front door, but the way the mirrors are set up you can see it from almost anywhere in the house. It's kind of freaking me out. Those beady black eyes, y'know.'

'What's the idea?'

'Dunno really. You know what she's like. Something brewing. You should ask her.'

I glanced at my watch. 'Hey, gotta go now, bro. Going out to collect cane toads.'

'Cane toads? Fuck, reckon you'd be better working in real estate than doing that, sis. Was that the kinda thing you had in mind when you went to uni?'

'Nah, I was aiming for dung beetles, but the market fell out of them.'

'Moo moo.' Brian chortled again and hung up.

I smiled. Talking to Brian always cheered me up.

Mac was supposed to be picking me up at six

o'clock so, camera on my lap, I settled on the steps to wait. The night seemed noisier with frog calls than usual. A symphony of crawks ricocheted around the garden like a Mexican wave.

It wasn't long before Mac's lights appeared in my driveway. I got to my feet. He must have seen me waiting, but he still beeped his horn; he wanted to make this hard for me.

I put on a big smile as I jumped in and just for a moment I thought I saw his lips quiver, but then he grunted — as usual.

His eyes flickered up and down my outfit. 'Might get cold,' he muttered.

I shrugged. 'I'll be right.'

A light rain started as we swung onto the highway, heading north. 'Shame about the rain,' I said, to break the silence.

Mac gave me one of his looks — not the 'total contempt' one, but the 'who is this idiot?' one. I like a man with range. 'You need high humidity to get them calling. No point in doing it on a dry evening,' he said.

'Oh. Right.' There was no need for him to sound so hoity-toity, not everyone can be a cane toad expert, can they? 'So, what's the plan?'

'Head up the Border Track. We'll stop every now and then — see if we can hear them. Keep your eyes open.'

'What do we do if we find one?'

'*You* take a picture. *I* collect it.'

'You collect it, and then what?'

'I dispose of it.'

Trying to have a conversation with Mac was like finding a parking spot in Pitt Street — frustrating and fruitless. I gave up and looked out the window.

He turned off onto a dirt track, pushing the gear stick into low range. The rain was falling harder now. I hung onto the door as we dropped into a deep hole in the track; I didn't think we were going to make it out again, but the car crawled up the other side easily.

We climbed higher and higher up this mountain track, rain-soaked trees thrashing against the car as we passed. Eventually Mac stopped near a gully, winding the window down.

'What are you …?'

'Ssh.' Mac waved his hand, listening. 'Great barred frog.' He pulled a laptop from the back seat and opened it. A throaty wark, wark, wark drifted in through the window as he tapped on his keyboard.

'What are you doing?' Almost everything he did was a mystery to me.

'Recording its location. Threatened species.'

I listened to the call drifting in from the rainforest. The air smelt mossy and ripe in the rain. 'Why do they call?' I said.

Mac flashed me his 'who is this idiot?' look again, but this time his eyes didn't leave my face. 'They want to have sex.' His voice was emotionless, factual, but his choice of words was telling.

Sex. He could have said mate. Wasn't that what scientists usually said? I showed no reaction. I had a feeling he was testing me. I looked out the window. The frog's call suddenly seemed very, very sexy. In fact, the whole rainforest was damned sexy — the smells, the noises, the tangled vines. It was the opposite of ordered; it was wild. And wild, I had only just realised, was about as erotic as it gets.

They want to have sex. Rain drifted in onto my face. I closed my eyes for a moment, feeling an inexplicable urge to leap out of the car, take off my clothes and let it wash over me. Maybe I even wanted to call for a mate, to croak, chirp and twitter until he found his way to me. *Oh yes, come and find me, I'm here …*

You must get that feeling all the time, René.

Putting the computer aside, Mac dug an MP3 player and speakers out of his backpack. As he pressed the power button, a noise like a telephone dialling tone filled the car. Brrr, brrr, brrr …

'Is that the cane toad's call?' My voice came out croaky. I coughed.

He nodded. 'The male — calling for a mate. If you play the sound and there are other toads in the area, they usually respond.'

Encouraged by his two-sentence answer, I pushed my advantage. 'Where do they come from?'

'Cane toads?'

I nodded.

'South America.'

'And what's the main problem with them here?'

He looked past me into the rainforest. 'Other animals eat them and die, because of their poison. They also eat native frogs and their tadpoles eat frog tadpoles. They're basically a hopping biodiversity muncher.'

Three sentences. I could have listened to his voice all night. 'That sounds bad.'

'They're right through this area and it's amazing frog habitat.' He paused. 'The Aboriginal name for this area means "a great place for frogs". Not such a great place now the cane toad's here, though.'

'A great place for frogs. I like that. How far south do the cane toads go?'

'The front is further down the coast — moving south about five k a year.'

'The front? You make it sound like a war.'

'It is a bit like that. Right now we're in enemy territory. We're dealing with a colonising movement that could sweep right across Australia.'

He'd forgotten to be grumpy — we were actually having a conversation. Could I have been right that the way to his heart was through his wildlife? I smiled. 'We will fight them in the trenches?'

'Yeah — we will never surrender.' His eyes met mine and — like a ray of sun breaking through clouds — he smiled back.

He smiled back!

It was a minor miracle, like taming a wild creature.

He had a beautiful smile. It hit me right in the heart —
bang. I turned my head, so he couldn't see the way my
cheeks were burning. *Goodness* — that was a powerful
smile. No wonder he saved it for special occasions.

He turned the engine on again and kept driving
up the road. The mist settled in around us as we got
higher. The headlights picked out clumps of hanging
moss, dripping with moisture.

'It's beautiful,' I said. My head was still spinning
from his smile. 'Very ... atmospheric.' *Very sexy.*

'It is.' Mac's voice was calm, tranquil.

I liked that new voice. It wasn't one I'd heard from
him before — I wanted more. 'What do you call those
things sticking out the sides of the trees?'

Mac followed my gaze. 'Buttresses.'

'Mmm, I like them — very *Lord of the Rings*.'

On the road in front of us a hunchbacked creature
hopped slowly along. Mac stopped the car and jumped
out.

'Toad?' I jumped out too, camera in hand.

He nodded, pulled a bucket and net from the back
of the car and draped a raincoat over his shoulders.
It wasn't coming down hard, but hard enough.

My first-ever cane toad was squat, with unblinking
black eyes and a disdainful expression. It wasn't the
monster I was expecting.

Mac pointed to the lumps on its back. 'Poison
glands, need to watch out for those.'

I took a few pictures as he scooped it up, shielding
the camera from the rain with my hand. I didn't have a

jacket, of course. Did Lara Croft ever wear a raincoat? I didn't think so.

Mac's eyes flickered to me and his hand went to his raincoat. I thought he was going to give it to me, but he just pulled it further over his shoulders. *So much for chivalry.*

'Why didn't you just run it over?' I shivered.

'Needed to double-check it's a cane toad — don't want to make any mistakes. Besides, humane euthanasia's the go.'

'According to the Geneva Convention for prisoners of war?'

'Yeah — that enough pictures for you?'

'I wouldn't mind a few more — if that's all right with you?'

'You're the boss.' His voice was sharp again, like he'd just remembered he was here under duress.

'Sorry,' I murmured.

'What?' He climbed back in the car and I followed him.

'Sorry. I'm sorry I made you take me out. Seemed like the only way I was ever going to get you to talk to me.'

He started the car up again, frowning.

'You hate me, don't you?'

'It's not a matter of hating.'

'What is it a matter of then? Ever since I arrived you've done your best to make things difficult for me.'

'There's a campground up ahead — might see

if there's some cane toads there.' He watched the windscreen wipers brush away the rain.

I wasn't going to let it drop. 'Snake in the toilet?' I said. 'Why?'

'I don't know what you're talking about.' He stared out at the night, fingers tightening on the wheel.

I reached over and touched his arm. 'Why?' His arm was warm. My fingers must have felt like ice against it, but he didn't flinch. I was soaked.

He glanced down at my hand where it rested on his forearm. Something passed over his face: annoyance and — if I wasn't mistaken, which I don't think I was — the 'd' word: desire. I know that look. It made my stomach jump. It was so quick, but I was sure …

On the other hand, perhaps not …

He pulled over at the campground. There were no tents, which was lucky considering the conditions. My hand fell off his arm as he reached into the back seat for a spotlight. 'You stay in the car. I'll have a look around.' He jumped out like the car was on fire.

I watched him walk away across the grass. In the beam of his spotlight the rain looked like snow. He liked it out there — I could tell from his face he was relieved to get away from me. Back into his natural habitat …

A toad was calling through the rain. In a way, it was a nice call — if you didn't know the creature that was making it. It was just an animal trying to find a mate. It wasn't its fault it was so far from home.

'Mac.' I jumped out of the car and ran towards him. In a moment I was wet through — my hair was sticking to my face, but I wasn't going to let him get away that easily. Not when I was just getting somewhere.

He turned, his spotlight shining in my eyes, blinding me.

'Don't run off like that,' I said.

'Get back in the car, you're soaked.'

I shrugged. 'Why do you hate me?'

He hesitated, then stepped towards me. He was so close — I thought he was going to wrap his arms around me. That's what it looked like. And when he spoke, his voice was low — almost tender. 'We don't need liars around here — I read the *Herald*, you know.'

Chapter Thirteen

High time to go

Neither of us spoke a word the whole way back. He picked up a couple of toads at the campground, added them to the bucket, then climbed back in the car. I was already there, shivering.

He turned the heater on as we headed down the mountain. That was considerate, I suppose. I was too miserable to bother trying to talk, but he opened his mouth a couple of times as if he was going to say something, then closed it again. In the back seat the toads jumped around in the bucket, banging against the plastic lid.

It was funny; I'd actually thought he was warming to me. We'd had a conversation — our first ever. Not much of a conversation maybe — no-one could call a discussion about cane toads romantic, but words had been exchanged. He'd even smiled. What if he never smiled at me like that again? I'd only had one hit, but already I craved it like an addict.

I'd felt something between us, I know I had — I've had experience at these things. I thought he was going to make a move. And then — that.

Now that I thought about it, I didn't know why it hadn't occurred to me before. It was the obvious reason for him to want to get rid of me. I'd thought he was hiding something. Really, he just hated me because I was a sneaky astroturfing spin-meister who had it in for the long-footed potoroo.

I watched the rainforest outside the window and, the thing was, I kind of got it. The way the mist hung among all those twisted branches — it stirred something in me. It was like that feeling you get now and then when you see a dress in a shop. You're just walking past, not even thinking about dresses … But then, there it is — the perfect frock — and suddenly it fills this hole you hadn't known was there.

I think I now knew how those people felt about the potoroo, about the rainforest, about turning trees into houses. I'm not saying I'd turned into a tree-hugging greenie. It would take more than that, but — I saw their point. It would be like someone taking a razor to my favourite dress — the whole wardrobe even.

I was just turning to Mac to try to tell him that, when I saw him stiffen. His eyes were fixed on the side of the road. I followed his gaze. Two dogs stood in the mist, beneath the dripping trees. As the car came closer they ran into the bushes. Across the back of their rumps were black stripes. I'd never seen dogs with markings like that before.

Still, I might not have thought much more about it if it hadn't been for the way Mac looked. His face was rigid and his hands gripped the steering wheel so hard his knuckles were white.

I looked from his hands to the rainforest and back to his face. He wasn't giving anything away. His blue eyes were cold. I suddenly remembered the tattoo of the tiger I'd seen on his shoulder that first afternoon.

I knew what he was hiding.

I wouldn't have done what I did if he'd said something — if he'd just asked me to keep it quiet. If he'd acknowledged what we'd seen. But he said nothing.

Even when he pulled up at my house and I got out, he didn't wave or say goodbye. I stood on the verandah, watching his lights disappear. I wanted to run after him, shake him out of that silence — why wouldn't he talk to me? I didn't, though.

Why are man–woman things so complicated? Why won't men talk? What goes on in their minds? Not much, possibly. But *was* this a man–woman thing? To *me* it was. To him, well ... I thought of those animals with their striped rumps. To him, it was probably something else. Were those animals *really* what I'd thought they were? Was that even possible? Weren't they extinct?

I pulled out my laptop, plugged the modem into the phone line and Googled Tasmanian tiger. The more

I read, the more excited I got. It was astonishing. Since the Tasmanian tiger, or thylacine, became 'extinct' in 1936 there had been 3,800 sightings in mainland Australia. Some of these seemed credible, others not so credible. None had provided any hard evidence, such as tracks or photographs.

But it was the location of many of these reports that really got my pulse racing. The wilderness area on either side of the Queensland and New South Wales border was a hotspot. *Here.* In my backyard. Since 1964 there had been fifty sightings of a striped animal like a cross between a dog and a kangaroo.

I thought about what I'd seen ... A Tasmanian tiger — now that was something. Two Tasmanian tigers — that was beyond *something*. It was spectacular. I was no animal expert, obviously, but you didn't need to be one to know that finding a Tassie tiger was like winning the lottery. I paced up and down in my kitchen as I thought about it. Long-footed potoroos and Hastings River mice were one thing, but Tasmanian tigers ... Now that was news — big news. I knew someone who'd be *very* happy to hear from me with this story.

And it would distract him from running that other story he'd mentioned ... PR queen goes feral was not a story I wanted to read in the Sydney papers.

I bit my lip. But Mac, it seemed, was trying to keep the tigers quiet. I reckoned he'd seen them before. That explained a lot, when I thought about it. Now why would he want to keep them quiet? Maybe he didn't want a media circus? Or … he was lining up a big media deal? Yeah, that could be it. Maybe he didn't want me to crash his party.

Something about that idea didn't square with the Mac I knew, but what *did* I know about him really? Stripping off my soaking clothes, I dropped them on the bathroom floor.

I looked towards the toilet, but of course you weren't there, René. I really did miss you then. A bit of philosophical wisdom was just what I needed.

As the shower ran over me, I considered my options. I knew what I had here was an entrée back into society of the highest kind. If I played my cards right *I* could be the woman who returned the Tasmanian tiger to Australia. Maybe there'd be an Order of Australia in it for me. That would be nice.

It was a pretty intoxicating feeling: finding an animal thought to be extinct. The idea of this tawny creature stepping out of the rainforest, out of the past … Yes, it was big news all right. But, should *I* be the one to break the story?

Towelling my hair dry, I sat at the kitchen table, listening to the rain. A drop seeped through the tin roof and landed at my feet, then another. I leaned down to fetch a saucepan to put under the leak and a cockroach the size of a matchbox scuttled out, across my wrist.

I screamed. I'd seen cockroaches before, but this one was a monster. Suddenly the room came into sharp focus: the crappy kitchen, the dirty stove, the cobwebbed windows ... Not to mention the animals in the toilet, on my roof and in my garden. Had these creatures never heard of boundaries? I didn't know how I'd put up with it so long. I wasn't meant for this kind of life. Wildlife and me just did not mix.

I *needed* that entrée back into society. This story would catapult me right back to the top of the A-list where I belonged. But, before I took any decision, I had to consult *Alice*. The book was on the floor beside my bed. I closed my eyes, opened the page and pressed my finger to it. When I opened my eyes, this is what I saw.

It was high time to go, for the pool was getting quite crowded with the birds and animals that had fallen into it ...

I read the words several times. *It was high time to go.* It was one of the clearest messages I'd ever had from *Alice*. I closed the book, nodding. *There were too many birds and animals.* That was it then, the universe had spoken. Time to go.

Simon McKechnie's number was on my phone. I pressed the buttons and waited. Maybe he wouldn't pick up. That would be a sign I wasn't meant to do this. Yes, I *was* still a bit conflicted, even with the clear advice from *Alice*.

I can't pretend I didn't know what I was doing. I'd had the epiphany in the rainforest — such as it was.

I wasn't totally the ignorant city slicker anymore — I didn't have that excuse. Maybe Mac's reasons for keeping the tigers secret weren't selfish. Maybe there was more to it I hadn't considered …

The phone rang and rang; I was about to hang up when he answered.

'McKechnie here.'

'Simon?' I coughed to clear my throat. 'It's Cassandra Daley. I've got a story you'll be interested in …'

It wasn't until we'd finished talking that I saw the fat black sausages dangling off my ankles. *Leeches!* They must have been there the whole time. I screamed and dropped the phone. I'd been right about rainforests — muddy and leech-infested pretty much covered it.

When I saw Mac's lights go off I knew this was my chance. Simon had suggested I search his house for photos or anything else that might count as proof. He'd been excited, but trying to hide it.

'I'll have to talk to my editor,' he'd said. 'See if he's interested.'

'Maybe I'll try the opposition instead …'

'Give me half an hour …'

'Gee, I don't know …'

'Twenty minutes then. I'll call you back ASAP.'

I looked out into the darkness towards Mac's house. Having come this far, it seemed stupid to baulk at breaking and entering. Hell, if Mac was going to treat me like a cross between Hitler and Judas, I may as well act the part. I should be able to duck over, case the joint and get back again in twenty minutes. The main problem was, it was wet out there — and I didn't have a raincoat.

My Tomb Raider outfit was lying in a sodden clump in the laundry. It seemed a shame to wet more clothes — the way this rain was going, who knew when I'd be able to dry them? Frog Hollow was sadly lacking in standard laundry facilities, like a dryer. Even the washing machine was one of those twin-tub models.

I took the only sensible option and pulled out my swimsuit. I'm not a bikini girl — less on show is always sexier. This season's strapless black retro fifties one-piece had turned heads at Manly Beach every time I'd worn it. I pulled my velvet dressing gown on top for warmth; no heads would be turning tonight.

Goosebumps popped up all over me as I stepped into the rain, my dressing gown flapping behind me in the breeze. I had a sudden vision of how I must look: like a cut-price Wonder Woman, minus the tiara.

I knew I'd have to walk — he'd wake up if I drove — but the bush route was out of the question. I'd end up in Brisbane if I didn't die in the jungle first. Not to mention the leeches. I'd just had an hysterical half-hour getting them all off. You could still see the lumps where they'd bitten me. A dribble of blood ran down the side of my foot and the theme music from *Jaws* ran through my mind as I leaned down to scratch my ankle. I imagined a pack of leeches circling, the scent of blood in their noses. Did leeches have noses?

My bare feet dug into the muddy track as I set off up the road, hand curled around my key ring torch.

I'd never experienced rain like it — not so much rain drops as rain container-loads. Croaks and ribbets followed me the whole way. Those frogs must have been yelling their guts out to be heard over the downpour. It was a great place for frogs all right.

Were you out there, René? I suppose you must have been, but I didn't hear you. You were being the strong, silent type for a change.

I listened for the call of the cane toad, but didn't hear it. There was something nice about being able to identify noises. It made you feel at home. I used to know the sound of the rubbish collectors, the neighbour's car and the Manly ferry, but now … I smiled to myself — toad identification was my specialty.

Stepping onto Mac's verandah was like climbing out of a pool. I breathed deeply, squeezing my hair to stop it dripping down my back. A blanket was draped over the hammock. Picking it up, I wrapped it around me. His door wasn't locked. The thunder of the rain lessened only slightly as I stepped inside, shutting the door. The noise was a good cover — he wouldn't hear me unless I did something stupid.

Mac's house was much the same as mine, only in better nick: the lino and wall paint wasn't cracked and peeling. In a narrow circle of torchlight I padded down the hallway, towards the kitchen — that's where everyone keeps their stuff, isn't it?

Like my house, the kitchen ran off the lounge room. I shone my torch around the lounge, looking for clues to the mystery man's life. No family photos or paintings decorated the walls. A couple of copies of a magazine — *Australian Zoologist* — lay on the coffee table. That was no great insight — I already knew he was into animals. An empty beer bottle beside them was also no surprise. A small guitar — a ukulele, actually — was propped up on the sofa. I imagined Mac strumming a Hawaiian melody. A dusty bookshelf next to the sofa housed a small collection of paperbacks. I flicked my torch beam over them — he seemed to favour thick books by Russian authors. I would have liked to investigate further, but knew I should move on.

There were a few dishes on the sink in the kitchen. A small jug of fresh herbs on the bench gave off the bewitching scent of basil and rosemary. A bowl of eggs stood next to them. I remembered the chickens. Compared to my kitchen, with its empty packets of Lean Cuisine and noodles, this one seemed used ... inviting. I felt a strange urge to make an omelette.

I opened drawer after drawer, carefully sliding them out to minimise noise. Top drawer — cutlery; next drawer — knives; third drawer — screws and a hammer; fourth drawer — *aha* ... There were no photos, but sitting in the bottom drawer was a white lump of plaster. Pulling it out, I ran my finger over the raised lumps in the block — it looked like an animal footprint. Could this be the evidence I was after?

A sheet of paper had fluttered out with it. Placing the plaster on the bench, I picked the paper up. A few words were scrawled on it, some scribbled out.

Lavender
You appear ~~from the sun ghostlike~~ pale in the twilight
Inhabit my ~~mind~~ dream
Sabotage my senses

A strange feeling came over me as I read it — like my mind had slowed down. I read it again. *Lavender* — it was about me. It had to be. Mac had written a poem about me. No-one had *ever* written a poem about me. I'd been given Valentine's Day cards with rhymes on them, but he'd made this up himself ... I didn't know anything about poetry — I mean it was probably total crap ...

No, it was nice. Even if it was crap, it was nice. I hadn't realised — poetry was so powerful. Just to think of him, thinking of me, writing that ...

I stared at it in bemusement. It was a total revelation — he had the hots for me? He'd done a pretty good job of hiding *that*. I read it again. It made me feel all, I don't know, deeply romantic and sexy at the same time. And the man who'd written that poem was in bed just down the corridor ...

I remembered his face when I'd touched him in the car — the way his eyes had flashed. My instincts had been right — it *had* been desire. And now, just thinking of his eyes, his hands, his voice, I felt a deep pull starting in my stomach and radiating up and down my body. My cheeks burned. I ached with longing; I wanted him bad. The poem had started a fire in my head that was rapidly setting my whole body alight.

Clutching the poem in my hand, I drifted on a tide of arousal towards his bedroom, not stopping to think that maybe he wouldn't be pleased to see me — he'd written the poem hadn't he? *Sabotage my senses* — he wanted me, all right. Pulling open the bedroom door, I coughed.

'Mac?'

There was no answer. I walked towards his bed. It was so dark, I couldn't see a thing. 'Mac?' I said louder.

Sitting down on the bed, I patted it.

He wasn't there.

Chapter Fourteen

A cat set loose

I sat on his bed in the darkness, wondering where he was. Where would you go on a night like this? Time passed slowly. Shivering, I waited, my clothes clammy against my skin, the blanket off the hammock still wrapped around me. All thoughts of getting back to fill Simon in on my discovery were forgotten. That didn't seem important anymore.

Mac's bed was unmade, the twisted sheets and blankets hung down over one edge, trailing onto the floor. I eyed the pillow hungrily. It wasn't so much the comfort I craved as the intimacy of lying where his head had lain. At last I couldn't resist and, dropping my blanket to the floor, I climbed in. His smell surrounded me — the same one I'd smelt on my shawl. What had he been doing with my shawl? Breathing him in deep,

I cocooned the covers around me, imagining they were his body.

The rain and the wind howled outside — I felt like I was on a tiny boat at sea. Closing my eyes, I imagined myself sailing to a distant shore. And on that shore was Mac. My heart fluttered at the thought, the possibilities crowding around me so thickly I could barely breathe. It was like an illness, this longing. But in its own way it was also delightful. It was painful, but I didn't want it gone.

I ran my hand across my stomach, imagining it was his. I craved his mouth, his chest, his belly against mine. Sometimes the anticipation can be as good as the act itself. More often, unfortunately, it is better ...

The front door opened. I jumped out of the bed and peered around the corner, into the corridor. A weak torch beam shone my way, fading into darkness before it reached me. Why didn't he turn the light on? He walked quietly as if he was trying to surprise someone. *Me?* Did he know I was here?

I waited. He didn't see me in the darkness of his bedroom. I could have touched him by the time I said his name. 'Mac?'

He stopped. 'Cassandra?'

I stepped towards him, reaching out my hand; it met his chest. His heart was beating fast. Did he still hate me? I didn't care really.

My fingers ran up the side of his face, wiping away raindrops as I went.

He didn't touch me. He didn't move away. He didn't say anything.

I hesitated, suddenly unsure. Had I misjudged this? Was the poem for someone else? Was I making a fool of myself? I let my hand drop.

He caught it. Held it. Wound his fingers through mine.

For a few moments I heard only the sound of his breathing. His thumb traced an arc across my palm. 'We shouldn't do this,' he said, but his hand was saying something else. His hand was saying the same thing as mine — *I want to touch you so badly it hurts.*

I dismissed his words; his body was speaking much louder. Curving my hand behind his head, I pulled him down towards me. I kissed him.

He wasn't reluctant. Not at all. He returned my kiss fiercely, almost bruising my lips. His hands were inside my dressing gown and sliding down my body. I shivered as his rain-wet fingers touched my legs. Pulling my dressing gown off my shoulders, he kissed the side of my neck. I moaned, my stomach turning over. His wet shirt pressed against my breasts. He slid his arms around my back and pressed his cheek to mine. I felt like I hardly knew where I ended and he began.

'I really shouldn't do this,' he whispered into my ear like a love song.

I believed only the tone, not the words. I licked his cheek, pressed my lips against his ear. 'I really think you should,' I breathed.

He let out his breath in a long sigh, as his hands ran down my arms, taking my dressing gown with them.

Then we sort of collapsed onto the bed and — well — it was … just the way it should be.

Crawk.

What — you want more details? All right …

There was just enough light in the room to see each other's faces. We touched noses, rubbed cheeks, gazed into each other's eyes. He rolled over, pulling me on top of him, stroked my face, my hair. He smiled, a long, lazy, wicked smile, his teeth white against his face.

My stomach flip-flopped. I leaned closer, caught his lip between my teeth, bit it lightly, traced the line of his mouth with my tongue.

He closed his eyes, exhaled, murmured something.

I didn't quite catch it. It sounded like 'I give up' but that didn't make much sense. I ignored it, which seemed the right thing to do as he didn't speak again.

My swimsuit vanished, like it was made of rice paper. Mac's clothes were there, and then they weren't. It was dreamlike, the kind of sex you have inside your head but never in reality. No, it was better than the sex I have inside my head.

That had never happened before. Usually the reality failed to live up to the fantasy.

You can learn a lot about someone when you make love. It makes you vulnerable, to be naked, to lose control. Some men resist that, the light goes out in their eyes and they give you their body, but not their mind. Mac wasn't like that. He never took his eyes off mine. Never. Not once. He didn't hide and he didn't let me hide either. It was almost scary, like falling into each other.

It was somehow completely ... pure. No masks.

That's the way it was for me anyway. That's how it seemed at the time ...

After we finished — *landed* — we lay in silence, legs and arms intertwined, our chests rising and falling against each other. I pressed my forehead to his skin, listened to the rain, my mind fluttering here and there like a butterfly drunk on nectar.

Mac didn't say anything, but I assumed, like me, he was sunk so deep in blissful torpor that he couldn't form the words. He expelled a deep sigh, then, extracting his arms and legs from mine, rolled over on his side and turned the bedside light on.

I blinked, shocked, wanting him back beside me. It was too sudden. I was still in the airlock from our journey. I wasn't back on Planet Earth yet. All I wanted was to wrap myself around him.

'I was just over at your place.' His hand was back, resting warm on my waist, but his voice had an edge to it.

A shot of alarm went through me. 'Why?'

'I wanted to know what you were going to do.'

I knew what he meant.

'There was a message for you while you were out. On your phone.'

Simon. I couldn't read his expression — the light was shining in my eyes — but his voice wasn't exactly warm. Not cold, but not warm either — neutral. You don't expect neutral at a time like that.

'A message?'

'Simon's got approval from his editor, you're not to give the story to anyone else, he's going to look after you and you're to search my house for proof.'

I felt like I'd been punched in the stomach. He was just so — *God* — gorgeous, and I'd done the one thing — the one thing he'd never be able to forgive.

He has the most beautiful eyes; have you noticed, René? No, I suppose he's not your type. But his skin — it's so soft. You wouldn't think it would be, but it is.

Crawk.

Yes, I know you prefer green, but we're talking about Mac here.

'I've totally blown it, haven't I?' I said.

He shrugged. He was back to unreadable.

How could he do that? Now. After what we'd just done. My body was still ringing like a symphony. Why wasn't it like that for him? I wanted to shake him, slap him about the head, pull him down and make love to him until he admitted there was something astonishing between us. Something miraculous even.

I hate the way men shut down like that. How hard can it be to say how you feel?

But violence was no solution — I was in the wrong, not him. 'What can I do to make it better? I can call Simon, tell him it was a hoax ...' My voice trailed off. Simon would never buy that — if anything it would just make him keener.

'There's nothing you *can* do now — you've opened the box, Pandora.' His hand slipped off my waist.

'So, why did you — why did we ...? If you knew ...' *I shouldn't do this.* He'd known, but he'd still made love to me.

He propped himself up on his elbow. I was acutely aware of the space between us. My eyes lingered on the tattoo on his shoulder.

'I'd have to be crazy not to want you, Cassandra. Turns out I'm not.' He gave a lopsided almost-smile. 'Not in that way anyway.'

My heart jumped with pleasure at this crumb, thrown my way. 'But don't you hate me?'

He took a deep breath, expelling the air slowly. 'No. I tried to, but I don't.' Rolling on his back, he looked at the ceiling. 'How long do you think it'll be before he gets here?'

'Simon?' I thought about it. 'If he can charter a plane he'll be here any minute. If not, first plane tomorrow morning. I wouldn't have done it if you'd just been a bit ...' I paused, '... nicer.'

Mac smiled briefly. It was a long way from his heart-melting sunburst in the forest. 'I'm not too good at nice. Sorry.' The whole time the rain was getting louder and louder. 'He won't be getting in here tomorrow. Rain like this, he'll be lucky if any planes are running, and even if they are, the roads will be cut.' He rolled over to face me. 'We've got plenty of time.'

I stared at him. What did he mean? 'Time for what?'

He smiled again; properly this time.

It had the same effect on me as before — a hot flush swept over my face.

'I love the way you do that,' he said.

'I hate it.' I did hate it — it was a relic from the shy Cassie I'd been unable to get rid of.

He touched my cheek. His hand felt cool. 'No, it's very cute. I meant, we've got plenty of time for whatever we want to do.' His meaning was unmistakeable.

'I didn't even know you liked me. I thought you wanted to get rid of me.'

'Who said anything about *like*?'

I winced, but Mac continued in a low voice. 'I wanted you from the moment I saw you ...'

'I thought you were dead.' I remembered the way he'd hung in the hammock.

'Mmm, I was pretty out to it ... You got all mixed up in my mind with dreams about Tasmania. It was only when you turned up in the office the next day I realised I hadn't dreamt you.'

'Why Tasmania?'

'That's where I'm from. And your smell, the lavender ... My parents grow it on their farm.'

'So, why the grumpy act, the snake ...?'

'It's a long story.'

'We've got all night.'

He smiled again — another burst of sunshine, such riches — and pulled me in to rest against his shoulder. 'Let's not talk about that now...'

We woke to thundering rain.

I curled into Mac's body. I wasn't used to it yet; I'd forgotten how thrilling it was, this intimacy thing. It really is everything you imagine it might be. That first flush of being with someone new; I'd leap mountains for it.

The crash of the downpour lent an air of unreality to the morning, like we were in a bubble, surrounded by water. I wondered if I should write a message in a bottle and throw it out the window — *it's me, Cassandra, help, help!* No, I had everything I needed right here.

'Do you think Frog Hollow is getting flooded?' I murmured to Mac as he stirred.

'Should be okay. You worried about it?'

I briefly considered my possessions, left behind in the house — clothes, magazines, iPhone, camera, my car parked outside ... 'No, there's nothing there I need.' The thought was liberating.

'It'll be cut off, though. Looks like you're stuck here for now.'

Turning my head, I drank in Mac's profile. It's funny how a face can seem like the answer, even when you don't know the question. There was still something impenetrable about him, though. I needed a can opener to get inside that man's mind.

'You still haven't explained the grumpy act,' I said.

'Haven't I?' He yawned and met my eyes.

'No.'

He sighed and rolled over to face me. 'You really want me to, do you?'

I nodded.

'Really?' There was an edge to his voice.

I wasn't sure if I did anymore, but I nodded again.

'You have no idea how out of place you are here, do you?' He sounded exasperated.

I bristled. How could he go from hot to cold in an instant like that? 'Yes, I do.'

'No, you don't. You think you're the city slicker in Hicksville —'

'No, I —'

Mac continued as if I hadn't spoken. 'What you don't realise is that Beechville, in its own way, has as much going on as Sydney. More, probably.'

'It has? You could have fooled me.' Part of me was hurt by his attack, but the other part rose to the challenge. That's what I'd wanted, wasn't it — someone to stand up to me? If he wanted an argument, I'd give him an argument.

'You just turn up here ... There you are — shiny hair, shiny nails, sparkling teeth. I'd never seen anyone so well groomed — horses maybe at gymkhanas, but not people.'

I blinked, tears rising to my eyes at the scorn in his voice. No, I didn't want to argue with him after all: he punched below the belt. I turned my back. I had no idea who he was. Why did I even care what he thought? Pulling my hand up, I looked at my nails. It wasn't even true anymore — the varnish was chipped and mud had lodged beneath my cuticles.

He took a deep breath. 'I'm sorry, Cassandra. I don't mean to be cruel; I'm just not used to women like you.' There was a long silence.

I didn't say anything.

'You could probably leave off those last two words,' he added. 'I've spent too much time with men. I just say what I think and that's not always the best thing.'

I rolled back over and met his eyes. 'Have you always been like that?'

He shrugged. 'I guess so. That's just me. I'm not like you. I'm a country boy at best; more of a wilderness boy, really. Especially lately — a year in Antarctica, two years in the desert — Beechville's about as cosmopolitan as it's got for me recently.'

There was so much more I wanted to ask him — *everything, tell me everything about you*. I wanted it *all* right now but I sensed getting to know Mac was going to be like an archaeological dig. I'd have to piece him together from bits and pieces; he wasn't going to give himself up whole.

'So, the grumpy act?' I murmured.

Mac reached out and touched my hair. 'You're not going to let it go, are you?'

I shook my head.

'Well, I figured you were used to getting your way ... with men, particularly. Am I right?'

I nodded.

'I looked at you and what I saw was — a cat set loose in the forest.'

'What do you mean?' Was it a compliment or an insult? Something about his tone implied the latter.

'A cat in the wild learns quickly. We had one we trapped autopsied the other day. It had thirty lizards in its stomach.'

I couldn't see the relevance. Just when I thought I knew where I was I'd dropped into Wonderland again. *It would be so nice if something made sense for a change.* 'I'm not a cat. I don't eat lizards.'

Mac didn't seem to hear me. 'I knew if you survived long enough to settle in you'd turn into a killer.'

Chapter Fifteen

It's more about the poetry

Mac met my eyes. He was serious.

What did he mean — I'd turn into a killer? My stomach knotted uneasily. 'This is about the tiger, isn't it?'

He tilted his head slightly in acknowledgement. '*Everything's* about the tiger.'

Everything? Something about the way he said that made the hairs stand up on the back of my neck. What did he mean, *everything*? I wasn't sure if I was ready to go there. 'So, where did you first see it?' I murmured.

'Near my chicken coop.'

'When?' It was like twenty questions — I was going to have to drag it out of him.

'Three weeks ago. Seems like forever.'

That was good; he'd volunteered some information. 'Did you only see it once?'

He looked past me. 'Once there, once somewhere else, and then once with you. I was watching every night but it never came back to the chicken coop. I was starting to wonder if I really saw what I thought I saw.' The dam had broken.

'So that's why you were so tired all the time? I thought you had a secret lover.'

'No … I was out there every night in the hammock with my camera. Sometimes I didn't know if I was awake or asleep. I kept seeing it, raising its head …' His eyes were distant. 'That first time … it was only about five seconds but in some ways … it seemed like more than the rest of my life put together.'

I knew what he meant. 'It was a defining moment?'

He nodded.

What was *my* defining moment? Maybe I was still waiting for it. 'What were you going to do with the photo?' I said.

'I don't know, but I couldn't think about much else. Until *you* came along.' His eyes came back to me. 'There I was in the hammock, night after night, drinking beer, wanting to think about it — the animal — wanting to sort things out in my head, wanting to have a bloody rest. But instead …'

'Instead?'

'Instead, I was thinking about *you*.'

My heart skipped a beat. 'Why is it so important to you?'

'The tiger?'

I nodded.

'The thing is, they're the Australian version of the wolf.' His eyes lit up. 'They're our only truly native top-end predator. Dingoes are just Johnny-come-latelys. And predators, well, anyone who's studied biology knows how important they are. To be honest, though, it's not only about the biology.'

I don't know what made me say it — a sudden flash of intuition … 'It's about the poetry,' I murmured.

Mac tensed, he stared at me. 'How did you know?'

'I found your poem.' I leaned over and picked it up from the bedroom floor where I'd dropped it the night before.

He laughed uneasily. 'And you still wanted me, after reading that? Poetry's not my strong point.'

'I loved it. Can you read it to me?'

Oh my, I had never realised … poetry is Viagra to the mind. Stimulate the brain and before too long, sigh, it travels south …

Some time later, with tousled hair and languid steps, we washed up into the kitchen. I'd wrapped a soft rug off Mac's bed around me like a toga.

The plaster cast was still on the bench where I'd left it. I ran my finger over it. There was a lump for the heel and four toe prints. 'Is this …?'

Mac nodded. 'Yeah, it's the tiger.'

I turned it in my hands, carefully, like a rare artefact or old masterpiece.

Mac leaned on the bench, his torso bare. 'It left its prints in the mud beside my chicken pen. If it wasn't for the footprint I'd have thought I dreamt it — or that it was a wild dog. The footprint, though, four toes and a heel print — nothing else makes prints like that.'

He gazed at the plaster cast. 'I pulled out my *Mammal Tracks and Signs*, took it outside and shone my torch on the mud …' His voice trailed off.

'That must have been amazing.'

'Amazing?' He shot me a quizzical look. 'Yes, I was amazed, but it was more than that.' His voice was quiet. 'It was like being in church.' He looked out the window. 'Not some pissy little country church either — Hobart bloody cathedral with the full choir singing.'

'A resurrection?'

He turned to me. 'Yes, a resurrection. Exactly.' His smile erupted.

It had the usual effect. *Oh my goodness*. Where was the valium when I needed it? I pressed my hands to my burning cheeks.

'It was lucky you weren't living next door at the time, Cassandra. I was jumping and hollering like an idiot. Anyone who'd seen me would have run a mile.'

'Then you took a cast?'

He nodded. 'I always have some plaster handy. You never know what will turn up around here; but not that, I hadn't expected that.' He ran his finger lightly over the cast in my hand. 'It's like touching a miracle.' His eyes lingered on it. 'I suppose it's kind of my religion — wildlife. And this one — it's the Holy Grail.'

I loved the way he said that — it was like he'd flung open the shutters to his heart. Mine, of course, had been wide open from the moment we made love; from the moment I'd read his poem. 'Did you get any photos in the end?'

Mac shook his head. 'That's another story. I think we'd better have a cup of tea first.'

'Any chance of a coffee?'

Mac looked in his cupboard. 'Might have an old tin of Nescafe here.'

I shuddered. 'Never mind — tea's fine.'

Mac made tea in a pottery teapot. He rooted around in the cupboards and extracted a packet of shortbread biscuits. 'I hope you like omelettes.' He gestured at the eggs with his chin. 'It's the only way I can keep up with the chooks.'

'I love omelettes.'

'That's lucky, because there's not much else.'

We settled ourselves at the table. He poured the tea into two mugs, pushed one towards me.

I leaned back in my chair and folded my arms. 'So, Mac, when do we get to the snake in the toilet?'

'Biscuit?' He held the packet towards me.

I took one. 'You're really spinning this story out, aren't you? Maybe I should call you Scheherazade. Do you think I'm going to kill you when you're finished?'

Shifting uncomfortably, he took a sip of tea. 'You know that anyone who hears the whole one thousand and one stories is supposed to go mad?'

'Should I be worried?'

Mac held my gaze. There was something in his eyes … Discomfort?

'What?' I said.

'What, what?' He smiled and it vanished.

Perhaps I'd imagined it. 'So, should I? Be worried?'

'Maybe. Anyway, what's the rush, Cassandra? That's the city in you, let it go. Slow down, enjoy the ride.' His eyes crinkled.

'Okay. We don't have one thousand and one nights, but I guess we've got all day.' I sipped my tea slowly. I hadn't had a cup of real tea like this since I'd left Blacktown. It was gentler than coffee, less of a shot to the heart. I could get to like it. 'Slow enough for you? Tell on …' I propped my head on my hands.

'That Sunday, after you went back to Sydney …' Mac said.

'After the snake incident.'

Mac nodded. 'That afternoon I went for a walk up an old fire trail that leads towards the tick fence on the Queensland border. It was slow going — weeds love a break in the canopy — there were blackberries everywhere. If it wasn't blackberries it was lawyer vine; once that gets hold of you it doesn't let go without a struggle. If I'd been thinking clearly I'd have worn long pants. I was ripped to shreds by the time I got to the top of Cougan Peak.'

I nodded — remembering how he'd looked the morning after I'd got back from Sydney. 'You looked like you'd been on the losing end of a fight with an echidna,' I said.

Mac smiled briefly. 'I was looking for tracks and scats all the way up but hadn't seen anything.'

'Scats?'

'Poos — thylacine poos.'

'Right.'

'Once I got to the summit I climbed up onto a rock to rest and a cloud of butterflies surrounded my head. There were all sorts: swordtails, swallowtails, blue triangles, even a Richmond birdwing, which was good to see — they're endangered. I knew why they were all there, around my head — the butterfly with the highest spot to mate gets the girl. But like I say, sometimes it's not the biology.'

I imagined a flock of butterflies around his head. 'Mmm, it sounds like poetry.'

'Yeah. It's not rainforest up on top of the peak, the soil's too thin — there's just a few grass-trees and some stunted eucalypts. But you're looking down on rainforest. I've worked in lots of different places and they all had their good points, but there's something special about the country round here, Cassandra. The Bundjalung people talk about a sacred triangle mapped out by three peaks. I'm no expert on that kind of thing, but I'd have to say you can feel it — it's in the air.'

I watched him talk, drinking it in. And I'd thought he was the silent type. He had plenty to say when he wanted to.

'Anyway, the sun was setting and it was so peaceful. Some of the butterflies came to rest on my head and the light was streaming through a gap in the clouds. My mind was as clear as it had been for days —'

'Because I'd gone?'

He smiled. 'Because you'd gone. Anyway, I kind of had a revelation.'

'All those blokes in the Bible, they always had their epiphanies on top of mountains, didn't they?' I said.

'Closer to God, I suppose … whatever. Mine was about the tiger, of course. I was looking out at all that country — we call it a wilderness area. It's not really wilderness, though — the Aboriginal people called it home. If you want real wilderness, you have to go to Antarctica. But putting that aside, it's rugged country — no-one goes there. They used to walk the tick fence, but that's pretty stuffed now. The closest inroad of civilisation is my house … and Frog Hollow, but at the time I thought I'd taken care of that.' He glanced at me with a wry smile.

'Ze snake in ze toilet, ve meet at last,' I murmured in a fake German accent.

'Yeah, the snake in the toilet. What can I say — sorry?'

'That would be a start …'

'It was just that, with the tiger, and you … I knew where you'd come from, the type of person you are.'

'Were,' I interrupted him.

'Were?'

'I've changed.' Even as I said it, I knew it sounded hollow. I'd called Simon, hadn't I?

'Have you?' Mac sounded doubtful. 'Anyway, you were the last person I needed around here.'

'Because of the tiger?'

'Because of the tiger.'

Outside, the wind was shaking the trees. They lashed against the house, scratching at the tin roof like fingernails. The rain was a sheet of grey; you couldn't see more than ten metres.

'They say we don't get cyclones this far south, but this is starting to feel like one,' Mac said.

'Don't change the subject.'

'It was only a carpet snake. It's not like I was trying to kill you.'

'It wouldn't have been very nice if it had bitten me on the bum.'

'It didn't, though, did it?'

'What about the snake? Isn't that against your ranger code of practice or something — putting snakes down toilets?'

'I did feel bad about it. It would have been fine, though.'

'I know, they can hold their breath for up to twenty minutes.'

Mac cocked his head. 'You're an expert now, are you?'

'I learn quickly when I have to. You didn't fix the hole at all, did you?'

'Of course not. I had to leave a way for the snake to get out again.'

I nodded, talking through a shortbread biscuit. 'So, back to Cougan Peak. There you are, you think you're rid of me, the butterflies are creating poetry around your head …'

'Yeah, there I was … it suddenly occurred to me that no-one needed to know. The only proper way to deal with the tiger was to do nothing. I wouldn't take a photo; I'd keep my mouth shut and destroy my plaster cast.'

'Why?'

'Any publicity will destroy it. People might say they want to help preserve it, but they'll want to trap it, chase it, round it up — "for its own good".' He avoided my gaze.

The remains of my biscuit congealed in my throat. What was going to happen when Simon arrived? I swallowed with difficulty. 'How do you think it's survived here for so long without being seen?'

'Two hundred years is not such a long time when you think about it. Not a long time to stay hidden in country like this. There's no reason it can't remain hidden a lot longer …' Mac finished his tea and gazed out at the rain.

'Did you see the tiger up there?'

Mac started, like he'd been miles away. 'Didn't I say? As soon as I'd made up my mind, they appeared. If I believed in God, I'd call it divine intervention.'

'They?'

'There were two of them. Probably a male and a female, I can't be sure. My camera was right beside me. My hand was on it, but I didn't move — I'd made a pact. They froze as they saw me. I love the way wild animals do that, just look at you — judging your intentions. There's something so innocent about it. Maybe they would have run off if I'd tried to take a photo. Maybe they wouldn't. I'll never know.

'After five minutes they turned and vanished into the forest. They're pretty hard to see if they don't want to be seen. I don't know how long I sat there for and I don't remember much about the walk back down. I woke up in my bed feeling like I was five years old and it was Christmas Day.' Mac's face was soft as he talked.

I wanted to keep on listening to him, but he seemed to have finished. 'So there you were, tucked up in bed, waiting for Santa, but then the big bad wolf came back.'

'Yeah, that's where my head was, still on top of that mountain, when I saw the note you'd left on my computer. There I was thinking, problem solved, when it was just starting up again.' He nodded at the cast. 'As you can see, I haven't got around to destroying it yet. I don't know why.' His eyes lingered on the footprint.

I turned it in my hands. 'So, this is the only proof there ever *was* a tiger?' *This was the proof Simon was after.*

Mac nodded.

I loosened my hands and let it fall to the ground. The brittle plaster shattered into fragments that skittered across the floor. 'Oops.'

Mac winced.

Chapter Sixteen

Pre-Headline-Tension

My God how it rained. It seemed there'd never be an end to it. Was it three days, four? It was frog weather, duck weather, build-yourself-an-ark-and-get-inside-it weather.

By the second day there was water as far as we could see. It crept closer and closer to the house — a brown tide of ribbets and croaks. It was frog-tastic. Maybe I should have been worried, but I wasn't. Mac was absorbing all my thoughts.

I'd never known a man to be so hard to figure out. He was one minute hot, the next minute cold …

In the hot periods, we spent a lot of time in bed — ribbet, ribbet, kiss, kiss. Frogs everywhere, but here was my prince …

Crawk.

We also talked. It was funny, for two people who'd
hated each other, we really got on — some of the time.
I found out what the tiger meant to him.

'There was a thylacine skin in the attic of my
grandparents' farm in Tasmania,' he said as I traced his
tattoo with my finger. 'My great-grandfather shot one
— not when they were almost extinct, but still … It
was disturbing his sheep. When I was a kid I'd roll that
skin out and play games with it, pretend it was alive.
I couldn't believe it when they told me we'd killed
every last one.'

'So, you're trying to make amends?'

He gave me a funny smile — one that hinted there
was more to it than that. 'I suppose it became kind
of a quest for me … protecting animals. But always,
there was this hope, that I might find one.'

'And then you did.'

Mac nodded. 'And then *you* turned up.'

In the cold periods, we argued, often also in bed.
He seemed like a different person at these times. It
was like he was wearing a mask, and even though I
knew the Mac I wanted was underneath, sometimes
I couldn't find him.

'You gave me a pretty hard time, you know,' I
said.

'I needed to get rid of you. You were your own
worst enemy too. Anyone could have told you how

the feral pig morning was going to turn out if you'd asked. But you're not the kind of person who asks for advice, are you?'

'The animal libbers mightn't have turned up if you hadn't geed them on,' I muttered.

'No, but you still would have had ten journalists staring at an empty hall.'

'It didn't work out the way you thought it would, though, did it, smarty-pants?'

'I'm not in your league when it comes to deception, Cassandra. Nothing turned out the way I thought it would.'

'Including us?'

'Us?' Mac's face was hard to read. 'No — that wasn't planned. Tell me, how did your big PR success go again? You had a group set up lobbying for development? Where did you find these people? How much did you have to pay them? And you made it seem like Rainforest Runaway was only part of what they wanted, didn't you? Good thinking.'

I had nothing to say when he attacked me like that. It made me feel small and lost. 'I've changed.'

He laughed sarcastically. 'Right, you're going to use your skills for good, not evil now?'

'I am.' Right then I would have said anything. I wanted my nice Mac back.

'You are?' He looked at me intently.

'I am.'

He had a funny look on his face and I could tell he didn't believe me. In a strange way, I didn't mind. I'd had too many men who were pushovers in my life and Mac was far from that. He was keeping me honest, making me work for his trust — if that was the right word. I admired that.

'If I'd deceived people for a good cause, would that make it all right?' I said.

Mac looked away for a moment. 'What do you think?' His voice was soft now.

'I don't know. A lie is still a lie. Isn't it?' I said.

'And is it always wrong to lie?' he asked.

'Depends what rulebook you're running your life by, doesn't it?'

'People use words in different ways,' he said.

'What does that mean?'

'Well, one person might call something a lie, and someone else might call it a necessity,' said Mac.

'You sound like you could be in PR. *When I use a word it means just what I choose it to mean.*'

'Humpty Dumpty, right?' Mac turned back towards me.

I laughed and met his eyes. 'Yes. That's amazing. You do know your *Alice*, don't you?'

'Grew up on it. *We're all mad here.*' He smiled.

So that was something else I learnt about Mac — he knew his *Alice in Wonderland*. Could any man be more perfect?

Mac stretched out his hand and took mine. 'These are big questions, Cassandra. Do we have to answer them right now?'

As it turned out, we didn't.

Neither Mac nor I had a watch or any other means of telling the time. I'd left my mobile at my house and he, of course, had never had one. After the first day I was fine with it — who needed to know what time it was?

We didn't talk about what we were going to do next — not while it rained, not while the outside world was safely barricaded behind a moat of floodwater. I don't know why. Maybe we thought it would never end.

Although, as it turned out, Mac *was* thinking ahead.

On the third day, or maybe the fourth, we woke to a different kind of light. 'Look, Mac.' A single ray of sun poured through a gap in the clouds. The rain wasn't crashing anymore; it was polite suburban rain.

'Time to get ...' A loud choonka, choonka, choonka drowned out Mac's words.

Outside the window a helicopter headed for a high patch of land a couple of hundred metres away. We sat up in bed, pulling the covers with us for warmth. A familiar sandy-haired figure in a blue raincoat jumped out of the chopper as the blades were still turning.

'It's Simon. What are we going to do?' I said.

Mac eyed the inflatable dinghy that followed Simon out of the helicopter. He swung his legs off the bed and pulled on his pants. 'Follow my lead.'

I should have asked him then what he meant, but it seemed like there was no time. All those days together and suddenly there was no time at all.

As I got dressed — swimsuit and velvet dressing gown again — Simon and another man rowed across the muddy water to Mac's house. Strolling down the corridor, I opened the door. Simon jumped out of the dinghy and ran up the stairs.

He had that look journalists always have when they're frustrated on a story. Pre-Headline-Tension I call it. After they've got the story, it's all fab — cigarettes in bed, love you, dahling, that was the best ever, et cetera.

Simon had the most severe case of PHT I'd ever seen. 'God, Cassandra, I've been holed up at the Paradise Resort in Surfers Paradise for three days. You look terrible,' were the first words he said to me.

I didn't respond; he was talking too fast. Mac had told me to slow down and I had. I was now so slow you could have fitted an ad break between each of my thoughts.

Leaning against the doorway, I looked at Simon for a long time. 'Simon, goodness ... haven't seen you since ... hmm, must have been when you rocked up at my doorstep with all those TV crews.'

'Yeah, great story — think I'm in the running for the Walkley. Thanks for that. Still, moving right along — where's this thylacine?' He looked behind me as if it might be lurking in the corridor.

'Can you ... slow down a bit? I'm not used to much stimulation at the moment. If too many things happen at once, I might freeze up, or something ...' I suddenly remembered Simon's veiled threat to do a follow-up story on me. 'Hey — that phone call, you're not really thinking of doing a follow-up, are you?'

Simon's shoulders lifted slightly. 'Nah, not really. I was just calling to say hello. After all, we're old uni mates.'

'I suppose that's one interpretation of our relationship.' I nodded slowly. 'I hadn't considered it that way before. So, do most "old uni mates",' I bent my index fingers around the words, 'run exposés in the *Herald* on each other?'

But I'd lost Simon's attention — Mac had appeared behind me. He hadn't put a shirt on, just his loose khaki pants. His shoulder pushed lightly into mine. His chin was black with bristles and his hair stuck up in wild corkscrews. He was dissolute and totally gorgeous; my body ached just looking at him. I waved my hand in his direction. 'This is Mac, ranger extraordinaire.'

The cameraman jumped out from behind Simon and let off a volley of flashes.

'Rein in your dog, mate,' said Mac. He leaned casually against the door frame.

The cameraman bristled. 'Who the fuck —'

'Cool it, Chris,' Simon said quietly.

The cameraman lowered his lens reluctantly.

Chris seemed a nice enough guy — longish wavy hair, combat trousers with twenty pockets and one of those waistcoats with a million apertures. The same air of anxiety seeped out of his pores, though.

It had never occurred to me before, but I realised

now that people in Sydney were often like that. *I was often like that. Hard to imagine.* Right now, I was so slow I could barely talk. 'Would you ... like a cup of ...?'

'Coffee, great,' Simon jumped in.

'Water,' I finished. 'Mac doesn't um ...'

Mac took my arm and pulled me gently aside. 'Come in. I might have a beer left ...'

'So.' Simon sat down reluctantly in Mac's lounge room. His knee jiggled up and down. He looked from Mac to me.

We sat down on the couch, shoulders touching — separation didn't seem possible. Mac picked up his ukulele and strummed a few notes — giving an implausibly Polynesian vibe to the situation.

Simon frowned as Mac segued into 'Ain't She Sweet'.

The cameraman prowled around — itching to take photographs, barely restraining himself. I could see him setting up the angles in his head.

'You two,' Simon continued. 'I take it you're *friends* now? That's a new development.' His face didn't give much away.

'Yes,' I simpered and took Mac's hand. Where once were brains, there now was fluff. I just wanted Simon to piss off so we could curl up in our nest again. I knew that wasn't possible, though. Not yet. I yawned the longest and widest yawn of my life. In three days I'd gone from Alice to the Dormouse. *I breathe when I sleep is the same thing as I sleep when I breathe.*

Mac squeezed my hand, winked, then placed it back on my lap. He seemed more on top of it all than me. He strummed a few more bars, 'Tiptoe Through the Tulips' this time. He must have known it irritated Simon. 'Cassandra's talked me round,' he said. 'We're going to help with this thylacine story.'

We were? That was the first I'd heard of it. I flashed Mac a quick look, but his eyes were on Simon.

Simon nodded, quietly triumphant. 'She's a pretty persuasive little lady, isn't she?' His tone was a blokey nudge, nudge, wink, wink — not at all his usual style. He was trying to bond.

Mac didn't respond.

Simon's mouth twitched. He leaned over and pulled a wad of paper out of his funky go-gear briefcase. 'I'll need you to sign here, here and here.'

'What's this for?' said Mac. He strummed again.

'Exclusivity contract — didn't Cassie tell you?'

'Cassandra,' said Mac.

I smiled at him dreamily.

Simon's nostrils flared, but he kept a lid on his temper. 'It just means you talk only to me until the story's broken. After that — it's open slather. You can negotiate any deals you want.'

'And what do we get?' said Mac. *Strum.* 'For talking to you?' *Strum.*

'I'm authorised to go up to fifty.' Simon's hands whitened around the contract.

'I suppose that'll buy a few beers,' said Mac. *Strum.* 'Doesn't seem much, though.'

'Fifty thousand,' I whispered.

Mac put down the ukulele, stretched his hands behind his head and yawned. 'I guess that's fair. It's a big story. Okay, where do I sign?' He smiled at me.

I had no idea what was going on. He was selling the story? Didn't he want to keep it secret? Why hadn't we discussed this while we could? The last three days together vanished with a bang that left me breathless. I was back to where I started with the man of mystery.

Despite his casual attitude, Mac read the contract closely before signing on the last page and handing it back to Simon.

The tension lessened as Simon slid the papers back into his briefcase.

'Can I take a few pics now?' said the cameraman.

<h1>Chapter Seventeen</h1>

Grumpy boredom

Mac was suddenly all business. While Chris wandered around snapping to his heart's content, Mac pulled on his shirt and grabbed a few maps from the bookcase.

He stretched the maps across the coffee table. 'You've got a chopper. That's good, it'll speed things up. Okay, I've sighted them, here, here and here.' His pencil slashed crosses into the map. 'Given the floodwaters, it's a fair bet they'll be here.' His pencil came to rest on the map. I read the place name — *Cougan Peak*.

'How many does the chopper hold?' he said.

'Three plus the pilot,' said Simon. 'You, me and Chris.'

Mac shook his head. 'You, me and Cassandra.'

'Come on.' Simon pulled at his hair. 'I need the visuals. Cassandra's excess to needs, Chris isn't.'

'You can take a photo, can't you?' said Mac.

Chris had gone pale — his Pre-Headline-Tension, which had gone briefly into remission, was now about to explode. 'I need to be there,' he stuttered.

'Just hang on while we do the reccie,' Mac soothed him. 'You'll get your visuals. I want Cassandra there.'

Chris looked at Simon beseechingly.

Simon rolled his eyes. 'What, you two can't bear to be separated, is that it?'

'That's right.' Mac's voice was matter of fact.

'Jesus.' Simon looked from Mac to me.

I smiled sweetly. I didn't know what was going on, but at least Mac wasn't leaving me behind.

Simon grimaced and turned back to Mac. 'Okay, you, me and Cassie — just for the reccie, then we come back and get Chris.'

Mac smiled. 'It'll be fine — you'll see.' He glanced at my swimsuit and dressing gown ensemble. 'I'll find you some clothes.'

'I'm all right.' It was all going too fast. I wanted to rewind — back to just me and Mac. I had a panicky feeling we'd never get back there. I looked at Mac to see if he felt it too, but it was like he'd flicked a switch from slow to fast — I was still stuck on slow.

'You'd better have some shoes.' He tossed me a pair of overlarge boots. 'Here.' A long-sleeved shirt and pants also flew my way. I eyed them dubiously and tucked them under my arm. I wasn't ready to look like Charlie Chaplin just yet.

'I'll just be a minute.' Mac disappeared into his room, reappearing shortly afterwards with a backpack over his shoulder.

We rowed over to the helicopter. Chris peered after us from the verandah like a dog watching a disappearing bone. Simon ignored him; he was still wound tight, pulling at the oars like he could will his world headline article into existence with the strength of his shoulders.

Mac didn't offer to help — he was off in his own world, gazing out over the floodwaters with an unreadable expression. I perched on the seat of the rubber dinghy and wondered where this was all going. Why was Mac taking Simon to see the thylacines? Or was he? I wrapped my arms around my knees and gave myself a hug. Mac caught my eye for a moment, but looked away quickly. Not touching him felt like being deprived of oxygen.

My mood picked up once I was inside the chopper. I'm like a kid that way, I guess — easily distracted by gadgets. Buckling my seatbelt, I pulled the headset over my ears. The choonka, choonka, choonka started and we lifted straight up and raced across the floodwaters towards the mountains.

God I love helicopters, René. I should have been a helicopter pilot. It has to be the next best thing to being Superman, zapping across the sky like that. Maybe it isn't too late?

It was only a couple of minutes before Mac leaned forward and tapped the pilot on the shoulder. He pointed downwards and spoke into his headset. 'Just let us down there. Come back tomorrow morning.'

Simon flinched and pulled his mouthpiece towards him. 'Tomorrow morning? I'm not prepared for an overnight stay. I thought this was just a reccie — what about Chris?'

'No point in trying to see them unless you stay the night,' said Mac. 'I've got a bit of food and a tarp to keep the rain off. We'll see if they're here, then you can come back with your cameraman.'

The sound of Simon's teeth grinding came through the headset.

The helicopter hovered over the top of a peak that jutted out of the rainforest like a bald head. 'I'm not going to be able to land,' said the pilot. 'Too rocky. I'll hover as low as I can. Try to climb out like you're getting out of a canoe — don't tip the boat.' He dropped the helicopter down, down, down, until the struts were a couple of feet off the ground.

Mac climbed out first, carefully. I passed his pack to him. Simon, despite the warning, jumped out. The helicopter swayed and Mac ducked down, pulling Simon with him as the blades tilted towards them.

'Gently,' yelled the pilot, steadying the helicopter.

I climbed out carefully, the noise and the wind buffeting me, and crouched on the ground next to Simon and Mac. The pilot gave us a thumbs up, lifted, and was gone.

No-one spoke for a while — even after the noise of the helicopter died away. It was still raining; I tightened the cord on my all-weather dressing gown as I looked around. The oversized clothes Mac had given me were still tucked under my arm. I wasn't tempted to put them on yet, though. A girl has to maintain some standards. Thick, grey clouds gathered below us in the valley, but up here it was just misty. Spiky trees hovered at the edge of our vision — it looked primeval, lonely. I shivered and folded my arms. We were going to spend the night up here?

Mac went into pioneer mode — erecting a tarp using sticks and bits of string. He fussed around with it for ages. Simon, meanwhile, paced up and down like his plane to New York was running late.

Every time he turned at the end of a lap he'd glare at me like it was my fault. 'There'd better be a thylacine,' he growled as he went past. 'Or I'll see to it that you never work in Sydney again.'

I considered his threat as he stalked up to the end of the clearing, turned abruptly and stalked back again. His Gore-Tex jacket hood was pulled up over his head. He looked like a mad monk.

'Like I care,' I muttered as he strode past. Not much of a comeback, but the best my fluffy brain could manage.

He stopped, the raindrops running down his face, and gave a sarcastic smile. 'Think you're going to stay in the bush forever with Ranger Rick, do you?' He jerked his head at Mac. 'Don't suppose you'd get a job back in Sydney anyway. Who'd have you?'

'You would.'

He laughed, but I'd hit my target. He thrust his hands deeper into his pockets. It might have turned into a cat fight if Mac hadn't called over to us. 'Come and get out of the rain. You'd better shut up too, if you ever want to see the tiger.'

Simon glared at me. I glared back, tossed my head and clumped over to the tarp, my boots squelching in the mud.

Mac had spread a plastic sheet over the ground, but it was still rocky and spiky. I moved next to him and he put his arm around me. Simon sniffed and stared out at the rain. His whole body radiated impatience.

I tried to signal Mac with my eyes in a 'what's going on?' way. Either he didn't understand, or he chose to ignore it. I contented myself with squeezing his hand. He squeezed back.

'No talking,' he whispered. He paused, then whispered even softer — so soft it was just a breath. 'Try to trust me.'

I searched his face. He was a hard man to read, when he didn't want to be read. I thought I saw discomfort there, maybe guilt. Why 'try' to trust me? Why not just 'trust me'? Was it going to be so hard?

Crawk.

Well, it was even harder than I thought, as it turned out, René — trusting Mac.

Hours passed.

Mac pulled some sleeping bags out of his backpack and we wrapped them around us to keep warm. He also passed us each a drink bottle. I didn't think I'd be thirsty, but for lack of anything else to do, I did sip at it occasionally. Mac had put some strong-tasting energy supplement in it. It wasn't bad.

The rain eased, but didn't stop. Mountains came and went in the mist like they were playing a slow game of grandma's footsteps. Simon's nervous energy — unable to find an outlet — congealed into a grumpy boredom. Every now and then he sighed loudly and drank from his bottle.

It's amazing how time passes, even when you're doing nothing. Slabs of time vanished, unaccounted for. I spent the period between one and two o'clock watching a cloud and mentally humming 'Raindrops Keep Falling On My Head'. It was restful — a bit like one of those meditation retreats where you're not allowed to speak for ten days. It had been a long time since I'd done nothing for so long.

I fell asleep at one point, curled up on the groundsheet, and woke to find Mac scribbling in a notebook. I raised my eyebrows in a question, but he just put his finger to his lips, slipped the pen inside the pages and stuffed the notebook back inside his backpack.

It was getting darker by that stage — we'd been there all day.

Simon had sat bolt upright the whole time, his

hand on his camera, hood pulled over his head. At one point I noticed him nodding his head. I figured he was listening to his iPod, but he turned, frowning, as I made a rustling noise and there were no headphones in his ears. Mac passed around a couple of muesli bars, but no-one ate them. Simon unwrapped his and played with the foil wrapper. The waiting must have been getting to him. He gulped at his drink bottle again.

There'd been bird noises all around us the whole time: one, a tinkling bell; another, a whip cracking; another, a lovely up and down warble. Mac would have known what they all were. I jumped slightly as a brown bird with long tail feathers burst into the clearing.

'Liar bird,' Mac breathed in my ear, his voice barely audible.

I turned to him — was he having a go at me? 'Liar bird?' I whispered back.

He nodded. 'It mimics noises. Anything.'

I smiled. *Liar bird.* So it wasn't only people who pretended to be something they weren't. The liar bird fussed around for a while, pecking at invisible bugs. Finally it spotted us and scuttled into the bush, its tail dragging behind it.

Then, all of a sudden, everything happened. We'd been sitting there so long with nothing to do and then — *whoompa* — action stations.

The sun, not that we'd seen it, had well and truly set. In the clearing there was just enough light to see my hand in front of my face. Beyond that it was shadows.

It was that almost-dark where you fool yourself into thinking you see things. Maybe you do, maybe you don't. Is that a tree, or a person? A rock or a kangaroo? It was that kind of dark.

The bushes rustled. A few sticks broke. Simon tensed beside me. The arm that was holding his camera twitched.

The rustling came closer — I thought I saw something move. A lighter patch appeared between the leaves. Next thing a flash went off — Simon had taken a picture.

My eyes were still seeing spots when two dog-like creatures bounded across the clearing. They were only there for an instant, before disappearing into the forest on the other side. The stripes on their backs were the last things to vanish. I was oblivious to anything else. *It was them.* Time expanded — I felt like I was floating in the moment. Like Mac had said, it was only a few seconds but it felt so much more.

After they'd gone I looked around. I expected to see Simon all flushed with Post-Headline-Rapture. Instead, he was sitting there with this look on his face — even in that light I could tell there was something strange about him.

And Mac? I don't know what I'd expected *him* to look like. Pleased? Guilty? Horrified? But Mac wasn't there anymore. He'd vanished while I was absorbed with the tigers.

At first I thought he'd followed them. I didn't want

to call out — to scare them away if they were still there. I thought he'd be back any minute.

It took me a long time to realise he wasn't coming back.

The whole time I was waiting for Mac, Simon just sat there, looking shell-shocked. I whispered, 'What's up? What happened to Mac? Did you get a photo of the tigers?' But he didn't reply. I didn't take much notice of him — I was too worried about Mac.

Try to trust me.

How can I, when I don't know what you're doing, or why?

Then, about the time I realised Mac wasn't coming back, Simon suddenly came to life.

It was definitely the worst night of my life.

Simon — I didn't have a clue what was wrong with him — went totally berserk. Okay, maybe berserk is overdoing it; he was basically harmless, but extremely annoying.

There we were, sitting in the middle of nowhere after two — supposedly extinct — Tasmanian tigers had just run past and what do you think he says? Not 'I'm getting on the phone and downloading these pictures to the *Herald*'. Not 'yeah baby, this is going to make my career'. No, the first thing he says is —

'Cassie, you look hot in that swimsuit.'

This, after he's already told me I look like crap. I looked at him sideways, pulling my dressing gown together. 'Are you all right?'

Simon pulled his hood down over his eyebrows
and smiled. 'Never better.'

'Did you see where Mac went?'

Simon glanced around at the bushes, then turned
back to me. An even bigger smile spread over his face.
'It's just you and me, baby.'

I tried to keep him focused. 'Where's your camera?
Don't you want to email some shots to your editor?'
I looked all around, but couldn't see his camera.
'Camera?' I said. 'Where is it?'

Simon gazed around vaguely and shrugged. 'Had
it a minute ago.'

'Simon. Where's your phone?' I wanted to make a
call. Get the helicopter back up there.

*Turns out they don't fly in the dark, René, but I
didn't know that at the time.*

I found his phone in his jacket pocket. His hands
were all over me while I looked for it. He was like
an octopus — a brain-damaged, sex-crazed octopus.
After all that there was no reception. Wouldn't you
know?

'Cassie, Cassie, why don't you fancy me? You
know I've always had a thing for you.'

It might have been flattering if he hadn't been
slurring his speech in a way that suggested a man with
too many whiskies under his belt.

'Have you taken something, Simon?' It didn't
seem all that likely — not his usual professional style.

Picking up his water bottle, I sniffed it, but could only detect the same fruity smell as my one. I considered taking a sip, but decided against it.

'Ever since that first day at university,' Simon mumbled, 'when you came in, in your miniskirt and ugg boots. You had earrings. Right up your ear. And you were wearing … a Led Zeppelin T-shirt.'

I shuddered. 'Guns N' Roses.'

'Doesn't matter. Point is … you were hot. You were so angry, all those protests you used to go to. Mmm, you were *so* hot when you were angry.' He leaned over towards me. 'You're still hot. Don't you fancy me a bit, Cassie? Cassiiiiiie,' he wailed, resting his head on my shoulder.

'Jesus, Simon. Pull yourself together. It's not that you're unattractive, but we've never got on, you know that. Anyway, like I'd fancy you, after you stabbed me in the back in Sydney.' I wriggled away from him.

'I only did it to get your attention.' Simon placed his hand on my leg and looked into my eyes. 'I *did* get your attention, didn't I?'

I pushed him off. 'You're joking. You ruined my career just to get my attention?'

'Pretty much.' Simon nodded happily. 'Do you still worry about globalisation, Cassie? I do. I worry about the world market and the way it squashes the underdogsh. The poor underdogsh. What about the workers, ey, Cassie?' He shuffled towards me and slumped onto my shoulder again. 'What about the workersh,' he mumbled as he attempted to grope my breast.

I elbowed him sharply and he pulled himself upright. 'Yeah, I *do* worry about globalisation, now you mention it, Simon.' I thought it was best to humour him. Globalisation — now there was something I hadn't thought about for a while ... *People and planet before profits; the banks have blood on their hands.* Those slogans used to roll off my lips very easily.

But that was before Dad left home and Mum had to take on extra cleaning just to get by. It was at that stage I realised I didn't have time to stuff around. If there were going to be 'haves' and 'have nots', I was throwing my hat in the ring with the 'haves'. Switching from journalism to PR, I left the protests behind with my ugg boots. People with Volvo-driving, Chardonnay-sipping North Shore parents, like Simon, could fly the flag for me.

Giving Simon another jab with my elbow, I looked around the clearing. Where *was* Mac? I couldn't believe he'd just left me here, stuck on this mountain. Maybe he'd fallen over a cliff, or been bitten by a snake? Prising myself away from Simon, I pushed my way into the bush, calling out for him.

It was disorientating in there; the bushes were so thick. I thought I was going in a straight line, but then I came across a prickly vine with a piece of my dressing gown on it. I'd been going around in circles. *Maybe I should just dig a pit and wait for Mac to fall in it?* I followed the traces of my dressing gown back to the clearing.

By the time I got back there Simon had started singing.

Do you know that song 'Cassandra' by Abba?
Crawk.
No, it wasn't one of their big hits, might not have made it to your frog-pond.

In between verses he'd lunge at me and I'd push him off. It was like being on an all-night date with some randy, deranged man, with no way of going home early.

Things got worse after that, as I should have known they would. He decided to do a striptease, pulling his Gore-Tex jacket down over one shoulder and then the other. It came off, and then his shirt. He danced around for a while with no shirt on. It reminded me a lot of my university party days.

'Are you hot for me yet, Cassie?'

He did have a nice body — sort of wiry and smooth. Given a different time, place, mood, mutual history and life, I might just possibly have been interested. 'No, not yet, Simon,' I called.

He took this as encouragement — the bottom half started coming off.

And, well, I saw more of him than I really wanted to.

I won't gross you out with the details, René.

After a couple of hours — thank God — he passed out. I still didn't really know what had got into him. Although — I eyed the water bottle — I had my suspicions.

I stayed awake all night, waiting for the chopper, waiting for Mac, keeping an eye on Simon to make sure he didn't jump me. Eventually I put on the clothes Mac had given me. There didn't seem to be any point in keeping up appearances anymore. My dressing gown went over the top. I covered Simon up with his Gore-Tex jacket to keep him warm. He looked pretty sweet, sleeping away.

Chapter Eighteen

He's a psychopath

I'd never been as pleased to see anything as I was to see that helicopter appear the next morning. I hadn't slept at all, just laid under the tarpaulin as far away from Simon as I could, listening to the rain patter on the plastic. And always there was the back beat: *Where is Mac? Why did he leave me here?* It was just inexplicable.

Of course he could have been lost in the forest. The fact that I would have preferred that probably said something bad about my character. But I didn't think he was lost; not Mac. He was too at home in the bush to disappear by chance. No, I'd been dumped. A cold lump settled like porridge in my stomach. *Why?*

I knew men did that: sleep with women, then spit them out. But it wasn't how I'd read our, admittedly brief, relationship. There'd been something real about it; hadn't there? He couldn't have faked it all. *Could he?* Talk about 'Fifty Ways to Leave Your Lover' — just leave her on the hill, Bill … Paul Simon, 1975. Before I was born, but my mother had the record.

As the helicopter rose up through the mist I prodded Simon awake.

'Caffè latte,' he murmured as he opened his eyes.

'We're going,' I called above the noise.

We climbed in, balancing on the hovering struts.

'Where's the third one?' yelled the pilot.

Simon looked at me blankly, as if he'd just realised there were only two of us. 'What happened to Mac?'

'Don't know — disappeared,' I yelled, pulling the headset on. 'Can you circle around to see if we can find him?'

I scanned the forest as the helicopter swooped around the mountain. Below the peak it was a dense and impenetrable mass of green. He could have been there, but there was no sign of him.

'I'll have to make a report for search and rescue,' said the pilot into his headset.

I nodded, but somehow I knew they wouldn't find him. He didn't want to be found. The helicopter dropped me off on the hill near my house. The floodwaters had gone down and only a few deep puddles stood between me and Frog Hollow now. I splashed through them, making a beeline for my bed, shedding dressing gown, Mac's clothes and boots and my swimsuit as I went, collecting my iPhone on the way.

Mum had left me a message a couple of days ago. 'Cassie? Are you there? Cassie?' There was a pause. 'I've been doing a ritual for you. With the frog goddess. It's supposed to help with fresh starts. I wanted to know if it was working yet. Call me back.' I pressed 'end' and placed the iPhone on the floor. 'I don't think so, Mum,' I murmured.

The helicopter swooped past outside just before I closed my eyes — Simon had collected Chris. Pulling my Mac-smelling pashmina over me, I breathed deep.

It could only have been a few hours later that my phone rang, waking me. I ignored it the first time, snuggling deeper into bed. It stopped, then rang again. Whoever it was, they weren't going away. Plucking my dressing gown off the floor, I picked up the phone and staggered out into the kitchen. I needed a drink.

'Lo,' I croaked.

'Can't believe that bastard pissed off with my camera.' Simon was back to his old self. 'Why'd he take me up there if he didn't want me to get a picture? We've still got a story, though. I need you to stand by me with an eyewitness account, okay?'

'Um ...' I wasn't sure where I stood. I hadn't had time to work it out. It was so confusing. On one hand, I'd thought Mac had wanted to keep the tigers secret, but on the other, he'd taken Simon up there ... I thought we'd been in it together, but then he'd left me stranded in the forest with a lecherous Simon ... *Why did he do that?*

'Cassie,' Simon snapped. 'I *need* you to stand by me.' There was a note of threat in his voice. He was reminding me that the 'failed PR queen meets feral pigs' story was still an option.

'Um —' I was about to say more but he cut me off.

'There'll be media all over the place today.'

I headed for the bathroom, the phone pressed to my ear.

'The story's broken, my phone hasn't stopped ringing. It's a pity I didn't get the photos but Chris is up there now — we might get lucky. It's still a fantastic story — the ranger who'll stop at nothing to keep a secret, et cetera, et cetera. Our eyewitness accounts of the tigers leaping from the bushes, eyes blazing — reporter tells how he was minutes from death, that kind of thing. I'll do something for the *Herald* first of course, but we'll be able to on-sell this all over the place. I'm hiring Harry M Miller.'

'But, no photo, Simon. I mean, people have sighted thylacines before ...'

'That was just punters, Cassie. This is you and me, the *Herald* journalist and the PR queen. And, sorry, but your reputation is only going to help here. You're not the normal greenie wacko people expect to see these things. That adds credibility.'

'Oh.' As I passed the hallway mirror an apparition startled me. Who was that white-trash hurricane victim? It took a couple of seconds to realise it was me. My highlights had grown out, leaving a dark runway down my part and my face was a makeup-free, washed-out blur.

Crawk.

  No, René, this isn't my usual look. Well, all right it is now, but it never used to be.

And it wasn't just my face. My velvet dressing gown was crusted in mud and torn where the vines had seized it. I half-heartedly picked out a few spiny seeds that had attached themselves in clumps. The person in the mirror wasn't Cassandra anymore — I'd reverted to Cassie, or even Cass.

'You know he doped me?' Simon's words cut through my reverie.

'What?'

'He doped me.'

'Get out of it.' I was trying to convince myself as much as him.

'My water bottle, it had something in it. Vodka maybe, disguised by that raspberry shit. Knocked me round a bit. Haven't drunk for six months so my tolerance is down. Got a shocking hangover.'

'Why would he do that?'

'Why do *you* think?'

'I don't know.' Actually, I did.

'I can think of a very good reason. He was hoping I'd pass out before I saw the tigers. But seeing as that didn't work, my camera's gone, therefore there's no evidence.'

'But … what about me?' The words burst out of my mouth before I could stop them. Moving Pictures, 1982; Shannon Noll, 2006. Pathetic. *Why hadn't he taken me with him?* was what I'd meant.

Simon laughed. 'You're well out of that one, Cassie. You should call the police if he makes contact.'

Contact — that would be nice. 'Uh, I don't know if he really doped you …' My protest sounded lame, even to myself.

'Come on, don't try to stick up for your boyfriend. He's run out on you now.'

I winced.

'Guess I just passed out, huh?' Simon continued. 'I can't remember anything after the tigers running past. I know I got a photo, but that bastard took it.'

'Well actually, Simon …' I twirled the cord of my dressing gown and decided to regain the balance of power. 'You did pass out, but first you groped me, sang 'Cassandra' by Abba, then performed a striptease. It was entertaining, but I don't know if I'd pay to see it.'

There was silence on the other end while this sank in. 'I wondered what happened to my boxer shorts,' Simon said eventually.

'And if you're looking for your mobile phone with inbuilt camera …'

'Cassie, we're a team now, aren't we?' Simon broke in. 'I know we've had our differences in the past, but …'

'You can have your phone back. I've downloaded

the images, though. Let me know if you want to see them and I'll put them up on YouTube for you.'

'You don't need to be like that. This is *our* story — your calling card back into Sydney. I'll give you equal billing. What's good for me is good for you.' Again, there was that note of threat in his voice.

My stomach churned queasily. Had Mac wanted to keep the tigers secret, or hadn't he? I wasn't sure of anything anymore. I couldn't believe I'd spent three days in bed with him and still had no idea what he'd been planning. I'd thought we were close, intimate even, but all he'd told me was what he'd wanted me to know. That hurt. I rubbed my chest, unconsciously.

And this was what I'd wanted, wasn't it — a soft landing back into the A-list? I picked a couple more seeds out of my dressing gown. Did I want to be stuck out in the sticks forever?

Not without Mac.

'Cassie,' Simon snapped. 'What's got into you? You're acting like you've had a lobotomy. Your boyfriend's double-crossed you and doped me.'

'You don't know that.'

'Face it, Cassie, he's a psychopath.'

'He's not,' I snapped. Mac was many things, but not, I thought, a psychopath.

'Look, Cassie.' Simon lowered his voice. 'I didn't tell you this before, but I've got the go-ahead from my editor on the PR queen gets porky spread. I'm not sure you'd be able to make a comeback from that one.'

Bastard. 'I'll wear it.' I tried not to think what that would mean.

'I'm also considering pressing charges against your boyfriend ...'

The breath rushed out of me; Mac could get sent to prison. 'You can't prove anything.'

'I've got a good lawyer. I've still got the bottle. There's also the missing camera. Something will stick.'

'You're blackmailing me.'

'No, I'm not. I'm highlighting the facts.'

'You know, Simon, you're a real arsehole sometimes.' I straightened my back. If I was going to do this thing, I was going to do it properly. 'My name before yours on all articles. It's only fair.'

'No way.' Simon sounded angry, but I sensed he was pleased to be dealing with the old Cassandra.

'Daley comes before McKechnie anyway — alphabetically.'

'That's ridiculous. I'm the lead journalist — you're just a PR.'

'You know, Simon — those photos — the cool air probably didn't do you justice. I'm sure you're much more ... substantial, usually. The boxers looked good on your head, though. I can think of a number of outlets that might be interested.'

'Jesus, Cassie.' He sighed. 'Okay.'

From the moment I got off the phone it was pretty much pandemonium. I attempted to spruce myself up — removed the mud and added a bit of lippy. When I looked in the mirror I'd progressed from hurricane victim to trashy TV confession show guest. I'm not sure if it was an improvement but I was beyond caring.

The only thing I could think of was Mac. Perhaps he really was lost in the bush. I imagined him waiting and waiting for help that never came. Was anyone looking for him? I rang the police. They knew he was missing, but didn't seem particularly worried.

'He's a good bush hand. He'll be right, love,' said the station cop, sleepily. 'If he doesn't turn up in a couple of days, we'll organise a search.'

'That's not very adequate,' I snapped. 'What if he's broken a leg? He could be lying in a hole, or fallen over a cliff.'

'I'm sure that's not the case, darling. He'll be found when he wants to be found.'

His implication was that Mac had left me. I slammed the phone down. He was probably right.

The Cassandra and Simon show hit the road — metaphorically. In fact, the road came to us. Half an hour after I spoke to Simon the first news van rumbled up outside. Simon jumped out — a broad grin on his face. His Pre-Headline-Tension was well and truly gone. It looked like his hangover had been dispatched as well.

Mine was just beginning. I had a fierce urge to slam and bolt the door.

Simon, possibly sensing this, strode forward and put his arm around my shoulders. 'Smile,' he whispered. 'You're committed now — make the most of it. It's going to be bigger than *Ben Hur*.'

A black umbrella emerged, then a blonde-bobbed woman in high heels. She stepped delicately through the mud towards my verandah, her well-known face pulling up into a smile as she saw me. Simon was right: if they'd got Marie from *Morning with Marie* onto it, it was a big story.

'Tell me *everything*,' said the morning show hostess, accepting the cup of coffee I offered her.

I eyed the yellow slick on the surface of her drink. I didn't think I was going to tell her *everything*.

She took a sip of her coffee. A stifled grimace confirmed my suspicion — the milk was off. 'That's usually the best,' she said. 'Tell me *everything*. We can figure out what's important as we go along.'

I smiled my PR smile back. It felt rusty as hell, but I don't think she noticed. What to tell? What to leave out? How much *can* you leave out without telling a lie? The memories — a rowdy bunch — pulled at my hands. *Pick me, pick me.* Maybe I would and maybe I wouldn't. Not everyone gets to be chosen every time. I mentally smacked at them — a harassed mother on the verge of a nervous breakdown.

And then I remembered the liar bird. I don't know why that came back to me then. *It can mimic anything.* Okay, maybe I didn't feel like the Cassandra who'd been the PR queen of Sydney anymore, but if a bird could do it, I certainly could.

I smoothed the hair back off my face, presented

my best angle to camera and inhaled. 'Really, it all began when Mac and I went toading ...'

Half an hour later I paused. Something was different. Ah, the rain had stopped.

'Do you mind if I open the window?' I said.

Marie shook her head, a few blonde locks escaping her stiff bob. Her smile, like her makeup, was undiminished. She'd done a good job coordinating her blue eyeliner with her blouse. The lipstick wasn't right, though. To me it said cheerleader, rather than journalist, but maybe that's the effect she was after.

After a struggle I eased the window upwards. Pushing my head out, I breathed deeply. Outside, the rain started again, but lightly now. The frogs carolled their joy in the puddles. Did they never tire of it? Five days of rain and they were still as thrilled as a beer drinker offered an unexpected free round. My eyes lingered on the rainforest. What was I expecting? Mac to pop out in his khaki shorts? I knew that wasn't going to happen.

I pulled my chair out and sat down again. 'Um ...' I'd lost my train of thought.

'Then you went to Cougan Peak,' murmured Marie. Her hand moved towards her coffee cup, then retreated.

'Right ...'

One interview merged into the next. Simon and I posed at my house, at Mac's house, pointed at the bushes, mimed the astonishment we felt when the tigers burst out of the trees. *Oh my, a Tasmanian tiger — did you see that, Simon? My word, Cassandra, a beast like that could bite your head off with one munch.*

Whenever I looked at the news feed on my computer or turned on the radio, there I was — the talk show queen. I could hardly bear to watch myself — it was like watching a train crash in slow motion. And I was the dummy tied to the front of the train, with no way to get off …

'Yes, I saw the thylacines. There were two of them. I saw them twice — once on my toading expedition with Mac Southern and once at the top of Cougan Peak before he disappeared.'

'Where do you think he's gone?'

I zoned out — where *had* he gone? That mysterious man who'd somehow got himself right under my skin. I'd never let a man affect me this way before. I'd always had the upper hand, but I guess that was because I'd never really cared …

How do you know if you're in love, René? Is it when you turn to someone twenty times a day to talk to them even when they're not there? When every time you lie down you imagine them beside you, below you, above you? When time without them seems like preparation for living, not life itself? That's the way it was for me. I was a rat on a treadmill, waiting for Mac.

Crawk.

Perfect men, like perfect numbers, are very rare?

How true, René, how true. Why did he piss off and leave me on a mountain with no explanation? Why? Philosophise that, frog.

When I looked back on those days in the flood they now had the shimmery feel of an illusion. Mac had disappeared without a trace but I hadn't forgotten the feel of his skin or his smell. I'd hold my shawl to my nose every night and breathe deeply. It made the longing worse, but I couldn't stop. *Sabotage my senses …* Yes, it *was* all about the poetry.

I held non-stop conversations with him in my head. In them he'd explain to me, somehow — the detail eluded me — exactly why he'd had to leave me on top of the mountain. *I knew you'd understand,* he'd say, pressing up against me. *Of course I understand, darling,* I'd murmur …

The problem was, I didn't. I *so* didn't.

'Cassandra,' the interviewer repeated, 'where do you think he's gone?'

I blinked. 'I don't know. I guess he'll be found when he wants to be.'

No matter how many times I said these words they still didn't ring true. Something niggled at me. There had to be more to it.

I wondered if Mac was watching. I didn't like to think of that. He'd brought it on himself, but … would a better woman have sold her story? Sure, I did it for him — he wouldn't know that, though. What would he think of me now? What he'd always thought probably: that I was a PR floozy with no scruples whatsoever.

Still, what difference did it make? If I didn't do it, Simon would. I figured I may as well get some mileage out of it, seeing as I'd sold my soul to the devil. Again. Make hay while the thylacine's news.

I went on so many helicopter rides I almost forgot how exciting they were. Simon and I relived our night on Cougan Peak with a TV crew, but the thylacines didn't reappear.

Simon left out the nude dancing part. It was almost a shame, really. Surprise, surprise, we were getting on well, Simon and I, now that our deal had been negotiated. I couldn't really hold his blackmail against him. After all, I'd have done the same thing myself, once. The story is sacred when it comes to journalism.

Simon was a master of the sharp city wit and repartee that I hadn't realised I'd missed. And my badly bruised ego needed a bit of judicious flirting to restore it.

Flirting might seem trivial, but it's not, really. This is the survival of the human race we're talking about here. It's also a lot of fun. I don't have to mean anything by it; it's just an instinct. *See man. Flirt.* I read a study once that said that all human achievement was a form of flirting. Rockets to the moon, Shakespeare's plays, the pyramids ... yep, flirting, flirting, flirting.

What do you think, René? Being French, you'll no doubt have an opinion on that.

Crawk.

What, you became a philosopher just to seduce women? You devil, René. Who would have thought it? Even philosophy, just so much flirting …

'I'll take you out to dinner somewhere swank when you get back to Sydney,' Simon said into his microphone headset as the helicopter rose up from Cougan Peak.

The pilot glanced around at us where we sat in the back seat.

'Not you,' said Simon. 'Any chance of you turning off your mic for a minute?'

The pilot winked, gave him the thumbs up and twiddled a button.

'Think you can keep your clothes on for it?' I said, pulling my mouthpiece closer.

'I've only got your word for it the striptease ever happened. I'm not so sure — it's not really my kind of thing.'

'Excuse me? I seem to recall you dancing shirtless on the tables at the refectory on many occasions.'

Simon laughed. 'That was a long time ago, Cassandra.'

'You think I'd make up something like that?'

'Yep.'

I smiled at him mysteriously, though my heart wasn't in it. 'You overestimate my abilities.'

'That, my dear, would be impossible.' He held my gaze for a long time as the mountains flashed past.

As I watched the helicopters swoop over the mountains day after day I wondered where the tigers had gone. What would they think of all the noise? Would they move on to somewhere else? An uncomfortable feeling lodged in my chest. It was a new one to me. It might have been guilt.

Okay, I had felt guilty before, occasionally, in my past. I knew I'd done things I shouldn't have done. It is very easy to justify actions you know deep down aren't right when you are rewarded and praised for them. But being with Mac seemed to have affected my heart. Something had cracked; it was too close to the surface now. This new guilt didn't bounce off the way the old guilt had.

And along with the guilt, I was angry — angry at Mac for taking the reformed Cassandra with him when he vanished. I hadn't even had the chance to do the right thing once before I'd been forced to revert to type. I glared towards his house at night. *I could have been a better woman if you'd stayed, Mac.* I was definitely turning into the type of person Oprah could use on her show.

When I rang the police to check up on Mac again they told me he'd called in. 'He's out of town — family emergency. Guess he'll be in touch with you if he wants to,' the cop said cheerfully.

Oh have a gloat, why don't you? 'Thanks.' I felt

like I'd been kicked in the stomach. That was it then, he'd left me. I needed to put him behind me and get on with my life. The trouble was, I couldn't. That ache just wouldn't go away. What's more, I didn't want it to. It hurt, but once it was gone, Mac was gone and *that* didn't bear thinking about.

Could I live without that smile?

Chapter Nineteen

I was a different person then

I hadn't been back to work since before the flood. I was too busy with all my media appearances. Everyone, myself included, assumed that the wildlife job was a phase that was now over.

'So, what's next for you, Cassandra?' one journalist asked me.

It stumped me really. Simon seemed to believe I'd be heading back to Sydney as soon as our media commitments wound up. He hadn't said as much, but I knew he thought he was in with a chance once that happened.

'What happened to that fellow you were living with in Sydney, the thick, good-looking one?' he'd said.

'Anthony isn't thick,' I'd protested. No-one except me was going to insult him. 'Turns out he's gay,' I said flatly. 'Bi, anyway.'

Simon's eyes flashed his amusement, but he restrained himself. 'Gee, how does that make you feel?'

'I'm fine with it,' I snapped. But now I thought about it, first one boyfriend turns gay, then the next one leaves me stranded on a mountain ... *Was this significant?*

I gazed in the mirror when I got home. My sexual attractiveness had been a constant from the day it kicked in at fifteen. I'd done nothing to acquire it — one day I was Plain Jane, the next a target of desire and envy. I thought I'd come a long way from that shy, fat kid, but maybe not far enough ...

I'd never realised I was a fat kid until Jessica brought it to my attention. It was the day of the school fete. Yes, the day I discovered *Alice in Wonderland*. This wasn't a coincidence.

I was happily jiving on to Tears for Fears under the shelter and feeling very cool in my leg warmers and miniskirt — it *was* the mid-eighties — when my 'best friend' turned on me.

'You look like Meatloaf when you shake your stomach like that, Cassie.' She meant the fat singer, not the mincemeat version. Flicking her blonde plait over her shoulder, she ran away, giggling.

It had been a good day before then, but suddenly it was a bad one. Jessica had turned against me; it was a familiar pattern. Now that I am wise in the ways of the world I can pick a Jessica a mile off. Most of the women on Sydney's A-list — as I had discovered — were Jessicas: fair-weather friends.

It was hard being a fat kid. Being chosen last for sport. Being the subject of scrutiny at the tuckshop counter: 'Are you sure you want that meat pie, Cassie?' It's especially hard for girls. A boy would just punch someone in the nose. That isn't an option for us girls; too shocking, too unfeminine.

I've heard people say once you know who you are, no-one can touch you. That's probably true, but not very helpful when you're a ten-year-old chubster who thinks she's Madonna.

But somewhere between ten and fifteen, a miracle happened. I morphed from Meatloaf into Marilyn. It was like I'd flicked a switch — suddenly male eyes were drawn to me like magnets. Strange ... I was the same fat, eager girl inside — at first, anyway. All power corrupts eventually.

Girls who'd ignored me in my fat and freckled phase now muttered bitchily behind my back that my jeans were too tight. Once, I could wear anything, but now every outfit was seen as an attempt to court male eyes.

I was uncomfortable with it initially. I learnt to wear tops that didn't show my nipples, pants that didn't hug my bum. I let my uniform skirt down, but it did nothing to stop the whispers that I was 'up myself'.

And then I discovered René Descartes and the other French philosophers. My black clothes and intellectual airs were an 'up yours' to those teenage princesses. Disguising my looks with goth makeup made me stand out, but it also made me invisible.

It took years to learn to ignore those whispers and take control of my new-found powers. There were many mistakes along the way. At first it seemed I could only be a slut or a frump; it was impossible to get it right. In the end I gave up and did what came naturally.

Now, as I looked in the mirror, I wondered: *have I lost it?* Was sexual attractiveness like a magic dust which appears and disappears on a whim? I *did* look kind of crappy — maybe I *had* lost it. I wasn't sure how I felt about that if so. Part of me was okay with the concept — maybe it would give me a chance to explore new strengths? The other part was freaking out.

I wasn't sleeping well either. The house seemed a bit empty. It took me a while to figure out what was wrong — I missed my frog.

I missed you, René. You hadn't been very talkative, but you were a companion, and that was what I needed.

I had, bizarrely, formed a close bond with an amphibian. This wasn't something I could ever have predicted would happen to me. But then, as far as I know, I had never met a frog until I met René. Wildlife was not a topic I gave much thought to before the long-footed potoroo hopped into my life. I cast my mind back, seeking wildlife precedents and omens, but it came up blank.

Perhaps this tendency was clear to others. In retrospect, these things often are. Maybe if you asked my primary school teachers, 'Which of your students would you most expect to form a relationship with a frog?' they would have nominated me.

If I appeared on *This is Your Life* the red book might reveal an obsession with *The Frog Prince*, an attraction to the colour green, a desire to hop as a toddler, even. I imagined people running into the studio, beaming, with stories of my early frog-loving ways. Perhaps.

> *Crawk.*
>
> *No, the snake was gone. I un-taped the toilet and looked, but there was no sign of it — even after I left it open for a couple of days. That meant it was safe for you to return. After all, I didn't need a functioning toilet — I had the portaloo. There was no reason why you couldn't enjoy your five-star accommodation.*

I wandered around the garden in search of René, but things had gone very quiet frog-wise since the rain had stopped.

Ominously quiet, you could say. If I was prone to an overactive imagination I could almost have thought the frogs were plotting. After all that croaking and ribbeting, it just didn't seem right. Was it the quiet before the storm? What form the storm would take, I wasn't sure. I hadn't heard that coughing animal that used to serenade me nightly again either.

The result of this lack of animal attention seemed to be that I couldn't sleep. Once I'd been kept awake by their noises, but now I needed them. How could I ever return to Sydney? I'd have to go and live next to Taronga Zoo.

I'd curl up in bed with my *PR Weekly*, but it didn't have the same effect on me anymore. When I looked at all those well-groomed smiling faces, all I could think of was how much trouble they must have gone to, to look that good. It was hard to believe I used to visit the beautician, manicurist, hairdresser, masseuse, boutique and gym regularly. Not to mention attending four or five glamorous social functions every week. How did I find the time? How did I find the energy?

It was like the Red Queen said: '... *it takes all the running you can do, to keep in the same place. If you want to get somewhere else, you must run at least twice as fast as that!*' Could I run that fast again? Would I care if I never attended another gala launch? I was flat out finding time and energy to comb my hair at the moment.

It was these kinds of thoughts that kept me awake at night.

The day after my Cougan Peak re-enactment aired on Channel Seven, my iPhone woke me. It was ten am but I was still in a daze. I stumbled out to the kitchen and picked it up. 'Hello,' I mumbled.

'Cassandra, baby. Aren't you the star of stage and screen?' The voice was familiar, but my overtired brain couldn't make the connections.

'Who is this?'

'Cassandra, never thought I'd live to hear the day you didn't recognise my voice.'

My synapses suddenly fired, or whatever it is they do. 'Wazza?'

'Who else, baby, who else? You sound a bit tired there, mate. Too many cocktail parties with the film crews, hey?'

This was so far from the truth it was funny. I ran my fingers through my lank hair and looked out over the cracked lino bench to the spider-webbed window beyond. Glamour this was not. Filling a cup of water from the sink, I sipped it, running my tongue over the fuzz on my teeth. 'What do you want, Wazza?'

'What do I want? An old friend rings you after a short break and that's the way you treat them? You've changed, Cassandra. Celebrity has gone to your head.'

'Celebrity? Yeah right.' A small brown bird alighted on the sill outside the window and pecked at its reflection. Was it some kind of metaphor for my life? I considered that, but it made my brain hurt.

'Come on,' Wazza interrupted my philosophical musing. 'You can't pretend you don't know your face is all over Sydney. Great hairstyle, mate — I've always liked that seventies rocker look. It's very you. Is Anthony still doing your hair?'

'No-one's doing my hair. What do you mean I'm all over Sydney, like where?'

'Cassandra, Cassandra, Cassandra, as if you don't know. *Woman's Daily*'s got you on the side of the buses.'

'*Woman's Daily*?' I paused. 'Buses?'

'You've knocked Terri Irwin for six. For that at least, you deserve a medal. I've got the magazine in front of me now. *Tasmanian tiger heroine tells — how the man I loved betrayed me.*'

'That's strange. I don't remember talking to *Woman's Daily*.' The little brown bird gave one last peck and flew away. Was it saying that celebrity is fleeting?

'Country living's blunted your brain, mate. They don't need to talk to you. You know how it goes — anonymous sources close to Cassandra, et cetera ... Are you all right? You don't sound like yourself.'

'Oh.' I gave that some thought. 'You never returned my call, Wazza.'

'Mea culpa, Cassandra. It's been frantic here, darling.'

A cockroach ran past and I slammed my mug down on top of it.

'Cassandra? What are you doing there?'

'Just killing a cockroach. You know, it's funny you should say that — about not sounding like myself — because I actually feel more like myself than I used to.' I paused, giving Wazza the chance to reply, but he didn't seem to have anything to say. 'Talking to you, though — I'm starting to feel less and less like myself again.' My friend the little brown bird was back, pecking at the window.

'Cassandra, you're starting to worry me, so I'll get to the point …'

I anticipated his question before he said it. In that moment hundreds of images flashed through my mind.

A triumphant return to Manly — celebrity of the week in Sydney — Wazza bringing me in as a partner — kick-starting my own business — cocktails at the Art Gallery — air kissing clients at Bel Mondo restaurant — fabulous parties on yachts staffed with men who looked like Anthony — or even … Anthony himself. Was he still gay? The bird cocked its head — it had seen me now, beyond the glass.

'Cassandra?' Wazza's voice implied he was humouring me, like a child who can't decide what flavour ice cream they want. I must have missed something he'd said. 'I'll bring you back on twenty thousand more, of course.'

'No thanks.' The words came from some part of my brain that seemed to have no trouble making decisions. *Good brain.*

'Okay, thirty thousand.'

'It's not about money.' *Did I really say that?*

'What do you mean it's not about money?' Wazza laughed. 'People only say that when they want more money. Everything's about money. You're not thinking of setting up in opposition, are you? That would be a big mistake; I'm still the best —'

I pressed the 'end' button. It rang again immediately so I turned it off. A surge of panic ran through me. Had I really just knocked back my old job with a thirty-thousand-dollar raise? How could I have done that? It ran against everything I'd been working towards for the last five years. What about my apartment in Manly, my social life, my lifestyle …? Was this the start of a slide into becoming my mother? This time next year, would I find myself in a size 26 aqua tracksuit at the Blacktown TAB?

A cold sweat broke out on the back of my neck. Breathing deeply, I resisted the urge to ring Wazza straight back and accept his offer. Instead, I yanked open the fridge, found the most calorie-intense item there — a chunk of cheese — and stuffed it in my mouth.

Refilling my mug of water, I picked up *Alice in Wonderland*, opened the front door and stepped out onto the verandah, chewing fast. The sun was out now and, above the trees, the tops of the ranges beckoned. A magpie warbled on the grass. It sounded like, *Where are you, Mac?*

Plonking myself on the steps, I opened the book at random, stabbing my finger onto the page. *'It's no use going back to yesterday, because I was a different person then,' said Alice.* I swallowed the cheese, staring out at the trees.

I was a different person then. I thought about it. I'd been a lot of different people in my time. I'd managed to let go of the shy, fat kid, the gothic punk teenager and the angry activist, hadn't I? So … I could let go of the city-slick PR exec too, right? *Maybe*.

But if I let go of that Cassandra, who would I become? I didn't know, and that was scary. If I wasn't a liar bird, who was I? Could I cope with working it out as I went along? The sun was warm on my face and a dragonfly whirred around my head. Was it enough to just be … me? I supposed it would have to be for now.

My heart slowly settled. I don't know how long I sat there for, but when I went back inside and turned my phone on, it didn't ring. I punched in the numbers and waited.

Sam answered. 'Beechville Wildlife Office.'

'Can I come back to work now?'

Chapter Twenty

What ranger is that?

Sam sounded surprised to hear from me. 'Cassandra? I thought you'd gone back to Sydney.'

'No. Sorry I haven't been in touch. I've been ... tied up.'

'I've noticed.' Her voice was dry, but not unfriendly.

'I didn't really mean to leave, though. It was just the flood, and then ...' I trailed off. 'So, can I? Come back to work?'

'Oh.' She sounded bemused. 'You want to come back?' There was a brief pause and I heard someone murmur behind her.

'Who's that with you?'

'Just Rodney,' she said quickly. 'Yeah, come back. Great. Today?'

'Is today okay?'

'Fine. It's pretty busy here actually — without Mac and all.'

'Have you heard from him?' I tried to sound casual.

'Yes, he's in Tasmania — bit of a family emergency, nothing too serious. Doesn't know when he'll be back, though.' Her voice was breezy, but I thought I detected an undercurrent of discomfort.

'Did he say why he took off? On the mountain ...' *Did he say anything about me?* was what I meant.

Sam sighed. 'Look, Cassandra ... There's something you should know about Mac.'

I waited. 'Yes?'

'He's ...' She seemed to be searching for the right words. 'Well, his heart's in the right place and he's smart, but he's a bit bloody unreliable. That's the sort of thing he does.'

'But ... why?'

'How should I know why? He just is. Always has been. I'd forget about him if I were you.'

I felt strange discussing Mac with Sam. Our relationship to date had been strictly professional. Besides, what she said didn't ring true — he didn't seem like that to me. I changed the subject. 'So, should I come in now?'

'Yes. You could probably start trying to work out what to do with this thylacine — from a PR point of view.'

'Like, publicise it, you mean?'

'You've been doing a good job of that already. We need to think how we can get some real benefit for conservation out of it.'

'Maybe a sponsorship scheme?'

'I *knew* you'd come up with something. We need to strike while it's hot. People have a short attention span.'

She hardly needed to tell *me* that. 'I'll be right in.' As I got dressed I wondered what I was doing. After Wazza's phone call, I knew what I didn't want, but was this what I wanted — to spend my working life in the Beechville Wildlife Office? A future full of feral pigs, cane toads, magpies, mice and survival-challenged shorebirds stretched ahead of me.

My mind flashed from one future scenario to the other. Feral pigs — Bel Mondo. Cane toads — harbour cruises. Magpies — champagne cocktails. I was a different person then ... I breathed deeply. *Little steps, Cassandra.*

As I pulled out of my dirt track onto the main road I slammed on the brakes. A small brown animal stepped cautiously in front of me. Flute-like nose stretched out before it, the echidna waddled slowly across the bitumen. When it was halfway across, a second brown face poked out of the bushes. Another echidna followed, and then another. Eventually eight echidnas followed in a train across the road.

I smiled as I gazed at their sedate procession. Now there was something you wouldn't see in Manly. A revving engine startled me — a car was coming fast around the corner from the other direction. Jumping out of my car and over the echidnas, I waved and held my hand up to stop them. Loud music blared from its windows as it came towards me. It didn't seem to see me — it wasn't slowing. I leapt up and down, waving and yelling — *was it going to hit me?*

At the last moment, the car screeched to a halt, metres from me. I strode over and yelled in the window. 'Slow down, why don't you? Can't you see there's wildlife on the road?'

It was Tyler — the boy from my cane toad focus group. He turned his music down bashfully, his hair hanging over his eyes. 'Sorry.'

We watched in silence as the echidnas continued their slow march. As the last one disappeared into the bushes, I waved him on. 'Take it easy from now on.'

He nodded and continued down the road at a more moderate pace.

I hummed as I got back in the car, with the satisfaction of a job well done. As I neared the outskirts of town I noticed something new. Easing my foot off the accelerator, I stared. *Welcome to Beechville — home of the Thylacine.* A Tasmanian tiger snarled below the words on the sign. They sure got that up quick; these Beechville people were more efficient than I'd thought.

A couple of journalists and photographers lurked in the main street. The big names had gone back to Sydney, but the story was still ticking over. Everyone was after the money shot — the beast itself. In the meantime there was the personality angle — me. Averting my face, I walked casually into the office. They didn't notice me.

My mind was on Mac as I climbed the stairs to the office. And then — he was there.

His name slipped from my mouth before I realised what it was. I glanced around to make sure no-one had seen. The collateral for my What Ranger is That? campaign had arrived. A life-size cardboard cut-out of Mac holding a blue-tongue lizard graced the foyer.

They'd done a good job with the airbrushing — his smile looked almost natural. Folding my arms, I narrowed my eyes at him. There was nothing about his face to suggest a double-crossing love rat. A lump lodged in my chest as I touched the cardboard. It seemed no less impenetrable than the man himself.

The merchandising had also arrived. I ran my hand along the T-shirts, mugs, caps, badges ... It felt like another lifetime that I'd ordered them so enthusiastically. I took a deep breath — I was a different person in more ways than one.

'Hello, stranger,' I said as I opened the door.

Rodney blushed. He seemed unusually bashful, even for him.

'Been surfing?'

'No, ah. Been a bit flat lately. Saw you on the news ...' His hand moved quickly to cover something on the desk.

'What have you got there?' I peered over the counter. The corner of a magazine poked out from beneath the papers Rodney had pushed over it. The words *heroine tells* were visible. 'You haven't been reading *Woman's Daily*, have you? I didn't even know you got that in Beechville.'

Rodney blushed again. 'They got a big order in — down the supermarket.'

'Did they now? Give us a look.'

Rodney reluctantly pushed the magazine across the desk.

They'd photographed me sitting on my verandah gazing out at the bush with a look that could only be described as forlorn. The picture was blurry — taken with a telephoto. I touched my hair. Wazza was right — I did have a bit of a grunge rocker thing going on. *Tasmanian tiger — love victim tells all*, was splashed across the cover. It made me sound like I'd been mauled. I suppose, in a way, I had been.

I'd always assumed celebrity would be a good thing, but reading about myself like that — it made me feel like my breakfast was about to come up again. And Eggs Benedict Lean Cuisine was bad enough the first time around. There was a photo of Anthony with the caption: *She left her loving boyfriend to take up with love-rat ranger, Macaulay Southern.* Macaulay? How strange — I'd never even known Mac's full name. Trust *Woman's Daily* to focus on the romance angle. I wondered who'd filled them in on all that. Simon, probably.

I smiled at the sight of Ant, posing outside his salon. Naturally, he wouldn't waste the chance for a bit of product placement. *She called me snookiepants, but everything changed once she met that ranger*, said his quote. I shook my head. *And you turning gay had nothing to do with it?*

I couldn't stay angry with him, though. To someone like Ant, this was a prime opportunity for exposure.

He'd even got them to put a 'before' picture of me —
*I used to do Cassandra's hair, but she's let herself go
now*, he said. I frowned — that wasn't very nice. I still
washed my hair, didn't I? In Anthony's books, allowing
your highlights to grow out one centimetre was a
crime on a par with armed robbery. For many years,
I'd agreed, but now I wasn't so sure. Maybe there were
more important things …

My eyes slid from the magazine to a car battery
next to Rodney's computer. 'What's that for?'

'My Ross River fever's playing up.'

'Oh, that's pretty bad, isn't it?' I'd heard of Ross
River fever, but thought it was more of a North
Queensland thing. 'Where'd you pick that up?'

'Here. There's lots of it around. Lots of mozzies …
after the rain.'

I scratched my ankle, thinking of the number of
mosquitoes that had bitten me recently. 'Right — so,
the car battery?'

'Trev — the barman at the pub — told me electric
shocks are the way to go. You get these aching joints.
Bit of electricity loosens 'em up. An electric fence is
best, I think, but you can't always find one when you
want it.' He placed his hands on the battery terminals
and jolted back. 'Jeez. Hurts, though.'

'Does it work?'

'Not yet,' Rodney admitted. 'But I figure if I do it
regularly enough …'

'Right — good luck with that. Oh, hey — I saw
eight echidnas crossing the road this morning.'

'Yeah?' Rodney nodded. 'Must be mating season again.'

'What are they doing?'

'The boys,' he swallowed, 'follow the girl …'

I nodded. 'Love is in the air, hey?' John Paul Young, 1978 … 'Might do a news release.'

Rodney blushed and shuffled his papers in an earnest way. I smiled — he was so easy to embarrass.

On the way to my desk I pulled up in surprise. Sam was at her workstation; her broad shoulders leaned over the keyboard as she typed furiously. She was humming. It sounded like 'High on a Hill was a Lonely Goatherd', but it was hard to tell over the rattle of the keyboard.

That was a first. I glanced back at Rodney.

Every day this week, he mouthed at me.

I held my hands palm up and Rodney shrugged, then mouthed again, *no ranger, very busy.*

Sam looked up and smiled. 'Good to have you back, Cassandra.'

By the time I'd turned my computer on, she was out the door.

Yodelley, yodelley, yodelley …

It was the busiest day I'd had in there. In the absence of Mac, Rodney diverted all the calls to me.

Each time I'd start work on a plan for a public awareness campaign around protecting the thylacine, I'd get calls like these:

'One of your kangaroos ate my lunch while I was bushwalking. Can I be reimbursed?'

'There's feral chickens in the bush next to us. Can you come and get rid of them?'

'We have feral chickens in the bush next to us and I'm worried the neighbours are going to kill them. Shouldn't you be protecting them?'

'What time do they let the animals out in the national park?'

'Where can I buy a possum? I want one for a pet.'

'The flying foxes in the trees next to me keep me awake all night with their noise. Can you come and get rid of them?'

'I'm worried our neighbours are going to do something to the flying foxes next to us. Can you come and give them a warning?'

It was a yin and yang thing. Almost every call would be followed by one expressing the opposite opinion.

Was this what Mac had to deal with?

By midday, I had a full diary of house calls to make the next day. God knew what I'd tell these people, but my PR skills were going to come in handy.

I scanned the *Beechville Star* as I had a quick bite to eat. The *What's On* section highlighted an enticing array of diversions for the weekend. Lawn bowls, soccer, line dancing, craft collective, dog trials ... I couldn't wait. Each of the activities had a little spiel next to it.

Lawn Bowls — reigning champion Rodney Speers will lead the Beechville side ...

Sam. That woman was amazingly talented —
whale rescues, musicals, now dog trials. What couldn't
she do? I contemplated the list of activities. Practically
everyone I knew in the town got a mention. Some
popped up in several activities. What a diligent group
of pleasure-seekers they were.

I thought back to my weekends in Sydney. Usually
I'd have a work function on Friday and Saturday
nights. Sundays, Ant and I would have breakfast at
Manly Wharf. Sometimes we'd go sailing with Jessica
or do lunch with Wazza but mainly weekends were
about work and recuperating from work.

But these Beechville people really worked their
hobbies hard. The column hinted at a weekend frenzy
of fun. I wondered if I could ever develop an interest
in line dancing or arts and crafts. Strangely, the idea
didn't seem all that far-fetched.

I returned to my desk mentally swinging my skirt
and tapping my boots. *Yee-hah.* The phone was still
running hot. Finally a call came through I couldn't put
off until tomorrow.

The voice of the woman on the end of the line was
shrill, hinting at a lurking hysteria. 'I've got a snake in
my house and I've caught it under a bucket. Can you
come and get rid of it?'

Chapter Twenty-one

Mortality rate second only
to the black mamba

I put the phone down on the snake call and looked around the office. Sam hadn't returned. Of course.

'Checking on a turtle that's being rehabilitated,' said Rodney when he saw me looking for her.

I told him about the snake call. 'Can you go?' I asked.

Rodney shook his head fervently. 'Not an admin job, sorry. Love to, but it's outside my job description.'

'Is it a PR job?'

'Well …' Rodney's eyes met mine uncomfortably. 'It's more a PR job than an admin job.'

I couldn't dispute that. PR is one of those job descriptions that can expand to anything involving contact with people.

'Isn't there someone else around here who does this kind of thing?'

Rodney shook his head. 'Mac usually does it ...' His voice trailed away and he blushed.

I rolled my eyes. 'It's all right, you can mention his name. I'm not going to cry or anything.'

Rodney shifted on his seat, then reached into the filing cabinet. 'Here.' He pushed a booklet across the desk towards me. 'All the deadly snakes are on the pages with red borders. If it's not one of them you can just chase it outside.'

'What if it *is* one of them?'

'Um.' Rodney gave himself another electric shock before replying. 'Jeez, I think it's working. Don't let it bite you. Here, you'll need this.' He pulled a pronged stick from behind the desk. 'That's what,' cough, 'uses.'

I tucked the stick under my arm.

'Take a first aid kit too.' He pulled a box with a green cross on it out from under the desk. 'There's a pressure bandage in there if you need it.'

I looked from the box to him.

He blushed, then picked up the phone.

'Right.' I picked up the first aid kit and walked out.

The house was a Queenslander, like all the others in Beechville. This one was in good nick, though — a well-kept garden and neat lawn stretched behind the picket fence. A middle-aged woman in a tracksuit was

standing at the gate as I drove up. My stomach sank —
it was Christine Bowles, the mouse woman. She hadn't
given her name on the phone.

She nodded as she saw the uniform. 'Took your
time,' she said in a clipped voice.

No need to thank me. I slid out of the car and into
my snake-catcher persona. I adjusted my Akubra hat,
pushed my hands into the pockets of my pants and
resisted the urge to spit on the ground. *All in a day's
work, ma'am.* That was the fun part — the seriousness
of the situation hit me as we went inside.

An upside-down bucket with a packet of rice on
top stood in the middle of her spotless kitchen floor.
It was as ominous as an unexploded bomb. I nodded
slowly. 'Snake's under there, huh?' Isn't that the kind
of thing the bomb squad usually says?

She nodded, her grey bob swinging about her
head. 'It came out from under the fridge. Almost gave
me a heart attack.'

'You did the right thing, calling me.'

She looked at me sceptically. 'What happened to
the other ranger?'

I stared at her. Surely she'd heard? Was it possible
that *anyone* didn't know the story? I sensed she was
testing me, but her face wasn't giving anything away.
'He had to leave for a bit,' I said shortly. Pulling out
my booklet, I handed it to her. 'Recognise any of
these, Ms Bowles?' So far, so TV procedural.

She turned the pages slowly, peering closely at each
picture. A tapping sound came from the bucket — the

snake was trying to break out. The bucket shuddered; there was something big in there.

At last she finished the red-edged pages and continued on to the green ones. I breathed a sigh of relief. But then she shook her head. 'No, I was right the first time.' Turning back to the red pages, she held the booklet out to me, her sun-tanned hand pointing at a picture of a coiled snake. 'This one.'

The taipan. I read the description. *Taipans grow to four metres long. They have the most toxic venom of any snake in the world. Mortality rate is second only to the black mamba, reaching one hundred percent.* My hands began to sweat. 'Are you sure?'

She nodded. 'Definitely. You've done this before, haven't you?' She looked at me doubtfully.

'Hmm.' I nodded in a non-committal way.

It was stupid, René, but, having got here — wearing the uniform and all — I just didn't feel I could back down.

You are *amazed how weak your mind is and how prone to error?*

Tell me about it.

I knew Christine Bowles' reputation. She'd be onto the *Beechville Star* in no time if I didn't help. *Wildlife Officer leaves woman stranded with deadly snake ...* No, this was my Waterloo and I couldn't surrender.

'Okay, stand back, I'm going in.'

A Zen-like calm descended on me. Maybe this was

what happened to soldiers when they went into battle. Once you've made the decision to act, you just go with it. My vision narrowed — there was no-one in that room except me and the snake.

I strode forward, flexing my fingers around my stick. *Pin it right behind the eyes. The way Steve Irwin does ... did, before he got too close to one too many poisonous animals.* With my left hand I reached forward and pulled off the bucket.

With lightning fast reflexes I pinned, crouched, grasped, lifted. A scaly creature wriggled in my hands, its legs waving frantically.

Legs?

The adrenaline leached away, leaving my legs weak and palms sweaty. An attack of hysteria rose to fill the void. I giggled. I spluttered and snorted until it hurt. My free hand clutched my stomach as I doubled over.

'What is it?' Christine backed away. 'Did it bite you?' She must have thought I was having a fit.

Walking towards her, I thrust the lizard out. Its violet tongue licked its lips. 'Do taipans have legs?'

'Does it have legs?' She squinted at the reptile. 'I can't see them.'

I looked at her incredulously. 'Have you ever thought of getting glasses?'

'I do *not* need glasses,' she snapped. 'Everyone in my family has excellent sight.'

The lizard twisted in my hands, its body unexpectedly warm and smooth. I ran my finger over its scales. 'It's a blue-tongue.'

Christine jumped backwards with a gasp. 'Get it away. Their bite is stronger than a lion, you know.'

I looked at the creature, now sitting placidly on my arm. 'Really?'

Christine nodded. 'One of the most underestimated creatures ever.'

The lizard opened its mouth, displaying rows of teeth. Well, it *seemed* pretty harmless, but who knew? I tightened my grip on its back. 'Right then, I guess I'll be off.' I paused, waiting for an offer of refreshment, or at least a word of thanks, but they weren't forthcoming.

Outside, I placed the lizard on the grass. It thrust out its tongue at me, then scuttled into the bushes.

Christine raised her hand in a gesture of dismissal as I drove off.

'What sort of snake was it?' asked Rodney as I came back into the office. He looked guilty. As he should.

'Taipan.' I swaggered nonchalantly to my desk. 'Took care of it. Pinned it behind the eyes — that's the best way.' Propping the snake-catching stick next to my desk, I balanced my Akubra hat on top of it. All I needed now were some maps and animal traps and I'd really have it going on.

'A taipan?' Rodney sounded awed. 'I've never heard of those being found around here before. Thought they were further north.'

'Just goes to show, doesn't it?' I swung my feet

up on the desk and admired my dusty riding boots. 'Wildlife is very unpredictable.'

'A taipan, wow. And you just grabbed it?'

'Mmm, right behind the head.' I stretched and leaned back in my chair, with my hands behind my head. 'Big one too, coupla metres, probably. They do get bigger, of course. Mortality rate second only to the black mamba, y'know.'

Rodney's mouth dropped. 'That's amazing.'

'Ah, it's nothing.' I lowered my legs to the floor and switched my computer back on. 'They can't possibly be as toxic as most of the people I dealt with in Sydney. Red pages all the way there.'

Rodney shot admiring looks my way all day.

I pretended not to notice as I did some reading about thylacines. It was interesting. While they were supposedly extinct, like the yowie they'd been sighted all over. I remembered that night on Cougan Peak — those stripy rumps vanishing into the bushes. They were etched into my memory forever. A warm glow spread over me as I thought of them. It *was* good to know they were out there.

At four thirty Rodney braced himself with one last shock and approached my desk, his sun-bleached hair still bristling with electricity.

I knew he was going to ask me out. He had that look about him — like he might explode any minute. I picked up my bag — I'd save him the trouble. I could do with a night out. Anything would be better than Lean Cuisine in my empty house. 'Where do you want to go?'

'Do you want to ...' He stopped, realising what I'd just said. His tension seeped away like someone had pulled the plug. 'Cool — the pub?'

'Is there anywhere else?' I didn't think so, but perhaps there was a secret gourmet restaurant that only locals knew about.

'No.'

'The pub it is then.'

The Beechville pub was almost empty. A few men in cowboy hats leaned against the bar and a group of teenagers, including Tyler, was playing pool. I hadn't been in there before. I'd thought about it a couple of times, especially when I'd forgotten to take my frozen dinner out of the freezer. Life's tough without a microwave. I'd kind of sensed that a woman on her own would be a cause for discomfort among the locals, though.

All heads turned as I came in — I felt like Angelina Jolie on the red carpet. Rodney's shoulders straightened — proud to be the escort of the local celebrity.

The barman — a huge red-cheeked man in a battered hat — leaned over the counter and nodded. 'Rodney.'

It took me a little while to realise where I'd seen him before. He was the lead farmer from the feral pig morning, the one who'd faced off the animal libbers.

'Hi, Trev. This is Cassandra,' said Rodney.

His washed-out blue eyes fixed on me intently and

then he nodded. 'Reckon I knew that already. You doing the electric shocks like I told you?'

Rodney nodded. 'Yep. Think it's working.' He rolled his shoulders. 'I'm loosening right up.'

'What'll it be?'

'What do you want?' Rodney reached for his wallet.

'Hmm.' I hadn't had a drink for a while. I could do with one. Come to think of it, I could do with quite a few. 'I'll have a schooner of beer with a rum chaser.'

Rodney looked startled.

Trev's eyes met his. 'Rodney?'

'I — I'll have the same.'

While Trev got the drinks, I eyed a map pinned up behind the bar. Red-tipped pins clustered here and there in a vaguely military way.

I nudged Rodney with my elbow. 'What's that?'

'Cane toads,' Rodney muttered. 'Trev's obsessed with 'em. Goes out collecting most nights — marks the locations with his pins.'

I remembered the article in the paper — *Local man nets record cane toad haul*. That, I now realised, had been Trev.

Trev returned, sliding the drinks across the counter. He noticed our gaze on his map. 'Bastards are getting better. More cunning, harder to catch, even got longer legs.' He glanced back at the map. 'I'm trying to work out what their strategy is — then I can cut 'em off as they come down the hill from Queensland. Bloody Queenslanders — should've stopped 'em at the border years ago. Put up a fence or something. They did it for the rabbits over west. All you need is a bit of mesh; they can't jump like frogs, y'see. Even cattle grids on the road would have helped — they're lazy, like to follow the highway. But no, just let 'em on through. Come right in and take over New South Wales. Bastards.'

I wasn't sure if he was talking about the Queenslanders or the cane toads. It probably didn't matter.

'Onya, Trev,' said Rodney, picking up the drinks.

A few beers later, I was getting hungry. Rodney and I had exhausted our conversation. I'd found out his main interests — surfing, watching car races and playing lawn bowls for the Beechville team. Apparently he was the star player.

'There's a lot of money in lawn bowls if you take it to the elite level, Cassandra.' The alcohol had reduced his shyness, but increased the redness of his sunburn. 'It's not a sport where you burn out after your twenties either. I've got at least another twenty years until I reach my peak.'

'Is that right? Fascinating. I never would have imagined.' It was hard to know where to take it from there. 'What's to eat here?' I glanced around, but there was no sign of a bar menu. 'Any chance of a curry or something?' I was missing my Thai food.

Rodney frowned. He leaned towards me and whispered, 'No Asian food.' He sounded like a spy imparting a secret code.

'Oh, okay, but what's the big secret?'

'Ssh.' Rodney tilted his head towards the bar. 'You don't want to set him off.'

'Huh?'

'He was in Vietnam. He gets flashbacks. Asian food sends him wild — even the smell of it. You don't want to mention curry in here.'

I glanced over at where Trev leaned against the bar, watching the news on TV. He was a big man; I wouldn't want to get on the wrong side of him. 'That's strange it's lasted so long.'

'Yeah. Hits different people differently. My dad was there too. With Trev. He's fine. Loves a curry. Won't talk about the war, though. They have these get-togethers, him and all the other vets. Go bush, canoeing, that kind of thing.'

'I suppose it helps them to talk about it. With people who were there.'

Rodney nodded. 'He's a wonder with the cane toads, old Trev, that's for sure.'

'Okay, you order then.' I lowered my voice. 'No curry.'

Another beer later, two plates overflowing with sausages, bacon, steak and mushrooms arrived — the mixed grill. I found it was just what I felt like. You can overdo Lean Cuisine — sometimes a big plate of fat is just what you need.

'Mmm, delicious.' My fork moved rapidly from plate to mouth and back again. I paused halfway through — Rodney was watching me like a spectator

at the tennis, his head going up and down. 'What?'
I spoke through a mouthful of bacon.

'I've never seen a girl eat like that before. Usually
they just pick.' He sounded admiring, rather than
judgmental.

'Waj hungry,' I muttered through my steak,
washing it down with the beer. Another glass arrived
as if by magic. I nodded at the barman. 'Thanksh.
This is a great pub. Don't know why I haven't been
here before.'

He tipped his hat back on his round, red face
and smiled, sliding a fresh coaster towards me. 'Was
wondering when you'd drop in.'

A sudden coughing fit from Rodney made me
swivel in my chair. 'You need to chew that steak,
Rodney. Gets shtuck otherwise.'

But Rodney's eyes were flicking from the coaster to
the barman and back again like he was signalling.

Trev's face turned a deeper shade of red. 'Sorry,
old stock. Past its use-by date.' His hand reached out
and an enormous fist covered the coaster. He walked
back to the bar and pulled out a Fourex coaster.
'Here.'

'Whatsup?' I'd had a few drinks, but the old PR
antennae never sleep. These men were trying to pull
something over on me. 'What was wrong with the old
coaster?'

'Nothing,' said Rodney and Trev together.

'Yeah right. It was probably some porno thing,
huh?'

Big smiles spread over their faces — I'd handed them their answer.

'You don't want to see that stuff, Cassandra,' said Rodney.

'It's not for the ladies,' said Trev.

I nodded like I believed them. I'd let it pass for now. Someone started up the jukebox. A boppy little number by a forgettable boy band blared out. 'Come on, Rodney, let's dance.' I pulled him up, determined to have a good time. I might not have been drinking cocktails with the film crews as Wazza imagined, but at least I was dancing in the pub. I'm not the kind of girl who sulks in a corner when she gets dumped — not that it had ever happened to me before.

The good thing about being love-sick in a place like Beechville is that you don't keep thinking you see the object of your desire in a crowd. There *were* no crowds, and there was no-one here who looked the least bit like Mac. It didn't stop me thinking about him constantly, though. *Try to trust me.* Why did he say that? It was a big ask from someone about to dump me on top of a mountain. *Bastard.* If only I could get him out of my head.

Several songs later, Rodney and I were slow-dancing to a romantic number. Inspired by our example, Maureen took to the floor with Trev. Tyler used the song as an excuse to lock face with his girl. All in all, it was turning into a raging kind of night — for Beechville.

Glancing over Rodney's shoulder I saw that Tyler was wearing the same T-shirt he'd had on at the feral pig morning. I gazed at the letters on the back. 'What does that mean — LOVA? I've seen it all around the place.'

'Oh, it's just this kids' band. You know, Cassandra …' Rodney raised his voice over the music. 'You have beautiful eyes.'

Uh oh.

His hands had been on my hips, but now they were sliding lower, towards my bottom. Maybe this getting-over-his-shyness thing wasn't such a good idea.

'Thanks, Rodney. You have nice eyes too, but just at the moment, I'm getting over — you know.'

'Mac?' Rodney's voice was loud. 'You shouldn't worry about Mac. He's not what you think, he's— ow.' Rodney jumped backwards.

'Sorry, Rodney, did I step on your foot?' Maureen's hair glowed pinkly in the fluorescent lights. She sounded distinctly unapologetic.

Rodney's face flushed a deep red. 'It's all right, Maureen.'

'Might be time for you to be heading home, son,' said Trev.

Rodney nodded. 'Yes, you're right.' The red tinge spread up to his ears.

I looked from one to the other — what was going on? They were giving Rodney the heavy. Why? Was it because of what he'd been about to say? *Something about Mac.* Behind Maureen, Tyler and his girl stopped pashing to glare at Rodney too. The mood had turned distinctly sour.

Whatever he had to say, I wanted to hear it. Lifting my chin, I put on my sexiest voice. 'Don't go, Rodney, the night is still young.' I slid my hand onto his elbow and fluttered my eyelashes — a cliché, I know, but it works. Usually.

Rodney looked from me to Maureen and Trev. 'Sorry, Cassandra — better go,' he mumbled. Turning, he stumbled out the door.

Huh? I was definitely losing it. Ant was right: I must have been letting myself go. That was another first — being deserted on a date. 'Well, guess *I* can still party on,' I said brightly. 'Who wants to dance?'

As I said that, someone flicked a switch and the music died. 'Closing time, I reckon,' said Trev, picking up glasses.

'Oh, but it's only ten o'clock.' I looked around. Maureen — already a pretty scary woman when she had a mind to be — was clutching her glass like she might shove it in my face. *And I'd thought we were friends ...* The teenagers were stumbling out the door. Perhaps it *was* time to go.

'Okay, bye then.' I picked up my purse and tottered into the street.

Chapter Twenty-two

I'm in a Stephen King novel

My car was parked outside, but I was too drunk to drive — even in a town with no cops. I wouldn't want to be responsible for the death of any small animal that might be romancing on the road. *Darling, you have the most beautiful bristles. I love the way your nose shines in the moonli— splat.* Maybe I could crash out in the office, then duck home for a shower before work?

I let myself in. The office had that spooky air that places usually full of people have when they're empty. I didn't want to turn the lights on — people would be able to look in from the street and see me — so I pulled out my key-ring torch.

I jumped as its feeble beam flickered over the cut-out of Mac. For a second, I'd thought it was him again.

*Here's a hot tip, René — erecting life-size
replicas of a guy, or frog, who's dumped you
is a bad idea. You'd never do that, would you?*
    Crawk.
    No, you're way too sensible.

'Whadda you looken at?' I put my hands on my hips.
'S'pose you think I'm heartbroken? Wasting away
without you? Well, that's all you know. I was just about
to end it too. Yeah, whadda you think about *that*? If
you hadn't left me on the mountain, I would have left
you. Fact is, I can have any man I want.' I prodded him
in the chest. The cardboard swayed. 'Rodney thinks
I'm hot.' I paused. *Although, hadn't he just dumped
me too?* I moved on. 'And Simon.' Yeah, I was pretty
sure I still did it for him. 'Why would I want a grumpy,
lying bastard like you?' I peered at his face. 'You're not
even that good-looking. You've got a funny nose. And
I've never liked curly hair. Ever. Don't know what I
saw in you — must have been the uniform.' I prodded
the cardboard again and it fell to the floor. I kicked
it aside and, for good measure, stamped on it. It was
satisfying. I stamped again. Maybe the cardboard
replica wasn't such a bad idea after all.

Now, where to sleep? I peered around the office — it
wasn't exactly designed for impromptu slumber parties.
Where were the comfy couches? There was a storeroom
up the back I'd never been in. Maybe there was
something soft in there. I went up and felt the handle. It
was locked, but I knew where Rodney kept all the keys.

I opened the little cupboard next to his desk and pulled out the key — obligingly labelled 'storeroom'. *Okay, where have you hidden the comfy pillows, Rodney?*

Fitting the key in the storeroom door, I pulled it open and screamed. Masses of shining red eyes were looking out at me, glowing in the light of my torch beam. I screamed again — my voice echoing eerily around the empty office. This freaked me out even more. I backed away, expecting the eyes to come after me. What were they keeping in there? It could be anything. Feral pigs, maybe. I remembered the newspaper article about the pig as big as a pony. *Omigod, it could be the giant hostage-taking pig.* No wonder they kept the door locked.

After a few steps I realised the eyes weren't moving. They weren't chasing me. Were they just biding their time, ready to pounce? Heart pounding, I stepped forward, directing the beam of my torch at one of the sets of eyes. It was a fox, but an unnaturally still one. Gradually, realisation dawned. That fox wasn't going anywhere. It was stuffed.

I ran my torch beam around the shelves. A black pig, a mouldy-looking koala, an eagle that looked about to bite and a small wombat stared back at me. It was still pretty spooky, but I could deal with it. I stepped inside.

Sun streaming through the office windows woke me. It took a while to work out what I was doing with my head on a wombat and a small pig cradled to my chest. I got there eventually.

I sat up, shifting my neck from side to side. That was a bad idea — my brain hurt. My head felt like it had been put on backwards. *That's the last time I'll use a wombat as a pillow.* I felt bad. *They should just stuff me and leave me in the cupboard.*

What a night. I felt like I hadn't slept at all. *But I'd dreamt about Mac.* It just came back to me in full emotional and visual detail. *Oh god, dreams, they mess with your mind.* It had been so real. I'd even smelt him. What a stupid dream, though; he'd just stood there looking at me. Considering the possibilities available, it wasn't terribly imaginative. I squinted my eyes against the sun, slowly coming to my senses.

Actually, now I thought about it, it had been a good dream. He'd smiled at me: the special smile — the one that fried my brain. The feeling lingered, a heat in my chest. A snippet from *Alice* wafted through my mind. *He was part of my dream ... but then I was part of his dream too.* Was I part of his dreams? He'd said that before, but now? It didn't seem likely. My chest ached. I wished it wouldn't. I wished I had a pill to make these feelings go away.

Getting slowly to my feet, I picked up my sleeping companions and placed them back on the shelves. 'There you go, guys — don't go bragging now. Good pigs don't kiss and tell.' I scanned the shelves. Apart from the animals, the storeroom seemed mainly to contain rolled-up posters.

I looked around the office. I was getting pretty sick of the posters we had up — we could really do with some new ones. Bound to be more wildlife, but at least it would be *different* wildlife. Maybe a change would cheer me up. I picked up the nearest roll and began to uncurl it.

'Old stock.'

'Huh?' I turned around, my head thumping. Sam was there. I glanced at my watch — it was seven am. 'You're in early.'

'Could say the same to you.' As always, Sam was inscrutable. Her suntanned face was friendly, but only up to a point.

I sensed tension in the air between us. Was it the posters? I let the end of the one I was holding roll back.

Sam smiled. 'Should do a cleanup — lots of junk hanging around here. So, what are you doing here at this time of day?' Her eyes flickered up and down my crumpled uniform. 'Or, haven't you gone home yet?'

I yawned. 'I worked back late — trying to get the thylacine strategy together. I'm thinking of a "friends of the thylacine" type of thing. Get some big corporate donors, put the money into threatened species protection work here.' I sounded like I had a brain — amazing.

'Sounds good.' Sam's voice was neutral.

'Yeah, anyway, I was tired, so I crashed out on the floor. Might go home for a shower now.' I started walking towards the door. 'I caught a taipan yesterday,' I couldn't help adding.

Sam raised an eyebrow. 'That would be a first for this area.'

I twitched my mouth into a smile. 'There you go then.' I stumbled into the foyer. The replica of Mac that I'd knocked over last night was now standing again. Sam must have picked it up on her way in. I pushed against it with my shoulder as I went past. 'Whoops,' I muttered as it toppled over, but the sense of satisfaction it had given me last night didn't return. *Damn that dream.*

Out in the street, the media contingent was gearing up for the day again. Their movements had become predictable. They decamped at sunset to the restaurants and nightclubs of Byron Bay, returning each morning with bloodshot eyes and weary yawns. They raised their cameras as I stepped out of the office. I could see the headlines now. *Heartbroken Cassandra works through the night to try to forget.* 'Hi, guys.' I waved my hand at them ineffectually. 'Any chance of skipping this photo opportunity?' But the flashes were going off as I spoke.

I pulled my rear-view mirror towards me as I got in the car. As I'd suspected — it was a bad look. I was beyond caring. My mind was on overtime.

I hadn't had a good look at the posters in the storeroom, but an image had registered. What was intriguing was it was the same image I'd seen briefly on the coaster in the pub before Trev had pulled it away from me. A triangle with words inside it — I tried and tried to remember, to imagine, what the words were, but I couldn't. All I'd seen was a jumble of letters. Why didn't they want me to see them? It was weird. What could be secret about a bunch of old posters and drinks coasters?

There was something going on, and it seemed like everyone except me was in on it. Across the road, Maureen was just opening the doors of the supermarket. She nodded coldly. Our relationship had gone downhill fast. Over at the petrol station, the attendant leaned against the pump, observing me. A cow mooed from the paddock on the edge of town.

I was tired, hungover, grumpy and sad, but that wasn't all. I was also a little bit nervous. It was in just these kinds of towns that the freakiest things happened. *Like the people who ended up in barrels of acid.* I was starting to feel like I was in a Stephen King novel; maybe the one where a crazy woman holds a man captive and cuts off his appendages one by one …

The paperboy glanced in my car window and smiled as he cycled past. It seemed a sinister smile — the kind you give to a kid who doesn't know the secret language all the other kids are talking. My eyes lingered on his T-shirt. *LOVA* — where *was* this band then? Why hadn't *I* ever seen them?

A shiny silver car stood outside Frog Hollow when I got home. My first thought was that it was Mac. No matter that he didn't seem the kind of person to drive a car like that; I had a one-track mind. My ridiculous heart sped up as I climbed out of the car.

I practically jogged to the house and leapt up the steps onto the verandah. An exotic smell stopped me in my tracks as I stepped inside the open front door — expensive perfume mingled with cigarette smoke. I knew that smell. It wasn't Mac.

I stopped, about to backtrack, run away. To where, I didn't know, I hadn't thought beyond the fact that I didn't want to see her. The kitchen door creaked open.

The familiar hourglass shape was shadowy in the backlight from the kitchen. Cigarette smoke curled up around her outline. Sunglasses protruded, horn-like, from the top of her head. I wouldn't have been surprised if a clap of thunder and the smell of sulphur had accompanied her entrance.

'Cassandra.' Jessica flung open her arms. 'I'm here.'

I stood poised at the front door, wondering if I could just run away. I felt like a bear whose cave has been occupied in its absence.

'Got a hug for your old mate?' Jessica took her cigarette from her mouth and blew out a jet of smoke.

I stepped forward reluctantly, ready for the air kiss.

As I got closer, Jessica eyed my dirty uniform. She stiffened, her arms going rigid in an attempt to hold me off.

Contrarily, this made me want to go in for the big one. I hugged Jessica's close-fitting pink linen shirt, catching a glimpse of her mid-calf white pants and spray-tanned ankles. Her sailing outfit. I had seen numerous variations on this theme when she had invited me out on the harbour in her boyfriend's yacht, *Success*.

'What are you doing here?' Seeing her was giving me a schizophrenic feeling. Jessica and Frog Hollow did not go together. Not to mention that I hadn't spoken to her since the night she dumped me from the perfume launch.

Jessica brushed at her shirt. 'Had a marketing meeting on the Gold Coast. Thought I'd drop in.' Her eyes flickered around the hallway. 'Nice place you've got.' She raised her eyebrows at the peeling paint and warped wooden walls.

My mouth twitched, seeing the house through her eyes. I felt protective of Frog Hollow, which was weird. Was it starting to grow on me? 'The birds are nice,' I said.

Jessica nodded slowly. 'You live here alone?'

'Not really.' I wasn't even sure why I said that. 'There's a lot of wildlife: birds, frogs, snakes ...' I trailed off.

Jessica puffed thoughtfully on her cigarette. 'You going to offer me a drink or something?'

It was the last thing I wanted to do, but here she was, she had driven from the Gold Coast ... 'I've only got water.'

'Water's fine.' Jessica stepped aside and followed me into the kitchen.

I pulled two grimy glasses out of the cupboard, filled them from the tap and slid one towards her. We sat down across the table. I sipped mine, tilting my head from side to side to try to get the stiffness out.

'Rough night?' said Jessica.

Was it that obvious? I glanced down at my crumpled uniform. Some of the tomato sauce from last night's mixed grill had adhered to my chest. I looked across the table at Jessica. It was hard to know what she was thinking. Seeing her there in her pink linen at my peeling lino table was disconcerting. It was hard to present my current lifestyle as a step up in the world. I sighed. 'Had a few drinks at the pub.'

Jessica drummed her perfectly rounded pink nails on the table. 'Our last conversation ...' She drummed again. 'Didn't go all that well.'

I shrugged. It was funny to think that Jessica's perfume launch had seemed important at the time. I gazed out the window at the place in the forest where Mac had appeared that night ...

Jessica coughed, took a sip of her drink and mumbled something.

'Pardon?' I looked at her. Was she blushing?

'Sorry.'

I waited for her to repeat what she'd said.

'Sorry,' she said again.

'That's okay, Jessica, just say it more clearly.'

'No, sorry is what I said the first time. I'm sorry I dumped you after that potoree thing.'

'Potoroo. Long-footed potoroo.'

'Potoree, potoroo, whatever.'

I flapped my hand. 'Makes no difference now.'

'No — I feel bad about it. Let me make it up to you.'

I leaned my elbows on the table, gazed at her, waited with faint interest for her to speak again.

'You're like a sister to me, Cassandra.'

I laughed.

'What?' said Jessica.

I opened my mouth, shut it again. I didn't know what to say. Do sisters dump each other at the first sniff of trouble? Maybe they do.

'I'm worried about you,' said Jessica. 'Why don't you come home?'

'Home?'

'Sydney. Cosmonauts is looking for someone to head up their international PR division.'

'Oh.' So that was why she was here. Her company had sent her on a head-hunting mission.

Jessica pushed her glass aside and leaned forward. 'You'd be managing Sydney, Paris, Berlin, Tokyo, London. The job's made for you. You'd be a shoo-in with your profile the way it is now.'

My profile. I laughed again, gazed out the window. My small brown bird was there again.

'What?' said Jessica.

'I don't know — my profile. I find it hard to grasp what that means anymore. It doesn't seem to belong to me.'

Jessica looked confused. 'But your profile's fantastic at the moment, Cassandra. You're on the side of the buses.'

'Yeah, Wazza said.' I met Jessica's eyes; maybe she would understand. 'It's not *me*, Jessica. It's just a figment of the media's imagination. There's nothing real about it.'

Jessica frowned. 'Yes, I know that.' She sounded like this was beside the point. 'But you're gold at the moment, Cassandra. You have no idea. *Everyone's* talking about you.'

The little bird tapped on the glass. I winked at it.

Jessica swung around and looked at the window.

'See, I've got lots of friends,' I said.

Jessica puffed on her cigarette. 'You're not turning into one of those hemp-robe-and-sandal types, are you?'

Maybe I was. I leaned my chin on my hand, imagined myself strolling through a grassy meadow, my naturally brown hair blowing out behind me in the breeze …

'This Cosmonauts job.'

I jumped. Jessica had interrupted my daydream.

'We'd be working together. It would be fun. We'd be a team again, like in Blacktown. We had some laughs, didn't we?'

I looked at her blankly. *What laughs?*

Jessica was unperturbed. 'Best years of my life.'

'Why don't you go back there then?'

Jessica hesitated, then laughed. 'God, you're funny, Cassandra. Like I'd go back to Blacktown. Would you?'

'No. Never. But I didn't like it in the first place.'

'What are you doing here?' Jessica gestured around the kitchen. 'This is a dump, Cassandra.'

'It's not that bad.'

'It's a dump.' As if to prove Jessica's point, a cockroach scuttled across the bench.

'I'm used to it.' Jessica was making me anxious. While I'd had no trouble hanging up on Wazza, having Jessica here in front of me was a different story.

'This job — it's what you're good at. You were so good, Cassandra. You're wasted up here.'

I nodded. *Paris, Berlin, Tokyo, London.* 'Yes, I *was* good, wasn't I?'

'The best. And think of Paris in the spring. Oh my god, the fashions, Cassandra.'

The fashions. I glanced down at my uniform.

'I can't believe you'd pass up a job like this.' Jessica's pert nose wrinkled. 'Tokyo — don't you love Tokyo?'

I nodded. 'Tokyo's cool.'

'Harajuku, Ginza, the nightclubs, the shopping ...'

I nibbled one of my hangnails, noticed the grime under my cuticles. *Tokyo.* I'd have to get my hair done, my nails, return to the gym ... 'I don't know, Jessica. I'm not sure if I can do it anymore.'

'Cassandra, you don't look well. You look tired.'

'I *am* tired.' I sipped my water, wondered if I had anything in the fridge for breakfast.

'Brainwashing.' Jessica snapped her fingers.

'Huh?'

'They've been brainwashing you.'

'No, they haven't.' Now that she mentioned it, though, my brain did feel kind of rubbery.

'I studied brainwashing as part of my marketing degree. It's the only explanation. You never used to be like this.'

I considered that statement. I wasn't sure if it was true. 'Like what?'

'You're so slow, and placid.'

'You make me sound like a cow.' I yawned, chewed my lip.

'It's classic brainwashing — sleep deprivation, harsh conditions.' She glanced around the room. 'Do you have a sense of powerlessness, a feeling you can only gain acceptance by complying with the norms? Are you eating unusual foods?' She ticked the points off on her fingers.

I thought of the mixed grill in the pub last night. That hadn't been the kind of thing I'd normally eat at all. I nodded.

'Is there an in-group language you're not party to?'

LOVA. I nodded again.

'I knew it. Open and shut case,' said Jessica. 'They're trying to grab you for some weird country town cult thing. Happens all the time.' She gave me a serious look. 'Friend of mine went to the Tamworth Country Music Festival once.' She shook her head. 'Great girl — worked in advertising. Slick as they come. Never came back. Heard she buys all her clothes from RM Williams now.' Jessica cast her eyes over my ranger outfit. 'It starts with the clothes, Cassandra. Before you know it you'll be dancing around the street singing country and western songs and playing a ukulele.'

A ukulele. I remembered Mac. 'I like the uk—'

'Sooner I get you out of here, the better. That ranger, he's probably the cult leader.' She half stood. 'I'll help you pack your bag.'

'No, I —' I gazed out the window at the rainforest. 'I can't leave yet, Jessica. I don't know why. I just can't.'

I knew I should say yes, René, but something was stopping me. What was it? Was it just Mac?

Crawk.

Assume there exists an evil demon capable of deceiving us? That's not a very nice thing to say about Jessica, René. Or are you talking about Mac?

Jessica stood up and sauntered to the sink. She ground her cigarette out on the draining board. The sun caught her hair, making it blaze. 'I'm taking a room at the Amble Inn for tonight. I've got a flight back to Sydney from the Gold Coast early in the morning. You should come with me.'

'You can stay here.'

Jessica laughed, brushing off some dust that had adhered to her linen shirt. 'I don't think so, Cassandra.'

Chapter Twenty-three

Is that a PR job?

After Jessica left I noticed a blinking light on my home phone. I picked it up and listened to the message.

'Hi, Cassandra — it's Anthony. I saw you on the cover of *Woman's Daily*.' He paused.

I already knew what was coming next.

'Your hair — I wondered if you'd mind telling people that I'm not doing it anymore ... if they ask. It's just — my reputation. I know you'll understand. Um ... I'm still seeing Damien. Thanks for being so ...' The message bank beeped. He'd run out of space.

I wondered why he hadn't called me on my mobile, then figured it out. He didn't really want to talk to me. I glanced in the hallway mirror. *Like I'd give you credit for this hairdo, Ant. This one's all mine.* I smoothed down the sticky-up bits. *Although ... I do owe him one.*

After a shower, a coffee and a fresh uniform, I felt capable of facing the office again. I fiddled with my hair in the mirror, getting the right AC/DC look.

I found myself singing along to 'Achy Breaky Heart' on the radio as I drove back to work. I stopped suddenly. Was Jessica right? Had I been brainwashed? *Paris, London, Tokyo.* It was tempting. And she was right, my talents *were* wasted here. I glanced over at the Amble Inn Motel and tapped my fingers on the wheel. Maybe I'd pay a call on her later.

The media contingent was still there outside the office. I strode towards them. 'Press conference, guys.'

They pulled out their notebooks eagerly. The photographers raised their lenses.

'I just wanted you to know …' The shutters clicked excitedly. 'My hair is, like, totally done by Anthony Karras of Anthony's in Surry Hills.' I twirled on the spot, model-like. 'That's all, folks.'

They were already on their mobiles, delivering the news as I strode off. It was a cheap shot, but I couldn't resist. It's not true what they say about revenge; it's *much* more fun than turning the other cheek.

Rodney started typing furiously as I came in. His freckles were standing out like pebbles in off-white snow today.

I stopped in front of his desk. 'Hi, Rodney.'

He looked up, turned even paler and smiled weakly. 'Hi, Cassandra. Sorry about last night.' Placing his hands on the battery terminals, he jerked backwards, moaning.

I cocked my head. 'Which part?' I wasn't really being smart, I was interested to know.

'Leaving like that. I should have taken you home or something.' A red tide washed across the snow. 'I don't mean to my home ...'

'It's okay. I know what you mean. So, what was going on — why did we get the bum's rush?' I stepped forward and leaned on his desk, peering around the side of his computer.

Rodney flinched as if he thought I was going to hit him. 'C-c-closing time?'

'Closing time.' I pursed my lips. 'Seems to me there was more going on than that. I thought Maureen was going to punch you out for a moment there.'

Rodney shook his head rapidly. 'I think they just wanted to go to bed. The pub always shuts at that time.'

'Really?'

Rodney nodded, like one of those dogs with a head on a spring.

'Good morning again.' Sam strolled up to the desk. She turned from me to Rodney. 'What's going on? Looking a bit peaky there, mate. Had a big night?' She swivelled back to me, putting two and two together. 'You both had a big night?'

'No, I ...' Rodney began.

She waved her hand to stop him. 'I don't need to know. Cassandra — Trev Benson just rang. Said you were coming out to look at those feral chickens?'

Shit. I made a lot of promises yesterday — now I needed to deliver. I nodded: another head on a spring.

'Good,' said Sam. 'Those chickens need to go. You should get out there tonight when they're roosting and catch a few.'

My mouth dropped open. *Was that a PR job?*

'Take a few photos for the paper while you're out there.' Sam made the tenuous link.

The amazing versatility of my job description was just sinking in. Was there anything that couldn't be classified as public relations? My phone rang and I jogged over to my desk.

'Are you going to come out here today and look at these flying foxes?' said a woman's irritated voice. 'I didn't sleep a wink last night with the racket.' Her voice sounded familiar, but I was too frazzled to work it out.

I glanced around the office. Sam had disappeared. 'Okay, sure, I'll be right there.'

There was just one thing I needed to do before I left.

Rodney's eyes burnt into my back as I walked towards the storeroom. I pulled at the handle but it was locked again. 'Have you got the key there, Rodney?' I sang out, trying to maintain the right tone of naivety.

'What do you want in the storeroom?'

Was I imagining it, or was there an aggressive note to his voice? I met his eyes, but he didn't look away or blush — *interesting.*

I thought quickly. 'I need the stuffed pig for a news release about feral pigs. I want a photo to send out with it.'

Rodney leaned down and took the key from his cupboard. 'I'll get it for you. Sam likes me to keep an eye on what goes in and out.'

I rolled my eyes. 'What, are they stuffed with diamonds or something?'

'It's just good administration procedure,' said Rodney stiffly.

I was seeing a whole new side to him today. He wasn't as much of a pushover as I'd thought. Peering over his shoulder as he opened the door, I ground my teeth. Sam had been busy — the shelves were empty. 'What happened to all the posters?' I said.

'What posters?' Rodney's reply was a little too quick. He handed me the stuffed pig.

I tucked it under my arm. 'Weren't there some posters there? I thought if no-one needed them I could use them for a kids' activity or something. Get the kids drawing pigs on the back.'

'Guess they've all been used up.' Rodney didn't meet my eyes.

I took a deep breath. 'Rodney. Look at me.'

He turned his head, but his eyes were on my nose.

'Look at me,' I repeated.

He met my eyes, his mouth setting in an obstinate line.

'What's going on?'

'Noth—'

'Don't give me that shit, Rodney. You couldn't lie your way out of a paper bag.'

Rodney's eyes widened, then slid from side to side.

I lowered my voice and stepped towards him. 'Sam's not here to save you now. Last night, you were going to tell me something about Mac.' I reached out and grasped his wrist with both hands. 'Tell me or I'll give you a Chinese burn.' He probably thought I was joking. I wasn't — ask any of my primary school compatriots. We fat girls have strong hands.

Rodney blinked. He looked like he might be about to cry. 'There's nothing, Cassandra. I was just trying to say …' He gulped. 'He's no good for you, that's all.'

I twisted and he yelped. 'Why,' twist, 'isn't he,' twist, 'any good?' I did feel a bit mean, but he had it coming.

He pulled his arm away. 'Look, you've left a mark.' He rubbed at his wrist.

A bell tinkled on the front counter. 'Helloo.' A sunburnt farmer peered over and saw us.

Rodney scampered away like a frightened hare.

As I drove away from the office, I saw Jessica lying on a sun lounge next to the tiny blue motel swimming pool. She was wearing huge sunglasses and a red bikini and sipping an orange juice. A pair of high-heeled slip-ons lay on the ground next to her. She looked as incongruous as a flamingo in a suburban street. I recognised the magazine in her hand — French *Vogue*.

Paris in the spring ...

The man in the garage opposite leaned on his pump, watching Jessica sip her drink. He looked hypnotised. He didn't even notice me. I'd obviously lost it.

Half an hour later I was standing in a gutter. An odour like month-old dirty socks assailed my nostrils. A flying fox colony had recently taken up residence in the rainforest at the western edge of town. On arrival, I'd discovered that the woman who'd called me down here was Maureen from the supermarket. Why I hadn't made the connection on the phone I'm not sure. It unsettled me; it was like I was missing things. Yesterday Christine Bowles had taken me by surprise, today Maureen ... Was it them or was it me?

Maureen didn't seem surprised to see *me*, though. 'My morning off from the shop,' she said flatly. 'Got the assistant in.' A milky-eyed old dog with moth-eaten bristly hair pushed itself between her legs as she spoke. The black and brown bodies of the bats dangled like smelly washing from the trees above. Chattering and screeching, they jostled for position, their leathery wings flapping. Maureen pointed triumphantly at a pile of sloppy brown poo. 'Look at that — dirty things. What are you going to do about them?' Strangely, she sounded like she had complete faith in my ability to solve her bat problem.

I peered up at the bats with a suitably intelligent expression, then turned back to her. 'Do you have any suggestions?'

She laughed, her plump face crinkling up under her frizzy hair. 'Do *I* have any suggestions? *You're* the ranger.'

I waggled my head from side to side in a way I hoped implied that I could be the ranger, but then again I might not be.

'You *are* a ranger, aren't you?' She eyed my badges. 'You *look* like a ranger.'

'Actually, I'm a PR officer.'

'PR? As in public relations?'

I nodded and gave my winning smile.

She didn't return it. 'So, you're here to be nice to me until I feel better about the bats, is that it?'

She'd hit the nail right on the head — she was smarter than she looked. 'That's about right — unless you have any other suggestions?'

'Can't you shoo them away?'

I glanced up. Every tree in the forest was bowed under the weight of its furry burden. 'How many do you think there are? Two thousand? Four thousand? They're going to take a lot of shooing; besides, they're endangered, you know.' I'd looked them up in my book before I came.

'Endangered?' Maureen screwed up her face. 'How can they be endangered? Look how many there are.'

'Yes, it *looks* like there's a lot of them, doesn't it? But that's just because they're all *here*, rather than somewhere else. There's not nearly as many of them as there used to be. A hundred years ago they'd fill the sky for hours on end when they flew out in the evenings.' I may have been using a bit of poetic licence there. 'It's like the passenger pigeons in America. Have you heard of them?'

Maureen shook her head. 'What have they got to do with it?'

I'd come across the sad story of the passenger pigeon on the internet while I was looking for a bit more guff on flying foxes. 'There used to be billions of them — literally. When they migrated, the flocks were over two kilometres wide and took three days to go past.'

Maureen gazed up at the sky, possibly imagining a flock of birds blotting out the sun for three days. 'What happened to them?'

'Extinct.' The word hung in the air for some time. 'Same reason that the flying foxes are endangered — loss of forests. They just don't have as many places to go these days.'

Maureen still looked unconvinced, but I could see she was thinking about it.

'They're also really important for the forests — they pollinate trees. The eucalypts would probably die out without them.' I slipped my hand into my handbag before she made a comeback. 'Have you ever tried earplugs? I find these ones are particularly good.'

Narrowing her eyes, she took the earplugs from me, crossing her arms. 'Is that the best you can do? Earplugs?'

'I could give you one of our new range of mugs ... I've got a few in the car.'

Maureen eyed me like I was a cockroach she might stamp beneath her slipper-clad foot.

I returned her look meekly. 'We also have T-shirts ...'

Surprisingly, she smiled. 'Look, don't worry about the bats for now.' She waved her hand in their general direction. 'I've been reading *Woman's Daily*. Fascinating story. Come inside and have a cup of tea. You can tell me all about it.'

'The thylacine?' I said hopefully.

She puffed air out through her lips disdainfully. 'No, not that — the love-rat ranger part. That's a story I'd like to hear. Better than *The Bold and the Beautiful*, I reckon, which is what I normally watch at this time of day if I'm not in the shop.'

'Oh.' I hesitated.

'Unless you want to try to move them?' Her eyes swept the bat colony.

I followed her gaze; there were so many of them. And they didn't look like they'd scare easily. Not to mention that they needed a break. Tough choice — spill my guts to a relative stranger or try to move a flying fox colony? I followed her inside.

As I came into the lounge room I pulled up short. The curtains were drawn and it took a moment to work out what I was seeing. It was like a medieval arsenal in there: weapons were arrayed across all four walls. Not guns, but swords, maces, double-sided axes and other lethal-looking things I couldn't identify. *Barrels of acid* ... I took a step backwards. 'Maybe I should have a closer look at those flying foxes ...'

Maureen chuckled. 'It's all right, dear. It's just my hobby.' She eyed the wall proudly.

'That's an interesting hobby.' I hovered on the threshold. 'What made you pick weapons?'

Maureen gestured at a stack of DVDs lined up in a bookcase next to a huge television set. 'They go with the movies.'

I took a step closer. There was the complete set of *Lord of the Rings*, *Star Wars*, *Harry Potter* and numerous medieval-themed movies I'd never seen. It's interesting what people are into. 'Fantasy, huh?' Maybe she wasn't planning on chopping me up and putting me in a barrel just yet.

'Much better than real life.' Maureen's eyes shone. She took a sword down off the wall and handed it to me.

I swished it experimentally. 'Mmm, I see what you mean.' It was strangely thrilling. I swished it again. If only I had some dragons to slay. That would be satisfying. Those knights had it easy — no struggling for a sense of purpose. Just find a maiden in distress and rescue her. *Easy.*

'And it's not just the weapons ...' She pointed her chin at a poster of Orlando Bloom as Legolas.

'Yes, nice hair. Aragorn was my favourite, though,' I said.

'Oh no, dear, he was already spoken for, wasn't he?'

'Yeah, that elf girl.' I frowned.

'You're right, she wasn't anywhere near good enough for him. But at least Legolas was single. There's no point in trying to compete with elf-queens, is there?'

The conversation was taking a strange turn, but I played along, thrusting and parrying with my sword. *I could get to like this.* 'No, I suppose not. I still think, though, if the right girl came along … Maybe someone who shared his interests in …' I glanced at the walls, 'weapons and so on. I'm not sure that Aragorn and Arwen had a lot in common, really.'

Maureen laughed and lifted the dog off the sofa. 'You know you're not allowed up there, you silly old thing. What I'd really like is one of those swords from *Lord of the Rings*; might have to take a trip to New Zealand for that, though. Look.' She picked up a photo from the sideboard. 'Here's me at the last North Coast Medieval Jousting Tournament.'

The photo showed Maureen in chain mail, looking slightly flushed. 'Nice.' I handed it back to her. 'You look very … formidable.'

She nodded. 'I won my section. Why don't you take a seat; I'll put the kettle on.'

'It must be getting near tea time; leastwise in decent places where there is still tea time,' I said, quoting Sam Gamgee.

'I like a girl who knows her *Lord of the Rings*,' said Maureen.

Our cup of tea took most of the morning. I told her about the night on Cougan Peak and how Mac had disappeared. It actually felt good to talk about it. She was a good audience: sipping her tea, munching on scones and making encouraging noises when I paused.

At the end of my story Maureen had some advice to dispense on the subject of Mac. 'You gotta look after yourself. No-one else is going to.' Her eyes bored into mine. 'You hear what I'm saying, dear?'

I nodded doubtfully — I didn't, really. First Rodney, then Sam, now Maureen ... Who was going to be next to warn me off Mac?

'What I mean is, men ... they're not always what they seem. Not everything is as straightforward as *Lord of the Rings* in real life.'

Was my life now more complex than a twelve-hundred-page trilogy? If so, it was beyond me. I wasn't sure if she meant that Mac: (a) wasn't what he seemed in the first place, or (b) wasn't what he seemed after I thought I'd got to know him, or (c) wasn't what he seemed now, that is, a love-rat psychopath, or (d) none of the above, or even possibly (e) an elf in disguise. Telling me that Mac wasn't what he seemed may have been one of the least useful bits of advice I'd ever had.

'Mac and I,' Maureen continued, 'we're kind of close.'

I remembered Rodney's comment about the hall key: *she's got a soft spot for Mac.* I nodded encouragingly.

'He's like the son I never had and I love him dearly, but he's not good news for girls like you.'

'Why's that?'

Maureen eyed me thoughtfully, like she was weighing her words. 'Emotionally unavailable, I think they call it these days.'

'What do you mean?'

'He's a slippery fish.'

I looked at her blankly.

'A greased eel, a melting popsicle …'

'Huh?'

'He has girls, but they don't stick. That disappearing thing he did, well, that's what he does. It's not the first time.'

'It's not?' That explained the casualness of the police. They'd been there before. I felt like I'd been kicked in the stomach. Was I just one of a long line of jilted lovers? 'But why?' It was a stupid question, but I couldn't help it. A slippery fish was a slippery fish and that's all there was to it.

'I don't think it's my place to say.' She clamped her mouth shut. It was obvious I wasn't going to get any more out of her.

Still, we parted on the best of terms. 'Sorry I can't do anything about your flying foxes,' I said. 'And thanks for the scones.' My head was still trying to absorb what she'd told me about Mac.

'No, no, don't you worry about that, dear.' She wiped her hands on her apron. 'I'll try the earplugs. If that doesn't work, I'll give you another call. Fancy a bit of jousting some time?' She said this in the casual way someone in Sydney might have suggested meeting up for lunch.

'Sure. Why not?' *Unless I'm shopping on the Champs Élysées.* That was beginning to feel more and more likely.

'Rightio — I'll let you know when the next tournament's on.' She stood on the street and waved as I drove off.

Another surprise was waiting for me at the feral chicken encounter. Trev Benson, who I'd spoken to on the phone, was Trev the barman. It was obvious in retrospect, but there seemed to be something wrong with my phone skills at the moment. Why didn't I ever know who I was talking to?

Maybe it wasn't me, it was them. Were they trying to unsettle me? Perhaps my conspiracy theory wasn't so far off the mark.

'Hello, hello, small world, in't it?' Trev said as I got out of the car. A couple of sleek cats twined themselves between his legs.

I put my hands on my hips and sniffed. 'Where are these chickens?' I'd had enough of being mucked around.

Trev took me behind his house to yet more rainforest. Sure enough, ten or so roosters were scratching around among the vines. The cats, which had followed us, pricked their ears at the sight of them, but didn't move.

'They look happy,' I said.

'They're digging up the plants. It's a nature reserve, you know.'

I didn't, but I nodded. 'Okay, looks like it's going to take a night-time operation.'

Trev pulled his cowboy hat down to shade his eyes. 'Didn't pick you for a girl who knew her chickens.'

I stared him down. 'I know my chickens, all right. And that's not all I know.'

He cocked one eyebrow. 'Yeah?'

'Yeah.' I hoped I sounded more knowledgeable than I felt.

'Meaning what?'

'Meaning ...' I didn't really have anything to add. 'Meaning, you'll be hearing from me about those chickens.'

'Do you want a cup of tea?' Trev asked abruptly.

I sighed. I was pretty tea-ed out, but you should never refuse hospitality. 'Maybe a cold drink?'

'Come in,' said Trev.

After Maureen's house I was a bit worried what I would find. But the main decoration in Trev's little Queenslander was a huge map of the area with pins all over it, similar to the one in the pub.

'Your cane toad map?' I said.

'Who told you about that?' He sounded cross.

'Rodney ... at the bar ...'

'Oh, right, yeah.' Trev eyed his map. 'Shocking things. His bushy eyebrows dropped. 'Think I've got 'em worried, though.'

I followed him into the kitchen. He pulled a glass out of the cupboard and filled it with water from the tap. The phone rang. 'I'll just get that — ice is in the freezer.' He pointed as he left the room.

I opened the freezer and jumped backwards. It was like a scene out of *Alien* — frozen little bodies in plastic bags filled half the cabinet. The cane toads' warty heads pressed forlornly against the plastic, ice cubes resting on top. I slammed the freezer door before they could defrost and attack.

'Actually, just out of the tap is fine,' I murmured as Trev came back in.

He chuckled. 'You don't need to worry about them. They're only dangerous when they're alive.' He opened the fridge — here two shelves were also stacked with toads in plastic bags. These ones were less rigid — one of them moved a leg slowly. It was creepy and a little sad, but I suppose they had to go. Beside the waving leg nestled some milk, cheese and tomatoes. I wrinkled my nose — there was no way I was staying for lunch.

'I put them in here first — then into the freezer once they've gone to sleep. It's the most humane way.' Trev gazed at the cane toads, then added, 'Poor buggers. It's not their fault they're so far from home. They're just in the wrong place at the wrong time.'

Something about the way he said it reminded me of what Rodney had said about Trev's experiences in Vietnam. *Wrong place, wrong time.* Did Trev relate to the cane toads somehow? 'You're doing a great job,' I said, rather feebly.

'Someone has to do it.' Trev spun around to face me. 'Don't they?' He slid open his cutlery drawer and extracted an envelope. Pulling out a photo he pushed it across the table to me. 'That's my biggest one.' The toad was lined up next to a ruler.

I peered closely. 'Twenty centimetres — that's almost as big as a cat.'

'They get bigger. Only good part is, if they keep getting bigger they might start eating rabbits.'

I glanced at Trev. 'You're joking?'

'Nup.' His face was straight.

I gave the photo the right amount of respectful attention, then slid it back in its envelope. I didn't like to imagine a cane toad bigger than that one. 'Better head back to the office, I guess.'

'Do you want a cheese and tomato sandwich before you go?'

'No thanks, I just ate,' I lied.

Trev laughed uproariously. 'Thought you'd say that.'

He was making himself a sandwich as I let myself out.

Ant's CD was still on constant rotation in my car. I pricked up my ears as 'Khe Sanh' came on. Cold Chisel, 1978. I'd never paid much attention to the song before, hadn't even really registered it was about the Vietnam War, but now its words seemed particularly apt. Instead of taking to drugs like the vet in the song, had Trev turned to cane toads? I figured we all had our demons, and catching cane toads was a better way of coping than many others. In fact, there was something quite admirable about it.

By the time I got back to the office, the day was nearly over.

'G-g-girl called in here for you,' said Rodney.

'What did she look like?'

Rodney blushed the most vivid red I had ever seen him. 'B-b-b—'

He didn't seem to be able to go on. 'Blonde?'

He nodded. 'And b-b-b—'

'Beautiful.'

He nodded again, his tomato red turning burgundy. It was stupid, but I felt a bit jealous. Making Rodney blush was *my* thing. But Jessica, it seemed, was even more overwhelming. What was I, meatloaf? I was about to return to the question of the posters when Rodney's phone rang. He grabbed it with relief.

Rodney managed to be terribly busy on the phone for the remainder of the afternoon. He darted nervous looks in my direction between calls. Giving up on any answers from that source, I picked up my bag and stalked out. The Amble Inn beckoned like a cocktail at the end of a hard day. Maybe I'd just talk to Jessica about the job a little more …

But out in the street I had a visitor — Simon was sitting on the hood of my car. He aimed a camera at me as I approached. I struck a pose, one hand on my hip. 'Reduced to taking pictures of me, hey? Can't you find the thylacine?'

'Heard the breaking news about your hairdo. Came to check it out.'

I laughed. 'I owed Ant one. Anyway, it's not that bad, is it?' I patted my hair.

Simon smiled. 'Not at all. Personally, I'd turn gay for Angus Young.'

I punched him on the shoulder and he winced.

'Hey, guess what turned up in the mail today?' He turned the camera over in his hands.

I eyed it in surprise. It looked like the one he'd had on Cougan Peak.

Simon held the display towards me. 'Recognise this?'

Leaning against the car, I gazed at the image on the screen. The Tasmanian tiger ran towards the bushes, its striped rump facing the camera. In an instant, I was back in that moment. 'You've got a picture?' I didn't know how to feel.

'Looks like it,' said Simon.

Chapter Twenty-four

A gigantic conspiracy

Simon passed me the camera. I looked more closely at the image lit up on the screen. I knew what I'd seen, but having the picture in front of me … it took my breath away.

'This *is* the camera you had on Cougan Peak, isn't it?' I said.

Simon nodded, his smile grew broader. 'Fantastic shots — I've emailed them off to my editor.'

'Wow. How did you get it back?'

'Like I said, it turned up in the mail, addressed to me at the newspaper. They forwarded it on.'

'Did Mac send it to you?'

Simon shrugged. 'I assume so. He didn't leave a calling card.'

My stomach lurched. 'Was there anything … with the camera?'

Simon raised one eyebrow. 'Like an apology maybe? No.'

'Where was it mailed from?'

'Sydney CBD.'

Not Tasmania. Wasn't that where he was supposed to be? I felt an almost irresistible urge to get on a plane and hunt him down. But where would I start? 'So ... that's great, Simon, photographic proof, big time.'

'Yep, it's what we needed, all right.' Simon glanced around him — checking for rival journalists — and lowered his voice. 'I've heard a rumour there's a big political announcement on the way.'

'About the tiger?' My voice rose, and Simon frowned. 'What kind of an announcement?' I whispered.

Simon tapped the side of his nose.

'You don't know, do you?'

He smiled. 'No frigging idea. Come and have a drink, Cassie — to celebrate.'

'You're not off the wagon, are you?'

Simon shook his head. 'Not after that night on Cougan Peak. Jesus, what a hangover. I'll celebrate with a lemon, lime and bitters.'

I didn't feel like celebrating. Why hadn't Mac sent *me* a letter? I knew this was irrational; why would he, after all those media interviews? He'd hate me now. He wouldn't understand. 'I wish I hadn't done all that media stuff, Simon. I didn't want to. You forced me into it.'

Simon cocked his head to one side. 'It was for your own good, baby.'

'Don't call me baby.' Madison Avenue, 1999. I crossed my arms. 'Exactly *how* was it for my own good? And who told *Woman's Daily* about me and Mac? You were the only one who knew. Now my love life's a public joke.'

'Cassie, I'm the best friend you've got. How much publicity have you got out of all this? You're set up for life now. And you know the media loves that romance angle. I had to play it, wouldn't have been doing my job properly otherwise. Anyway, why are you still here? I heard Wazza made you a very generous offer.'

'Who have you been talking to?'

'Your friend Jessica, over at the Amble Inn.' He raised his eyebrows suggestively.

'Do you have to do that?' Jessica obviously hadn't mentioned the Cosmonauts job. Head-hunting was a covert operation.

'What?'

'I'm just over it. All this eyebrow raising, blushing, leering. She's not all that fabulous, is she?'

Simon cocked his head to one side. 'Not half as fabulous as you, Cassandra. In my opinion. So, why are you still here?'

'Oh God, I don't know.' I looked up and down the street. Why *was* I still here? The place was a dive — all it needed was tumbleweed blowing by and it could have been a ghost town movie set. Five o'clock and the only place open was the pub. But yet, here I was, with no firm plans to leave. I wasn't sure if that was due to inertia or something more intangible. 'Unresolved issues, I guess.'

That took me back to Mac. There *had* been something special about what we'd had. *Hadn't there?* I didn't really know anymore — maybe it was all in my head. 'You know, Simon, sometimes I really hate men.'

Simon looked alarmed.

'Why are they so bloody secretive? I mean, they might not all disappear like Mac, but they may as well a lot of the time ...'

Simon shrugged. 'Maybe it's that nomad instinct. That man versus wild —' He stopped, seeing my lowered brows. 'Hey, *I'm* here.'

I gazed past him down the street. Beechville might be boring, but the thought of Sydney didn't grab me either. *And what about Paris, Tokyo and Berlin?* That should have made me excited, but instead it made me feel tired. I felt like I didn't fit in anywhere anymore.

I didn't know what to do with my life, René.
Crawk.
You just keep pushing. You just keep pushing?
Did that work for you? I don't think so. Weren't you banned by the Church and then poisoned?

'Cassie?' Simon tapped me on the leg with his foot. 'Pub?'

Pub? It was the last thing I felt like. Although … I had a brainwave. I might be able to get hold of one of those coasters. It was driving me crazy, not knowing what was on them. And I'd be less conspicuous with Simon than by myself. 'Maybe just one drink — I've got to catch some chickens later.'

'You mean count some chickens? As in, before they hatch?'

'No, I mean catch some chickens as in pwuck pwuck chicken.' I flapped my elbows. 'They're in the rainforest. I need to get them out.'

Simon frowned. 'Is that what you do these days?'

'Yeah — chickens, snakes, flying foxes — you name it, I catch it.'

'Huh — never would have picked you for a critter catchin' gal.' Simon tilted his head to one side and gave me a long look.

'Buy me a drink and shut up, Simon.'

He smiled. 'That's the Cassie I know.'

'Cassan— never mind.'

Simon slid off the car and we strolled companionably towards the pub. The sun was just going down and Maureen's supermarket cast a long shadow across the road.

Something occurred to me. 'Simon. That feral pig story you were thinking of running?'

'Mmm?' He flashed me a glance out of the corner of his eye.

'How did you find out about it?'

'You know I can't reveal my sources, Cassandra.'

'So you had a source? Someone tipped you off?'

'Mmm.'

'Anonymously?'

'Mmm.'

'Male or female?'

'I'm not saying any more.'

'It was Mac, wasn't it?' I'd just remembered the way he'd looked at me the day Simon had rung me in the office, like he'd known what was going on.

Simon gave me a sharp look. I could see his brain whirring, making connections.

'It's all right. You don't need to tell me.' It was Mac. I was sure of it. Why would he do that? What would make him contact Simon? He said he'd wanted me gone, but wouldn't ensuring I could never return to Sydney have the opposite effect? He was worse than a Rubik's cube, that man. I could turn the facts this way and that, but whichever way I looked at them they still didn't line up.

Simon looked thoughtful as we approached the pub. I assumed he was pondering the same question as me, but in fact his mind was on other things.

'You used to fancy me in uni, didn't you?' he said as we neared the door.

He'd spoken so casually it took a while for what he'd said to sink in. When it did, I was so flabbergasted I almost elbowed him in the stomach as I swung around. '*I* used to fancy *you*? Excuse me? I think it was the other way around.'

Simon laughed. He was in a jovial mood — the

exact opposite of Pre-Headline-Tension; nothing like some 'extinct tiger returned to life' photographs to brighten up your day. 'Well, of course I used to fancy *you*. Still do. But, what I meant was — you *did* used to fancy me a bit. Didn't you?'

I crossed my arms and looked at him. There was something appealing about him tonight — his excitement was infectious. Anyway, it was almost true. I smiled. 'Okay, I did. A bit.'

He jumped in front of me, blocking the door to the pub. 'Did? Or do?'

I pushed at his chest with one finger. 'Did, a little bit — until you turned into a wanker.'

'What do you mean, wanker?' He looked genuinely shocked. 'I'm just a good journalist.'

'Good journalist to you, wanker to me. Good PR to me, scheming spin-doctor to you. I rest my case. Now, are you going to buy me this drink, or what?'

Simon backed away. 'Touché, my spin-doctor.'

I took a seat at a table and Simon strode off to buy the drinks. Trev was behind the bar in his cowboy hat. I tried to catch his eye, but he didn't look over at me as he handed Simon the drinks. That was strange, considering we'd been on cheese-and-tomato-sandwich terms not long before. Maybe he didn't like journalists. That would hardly be unprecedented.

Simon slid the drink across the table to me — I was back to my more usual whiskey and soda. I wasn't sure if I ever wanted to drink another beer — certainly not with a rum chaser.

'What's the go with the map?' Simon inclined his head towards the bar. 'I would have asked him, but he didn't seem to be warming to me.'

I explained about the cane toads and the Asian food phobia.

'Post-traumatic stress, huh? Amazing it's lasted so long.'

I could see his brain ticking over, wondering if there was a story in it. *Vietnam vets — where are they now?*

We were silent for a while, but it was a good silence. It was the kind of silence you have with someone you've known for a long time. Did that mean I liked Simon? I turned from gazing out the window and found him looking at me in a speculative way.

I shifted on my seat. 'What?'

'You've changed, haven't you, Cass?'

I let it pass. Hadn't I already decided that I'd reverted to Cassie or even Cass? I shrugged. 'Have I?'

'You're not such a bitch anymore.'

Harsh words, but they weren't said harshly. *Did I used to be a bitch? I suppose I did.* I smiled. 'Don't worry, Simon, I'm still a PR bitch at heart.'

'Thank God for that, I was starting to worry.' The bar lights shone on his sandy hair, creating a halo around his head.

Simon and I had been opponents for so long that this truce felt very strange. I cocked my head to one side. I hadn't looked at him — not really looked at him — for a long time.

He had the face of a religious crusader — a pale, angular, sandy-haired, green-eyed knight. His shirtsleeves were rolled up and golden hairs curled on his forearms. His long legs stretched under the table towards me.

Was I starting to warm to him? I gave myself a mental slap around the cheeks. What was I thinking? This was *Simon,* for God's sake. Simon McKechnie — environmental journalist extraordinaire. This son of a bitch was the reason I was here. If he was being nice to me, it was because he wanted something: either sex, or a story, or both.

Journalist extraordinaire. Of course — son of a bitch or not — Simon's was just the mind I needed to bring in on this problem of mine. I glanced over at the barman. 'Simon — I keep feeling there's a gigantic conspiracy in this town that everyone's in on, except me. And no — I'm not paranoid.'

'I wouldn't say that, Cass.'

I narrowed my eyes. 'What, you wouldn't say I'm paranoid, or you wouldn't say I'm not paranoid?'

'Either.' He leaned over towards me and lowered his voice. 'So, what makes you think there's a gigantic conspiracy?'

'Don't humour me.'

'You know I wouldn't do that. Humouring is not what I do — stabbing in the back is what I do.' He smiled. 'Spit it out.'

I told him about the coasters and the posters. 'It sounds pretty weak, doesn't it?'

But Simon had that look he gets when he's onto something. It's like a missile locking on its target. I was glad it wasn't me he was after — this time. 'I trust your instincts.'

'You do?'

'Of course I do.' His green eyes met mine. 'You were the best PR in Sydney for a while there. Still could be, if you wanted.'

'Seems like a long time ago.' I ran my fingers through my Angus Young hairdo.

'You *have* changed. You never used to doubt yourself, did you?'

I shook my head.

'Well, in my game I trust my gut instincts. If you think something's fishy, it probably is.' He glanced up, scoping the room. 'Tell you what — you distract the barman, I'll try to get a few of these coasters.'

A couple of seconds later I tottered to the bar. 'Could I have a … a glass of water, please,' I whispered. While Trev was filling it, I sank in a graceful swoon to the floor. Eyes half-closed, I saw the barman's legs run out from behind the counter.

He knelt down beside me. 'Are you all right? Here's your water.'

I kept up my dying swan act for a few minutes. When I finally rose, with a feeble, 'Oh, thank you, I don't know what came over me,' Simon was out on the street giving me a thumbs up. 'I think I'd better go now,' I murmured, walking unsteadily to the door.

We scuttled around the corner, out of sight of the

bar and paused under a street lamp. Simon held the coaster up to the light. Inside a green triangle was written: *No Dam for Beechville.* His eyes met mine. 'Mean anything to you?'

'Nuh-uh.'

Simon looked thoughtful. 'It's ringing a few bells for me — I'll check it out tomorrow.' He looked at the coaster and back at me, then took a deep breath. Stepping forward, he placed his hands on my shoulders and kissed me.

Chapter Twenty-five

That chicken just gave me a smile

I squawked and jumped backwards, my hand coming up to my mouth. 'What are you *doing*?'

Simon stepped forward. He reached out and grasped my wrist. 'It's time you admitted it — we're made for each other. I know you, Cass.'

It sounded pretty profound the way he said it — way too profound. 'What makes you think you know me? *I* don't even know me.'

Simon's hand encircled my wrist loosely. 'You're smart, but you act dumb. You're soft, but you act hard. You're shy, but you act confident. You want me, but you pretend you don't. I know the way your mind works. Am I right?'

'You're off your head. *I* want *you*? *You* want *me*, you mean.' He was spot-on with some of the other stuff, though. Could he actually be right?

But there was still Mac. He might have left me, but I wasn't ready to let go of the idea of him yet. We'd only had a few days together, but it seemed like much more. I thought of what he'd said about the thylacines: *a defining moment.* Was he *my* defining moment — the yang to my yin, the puzzle piece that would fit me perfectly? Is anyone ever? *Try to trust me.* It was so confusing. Part of me really wanted him out of my head. I'd had enough of trying to figure him out. It gets wearing after a while.

Simon ran his thumb up my arm and I didn't pull away. '*I* want *you*? There's never been any doubt about that, has there? I've always wanted you, from the moment I saw you in first year — when you were still Cassie in ugg boots and a miniskirt. When did you become Cassandra?'

'End of first year.' I'd shed the girly name along with my ugg boots. Cassie went with checkout chick. Cassandra was a name to spin possibilities with.

Simon's hand dropped to his side, but he was still standing so close I could feel his breath on my face.

'So, why did you dig the knife in — in Sydney?' I said.

'I thought it would be good for you.' His green eyes didn't falter.

'You thought it would be good for me — to be publicly shamed and humiliated?'

'It has been, hasn't it? I can tell — looking at you.' His voice was steady.

'Jesus, Simon. Talk about tough love. What's your next trick — shoot me through the kneecaps?' It was dark now, and I had things to do. 'Do you want to come and catch some chickens?'

Simon smiled. 'Sure. Sounds like fun.'

It wasn't far to the chickens' rainforest home. We walked in silence, not touching. But it was that kind of not-touching where you are conscious of every centimetre between you.

'So, what's the go with these chickens?' said Simon, as we got near. 'What are they doing in the rainforest?'

'They're all roosters. People let them go because they don't lay eggs. They're no good for the forest, though; they scratch around and dig up all the seedlings.'

Simon raised one eyebrow. 'You really know your chickens, don't you? So, what's the plan?'

'Huh?'

'How are we going to catch them?'

It only then occurred to me that I was woefully underprepared for this expedition. 'I don't know. I should have brought something to put them in.'

'How about we just catch one each? Think of it as a reconnaissance. We can come back tomorrow night and catch some more, once we've established their modus operandi.'

'I like the way you say that, Simon — modus operandi.'

'I always think, with these types of expeditions, it's important to set the tone.'

'It's a good tone. Now I feel like a super sleuth on the trail of some desperate criminals.'

'Those feathered wascals won't escape the claws of justice,' Simon murmured.

We'd reached the rainforest patch near Trev's house now; pale shapes of chickens dotted the trees above us. The ground squelched underfoot as we stepped beneath them. It was interesting; seeing chickens in trees gave a whole new facet to their character. I'd never be able to look at a chicken now without seeing the wild jungle bird inside.

Simon spoke out of the corner of his mouth, barely moving his lips. 'That chicken just gave me a smile I could feel in my hip pocket.'

I matched his drawl. 'From thirty feet away, that chicken looked like a lot of class. From ten feet away it looks like something made to be seen from thirty feet away.'

'Hey, I didn't know you were a Raymond Chandler fan,' said Simon.

'I thought you said you knew me.'

'I know you enough.' Simon gave me a brief smile, then grasped the lower limb of one of the trees and pulled himself up. He dragged himself on his stomach along the branch. The chicken's head was tucked under its wing — but as Simon lunged towards it, it woke and flew down, squawking. Its squawks woke up the rest of the neighbourhood and cock-a-doodle-doos rang out across the forest.

'Nicely done,' I called up to him. 'Are you a professional chook catcher, by any chance?'

'Years of experience, darling.'

From then on, it was pretty much a run-and-grab operation. Simon attempted several flying tackles. I was more of a sneak up and pounce girl, myself. It took a long time, but eventually we each had a rooster tucked under our arm.

'So, I think we've effectively established their modus operandi,' I said. 'Shall we call it a night?'

Simon and I were just coming to the edge of the rainforest when a stick snapped behind us. As we turned, a tawny shape dashed past. There was a loud squawk as the animal grabbed a rooster and vanished into the shadows, the stripes on its rump blending into the leaves.

We stood there speechless for a few moments.

Simon spoke first. 'Wow. Wow.' He shook his head in amazement. 'Wow. That was it, wasn't it?'

I nodded.

'That is so …' He shook his head again. 'Wow. I've got to come back here with Chris tomorrow night for a stakeout. See if we can get some footage. Keep it quiet, will you? I don't want all those other journos all over it.' His voice exuded excitement.

I nodded again. *It was right here. In Beechville.* There didn't seem much point in trying to stop the media juggernaut now. The sight of the tiger had pulled me straight back to that night on Cougan Peak. My stomach clenched. Where *was* Mac? Why hadn't he contacted me?

Simon shook his head. 'How about that, eh? The Tasmanian tiger hits the town.'

I gazed at the place where the animal had vanished. The forest was as dark as a cave.

'Well, these chickens should put you in solid with your boss,' said Simon as we strolled down the street, chickens under our arms.

'Pardon?' I pushed the thoughts of Mac aside. I was an idiot to keep thinking about him. I needed to stop it. 'Are you still quoting Raymond Chandler?'

'Sam Spade — *The Maltese Falcon.*'

'You're a real hard-boiled detective fiction fan, aren't you, Simon?'

'Yep, I love a tough-talking man with a gun.'

'Who would have thought?'

Simon flashed me a glance. 'Guess there's lots you don't know about me, Cassie. Why don't you make it your mission to find out more? Here's something else you didn't know,' he waggled his eyebrows suggestively, 'I make a great breakfast in bed.'

'Simon, I rank that about one out of ten on the flirting subtlety scale. Next you'll be asking me where I left my wings, because I must be an angel who fell from heaven. Am I right?'

He laughed. 'It was just on the tip of my tongue. I'll have to lift my game, won't I?' We stopped beside my car. 'Where do you want your rooster, ma'am? In the boot? Or would you rather have it home delivered?' He waggled his eyebrows again.

'Jesus. You're going downhill. I didn't think that was possible.' Something caught my eye. 'Simon.' I stared over his shoulder. 'What's going on in there?' It might have been quiet on the street, but inside the office the lights were blazing. Silhouettes of a crowd of people moved to and fro in front of the lights.

'Looks like your party invitation got lost in the mail,' said Simon.

The dark shapes shifted around in the office like shadow puppets. I couldn't believe how many people were in there. It looked like it was standing room only.

'Quick,' I hissed. 'Let's get up there and see what's going on.'

Simon looked up at the window. 'You think this is the big conspiracy at work?'

I nodded. 'What else could it be?'

'A community meeting?'

'Why wouldn't they have invited me, then? And what sort of community meeting attracts that many people? I only got five to mine. Besides,' I glared in the direction of the office as some music drifted towards me, 'they're dancing. Come on.' I waved my arm towards the steps.

'What about the chickens?' Simon held up his rooster.

'Just take them. They're no trouble.' Indeed, the roosters were extremely docile now they'd been caught. They sat quietly, taking in the scenery from under our arms.

The front gate was locked but I had my key. We sneaked up the steps, although there was probably no need — the noise doof-doofed from upstairs; they wouldn't have heard a thing. It sounded like the party was in full swing. When we reached the office foyer, I beckoned to Simon to crouch and we scurried over to the front counter and huddled under it.

Simon raised his eyebrows at me questioningly.

I shrugged.

With his free hand, Simon reached towards his camera, which he'd stuffed in his jacket pocket. He couldn't get it out with one hand. Shuffling towards me, he transferred his rooster to my other arm.

'I'm a Texas chicken-slinger,' I whispered, cradling a rooster on each hip.

Simon smiled. 'You're lucky I left my firearms at home. Usually I pack a coupla mean bantams.' He cocked his head up questioningly.

I nodded.

Rising slowly, we peered over the top of the counter. The roosters peered over too. It took me a few seconds to process what I was seeing.

The office was packed. I think there were about fifty people. Music was playing — whoever was doing the selection had a fine taste in eighties disco hits.

Maureen, in a tight purple dress, was dancing with a man in a loose blue shirt and black pants, who had his back to me. Her hair, also purple now, glowed under the fluorescent lights.

Sam — a champagne glass in her hand — was wearing tight leather pants and a red singlet. She looked like she'd had a few — her cheeks were flushed and her arm was draped over Trev's back. Trev was talking to Hannah, the animal liberationist. Weren't they enemies?

Mismatched pairings seemed to be the order of the night. Rodney — in a Billabong T-shirt and board shorts — was dancing with Christine Bowles.

Tyler and the other teenage boy from the feral pig morning were slumped on the floor, passing a bottle of champagne between them. I scanned the room. Almost everyone I'd ever met in Beechville was here.

Why hadn't they invited me? I'd been snubbed before, but only at A-list events. This one spanned the whole alphabet.

Simon tapped my arm and pointed to the walls. He clicked off a few photos.

I followed his gaze. Pasted up all around the office were the posters I'd seen in the storeroom. Finally, I could get a good look at them. The message was the same as that on the coasters. *No Dam for Beechville.* Underneath were the words: *Leave Our Valley Alone.* *LOVA* — well *that* explained *that*; it wasn't a band at all. Why had it been such a secret, though? So there was a dam planned? Big deal.

As I was taking this in, the music stopped. The crowd on the dance-floor dispersed towards the drinks table. The man who'd been dancing with Maureen turned.

My heart accelerated like I'd grasped the terminals on Rodney's car battery. The man was gorgeous — smoothly shaved tanned cheeks, bright blue eyes, a sharp haircut and sharp clothes. It was Mac — but not as I knew him. Where was the three-day growth and slept-in hair?

Sam whistled and a dog bounded across the room towards her. She looked around. 'Where's your mate?'

Nails clattered on the steps behind us and a hairy shape streaked past, racing towards Sam. The dogs were tan-coloured and stocky with short hair and long tails. One had chicken feathers around its mouth.

'What have you been doing, you bad dog?' she said.

As they jumped up at Sam, wagging their tails, the recognition hit me like a kick in the stomach. The stripes on their backs were fading, but still clearly visible.

I'd been had, René. The bastards had conned me.

Chapter Twenty-six

If not for the roosters

Simon's camera clicked madly as he focused in on the dogs' stripy backs.

I knew instantly what had happened. There was no doubt in my mind — those dogs were the tigers. I just wasn't sure what that meant.

It would have been all right except for the roosters. Simon and I were ducking out of sight again when something set them off. Maybe it was the sudden silence.

Cock-a-doodle-doo, cock-a-doodle-doo, cock-a-doodle-doo.

It was obvious why those roosters had been dumped. Their cries were absolutely piercing — there's no way I'd want one of them living near my house.

All heads turned. For a moment there was silence, then Tyler nudged his friend and laughed. I had a vision of how absurd I must look — standing there with a chicken protruding from under each arm.

'Get them,' yelled Trev. His eyes opened wide. 'Get them, before they give the game away.' He looked like he was about to leap the counter.

Tyler jumped to his feet, flicking his hair out of his eyes. 'Easy, Uncle Trev. We'll handle it.'

His mate scrambled up, overturning the champagne bottle they'd been sharing.

'Get the camera,' yelled Trev.

'Run.' Simon took off for the door, camera in hand.

I hesitated. It was just a party — full of people I knew. Okay, they hadn't invited me, but that didn't mean I needed to run away. I scanned their faces — shock, hesitation and uncertainty were variously registered. My eyes returned to Mac; a flash passed between us. Well, it passed through *me*, anyway. My legs trembled. I stared into his eyes, unable to break away.

'Cassandra.' His voice was low, but there was an edge to the way he said my name. Was that guilt?

'Cassie,' Simon called from the door. 'Come on.'

Tyler and his mate ran to the counter and vaulted over it. Throwing the chickens at them, I ran too.

A large proportion of Beechville followed me.

We never stood a chance, Simon and I. Not with most of Beechville after us. Not with two athletic and inebriated teenage boys in the lead. Not with my weak legs and spinning head full of Mac.

Tyler crash-tackled Simon to the ground before he reached the door. He wasn't as big as Simon, but he sure had a mean tackle.

The camera slid from Simon's hand. 'Run, Cassie,' he yelled.

I might have got away if it hadn't been for Mac. 'Cassandra,' he called. 'Come back and talk.'

I froze halfway down the stairs, stopped and — like an idiot — retraced my steps. The pack that was after me — Tyler's mate at its head — backed away as I advanced. 'Talk about what?'

I was glad Mac and I still had the counter between us. I needed that space. He was so clean and well dressed; so breathtakingly good-looking. I didn't want him to be that good-looking. It made me uncomfortable. Here was I, my hair a mess, no makeup, chicken feathers and — I now realised as I moved beneath the foyer lights — chicken shit, all over me. It was like we'd changed places.

He ran his hands along the edge of the counter, taking in my appearance, then smiled. 'You look … different.' He spoke to me like I was the only person in the room. Everyone else had been photoshopped out of the picture.

'Yeah.' I puffed air out of my nose irritably. I knew I looked like crap; I didn't need him to tell me that. Why did I have to see him right now? 'Where have you been anyway — since you sneaked away on Cougan Peak? You might have told me where you were going.' I sounded like a nagging wife whose husband was late home from the pub. It didn't help that I had to yell to be heard over the dogs. They were running in circles around Simon, barking madly — nothing like a good chase. I glanced at them. 'The Tasmanian tigers, I presume?'

'Whadda ya wanna do with him, Uncle Trev?' grunted Tyler. He and his mate pushed Simon over the counter, pulling his arm up behind his back.

'There's no need to resort to violence,' Simon mumbled into the counter. 'I'm sure there's a way to resolve this … perceived problem. I'm a journalist. I should have immunity.'

'Fuckin' journalists.' Tyler slid the camera across to Mac. 'Spying on our base — let's tie him up and hold him for ransom.'

It was hard to know if he was joking or not.

'It's okay, mate.' Mac touched his arm. 'Why don't you go get a drink? I'll take over here.'

'You sure?' Tyler glanced at Trev for reassurance.

Trev gave a nod so subtle it was almost non-existent.

Tyler and his mate released Simon after giving his arm one last yank.

'Ow, lay off,' said Simon.

Trev handed the boys a beer each. 'Good job.'

'Thanks, Uncle Trev.'

Simon straightened up. 'Jesus.' He gazed after Tyler, rubbing his arm. 'He's wasted out here in the sticks. Should be playing for the big league.'

'Cassandra, Cassandra, Cassandra — what are we going to do with you now?' A suntanned hand reached out, taking the camera from Mac.

It was very strange to see Sam out of her khaki uniform. Even stranger to see the clothes she was wearing — and was that lipstick? Her hair was all fluffed up too — she seemed to be channelling Olivia Newton-John in her *Grease* period. That woman never ceased to amaze.

'I wouldn't have even been here except for you — you told me to go get the chickens,' I said. 'And then I saw the party.'

'That was probably a mistake on my part.' Sam flicked through the photos and deleted them, one by one. The dogs sat at her feet, watching attentively. She glanced up at me. 'I didn't realise you were so conscientious.'

'I thought it was important to get the chickens out of there. They were digging up the seedlings. It's a nature reserve.'

Sam smiled. 'See,' she said to Mac, 'told you.'

I would have liked to know what she meant, but I wasn't going to ask.

Mac flashed me a look I found hard to interpret. It was hopeless. There was no way I could talk to him with all these people around.

'How about you tell us what's going on, and we'll take it from there?' said Simon, flinching each time Sam pressed delete.

'I suppose we'd better.' Sam handed the camera back to Simon. 'Whiteboard.'

She'd only spoken quietly, but Rodney rushed down to the storeroom and pulled out an electronic whiteboard, wheeling it up to the front of the office. Sam inclined her head. 'Come in.'

The crowd who had rushed out into the foyer after Simon and I filed back into the office. There were a few moments of social awkwardness as we milled around. Small talk seemed out of the question, but so was everything else.

I bumped up against Maureen and searched my brain for a suitable topic of conversation. There are times when 'Do you like guacamole?' just doesn't cut it. I resolved to cross that question out of my conversation starters notebook as soon as I got home.

'Everyone sit down,' yelled Sam.

Simon shrugged and sat down next to the photocopier. I took up a position next to him. Mac leaned against the wall. His eyes flickered towards me, then away again.

I bit my lip to try to stop myself caring. *Get him out of your head, Cassandra.* It was easier said than done.

Sam stood waiting next to the whiteboard. 'So.' She picked up a whiteboard marker and turned it in her fingers. 'I suppose you've worked out what's going on.'

'There was no thylacine?' I murmured. My eyes were on Mac, but it was Sam who answered.

'Affirmative. There was no thylacine.'

'But you said ...' I trailed off.

Mac's eyes flicked towards the ceiling, like he wanted to escape. 'I wasn't totally … truthful.'

'Not totally?' My voice rose to a squeak. 'Take out the thylacine and what's left?'

Several people shifted uncomfortably. Maureen shook her head sympathetically. I remembered what she'd said. *Men … they're not always what they seem.* I glared at Mac; some men were even less like they seemed than others.

'The truth,' Sam fixed her eyes on me, 'is not necessarily solid. It can be liquid.' She took a sip of wine, as if to emphasise her point.

It sounded like something I might have said once.

At that moment, Simon's phone beeped. He glanced down at the text message. 'My editor — the Feds have intervened to stop the dam, but you knew that already, didn't you? Hence the party. I take it that was the purpose of the thylacine?'

'No-one's going to drown a thylacine,' Sam said.

My mind was still fixated on the lack of thylacine. If you took that away … I rewound the past few weeks. 'So, if there *was* no thylacine — why were you trying to get rid of me?' I sounded pathetic, like I was the fat kid no-one wants to play with again.

Simon touched my shoulder.

Mac's eyes followed his hand, but it was hard to know what he was thinking. He ran a hand up his immaculately shaved cheek. I'd never noticed it before, but he bore a more than passing resemblance to a curly-haired Hugh Jackman. I was a sucker for those *X-Men* movies. Let's face it, I was a sucker for *him*. There didn't seem to be anything he could do to stop me wanting him.

My eyes flickered up and down, absorbing his changed appearance. It's funny, he was gorgeous now, but I'd liked him better before. Pretty boys were a dime a dozen but wild men like Mac ... My cheeks burned at the memory. Mac looked at me like he knew what I was thinking. It didn't help.

'If there *had* been a thylacine — that's the way I would have played it,' he said.

'Played it? What *was* this, some kind of production?' Breathing deeply to calm myself, I turned to the rest of the crowd. 'What was *I* — an expendable extra?'

'The first casualty of war is truth.' Trev took a sip of his beer.

I frowned. '*Is* this war?'

'Look, Cassandra,' Sam intervened, 'no-one's sorrier than I am that we had to deceive you.' She didn't sound sorry. 'But your role as naive PR officer was essential to the whole script.'

'Naive?' I'd been called a lot of things, but naive wasn't one of them. 'Script? You're not making a reality TV show, are you?' I checked the room for a hidden camera.

Sam's eyes crinkled with amusement. 'Not a bad idea, but no.' She flicked the power switch on the whiteboard, then pressed a button; the screen moved to the left. Another screen came into view. Written neatly on it in black marker was: *Leave Our Valley Alone — no dam for Beechville.*

'We all know South-East Queensland is desperately in need of water,' Sam said. 'Their population's growing by twenty-five percent over the next twenty years. Where are they going to look for it? Not on their side of the border, that's for sure — it's a rain shadow. So, when the government announced a new dam in this area, I knew we were going to have a hard time stopping it. No-one here wanted it.' Her eyes swept the room.

'I've lived here my whole life,' said Christine Bowles. 'They said they'd relocate us, but I don't want to go. I love this town. People here know me. I know them. We don't always get along, but that's just the way it is.'

'And what about the animals?' said Trev. 'Where are they going to go, when the whole valley's underwater? One big cane toad breeding pond, that's what it'd be.'

'My supermarket,' said Maureen. 'That would have been flooded too. My father built that with his own hands.'

'Our football field,' said Tyler. 'What would we all do then?'

I stared at them. They really did love this town.

Sam put up her hand, to stop the outcry. 'We tried the usual stuff — lobbying, campaigning ...'

'The posters and coasters,' I said.

Sam nodded.

I glanced around at the posters on the wall. 'I don't see why they had to be such a big secret.'

Sam shrugged. 'They probably didn't. I just thought ... a clean slate was best. You'll understand in a minute. Anyway, it became obvious that none of that stuff was going to work. No-one cared. We needed to get smarter. We held a meeting and I suggested a new plan ...'

She pressed the whiteboard button again and the next screen slid out. Murmurs echoed around the room. Sam tapped the board with her marker and the murmurs died out. 'It's a five-point plan — all the best ones are.' She paused. 'You're probably going to find this a bit confronting, Cassandra. I'm sorry. But, as a person in the PR industry, I hope you'll appreciate that this is the way it had to be.' She gave me a wry look. 'You may also find that there is a certain symmetry here.'

I had no idea what she meant.

She read the first point, tapping her marker next to it.

1. *Engage PR officer, preferably one with high-profile contacts.*

'You exceeded our expectations there, Cassandra. We never imagined we'd get someone who'd just hit the media in such a big way.'

'You knew about that?' I said.

'We actually *do* read the *Herald*,' said Sam. 'Just not since you've been here.'

I looked around the room. 'Did everyone know?' I felt embarrassed.

Sam shook her head. 'No. Actually, it's only me and Mac who read the *Herald*. And we were the only ones who had the full picture about my plan. Others played their parts as required. They just had to trust me. I told them they would each have a role to play as events progressed. I didn't want everyone trying to act a part. It would have been too hard. It was hard enough for Mac and I as it was.' She gave Mac a meaningful look.

He avoided my eyes.

'Why did you pretend — '

Sam talked over the top of me. 'And it was obvious you had no scruples whatsoever, which was just what we needed. In fact, you were pretty near perfect for the position.' She beamed at me as if congratulations were in order. 'I thought so, anyway.'

That hurt — I'd changed, hadn't I? I stiffened my lips and looked over at Mac. 'So, what's his role?'

'I'll get to that,' said Sam. 'Mac was worried you'd be too smart, too devious. That being so used to deception, you'd sense it. I thought your profile and contacts,' she glanced at Simon, 'outweighed that concern. And I am the senior officer here.'

Sam tapped her marker on the board again.

> 2. *Raise suspicions of PR officer — make her think that ranger is trying to get rid of her. Manager must counteract influence of ranger to maintain credibility of this storyline.*

There was too much in that point to let it pass. I stared at the board, my mind spinning: *make her think that ranger is trying to get rid of her.* 'So, the feral pig morning debacle? Was that all staged?'

Sam nodded. 'Pretty much. Good cop,' she pointed at her chest. 'Bad cop.' She inclined her chin towards Mac.

There was an empty wine bottle on the floor next to where I was sitting. My hand curled around it. I didn't look at Mac. If I had, I wouldn't have been able to stop myself throwing the bottle at him.

Hannah, the woman who'd staged the protest, smiled proudly. 'Down with pig-killers,' she said, giggling.

My nostrils flared. One wine bottle wouldn't be enough. I couldn't believe it. What else had they staged? 'The seal stranding?' My voice came out in a croak.

Sam beamed, shaking her head. 'Sheer serendipity — the seal turning up then. Could never have planned something like that. It really added a terrific dimension to it all, though. Until then it was just a "get bogged on the beach" scenario.' She waggled her fingers around the words.

'But ... how did you know I was going to get bogged?'

Sam laughed. 'That was the easy part. Most novice four-wheel drivers get bogged down there. It's notorious. And you didn't even know how to engage four-wheel drive. I would have eaten my hat if you'd made it off that beach without getting bogged. I was going to turn up to save you, of course, but it was much better with the seal. Fantastic, in fact.'

'But, why? I mean, I'd got the message that Mac wanted me gone before then.' I couldn't believe it had all been an act. It was too weird. I looked around the room. No-one else except Simon seemed to think there was anything strange about this. If anything, they looked proud. I didn't look at Mac.

'It was important to keep the good cop/bad cop thing going at every opportunity,' said Sam. 'If you're going to do something like this, you don't do it by half-measures. You develop your scenario and you stick to it. It's like performing in a play — you stay in role until it's complete. We had to make you think Mac was trying to get rid of you, but somehow let things work out so it seemed you were doing a good job. We couldn't risk you leaving.' She glanced at Mac. 'I knew that snake in the toilet was a mistake. It was too much. We were lucky you came back.'

'But — isn't it all a bit extreme?'

Sam looked at me blankly. 'It wasn't hard. You did something similar yourself.'

'I did not.' Was that what she meant by symmetry?

'The fake committee?' Sam said.

'That's completely different,' I said.

Sam raised her eyebrows ironically. 'Is it?'

'You guys are mental.' I was trying to keep it together, but I felt humiliated. I glared at Maureen. 'You knew all this?'

She shook her head. 'Not at first. And never all of it.'

My mind raced. Scenes flashed through it — the

Hastings River mouse, the taipan … 'The flying foxes and the feral chickens. Were they staged too?'

'No,' said Maureen, quickly.

'Yes,' said Trev at the same time.

Maureen glared at him. 'Well, the flying foxes weren't. I really did want to get rid of them, until Cassandra explained how important they were.'

Mac flashed me a glance. I avoided his gaze.

'I didn't give a stuff about the chickens,' said Trev.

Sam waved her hand. 'Some stuff was planned, some stuff just happened. It's not like everything was totally sewn up. We needed to keep you busy,' she snapped. 'I thought you'd piss off back to Sydney at the first opportunity. Once you were the flavour of the month and all; what was keeping you here? I mean, you'd done your bit — the public totally bought the thylacine thing. So top marks to you two for that.' Her eyes slid to Simon.

That reminded me. 'You tipped him off about the feral pig morning, didn't you?' I said to Mac.

Mac looked at the ceiling.

That was confirmation enough. 'Why did you do that?'

Sam answered for him. 'We wanted to pique media interest, make sure you kept up your contacts.' She inclined her chin at Simon. 'Keep him sniffing around, ready for the big event.'

Simon bit his lip. He sighed heavily.

'But when you wanted to hang around … we were worried you'd start digging if we didn't keep you occupied. I was right, too. You did start digging, didn't you? Anyway, we're getting ahead of ourselves.' Sam tapped the board.

> 3. *Allow PR officer to see 'thylacine'. Make her think ranger wants to keep it secret — hostile relationship with ranger will ensure she contacts media.*

'Couldn't you just have told the media yourself? Or got me to publicise it? Why did it have to be so convoluted?' I said.

'Who's going to believe us?' said Sam. 'Thylacine sightings are a dime a dozen. Especially around here; there are lots of wackos — thylacines, yowies, panthers, you name it. The authorities would be suspicious of our motives too. The dam is not exactly a secret. But if it looks like we're trying to keep the tiger a secret and the news is broken by you, an outsider, someone with no stake in the dam — much more authentic.'

I nodded — I could see the logic. 'Smoke and mirrors,' I murmured. 'Lead with the left, punch with the right.' It was classic PR. Wazza would have had a job for Sam.

She nodded.

'But how did you get the dogs to appear on time in the right place?'

'We coordinated.' Sam inclined her head at Mac. He looked away. 'The toading expedition. I knew where you'd be and when.'

'And Cougan Peak?'

'Mac gave me a call. Told me you were heading up there.'

I remembered how he'd left the room for a few minutes before we got in the helicopter. I glared at him, but he refused to meet my eyes.

'It was a bit of a job getting up there,' said Sam. 'With the floodwaters and all. Took a few hours. My dogs are well trained, of course. We've been working on the "appear and disappear" routine for a while.'

I remembered the dog trials.

'You were a naughty boy tonight, though, weren't you?' Sam tapped one dog on the nose. 'Going after the chickens.' The dog banged its tail eagerly on the floor.

Sam gestured at the board again.

4. *Ensure media sightings of 'thylacine' and provide photos that can be authenticated.*

Simon turned his camera in his hands thoughtfully, his mouth pursed.

5. *Allow others to do 'No Dams' political lobbying. Locals stay out of this.*

'Anything else?' My stomach clenched, imagining — ranger to have affair with PR, then dump her to ensure she is so pissed off she follows through on media to spite him. Surely no-one could make a plan that twisted. Although … I did know of PR jobs where sex had been used as part of the strategy.

Sam's eyes flickered towards Mac.

He looked at the floor.

I ran my hand along the side of the bottle.

'No.' Sam's voice was dry. 'Everything else that happened was not to plan. In fact, it could have been extremely counter-productive.' She shot Mac a sharp glare. 'Luckily it all worked out anyway.'

'The thylacine signs at the town entrance — that's how you got them up so quickly. They were already made — weren't they?' I said.

Sam nodded briefly, as if this was hardly worth commenting upon. 'So, it's up to you two now.' She turned to Simon, eyeing the copious notes he was making. 'We can't force you to keep quiet.'

'We can try,' said Trev.

Sam put up her hand. 'Before you make up your minds … Mac, have you got anything to add?'

Mac straightened and nodded. He stood silently for a moment — a good presenter's trick to create suspense. His eyes met mine, then moved on to Simon. When he spoke, his voice was low, but totally compelling.

'I know what we did wasn't ethical, but it had to be done. Some people here are worried about the town and I wouldn't like to see it underwater either, but that wasn't my main motivation. Mainly, I was thinking about the animals.

'You might not know that Australia has the worst extinction record in the world. In only two hundred years, eighteen species of mammals have vanished. That's half of all mammal extinctions worldwide in the same period. Most of these were in the last forty to fifty years.'

Simon scribbled madly, like he was at a press conference.

I tried not to succumb to the persuasiveness of Mac's voice. I wanted to block my ears. Hum to myself. Stop his voice from pulling at my heart.

He continued. 'And it hasn't stopped yet. In the desert, ninety percent of small mammals are likely to be extinct within ten or twenty years.' He paused to let that sink in.

'There might not be a thylacine here, but the forest is no less precious for it,' Mac said. 'Twenty animals are hovering on the verge of extinction between here and the Queensland border. God knows how many plants. A dam could be just enough to push them over the edge. I didn't want that to happen.'

Simon and I stared at him in silence.

'So, do you have any questions?' Mac said.

I opened my mouth; but I had so many, I didn't know where to begin. I looked around the room. The whole setup was almost as bizarre as the courtroom scene in *Alice in Wonderland*. Had Sam cried *off with her head* I wouldn't have been too surprised.

My bedroom conversations with Mac flashed into my mind. He'd given me a hard time for what *I'd* done and meanwhile he'd been planning all this? 'My astroturfing is nothing compared to what you've done.

You haven't just formed a fake committee, you've formed a whole fake … town.'

'But in a good cause — that's the difference, Cassandra.' Mac's voice was gentle.

I loved the way he said my name, but still I wouldn't let myself succumb. 'Does it really make a difference? Isn't a lie still a lie?' I heard the tremor in my voice. *You're nothing but a pack of cards*, I wanted to yell. But it wouldn't be true. These people meant more to me than that. And that was why it hurt. Wonderland had grown on me. I wasn't sure if I wanted to return to the 'real world' anymore.

Whatever discomfort Mac had shown before, it was gone now. 'If the end doesn't justify the means, what can?'

'Doping me?' Simon's voice was cold. 'Where does that fit in?'

'You weren't doped.' For once Mac didn't sound convincing. 'A bit drunk maybe.'

'I could get you for assault. Not to mention fraud and probably a whole lot of other stuff,' said Simon. 'The only reason I haven't yet is that …' He glanced at me. 'Well, Cassandra can explain that part if she wants to.'

Mac looked at me questioningly. 'Cassandra?'

'Cassie,' I said.

Mac and Simon's eyebrows raised identically in surprise.

I shrugged.

Chapter Twenty-seven

Cunning counterplot

Simon fiddled with his camera. I knew the sign: Pre-Headline-Tension was rising. 'Are you going to tell him, or not?' he muttered.

Should I tell Mac the only reason I did the media stuff was to protect him from Simon? He was still waiting. So was everyone else. I couldn't talk about that now, here ... Did it matter, anyway? If he'd cared, he wouldn't have left me there. I almost felt embarrassed I'd done that for him. 'Nothing to tell,' I said.

'So,' said Sam. 'Like I said, we can't force you to keep quiet.'

Trev stepped forward. 'I still reckon we can try.'

Sam shook her head. 'We're not heathens. It's unfortunate you had to find out about the plan. It's not as clean as I would have liked.' She glanced at Simon.

'I read your column. I liked that piece you did about the pulp mill.' Her mouth opened as if she was about to say something more, then shut again.

Mac stepped forward and touched my shoulder as I stood up. 'Call me ... Cassie — if you want. I'll be at home.' He attempted a smile. 'Sorry. Sometimes you have to do things you don't necessarily ... want to. You'd understand that.' He tried to look into my eyes, but I avoided his gaze. I wasn't falling for that one.

Cassandra would have understood only too well the need to fulfil a brief, but Cassie ... Well, Cassie was an altogether different person and I was glad she was back. I briefly fought an impulse to kick Mac in the shins — then gave in to it. Swinging my leg back, I kicked him as hard as I could.

'Ow. Jesus. Cassandra, Cassie, I said I was sorry,' he gasped.

'Sometimes sorry isn't enough.' I turned and stalked from the room.

Simon's face looked pained as he ran down the stairs next to me. 'Did you have to do that?'

'What, you're not sorry for him, are you?' I turned with my hands on my hips.

'No.' Simon shook his head quickly. 'No way. As if I'd be sorry after he doped me and stole my camera. Good on you.' He smiled. 'I think I like it — I'm sensing the return of the old G8 Cassie.' He thrust his hand into the air. 'The banks ...'

'Have blood on their hands,' I completed the chant for him, but my heart wasn't in it. Kicking Mac in the shins had been satisfying, but it wasn't what I really wanted to do with him.

Crawk?

Yes, even after everything he'd done, René. What was I going to do with what had been done to me? That was the question.

We were out on the street now. A cold pre-dawn light was bringing the shops into focus. A rooster crowed loudly, followed by another one.

I jumped and looked down. The two roosters pecked in the dirt near our feet. I'd lost track of them in all the excitement and they'd wandered onto the street. 'I'd forgotten about you guys. What are we going to do with them?'

Simon put his hands on his hips and watched the chickens strut around, stopping to scratch every now and then. 'You know, Cassie, I think you and these chickens are a match made in heaven.'

'Oh, you're good, you're very good.'

Simon rotated his camera in his hands. 'What do you want me to do, Cassie?' He turned his green eyes on me, giving me a long, slow look, a lopsided smile on his face.

He was really quite a charmer. *This is Simon*, I reminded myself. *If he's charming you, it's because he wants something.*

'Cassie?'

'What do I ...? Oh, you mean about the thylacine?'

'What did you think I meant?' His eyes lingered on me — he always was one step ahead.

'Nothing. Right — the thylacine. Well, you're a journalist. I guess you'll just go ahead and journal. Great story — *Conspiracy in the country*. Feel free to use that.'

'I prefer *Cunning conspiracy in the country*.'

'Well, if you want to be a smartarse — how about *Cunning conspiracy of the country cabal?*'

'Or *Cunning conspiracy counterplot of the country cabal*.'

'You win.'

'But seriously, Cass.' He stuck his hands in his jeans pockets and, with the toe of his boot, gently pushed away one of the roosters that was pecking at him. 'I need to report this. I just wanted to know where you stood. Can I quote you?'

'Is there any chance you'd consider not reporting?'

Simon looked like I'd just suggested he eat a newborn baby. 'It's against my code.'

'What — journalistic ethics? Honesty, fairness, independence, respect for the rights of others and go for the jugular?'

'That kind of thing, yeah.' Simon gazed down the street. I could see the tension in his shoulders. 'You can't expect me not to report this. It's fantastic, once in a lifetime. It'll run and run.'

'They'll build the dam.' I eyed the shabby shops, the pub, the wildlife office. 'It's not much of a town, but it's their town.' *My town*. Where had that thought come from? I moved on. 'And there's all those animals ...'

'They lied. They got found out, tough titties.' Simon turned the full beam of his gaze on me. 'I can't be swayed by emotion, Cassie. Impartiality — that's the foundation I work on. You're asking me to cover it up?'

'Lying isn't the worst thing, Simon.'

He laughed and I flushed. I knew what he was thinking — I had a stake in convincing myself it was okay to lie. I'd certainly done my share in my time. But maybe this was different. Or was it?

'You can't go along with a conspiracy like this, Cassie. What about what they did to you? What Mac did to you? They made a fool of you. You can't want to protect them now.'

A wave of heat spread down my neck and chest. It was one thing for me to think it; it was another for Simon to say it. Did I think it was right, what they'd done? I wasn't sure of anything anymore.

'And what about your public relations code of ethics, darling?' Simon's voice softened. 'Aren't you worried about that?'

I caught the flicker of his mouth. 'Yeah, right — very amusing. Ethics are for those who can't handle public relations.'

'That's a Wazza quote, I take it?'

I nodded. 'If Wazza ever had an urge to think about ethics, he'd lie down until he got over it. Look, Simon, it's very late.' I glanced at the first rays of sun coming up over the buildings. 'Early, whatever … How about we sleep on it? Just for a bit?' I needed to rest before I could think about anything else. Wrestling with ethical dilemmas was a new thing for me. It made my brain hurt.

Simon glanced at his watch — I could feel a deadline looming. 'It's five o'clock; too late for the morning edition anyway. 'So, okay.' Simon scooped a rooster up under each arm and put them in my car boot. 'Can I call you at nine? I'll need to get a report filed by ten if I want to make the evening edition.'

'Look, come over at nine. Bring some coffee — I don't have any.' I climbed into my car.

Simon leaned over and rested his arms on the car window sill. 'Those chicken feathers in your hair — they really suit you, Hiawatha.' I pulled down the rear-view mirror. I looked like I'd been on the losing team in a down-filled pillow fight.

'See you in a few hours.' Simon straightened up and walked away towards the Amble Inn, checking his phone messages as he went.

I switched on the radio — 'Achy Breaky Heart' came on again. I sang along as I started the car.

'Cooee, Cassandra.'

Glancing out the window, I saw Jessica totter out of the Amble Inn on high heels, pulling a suitcase on wheels behind her.

I felt like I'd lived a hundred lifetimes since I last saw her.

Jessica leaned down and peered in the window. She frowned. She opened and shut her mouth.

'What?' I said.

'The feathers?' She sounded tentative.

I brushed my hand over my hair and a few chicken feathers fell out. 'I've been catching chickens.'

Jessica's eyes flickered over me. 'Where are they?'

I gestured with my head towards the boot of the car.

'Oh. What are you going to do with them?'

'I'm not sure yet.'

'I suppose there's no point in asking you why you caught them?'

'Not really. No. It's job related. You know how it is — client confidentiality.'

Jessica glanced at the radio. 'Are you listening to the country and western station?'

'Yeah, it's pretty good.'

'You really need to get out of here, Cassandra.' Jessica glanced at her watch. 'I called into your office to see you yesterday. That guy ...'

'Rodney.'

'Yes.' She giggled. 'I thought he was going to fall off his chair. It was kind of cute.'

'Yeah.' I smiled. 'Rodney is easily startled by a pretty face. Some woman is going to make good use of him.'

'So what shall I tell Cosmonauts — are you interested or not? They'll be wanting an answer when I get back to Sydney.'

I tapped my hands on the wheel in time with the music.

Outside, Jessica toyed with her sleek hair, adjusted the hem of her tight-fitting skirt.

'Give me a minute?'

Jessica sighed. 'I'll put my bag in my car.'

I turned up the radio. Some singer was now yodelling about outback sunsets.

How long had it been since I'd left Sydney? Almost four weeks? It seemed like longer. I looked out at the sun rising over Maureen's supermarket. Would I care if I never saw that supermarket again?

Maybe I would.

The sun bounced off the petrol bowser, casting a rosy glow on the white picket fence in front of the wildlife office. The glow moved down the street, lighting up the creek that ran beside the road. I remembered the day I'd come up for the interview, how I'd had that strange urge to paddle in the water. I hadn't had time then …

Climbing out of the car, I walked over to the creek, pulled off my boots and placed my phone on top of them. Rolling up my khaki pants, I ran down the bank to the creek. The water was cold. It made my toes curl. I kicked and spray danced in the sunlight. A strange feeling overwhelmed me. What *was* that feeling? Did I like it here?

Something splashed further up the bank as I waded through the shallows. A fish darted away in front of me. *Yes, I liked it here.* How had that happened?

The place had crept up on me and disarmed me. And it wasn't just the place; it was the people ... They were nutty, but I liked them too. Maureen and her weapons, Trev and his toads, Sam and her amateur theatricals, even Rodney and his lawn bowls ... Yes, Beechville was a 'make your own fun' kind of place, but maybe that was okay. People were allowed to be strange here.

I *could be strange here, René.*

'Cassandra, what are you *doing*?' Jessica was on top of the bridge. Her car keys dangled from her finger.

I squinted into the sun and spoke before I could think about it too much. 'Tell them no.'

'You're going to stay here?' Jessica sounded appalled.

I poked at a rock with my toe, shrugged and craned my neck to look up at her. 'Maybe. If they'll have me.'

'There might be eels in there, you know.' Jessica eyed the creek warily.

'There might,' I agreed.

'You're going to regret it, Cassandra. Your ten minutes of fame won't last forever.'

'Good.' I climbed up the bank towards her, the grass cold under my bare feet. 'I've had enough of it already.'

Jessica flicked her hair over her shoulder. 'Well, bye then. I'd better go catch my flight.' Her eyes fell on my phone where it lay on top of my boots. 'Hey, nice iPhone.'

I picked it up, fondled its shiny surface then held it out to her. 'Present.'

'Really?' Jessica took the phone, wrapping her long, red-coated nails around it.

'So you can keep in touch.'

'You sure?'

'Ain't no need for iPhones where I'm going, babe,' I drawled.

Jessica laughed. 'You always were a funny one, Cassie.' She leaned over and gave me a hug, enveloping me in an aroma of expensive perfume and cigarette smoke.

I hugged her back. 'Give my love to Paris.'

The iPhone flashed in her hand as she sauntered back to her car, hips swinging, hair swooshing, heels clicking on the pavement.

As I watched her go I wished that Jessica and I could replay our whole friendship but do it properly this time.

Despite the pressing concerns that jangled together in my mind — Mac, Simon, dam or no dam — a strange calm overtook me as I drove home. I felt like I was coming to the end of a journey. I wasn't sure of my destination, but I was pretty sure it would be an interesting place when I got there.

Climbing out of the car, I went around to the boot to let the roosters out. Dust flew in the air as I opened the lid. My red Ferrari, once the pride of Manly, wasn't the car it used to be. It looked shabby, worn in, a bit of a work horse ... rather like its owner.

I lowered myself onto the old couch on the verandah.

Taking a deep breath, I looked out at the hills. A multi-coloured parrot flew down and settled in a nearby tree. Another one followed. They squawked to each other as they jostled on the branch. The roosters, liberated from the car, pecked around my feet.

A rush of wings startled me as the parrots took off towards Mac's house. I had to admit it was beautiful here — thylacine or no thylacine. *Twenty animals on the verge of extinction between here and the border ...*

That seemed like a lot.

'Cassie? It's nine o'clock.' Simon's hand shook me awake.

The sun was right behind him and he looked like an avenging angel — his hair lit up in its glow. Instead of a golden staff, a mobile phone was in his hand.

'Simon?'

I'd been dreaming of Mac. We'd been sitting side by side on a couch, reading together. What was the meaning of these rather dull but strangely nice dreams? What was my subconscious going to come up with next? Would we play Monopoly? Maybe do a spot of household cleaning?

Sitting up, I shook off the lingering feeling of contentment. Here was Simon with a raging case of

Pre-Headline-Tension and I still didn't know what to do. I blinked into the sun, Simon's tension transmitting itself to me. *Mac.* There was so much that was hard to forgive, but in a way that was beside the point. There was more at stake here than just me and him.

I watched Simon pace up and down with his phone — he could barely contain himself. Pushing thoughts of Mac aside, I tried to focus. Right now, I needed to work out what to do about Simon. Should I back up his story about the conspiracy? Would he even consider not reporting it? Did I want to stop him anyway? Where was the ethical high ground? Did I care? My mind ran furious circles like a hamster on an exercise wheel.

'Sit down, Simon.'

He perched on the sofa next to me. He was trying hard to contain himself, but one hand drummed out a beat on his jeans, while the other fiddled with his mobile phone.

I smiled. 'You're incorrigible.'

Simon took a deep breath and stuck his hands under his legs. 'You know what it's like — deadlines.' He pulled his hands out again and reached down to his backpack. 'I picked up a paper on the way here.' He pulled it out and unfurled it.

I read the headline: *Dam blocked to save thylacine.*

Simon's picture of a thylacine covered half the front page. The image was only slightly out of focus. I stared at it. 'It doesn't look like a dog.' The animal had a pointier head than a dog and its tail stuck out stiffly behind it.

'No, it doesn't, does it? Funny that.' Simon's voice was dry. 'It's not the picture I took on Cougan Peak. I thought it was when I looked at it on the camera — but now that it's blown up … They've doctored it. Must have used a stuffed thylacine or retouched an old photo. You can do anything these days and it's pretty hard to pick up. Anyone who'd had a good look at the ones I took would have seen it was a dog, obviously. This one's much more authentic. That's why they gave me the camera back.'

'And you fell for it. That's not like you.'

'No, it's not, is it? I guess, like everyone else, I wanted to believe. And I saw them; I thought I saw them …' Simon's hands clenched the paper tightly. 'You're not the only one they made a fool of, Cassie. I guess there's just something about the tiger that clouds our judgment.'

'It's the poetry,' I said.

'Huh?'

'It's not the animal itself; it's the idea of it … A wilde beaste having claws like a tiger.' I held my hands up, claw-like.

'Huh?' Simon was strangely inarticulate.

'That's what Abel Tasman saw when he first arrived in Tasmania. I wish I'd been there then. Imagine.'

Simon eyed me. 'I deal in facts, not fiction, Cass.'

'That's why you're a journalist and I'm in PR.' I jumped up. 'Simon, can you wait here a minute?'

Simon's eyes flickered to his watch.

'It won't take long. Promise.' I glanced back at him as I went inside. 'Put that phone down.'

Simon's hand was still fiddling with the buttons.

'Down, that's it. Five minutes, I promise.'

'Five minutes?'

I nodded.

Simon put his phone on the couch and folded his arms.

'Good. See, you *can* do it.'

He attempted a smile, but it came out as a grimace.

I needed guidance and I needed it now. Running into my bedroom, I closed my eyes and flicked open *Alice in Wonderland*. Opening my eyelids slowly, I prayed for illumination as I pressed my finger to the page. *If you don't know where you are going, any road will take you there.*

I read it twice, hoping I'd missed the meaning the first time. But no, no matter how I looked at it, I couldn't see any applicability to my current situation. Just when I really needed it, my channel to the wisdom of the universe had broken down. Now what? All I could hope for was that Mum's hotline was working better.

Mum picked up the phone after three rings. 'Cassie? How lovely to hear from you. I've got the cover of *Woman's Daily* stuck to the fridge. I've seen better photos of you, though. Is Anthony still doing your hair? If so, you need to have a word to him. That ranger — he sounds like a bad one. How do you get mixed up in these things, Cas—'

'That's what I need to talk to you about, Mum. I need some advice.'

'Oh.' Mum sighed with satisfaction. 'I'm glad you've finally recognised that wisdom comes with age, Cassie.'

'Yes, Mum. Now, this is totally confidential. I'm not going to tell you unless you *promise* not to tell anyone.'

'Even Brian?'

'All right, you can tell Brian. No-one else.'

'Okay, Cassie, if you insist.' Mum sounded excited. 'Go on.'

'Tell her the one about the frayed knot,' yelled Brian.

'Tell her yourself,' said Mum.

I provided her with a rapid edited extract of the story to date, glancing at my watch. My five minutes were up. I peered out the window. Simon was pacing again.

Mum gasped as I finished. 'Goodness — it's like something out of Arthur Grisham.'

'John Grisham, Mum.'

'That's what I said.'

I let it pass; there was no time for point scoring. 'So, what should I do?' Simon caught my eye through the window and tapped his watch.

'Just let me make sure I've got it straight,' said Mum. 'You want to know if you should lie to stop this dam going ahead and should you get back with this mad ranger from the *Woman's Daily*?'

'He's not really a mad ranger, Mum.'

'Brian,' Mum called out. 'Do you think Cassie should lie to stop a dam flooding a valley with thousands of rare animals, and should she get back with that mad ranger from the *Woman's Daily?*'

'He's not a mad ranger,' I muttered. I heard Brian yelling in the background.

'Your brother says honesty is the best policy and definitely not the mad ranger.'

My mind was suddenly clear. 'You've been a big help, Mum.'

'Any time, darling.'

I was about to hang up when I remembered. 'What was that thing about the frog goddess? You left me a message.'

'Did I?'

'You said you were doing a ritual.'

'Oh, yes. It was an Egyptian resurrection and rebirth thing I was trying out. I thought you might be able to do with a bit of help. It's about starting over, finding your true path, that kind of thing. Those Egyptians were a very spiritual people.'

I smiled. 'Thanks, Mum. I appreciate it.'

'Glad to help, darling. The universe presents many possibilities; you just need to leave yourself open. Speaking of which, you know that job in the real estate agent? It wasn't my idea at all, it was Brian's. Sounded dead boring to me, actually. And that mad ranger ...'

'Mmm?' I'd given up on trying to correct her.

'My astrologer had a look at his picture. She can sense things just from photographs.'

'Uh huh?' I looked out the window, held up a finger to Simon to indicate one minute.

'She says he's a very passionate man. Is he a passionate man, Cassie?'

I exhaled slowly, remembering his poem. *Inhabit my dream. Sabotage my senses.* 'God yes, Mum.'

'Your father wasn't a passionate man. You know what he gave me for our tenth wedding anniversary?'

'No.'

'A new vacuum cleaner.'

'Oh, Mum ... Really?'

'Yes. I'm glad he left. No sense of curiosity, that was his trouble.' She lowered her voice. 'A bit like Brian.'

'But not like you, Mum.'

'No. And not like you either, Cassie.'

Chapter Twenty-eight

A mother's wisdom

There is no substitute for a mother's wisdom. Or a brother's, for that matter. As I put the phone down, I knew what I had to do.

> *The fact is, René, I'm still an unscrupulous bitch at heart. I like to think I'm a bitch with a heart of gold.*
> *Crawk.*
> *No, not everyone would agree.*

Throughout my time in Beechville I'd gained a new appreciation for certain things — frogs, birds, potoroos — but, basically, I was still the girl who'd been the PR queen of Sydney. They say a leopard doesn't change its spots; well, it's the same with us PR girls. Protest and passion are all very well, but sometimes good old unscrupulousness is still the go.

Simon was back on the couch again when I came outside. A magpie had landed near his feet and was regarding him with its intelligent black eyes. Simon had a speculative look on his face; the attitudes of both man and bird hinted at a discussion in progress.

I paused in the doorway, watching them, then took a deep breath and stepped onto the verandah. Simon looked up as I came towards him. His phone was in his hand and I saw his editor's number on the screen.

His phone slid to the floor as I undid the top button on my ranger shirt — I still hadn't changed out of my chicken-catching outfit. Undoing another button, I swung one leg over and sat astride his knees. 'I'm going to be honest here, Simon, because my mum just told me honesty is the best policy. Also, you're too smart for me to con. You and me — we understand deals, don't we?'

He nodded, his eyes boring into mine. The sun's glare lent an air of heightened reality to the moment. The magpie cocked its head, including me in its observation.

'How about a shag for a no-tell policy? No strings, once only.' Like I said, there's no substitute for a mother's wisdom. You just listen carefully to what they tell you, and then do the complete opposite.

What's that unit of time they use to measure swimming races in the Olympics, René?

A millisecond? A trillisecond? That's how long Simon took to consider my deal.

His hands were undoing my buttons so fast I think it might even have been a world record. Well, okay, that's the way I'd imagined it would go. In actual fact he surprised me.

Hands loosely by his sides, Simon smiled. 'You mean that, Cass?'

'Well, sure. You know, why not?' I was starting to feel a bit uncomfortable sitting on his lap. The scene wasn't playing out the way I'd expected.

'You'd have sex with me to save this valley?' Simon's head tilted to one side. He sounded amused. The magpie copied his movement; they were obviously in cahoots.

'Excuse me,' I said to the magpie. 'This is a private moment. Do you mind?' It shuffled a couple of steps further down the verandah, but didn't take its eyes off me. 'Shit, Simon, do you want to do it or not? I'm feeling like a whale steak at a vego barbie, here.'

He lifted his hands to the neck of my shirt and did up the buttons. 'Not under these conditions, no.'

My cheeks flushed and I sucked in a deep breath. Swinging my leg off, I sat down beside him, suppressing a giggle of relief. 'Well ... guess I can recognise a knock back — not that it's happened before. It would have been a bit kinky anyway.'

'It would? Maybe I'm warming up to the idea.' Simon's eyes crinkled at the corners.

'I mean there's something kind of kinky about having sex with someone you've known for a long time. It's sort of ... incestuous.'

'Yeah — all those long-repressed fantasies would be right there with me.' Simon's phone rang and he pushed it off the verandah with his foot. It lay among the bushes, ringing and ringing. Simon's fingers twitched, but he didn't pick it up.

'So, you're not ...?'

'I guess not.'

'What? But ...'

'I've had a change of heart. I think maybe journalistic ethics are overrated. There's other types of ethics too. The rulebook doesn't always work. Things change, you need to go with the flow.'

I gazed at him. 'Why, Simon, you *have* got a heart.'

He bared his teeth in a wolfish grin. 'I wouldn't go that far.' His eyes flicked out over the valley. 'It's important, I can see that, to you ... and the magpie ... and all its friends. So ... I'm making an exception; just this once. Besides,' he glanced down at the photograph in the newspaper, 'I've got my scoop right there. It's not exactly going to enhance my reputation if I turn around and admit I was duped.'

He leaned towards me until his nose was only centimetres from mine. 'About that offer you made me ... I've got a feeling you wanted it as much as I did.'

I held his gaze, testing my feelings. 'I did not. I could have had you any time. Anyway, I only made the offer because I knew you'd say no.' I was lying, of course, but he'd never know.

'How could you know I'd say no?'

'Intuition, our history together … I figured you'd rather have the chance to knock me back. We're even now.'

'So what would you have done if I'd taken you up on it, darling?' His face was still close to mine, his green eyes amused.

'You'll never know now.'

Simon's eyes crinkled. 'You know, Cassie, this is exactly why it would never work out with the two of us — we're too competitive. And there's another reason too.'

'What's that, Simon?'

'Next time you're tangled up in a big story, I'm going to have to report it. And there will be a next time, won't there?'

'You're right, Simon. There's always going to be a next time.'

Simon touched my cheek. 'When you've got over what's-his-name, give me a call.' He got up and walked to the car.

I leaned down to his window as he started the engine. 'You forgot this.' I handed him his phone.

'Cheers.' The phone rang and Simon glanced at his text message. 'I'm needed back in Sydney.'

'So, Simon?'

'Yeah?' His mind was already on the next job.

'Next time we meet — go easy on me, buddy.'

'No way.' He pulled me down and planted a big kiss on my cheek. 'That's it — opposite camps now, sweetie.'

'Okay — I guess I expected that.'

I waved as he drove off.

So, now you want to know what became of me and Mac, don't you, René? Could I forgive him? Could he forgive me? Did we have something special, or was he just one of those chance encounters life throws up? Was he a slippery fish, or a keeper? I didn't know.

Crawk.

Oh, I knew you would say that — it is easy to hate and difficult to love. I don't know that I agree. But then you are the philosopher, and me? I'm just a girl who likes men ...

The phone rang about ten minutes after Simon left. I eyed it like it might explode, for one ring, two rings, three rings ... On the fifth ring I picked it up.

'Cassie?' It was him.

I still wasn't sure how I felt about that. 'You're in the clear. Those spangled quokkas can sleep easy tonight.'

'Thank you.' Mac was silent for a moment. 'What did you have to do to pull that off?'

'What you don't know won't hurt you.' Just hearing his voice made my chest ache in a way I knew would only be cured by holding him tight. I would have been happy to listen to him talk, but he didn't say anything. I wondered which of us was going to be first to break the silence.

I cracked under the pressure. 'So, what next, oh man of mystery?'

'Can I come around and see you?' he said, at the same time.

'Um ...' Did I want to see him? *Yes, yes and thrice yes, but ...*

'I'll be there in ten minutes. I won't stay if you don't want me to.' He hung up.

I placed the phone down and looked out the window. On the verandah the magpie broke into a long, warbling song. Who knew what it was saying, but it was beautiful.

What was I going to do when Mac got here? I knew I wanted him. The way my body reacted to his voice was proof of that. But everything he'd told me had been one big lie from start to finish. I understood why he'd done it, but it still hurt. He'd been so good at it too ... the butterflies on the mountain — how could you make up something like that? I was a practised liar myself, but he was way out of my league.

Then there was the question of how he felt about me. In his eyes I was still the girl who'd sold the thylacine story to the highest bidder. And Maureen had said he was emotionally unavailable, whatever that meant. But he hadn't seemed like that in the flood ...

I sneezed — a chicken feather had gone up my nose. Glancing down at my feather-coated uniform, I sneezed again — it was time for a change of clothes. Stripping off, I pulled on a pair of shorts and a singlet. When I went into the kitchen for a glass of water, guess who was there? My gorgeous green friend — sitting on the window sill above the sink.

It was you, René. You'd come back.

'Hi there, shorty.'

René looked up at me and — I know I'm a tough PR bitch, but — I'd swear something passed between us. There was definitely some inter-species communication going on there.

'Crawk, crawk, crawk.'

'You're right — it's fab the dam's not going ahead. Tell your friends.'

'Crawk.'

I felt good about that.

Next thing there was a movement. Another little green frog hopped into view and perched next to René. It was so tiny — smaller than a five-cent coin.

'Your son or daughter? Congratulations, René. Or are you Renée? I think you might be.'

There was another movement — another frog.

'Twins? My, you are a lucky frog.'

Renée moved along the window sill to make room. Ten more frogs hopped into view.

'So that's what you were up to after the rain stopped, huh? No wonder you were keeping quiet. You've been busy.'

Thirteen pairs of black eyes looked up at me from the window sill. 'Crawk.'

'So, what am I going to do, Renée? About Mac? Any words of advice?'

Renée looked at me with her beautiful eyes. 'Crawk.'

'Never place complete confidence in that by which we have once been deceived? But, Renée, what about forgiveness?'

A hand touched me on the shoulder. I jumped. Mac had sneaked in while I was talking to the frogs.

'Just, you know, catching up with my friends.' I blushed. His hand was still on my shoulder. I stepped backwards and it fell to his side. He looked a little more like the Mac I knew. He hadn't shaved and his hair was sticking up in wild curls again.

'So ...' My heart was leaping about like it might burst out of my chest. I rubbed it unconsciously. Was I having a heart attack?

'So ...' he replied, a small smile on his lips.

'What have you got to say for yourself?' I don't know how I managed to get the words out. My brain had turned to fluff. It was all I could do to resist the magnetic pull dragging me towards him.

'You look nice,' he said.

'Nice?' I glanced down at myself. 'No, I don't.'

'Are you questioning my choice of adjectives?'

'No. Yes. Why are we having this conversation?'

'What should we be talking about?'

'God — where to start?' I pulled at my hair. 'Not with small talk, anyway.'

'Okay.' Mac pulled himself up to sit on the kitchen bench. 'You want big talk. Simon called me this morning.'

'Simon? Why?'

'He wanted me to know that he'd pushed you into doing the media stuff — that he'd have laid charges otherwise.'

'Simon said that?' The man was full of surprises.

Mac nodded. 'He seemed to think it was important.'

'Wasn't it?'

Mac half shrugged. 'Yes and no. We manipulated you. I pissed off and left you on the mountain. How could I have blamed you for doing what you did?'

I stared at him. Was this an apology?

'Sam's plan was a good plan. It seemed like a good plan before I met you ... What it didn't take into account was the way I ...'

I waited.

Mac gazed over my shoulder '... the way I started to feel about you. I kind of stuffed it up for everyone. That's why I had to leave you there — to get things back on track.'

'It worked. Well done.'

'I'm sorry. Does it help if I say it wasn't easy?'

'Did it actually mean anything to you? All those days in the flood ...'

He met my eyes. 'Of course it did. How could you think it didn't?'

I shrugged. 'Everything changed straight afterwards. It made it look different.'

'Those days with you … It was like we were in a cocoon, Cassie. But I knew it was about to break open any moment. The whole time I was trying to forget what I had to do next. Mostly, I did. I knew I'd gone outside the script with you. Once I'd done that there was no way to avoid hurting you … and me.'

'Maureen told me something … about you.'

Mac stiffened. 'What did she say?'

'That you're bad news. You don't stick … you're a slippery fish.'

Mac sighed. 'Anything else?'

'The words greased eel and melting popsicle were also used.' I tried to sound light-hearted, but I'm not sure I succeeded.

Mac reached in his back pocket and pulled out his wallet. He flicked it open and showed me a photograph. 'There's something I should tell you.'

Chapter Twenty-nine

It's all about the poetry

I don't know what I was expecting, a family photo of
a wife and kids, maybe. That would have explained a
lot. But the photo was of a teenage girl, about fifteen.
She had Mac's eyes and hair.

'She's lovely.' I looked up, trying to read his face.
'Your sister?'

'My daughter.'

'But, how old is she? Fifteen?'

'Seventeen now, it's an old photo. I was just one
year older than that when she was born.'

I gazed at the photo — the girl's long hair was
blowing across her face. She was laughing and holding
it back. 'That's young.'

'Too young. Her mother and I, we tried to make
it work, but we were just kids. We didn't even like

each other very much. In the end, I couldn't take it anymore. I pissed off. I'm not proud of it, but I wasn't any good to them. I was going crazy there.'

'Do you see her?'

He shook his head. 'She doesn't want to see me. Maybe when she's older ... Who knows? I can't blame her. I send money, of course.' He slid the wallet back in his pocket. 'So, that's me ... once a slippery fish, always a slippery fish, hey?' He attempted a smile.

I was lost for words. There was so much I didn't know about him. So much he didn't know about me. He had a daughter, a whole life I knew nothing about. I only knew him well enough to want to know him better ... 'Is that what you want?'

Mac met my eyes. 'No, it's not what I want. It's just the way it works out, the way it has worked out. I get scared and run. It's not what I want at all, not with you.'

'You don't know me very well.'

'Sometimes you know as much as you need to in the first five minutes ...'

'All those lies ... Why should I even talk to you?'

'Lies?' The word hung in the air.

The frogs looked up expectantly. I knew what he was saying. I'd lied, Simon had lied, Sam had lied, he'd lied — in the end, did it matter? Where did you draw the line, though?

'Were they really lies, Cassie? It all depends ... is the truth something to discover, or something to create? What do you think?' His eyes carried a hint of mischief.

'Mac, don't bullshit me. I'm in PR, remember. That's all very well, creating your own truth, but was any of it true — in the usual sense of the word? Any of that stuff you told me — about the tiger?'

'It was all true. I'm not that good a liar. Didn't it feel like the truth?'

I shrugged. 'It *all* felt like the truth. Every bit of it, right up until you disappeared.'

'That's because it *was* true; only the location changed. It all happened, the thylacine ... me. Just not here — in Tasmania.'

I looked at him carefully. 'You're not doing it again, are you?'

'No, I swear ... It was in south-west Tasmania. Other than that, it was just as I described it — the chicken coop, the epiphany on the mountain. All true, in every sense. Everything I said to you about what it means to me. I couldn't lie about that.'

'So you really saw one?'

Mac nodded. 'Two.'

I looked into his eyes.

'Do you believe me?' he said.

I nodded slowly. 'I'm gullible, huh?'

'Gullible is not a word I'd ever use in connection with you.'

Some facts from my research popped into my head. 'It's true that there *have* been a lot of tiger sightings by rangers.'

'You've been reading up, have you?'

'Uh huh. In 1982 a Tasmanian ranger watched one for three minutes during the night, but he never got a photo.'

'When he reached for his camera, it disappeared,' said Mac.

'In 1990 a park ranger saw one in Kosciusko National Park.'

'In broad daylight.'

'In 2007 another Tasmanian ranger saw two in the early hours of the morning ...' I looked at Mac; there was something about his face ... 'That was *you*, wasn't it?'

He nodded.

'So either you *rangers*,' I drawled the word, 'are crazy — which is entirely possible, if you're anything to go on — or they're out there.'

'They're out there. I've seen them. Once you see something like that, it never lets you go. It's like ... the *Titanic* missed the iceberg or ...'

'Romeo and Juliet rose from the dead?'

'Exactly.'

I smiled. 'So, you've rewritten a tragedy, hey?'

'And I'm going to rewrite plenty more ...'

The frogs on the window sill croaked enthusiastically.

'The last wild Tasmanian tiger was supposedly shot in 1930, wasn't it?' Sometimes I amaze myself — the way these facts stick in my head.

'By a chicken farmer. Get that — he shot an animal like that to save his chickens. People. There's no end to their stupidity. I booked a woman the other week who'd killed a three-metre carpet snake because it was trying to eat her guinea pigs. It would have been at least ten years old.'

'No-one thinks he needs more common sense than he already has,' I said.

'That sounds like a quote.'

'Yeah, it's René Tr—' I caught myself, 'Descartes.'

'I hadn't picked you for a philosopher.'

I shrugged. 'I used to be.'

'So you're an ex-philosopher?'

'Mmm, but I'm taking it up again.'

'I think you should. He was right, anyway,' said Mac.

Something just occurred to me. 'That plaster paw print …'

Mac nodded. 'It was the real thing, from Tasmania. I told you — all true.'

'Jesus. It was a real thylacine paw print and you let me drop it?' I winced, remembering the plaster scattering across the floor.

Mac looked at me quizzically. 'I don't remember being able to stop you.'

'You don't sound concerned. You're not a bit upset I broke your paw print?'

Mac shrugged. 'I never planned to go public with it.'

'But what if you wanted to do something like this again?'

'I never do the same thing twice.' His eyes lingered on mine. 'So, can you forgive me?'

I turned my head away, I couldn't think while I was looking at him.

'I've tried to get you out of my head,' he said, 'but I can't. When I saw you asleep in the office ... Well, I was pretty damn jealous of that pig you were curled up with.'

'You saw me with the pig? I thought I'd dreamt you.'

'No, I was there. Don't expect to be hearing from that pig again, by the way.' Mac smacked his fist into his palm. 'I picked up the cardboard cut-out of me you'd pushed over too.' He leaned in front of me and smiled.

It was a tentative smile, but I couldn't resist it. I smiled back.

Then my eyes fell on you, Renée. You didn't say anything, but I think if you had, you would have said that it's all about the poetry. And where would I find poetry if not with Mac? Your shiny, shiny eyes urged me on.

Part Three

go on till you come to the end:
then stop

The King, *Alice's Adventures in Wonderland*

Chapter Thirty

Liar bird

Renée and her twelve froglets perch expectantly on my window sill. Their eyes follow my every move. It is almost like a Disney movie. I will hardly be surprised if they burst into song.

I turn back to Mac. 'You said before I looked *nice*.'

'Ye-es.' He draws the word out. 'You want me to rephrase that?'

I nod.

'Okay. You look like someone I'd like to touch.'

My heart accelerates. 'I look like, or I am?'

Mac ignores my question. 'You've got your Lara Croft outfit on again.'

I glance down at my shorts and singlet. As it turns out I *am* wearing the same outfit I had on the night we went toading. There is something about the way he said it ... 'You're into Lara Croft?'

Mac's eyes rest on mine. 'A bit more than *into*. It's like you've tapped my fantasies.'

I back against the wall to support my legs. It's doing my head in, the way my body reacts to his face, his words ... I'm not sure if I like it. If I was hooked up to a heart monitor I'd be shooting off the graph. *Matron, sedatives, now!* 'Well ... that was certainly a lucky fluke on my part.' The words sound cool, in control. *Amazing.*

Mac leans against the sink. His eyes don't leave mine. 'You already *were* my fantasy — that just tipped me over the edge.'

'Why Lara Croft? I mean, I know she's hot, but it's a bit more than that, isn't it?'

Mac shifts uncomfortably. 'Do I have to say?'

I fold my arms. 'I think you'd better.'

He looks over my shoulder. 'A few years ago I over-wintered in Antarctica. You form some pretty intense bonds over a long winter ...'

I brace myself for a tale of passion. 'Go on.'

Mac's mouth twitches. 'It's not what you think. There were eighteen men, two women, both attached, and a small video library...'

'Including *Tomb Raider*?'

'One *and* two,' says Mac. 'I think they stopped adding to their video collection after 2004.'

I nod slowly.

'So ... no prizes for guessing whose body was pressed up against mine — in my dreams.'

My stomach turns over. The way he's looking at me ...

He smiles in an embarrassed way. 'I know it's nerdy. But, it's like you were reading my mind when you put that outfit on. I never stood a chance.' He steps towards me.

I step back. Twenty-six black eyes watch from the window sill.

'Not that I ever stood a chance anyway,' he adds. 'Cassie, you're the first thing I think of when I wake in the morning and the last thing at night. What else can I say?'

'Snap. Me too.' This time when he steps forward I don't step back.

Just then there's a coughing bark from outside the window. 'What *is* that animal? I hear it all the time,' I say.

Mac is already peering out. He holds his finger to his lips.

I join him at the window. The brown bird with the trailing tail that I saw on Cougan Peak struts across the grass. It makes the coughing bark once more, then vanishes into the bushes.

'The liar bird,' I say.

Mac gives me a strange look. 'What did you call it?'

'The liar bird. Isn't that what you said it was called? Because it mimics other animals?'

Mac stifles a laugh. 'Not liar bird, lyrebird. Lyre, as in musical instrument. It's because of the way the tail looks.'

'Oh.' I feel silly.

'Actually, I like liar bird better,' he says, meeting my eyes. 'Reminds me of someone ...'

'Not me,' I say. 'Not anymore. Uh uh — truth all the way now.'

Mac's eyebrow twitches. He doesn't believe me. 'Did you say you'd heard that noise before?'

'I used to hear it every night.'

'That barking noise it makes,' Mac says. 'It sounds like a thylacine.'

I stare at him. I don't understand why he's so excited.

'Don't you see? It might be mimicking a thylacine.'

It finally sinks in. 'So ...'

'So, maybe I wasn't lying after all,' Mac says. 'Who knows? There could be *anything* out there.'

'That's a nice thought, isn't it?' I look out at the forest. The bushes rustle. 'All that wilderness, and only you and me to call it home.'

And it feels like I've come a full circle, right back to my first night in Frog Hollow. Then, that thought had scared me, but now ...

'You, me and thousands of animals, you mean,' he says.

'How could you ever be lonely with all that company?' I smile.

Our shoulders are almost touching, there at the window. I can feel the heat radiating from his body.

Mac gives me a long look. 'Is there any chance we could ...?'

'Satisfy your erotic fantasy?'

He laughs. 'I wasn't going to put it like that, but —'

'As long as I don't have to pull a gun on you … And speaking of guns,' I add as his hands touch my shoulders. 'If you ever lie to me again, I'm going to kill you.'

He *really* smiles then — the full neuron-blasting one that shorts out my brain and makes my cheeks blaze. 'I'll have to take that chance,' he says.

My arms creep around him and I hold him tight, feeling his heartbeat, his chest rising and falling against mine. And yes, he is still a mystery, but at that moment he feels just right.

'Crawk.'

Renée and her offspring hop along the window sill and out of sight.

Acknowledgements

Writing a book turned out to be much more difficult than I imagined when I first set out on this path. Without all the people who encouraged, advised and inspired me, I never would have got there at all.

Particular thanks must go to the Varuna Writers' Centre for allowing me to complete *Liar Bird* among the lyrebirds. Peter Bishop and Helen Barnes-Bulley provided valuable advice. The Northern Rivers Writers' Centre has also done an amazing job of supporting me through thick and thin (mainly thin). Special thanks to Susie Warrick.

And then there are all the women who have helped me: Marele Day, Laurel Cohn, my agent Sophie Hamley and my magnificent writing coven: Helen Burns, Jane Meredith, Jessie Cole, Emma Ashmere and Jane Camens, to whom I owe the title of this book.

All writers should be so lucky as to have such clever friends as you. My book group was kind enough to read an earlier version of *Liar Bird* and provide comments and encouragement — particular thanks to our intrepid leader, Trish McCarthy. For the laughs and writerly chats beside the fire at Varuna, thank you to Brigid Delaney, Sarah Klenbort, Mif Hudson and Ilinda Markova.

The team at HarperCollins has been a pleasure to work with. First and foremost a very, very big thank you to the extremely astute Stephanie Smith, who picked me out of the pile. Anna Valdinger made my day by falling in love with my ranger, and the fine editing skills of Mel Maxwell and Kim Swivel saved me from looking foolish.

Also thank you to my hardworking colleagues in conservation who bear no resemblance to anyone in this book, being much more talented and, above all, fun to be with. And last, but by no means least, a big hug for Simon, Tim and John who have so graciously endured a mother and wife with her head in the clouds.